GATHERED UP

A Portland Heat Collection

Books by Annabeth Albert

The Portland Heat Series

Bundled Up:
Served Hot
Baked Fresh
Delivered Fast

Gathered Up:
Knit Tight
Wrapped Together
Danced Close

The Perfect Harmony Series

Treble Maker
Love Me Tenor
All Note Long

Gathered Up

A Portland Heat Collection

Annabeth Albert

LYRICAL SHINE PRESS
Kensington Publishing Corp.
www.kensingtonbooks.com

Lyrical Press books are published by
Kensington Publishing Corp. 119 West 40th Street New York, NY 10018

All Kensington titles, imprints, and distributed lines are available at special quantity discounts for bulk purchases for sales promotion, premiums, fund-raising, and educational or institutional use.

To the extent that the image or images on the cover of this book depict a person or persons, such person or persons are merely models, and are not intended to portray any character or characters featured in the book.

Special book excerpts or customized printings can also be created to fit specific needs. For details, write or phone the office of the Kensington Special Sales Manager:
Kensington Publishing Corp.
119 West 40th Street
New York, NY 10018
Attn. Special Sales Department. Phone: 1-800-221-2647.

Kensington and the K logo Reg. U.S. Pat. & TM Off.
LYRICAL PRESS Reg. U.S. Pat. & TM Off.
Lyrical Press and the L logo are trademarks of Kensington Publishing Corp.

First Electronic Edition: December 2017
eISBN-13: 978-1-5161-0796-4
eISBN-10: 1-5161-0796-9

First Print Edition: December 2017
ISBN-13: 978-1-5161-0797-1
ISBN-10: 1-5161-0797-7

Printed in the United States of America

To all the #PortlandHeat fans who have supported this series from book one, especially those who have shared their love for the series. Every review, like, share, mention, and note of support has been so appreciated. You all are the reason this series will always have a very special place in my heart.

Table of Contents

Knit Tight

Portland Heat

Annabeth Albert

LYRICAL SHINE PRESS
Kensington Publishing Corp.
www.kensingtonbooks.com

Chapter 1

"You're my favorite barista," the girl said with a self-conscious giggle. She was all of eighteen, if that, and reminded me of my sister, with her wispy hair and pale skin.

"Tonight I'm the *only* barista." I took a breath, kept my tone light, and didn't give in to the urge to sigh heavily.

I grabbed a mug to get her latte started. Wednesday nights were our busiest of the week, and I was stuck working alone because my coworker had called in sick. I *hated* Wednesdays, but I wasn't in a position to turn down hours. As it was, our boss had been slashing staff for the evening shifts, citing cost-cutting measures, so he hadn't seen fit to give me a backup.

"You're the best barista I've got, Brady. You can handle it," he'd said on the phone, in his usual offhand manner. He didn't like to be bothered with what he deemed trivial stuff. So I was alone to face Wednesday hell, better known as Knit Night, the weekly event in which a horde of women and their baskets of fibers descended on the coffee shop. But they all bought at least one drink and that meant tips in my jar.

And I was a damn fine barista, something I reminded myself as I put a little flair into making the girl's drink. She came here for this after all—the little bit of a show as I flipped the mug and steamed the milk, the latte-art smiley face I finished the drink with, the winning smile I dredged up as I handed it over. For an instant I made her feel like she was the sole focus of my attention instead of the line of traffic behind her. That was my skill, the one that was going to elevate me from Brady the barista to Brady the national-champion barista and alleviate a whole shitload of problems.

Buzz. From deep in my black apron pocket, my phone vibrated against my thigh. Hell. One of those problems was undoubtedly slipping into a crisis state, but I couldn't risk fishing the phone out with a line of customers. I'd have to hope that my sister could hold down the fort at home and that whatever it was could wait for a lull in the rush.

The next order was the girl's friend, another latte, another smiley face, but I made the mistake of glancing up at the door as I worked. The next customer to come in was the hottest guy I'd seen in a very long time. He had artfully styled black hair, the sort of purposefully messy cut that probably cost three digits and took twenty minutes in the morning to perfect. His slim-fitting jeans also looked designer—a rich color somewhere between brown and black and a subtle sheen to the fabric. A fancifully wrapped scarf over a close-fitting, long-sleeved shirt would probably get noticed by the Knit Night ladies, which was exactly what I did not want to have happen.

Our eyes met as I drew the latte art with a stirring stick, and he grinned widely at me. Gorgeous rose-pink lips and perfect white teeth straight out of a dental ad, and—

Frak me. I flubbed the smiley face, distracted by my efforts to memorize the handsome stranger. Rather than hand over a squiggly mess, I chucked the cup and started over. The girl didn't seem to care as she was deep in conversation with her friend at the end of the bar.

"Sorry about the wait," I said to the guy when it was finally his turn and he moved up to order. His intent gaze coupled with his polished appearance made me more conscious of my untrimmed beard and scruffy ponytail and made me wish I was wearing something a bit nicer than a faded People's Cup T-shirt.

"It is no problem," the guy said. He had a gorgeous voice—deep and polished, like a shiny piece of ebony. He had the fast speech and clipped consonants of an East Coast accent, but there was a lilt of something more exotic there, too. "I am happy to wait. Very peaceful in here."

Ha. I checked the clock as I tried to think of some flirty reply. The heavy glass door that led to Alberta Street swung open. It was 6:58 and Violet was first as usual, holding the door open for the herd of knitters. Not the steady trickle of a breakfast or lunch rush but twenty-plus women, all obsessed with punctuality and festooned with hats, scarves, and knit vests. Each ordered drinks for here with the sort of lengthy deliberation of someone who only ordered one coffee a week.

An older woman with the look and demeanor of a no-nonsense teacher, Violet made it her business to keep her fellow knitters in line. Knit Night was the brainchild of Iplik, the yarn store just down the street from us on Alberta, but Violet was the weekly event's unofficial hostess. As usual, she started giving her comrades orders about table rearrangement.

The People's Cup wasn't huge by any means, and Knit Night tended to fill the joint up. The space was longer than it was wide, with couches in front of the plate glass window, the coffee bar running along one wall, tables in the middle of the room, and a long wooden farmhouse bench and table for communal seating in the back of the room. The Knit Night ladies liked to turn the couches around and group the center tables together, creating a setup conducive to conversation but a tripping hazard for the rest of the patrons. And the arrangement resulted in an unholy din really, especially on nights when their ranks swelled to thirty or more.

"Remember to keep the aisle clear," I said to Violet and her minions. I'd warned them about creating tripping hazards with their knitting gear, but it was as futile as telling the twins and Jonas to keep their Legos in one area. Like my siblings, the ladies loved to spread out their projects.

"What'll it be?" I swung back to the register, no closer to having the right banter for the stranger, but no longer in a position to care. However, he'd stepped aside for Violet and her herbal tea order.

"I'll be back when the line clears," he said with a wink. He had a leather messenger bag, the sort meant to look like something Indiana Jones would haul around, for which one paid for every crinkle in the distressed finish. He'd probably come in wanting a quiet place to work.

He had the look and accent of a displaced New Yorker—working some cushy freelance job, no doubt. I liked thinking up little stories about my customers, but I didn't bother coming up with a lengthy one for him. He wouldn't be back once he saw how loud Knit Night got. And the ladies were likely to pester him about his intricately knit scarf with its pattern of interwoven cables. One time, I'd made the mistake of wearing a wool beanie I'd found for a buck at the thrift store. *Every* single knitter needed to remark on its construction. Dude was *so* going to be beating feet once Knit Night got underway.

Without a coworker, I was slammed, having to work both the register and the machine. While it kept me hopping, I didn't lose my rhythm until the triplets showed up.

They weren't really triplets. That's what I called them in my head—three middle-aged women who apparently texted each other every week to coordinate their outfits. This week it was cardigans—one yellow, one pink, one green—all in a similarly complex knit pattern. Each woman had long, grayish-brown hair, all carried identical hemp knitting bags, and they all were incapable of making a decision.

"Now, ladies, what are we ordering this week?" the first asked the other two. "I was thinking mochas?"

"Oh, I was thinking chai," said the second.

"Don't we want lattes?" the third asked. They couldn't each order to their own preference. No, they had to agree on that week's beverage, something they couldn't seem to do prior to holding up the line.

"Oh, yes," the first said. "We want some of Brady's art."

I immediately started thinking of what bit of whimsy would make the triplets happy. The smiley faces were better suited for the teen girls, but I could come up with something special just for the ladies. I was good at that, and the detail-oriented work itself always soothed me, even when the shop was busy. But what drove me batty was how the triplets were prone to changing their order as soon as I had it straight in my head.

Yellow gets skim.

Pink gets half caf.

Green gets picky.

Brady gets distracted by the sexy stranger texting on his shiny smartphone in the rear of the store...*No time for that.* I moved quicker, trying to ignore the fact that my eyeballs wanted to track his every movement.

"No, wait." Yellow cardigan stopped me in midpour. "Did I remember to say decaf?"

"Nope." I dumped the cup, ready to start over.

"And mine is sugar-free, too," Pink added.

Buzz. My apron vibrated against my thigh again. Behind the triplets, the line was at least ten deep. *Damn it, Renee. Just handle the kids. Please.*

Finally I had the three of them set. Green took a sip, then held out the cup. "Is this coconut?"

"You said nondairy, nonsoy?" I took the cup back.

"I meant almond breve." She sighed, like I should have gotten that at first, and if I wasn't distracted by what was going on back home, I would have remembered to ask her *which* nondairy, nonsoy option she wanted.

"Here, let me try again." I had just finished her new drink, complete with a leaf design in the foam, when a loud crash rattled the whole shop.

A two-seat table had tipped over, sending two coffees flying and leaving two women in tears.

"My Fair Isle sweater!" The younger of the two, a pixie with platinum hair and a hook nose, held up a dripping garment with half a dozen colors of yarn, still on long needles connected by a cable. "I've worked six months on this!"

"I'm sorry!" The rainbow-haired young woman in a roller derby T-shirt had tears streaming down her face.

"You never look!" The first wasn't having any apology.

"Hey, my hat got ruined, too!"

"Ladies." I stepped out from behind the counter, grabbing the mop we stashed against the wall. I approached the mess and tried to inject some patience in my voice as I said, "Maybe if you didn't move the table—"

"And what business is it of yours?" Oh, Miss Fair Isle was pissed and she was turning it all on me and the other knitter.

"Brady! Can we order?" someone called from the line at the counter.

"Did you forget to sweeten this one?" Green cardigan triplet was apparently still not happy, but I ignored her to set the fallen two-top to rights. As I straightened, I noticed a pair of expensive-looking desert boots: the brown leather staples of all Portland hipster men. And as my gaze traveled upward, I took in the handsome stranger who had somehow managed to find his way right into the middle of the Knit Night chaos.

"Is this always so...boisterous?" he said with a faint curl to his gorgeous full mouth.

"'Fraid so. Welcome to Knit Night." I finally gave in to that heavy sigh I'd been holding in for the last hour.

"It is not so bad." His lips curled as his gaze latched onto mine, not breaking away.

He didn't move, and I didn't scurry back to the counter like I should have. The air felt charged—

"Debbie. You ruined my Fair Isle! Two hundred dollars' worth of yarn! Ruined!" Anger. That's what the air was charged with. Fair Isle lady wasn't letting it go and was all up in the roller derby girl's personal space again.

Buzz. My leg vibrated yet again, this time the steady pulse of a missed call. This just wasn't my night. I had no idea when I'd get a chance to breathe, let alone check the latest message. A solo Knit Night was proving to be a special kind of hell. And, of course, the most attractive man I'd seen in weeks had to be dropped right into the middle of it. I gave him five more minutes before he scurried out to the chain place down the street. They were stealing enough of our business, why not him, too?

"Ladies. May I see?" Instead of fleeing, the man stepped closer to the arguing women.

To my surprise, the angry knitter handed over the soggy garment. "Evren! I thought I saw you over in the corner. You should have joined us! Is Mira with you?"

"I wouldn't miss it." One of my favorite customers stepped out of the line for coffee. The owner of Iplik, the yarn store, she was a neighborhood institution unto herself. And she'd been sorely missed the last few Knit Nights. I'd heard a rumor about some health problems, and I was very glad to see her, even if she did look thinner and frailer, with an elegant knit turban on her head. She was one of the very few people who knew my situation with the kids, and I still got all warm at the memory of the little knit ornaments she'd given me for them at the holidays.

"And what is all this fuss?" she asked.

I loved her lilting Turkish accent, and I realized that was what I'd heard in the man's voice—New York with just a hint of Turkish.

"There's no fuss," Miss Fair Isle said, flipping her long blond hair. She was too busy making goo-goo eyes at Evren. Not that I blamed her. He was handling her soggy yarn balls with such deftness and care that it made certain parts of me take notice. He had long, elegant fingers with blunt tips. Capable grace.

"I think this can be fixed," Evren pronounced, and the whole group exhaled. "Now, why don't we let the man get back to his coffee?"

"Evren, this is Brady, my favorite barista," Mira introduced me with a flourish, emerald tunic top rippling. "Brady, this is my nephew. He's come to…help with the store."

"That's great." I forced my voice to be bright and cheery, just like hers. But I knew his arrival couldn't be a good thing—her health must have been even worse than the rumors. "You must be the famous nephew she's always raving about."

Truthfully, I'd pictured someone younger from Mira's stories about her favorite relative. Evren was probably a bit older than me, perhaps in his late twenties. And if I was honest, I'd imagined someone diminutive and round, like Mira was before her illness, not tall, confident, and composed. And hot as hell.

"Perhaps *Hala* Mira exaggerates." He patted her arm before turning his attention to the bickering knitters. By the time I was back behind the counter, he had the two women sitting next to each other again, laughing, and he'd stowed the soggy mess of knitting in a shopping bag to "fix later." That pronouncement had drawn much awe from the Knit Night crowd.

There had been the odd dude at a Knit Night before, hipster types with scraggly-looking bits of scarf and an eye on a girlfriend or potential girlfriend, but I was still impressed when Evren opened his bag and pulled out a half-knit sock on the needles and a completed sock, which was passed around and oohed and aahed over by the ladies. It was indeed a nice piece of work—at least three colors that I could see, and some sort of complicated pattern that had him pulling out charts and diagrams.

His hands were so sexy that I kept spying on him as I finished the rest of the initial Knit Night rush. I liked watching his long, elegant fingers move rapidly with the teeny needles, liked how he gestured as he passed his scarf around, and really liked when he flipped his ridiculously thick, straight hair off his forehead with a flick of his hand. *Wonder what else he's good at with those hands...*

With the scarf on the table, his long neck was exposed, and he had the sort of prominent Adam's apple and faint scruff that never failed to turn me on. Maybe after Knit Night, I could say a few words—

Buzz. Hell. Finally, I had enough breathing space at the counter that I could check the texts, keeping the phone hidden behind the counter.

I discovered a series of texts from Renee, each more dire than the last.

Madison's stomach is upset. Should she eat dinner?

She's puking! All over the rug! Help!

Fever's 102!!!! Brady!!! What do I dooooooo? :(:(:(

I could hear Renee's wail just from the text. Yeah, eighteen wasn't a baby anymore and we could all do with fewer hysterics from her, but she was still munchkin-size, with a sweet voice and a sensitive attitude. It was hard to get those memories of us as little kids out of my head. I'd been five when she was born and I'd been the type of older brother who fell hard for the family's new addition—the tiny blond-haired toddler I'd begged my mom to let me push on the baby swing. The too-damn-cheerful kindergartner who'd held my hand so tight on the way home from school every day.

Renee and I had both grown up a lot faster than we'd wanted to when our mother and her second husband died last year, and now we were doing our best to raise our younger half siblings together.

Trying to keep the phone low and discreet, I frantically typed back.

Calm down. Children's fever reducer in the medicine cabinet. Top shelf. I circled the dose on the box for the twins. Give that. Home soon. Promise.

Cough. A throat clearing made me look up. Fuck. Evren loomed over me, and he was staring right at my phone.

"Sorry." I pocketed it, shaking my hand off like it was burning. "I don't usually..."

"Do not worry about it." Evren made a sweeping gesture. I was already a serious fan of his accent and the little bits of formality that crept into his speech just added to the appeal of that melodic voice. "You looked so serious and concerned. You must have had good reason. I saw nothing."

He patted my shoulder. A simple, friendly gesture, but not one most customers would make. Especially not most *straight* customers. I'd be lying if I said I hadn't been wondering which way he swung since the moment he came in, and the hot sizzle rushing down my arm only intensified those thoughts.

"Thank you." If word got back to Randy, my boss, that I was on the phone, it wouldn't go well. "What can I get you? On the house."

"Do not be ridiculous." Evren pulled out a handsome embossed wallet and slid out his debit card. "Large Americano. Extra shot. Extra sweet. And a chai for Mira, please."

I gently pushed the card away. "Mira drinks free. All the business owners who give us special events and customer referrals like this do. It's how we give back to Alberta Street."

It was a tradition started by my old boss, Chris, and one grudgingly kept up by Randy.

"All right. This time. Next time, I pay." He flashed me a smile full of gleaming teeth. His lips were wide without being overly full and the perfect shade of rose—the same shade as Mira's turban and, unlike the hat, the lips were sure to star in my private thoughts later that night.

"Oh, you planning on making this a regular thing?"

"We shall see, Brady. We shall see." He looked right at my lips as he said the words before he winked. Slow and deliberate. *Damn.* I swear I felt the buzz of his gaze all the way down to my Vans.

He hummed a bit to himself as he accepted the drinks and carried them over to Mira. He made sure she was settled with hers, adjusting a shawl around her shoulders. Oh, man. I was toast. The dude was the definition of masculine hotness with his thick, straight black hair, scruffy jaw, and lean build, and he was kind? And he could wrangle a room full of knitters? I wanted him back every week, and not just for the eye candy.

Buzz. I had to pretend to get myself some coffee to sneak a peek.

Fever down but she's asking for you.

While I had a chance, I grabbed a ginger soda from the cooler and shoved it in my beat-up messenger bag under the counter. Unlike Evren's pricey number, mine was more patches than canvas at this point. Just one more way we were from different worlds. With luck, I'd have time to stop for some electrolyte drinks and broth on the way home, particularly if tips were good. If Madison was sick, Morgan and Jonas were sure to follow. I was on the skateboard, so it would have to be a small trip.

Over at the knitting tables, a loud group laugh echoed through the coffeehouse, Evren's deep chuckle joining in. A low ache gathered in my gut. I should be a normal twenty-three-year-old, free to mack on the hot stranger, stick around and flirt with him after closing, but instead the text had served as a reminder of why none of those things were happening in my life, even with someone as intriguing as Evren. I had three kids depending on me, a sister who should still be a kid, too, and absolutely no room for anything else.

Chapter 2

"Fiber and color should match your mood. Don't underestimate the power of a cushy cotton to relax you or a sturdy wool to invigorate you. Likewise, look for spots of color, even on your darkest days."—Evren's Yarnings

The third time Evren came into the shop for an Americano, extra sweet, extra shot, I had the to-go cup waiting before he got to the front of the line. It was late morning, so I wasn't the only one on duty. Miracle of miracles, I hadn't caught the twins' plague and had made it through the full week. Audrey rang him up, but I waited until he was right in front of my end of the counter to put the drink up. Yes, I totally was hard up enough that I took pleasure in tiny little things like the brush of his hand against mine or the way he smiled with gratitude or how he always took the first sip before he left the shop, wincing a bit at the temperature, throat muscles working…

Fuck. He was sexy as hell. And he always took a moment to greet me by name and ask how my day was. Same question every day, but that small courtesy was almost sexier than the rest of him put together.

"Thank you, Brady," he said as he grabbed that day's drink. As usual, his eyes lingered longer than strictly necessary on my face. Man was going to give me a reason to take up shaving and hair product again. "I really should start bringing a reusable cup, yes?"

"We sell some." I motioned at the display near the entrance. "You could knit a cozy for it, maybe?"

"Maybe I will." His eyes went all thoughtful and his fingers drummed against his cup, like I'd been serious and not teasing. "Not a bad idea at all. Actually, what do you think about a cozy contest?"

"A cozy contest?"

"For Knit Night. I'll put up a flyer. We'll see how creative people can get." Something about the way he said *creative* made my mind go to dirty places. But then, his voice pretty much always had that effect on me.

"I can probably get my boss to donate a mug for the winner," I said. Randy was a bit unpredictable, and not as caring as Chris, Randy's ex-partner, who'd managed this location for as long as I'd been here before moving away with his new boyfriend last year. However, Randy was a keen businessman, and he'd see the value in such a promotion. "So you're coming to more Knit Night events?"

"Of course." He raised an eyebrow. Even his eyebrows were refined and elegant, dark slashes with a slight upturn. "And I think a contest like this will be just what Mira needs. Something to make her smile."

"One of the ladies said it's cancer?" I asked. Hell, I'd take up needles or hooks or whatever myself if I thought it would help Mira.

He nodded. "Pancreatic. She's started treatment, but…" He drifted off with a helpless gesture.

Even I knew that was a largely fatal cancer. "Fuck," I said, then remembered I was at work. "Sorry. I just mean—"

"No, that's exactly how I feel. *Fuck.*"

"So you'll be around a while, then?" I asked.

"As long as it takes to get her on her feet again. Which we will do. We do not care about such things as odds," he said firmly.

"She'll beat it," I said, forcing some conviction into my words. And if I felt a slight twinge at the news that Evren's stay might be temporary… well, such things were better ignored anyway.

"I believe so. I had to quit my job in Brooklyn when they wouldn't give me time off, but getting her better is more important." He sounded a bit wistful about the job, further underscoring that he'd be moving on soon enough. "I'm a freelance knitwear designer now, so I can work just about anywhere, but my main job is going to be keeping her well and keeping the shop running until she's ready to take it back over."

"Good luck," I said, because I wasn't really sure what else I could say…or do. On impulse, I grabbed another to-go cup. "Wait a sec. Let me make her a chai."

"Oh, that is so kind of you, Brady, but I just made her Turkish coffee a little while ago. Her appetite, it is not that good this week."

I paused with the cup still in my hand. "Wait. You *made* coffee. And then came over *here*?"

"Good-bye, Brady. Do have a nice afternoon." He gave me a little wave as he backed out of the shop.

Sneaky, sneaky man. Whom I had absolutely no time for but who had me smiling all afternoon long.

The next day, Evren brought over a flyer that he tacked to the community message board. On it was a photo of a cup cozy with a replica of Iplik's logo. He fished the real deal from his bag and showed it to me.

"You whipped this up in one day?" I fingered the soft, thick yarn.

He shrugged. "Mira watched a marathon of some teen paranormal show. There was a lot of time to pass."

I chuckled at the image of Mira, who had to be around sixty, desperate to catch the next episode of some teen angst drama. "Nice. You're a good nephew."

"She's a better aunt." Some distant sadness passed in his eyes, there then gone before I could suss it out. "You can keep the cozy if you want. I'm going to tweak the design before next week."

"Thanks. You know, for a guy who isn't planning on sticking around, you seem rather…invested in Knit Night."

"It is important to my aunt." He waved his hand like it was a simple matter, when I knew full well that cheerfully putting the preferences of others first wasn't easy. I loved how his hands moved as he talked—more expressive than most people but full of confidence, not drama.

"Mind if I give this to my sister?" I asked. If possible, Renee drank more coffee than I did, which was partly my fault, because I'd been slipping her free coffee since she was in high school. And she was a die-hard environmentalist who wouldn't dream of using a paper cup. She deserved way more than a cozy after a week of sick-kid duty, but I knew that adding it to her favorite reusable cup would make her smile.

"I would be delighted." He grinned at me, the most playful smile I'd seen from him yet, and it carried me all through the weekend.

* * * *

I had a plan when Knit Night came around the following week. Everyone was healthy, so I'd told Renee I might be a bit late home, and she hadn't grumbled as much as she did sometimes. I'd spent a little extra time getting ready, too—putting my favorite small wood gauges in my ears and pulling back my hair into a neater ponytail than my usual messy man bun. Trimmed the beard down from mountain man to quietly hipster. I might not have time for someone like Evren, but that didn't stop a guy from wishing.

Randy had blessed me with a second barista for the evening shift for once, so I wasn't so slammed with the rush of ladies and had more time to ogle Evren, who was wearing a loosely knit white cardigan. On any other dude it would have looked delicate and feminine, but on him it looked as regal as a military uniform. He admired each cozy with the same enthusiasm, even the ones that were a mess of knots and glitter.

"Brady, come judge," he called after the initial rush was done and he'd laid out all the cup cozies on a table.

"Which is yours?" I hissed, stepping closer than absolutely necessary. I didn't want to accidentally declare him the winner, because he'd told me earlier to take him out of the running. But mainly I just wanted the excuse to see what he smelled like. The scent was something I wasn't expecting— holly and pine. It was early spring and he smelled like a Christmas tree farm I'd visited long ago. And wool. It was a very comforting smell, and I had to stop myself from leaning in to him.

"That one," Evren said in a low voice and pointed. I should have guessed. It looked like interlocking Moroccan tiles—like something you'd see in fancy restaurant bathroom. Utterly elegant with a masculine vibe. Utterly him.

"I love it," I said.

"And that one." He indicated the one next to it, identical to the cozy I'd given Renee, except he'd done something to make the logo stand out in relief more. "Pick any others."

"Ah." I studied the rest of the table. "My second favorite is that one." I pointed at one done to look like a little zebra, complete with ears on the sides and a tail in back.

"I concur." He smiled, and something passed between us, something so palpable I could almost grab it with both hands.

The winner was an elfin young woman who wore a zebra-inspired cardigan, hat, and fingerless mitts. At least she was committed to a theme. I got her a mug and returned to the counter.

"I'm so happy Randy asked me to work tonight," Audrey said, touching my sleeve. Her blueish-purple hair shook as she spoke, and she had this habit of touching me or brushing against me while trading places behind the counter that I really didn't like. "He was *so* sweet and gave me some extra hours at the Northwest store next week because I'm saving for my summer trip to Greece."

Yup. That sounded like Randy. He knew I needed the hours in the worst way, but he liked to play favorites with the baristas of both genders who got flirty—as well as the ones who could be the most flexible with the schedule. I didn't flirt, and I could no longer be as available as I once was.

I was, however, a damn good barista, and I really needed Evren to order something other than an Americano so I could show off my skills with flair. I'd won a regional contest with my ability to make pictures in cappuccino foam as well as other skills, and if all went well, I'd be heading to the national coffee championships in a few months. We *needed* that win—Renee, the kids, and I were crammed into a tiny two-bedroom apartment. The cash prize of the contest would let us get enough float in the bank account for a bigger rental.

Yet another reason why I shouldn't be daydreaming about Evren or reworking the plan I'd come up with earlier. I needed to focus on the kids, the contest, and keeping it all together. But that didn't stop me from grinning big when Evren came back for a second drink and a big cookie.

"I'm hoping to get Mira to eat part of this," he said as he paid. "They said her appetite would come and go, but I'm having such a hard time getting her to eat anything."

"You have to get her home after Knit Night?" I asked. I already knew Mira lived above her store, and that she owned her building. The Alberta gossip loop kept close track of who bought, who rented, and who was looking to sell to one of the higher-end places moving in as the area became more and more gentrified.

"Yes." Evren rubbed his lightly stubbled jaw. "She's probably exhausted even though she'll never admit it."

"You ever go out again after she's settled?" I asked, sticking my toe in waters I had no business swimming in.

"I have not yet." Evren didn't sound disinterested and his eyes watched me intently. My heart beat double-time.

"You haven't had much chance to explore the neighborhood. I was wondering if you might want to grab a beer—"

"Evren! How do you do a cable again?" A busty woman with half a sweater on giant needles interrupted us.

He gave me a pained expression, and his mouth moved like he wasn't sure who to reply to.

"It's okay. You can get back to me." I grabbed a rag and started wiping down the counter, freeing him to answer the knitting question. I had a feeling the electricity zooming between us was mutual, but I had no way of knowing how open he was about his sexuality and didn't want to presume.

As I was watching Evren help the knitter, Audrey came up from behind and wrapped her arms around me.

"What the heck?" I stepped to the side and kept my voice low.

"Oh you. I was just having the *best* daydream, thinking about the last time we worked late together." She touched my neck with a hand that was far too familiar. Her voice wasn't a whisper, nor was the memory she alluded to welcome. "I was thinking about a repeat?"

"I've got plans," I said curtly.

"Bah. Another time." She flitted away. She wasn't a bad person by any means, but she did have the worst timing on earth. Evren glanced over at me and frowned. More than just irritation, there was disappointment in his expression. *Fuck.* He'd heard or seen too much. A heavy feeling descended on me, one that didn't lift as the knitters started drifting away. Evren started straightening tables, which was not his job, the perfect excuse for me to leave the counter and go help him.

"You don't have to do that," I said, moving some chairs out of the way. The ladies always ended up shoving most of the tables together and pulling chairs every which way.

"No, it is fine," he said as he straightened a table. "We should be courteous to the shop."

"Appreciated," I said. He wasn't looking at me, and I had a feeling I knew what the answer would be, but I had to ask anyway. "So, a beer?"

"Thanks, but…no." That pained expression was back. He glanced over at Audrey, who was cleaning the machines behind the bar.

Hell. "I'm not…" I moved my hands restlessly. "I'm not involved with anyone, if that's what you're worried about. And the invitation was totally open as friends, too."

"You were involved, though?" Evren kept his voice low. "You and the female barista?"

"We…collided a few months back." That was the best description of it really. We'd been working late together, she'd been flirting heavily, and I'd been almost a year without touch from either gender. She was vivacious and knew exactly what she wanted—something I found hard to resist in either gender. But she'd caught me at an exceptionally weak moment, as I'd left my random hookup days far behind, or so I'd thought. "Nothing repeated. Nothing serious."

Evren's frown deepened. "I do not usually do casual. Or bisexual."

"You don't do bi?" I gaped at him, my jaw seriously hanging open. I could get not doing casual—more power to him. If my life had any room in it, which it most certainly did not, I wouldn't do casual anymore either.

But bi? What the fuck? Bi erasure was so five years ago. Ev needed to join this decade.

"Let's just say I have my reasons. And I don't mean to be rude—"

"But you *are*." I shoved a chair in with more force than strictly necessary. "It was just a beer, man."

"No, it wasn't." Evren shook his head sadly. "Good night, Brady."

Fuck this. I finished the rest of the closing with a lot of stomping around and minimal talk with Audrey. I was being ridiculous. I really had no time for someone like Evren, especially not someone with bizarre prejudices, but damn if I wasn't more than a little put out.

Chapter 3

*My friends, you keep asking for an update on how I like being
back in Portland, and if I miss Brooklyn. I do miss Brooklyn,
and adjustments are...complicated, but my focus now is on my
dear Hala Mira's health. And to that end, I share with you the
restorative silk and merino shawl I've designed for her for the
drafty treatment rooms at the hospital. —Evren's Yarnings*

Not surprisingly, Evren dropped his near-daily coffee habit, which
shouldn't have depressed me, but it did. It meant he *had* been coming around
to see me, and my mouth filled with a sour tang that he was rejecting me
for something over which I had no control. But after a few days of silence,
Mira came over by herself.

Even if the lack of Evren made me grind my teeth a bit, seeing her
out and about with a good appetite for our soup and bread and a chai tea
brightened my day. Because she seemed so small and frail, I took advantage
of the fact that we were a little slow to carry her food to her table for her.

"Thank you, dear. My Evren cooks such nice food for me, but I just
had a craving for your split pea today."

"You should get whatever you crave," I said. She shivered and pulled
her lilac shawl closer around her. "You warm enough?"

"Yes, dear. You're as bad as Evren with your hovering. Get back to
work." She made a little shooing motion and I went back to the counter,
but I kept an eye on her.

Her shivering got worse, not better, and her hand trembled holding the
soup spoon. She brushed the tails of her head scarf off her neck, and there
was sweat along her brow line. Her color wasn't looking so good either—

the usual dusky olive skin tone that Evren shared had been replaced with a pale, sickly gray.

"Mira, are you all right?" I hurried over to her.

"I'm fine. Perhaps I should be getting back to the shop, though." She started to rise, then wobbled and sat down fast. "Or maybe not." She gave me a shaky smile.

"Let me call Evren for you."

"I don't think that's…" she trailed off, rubbing her neck.

"Mira. Give me your phone." Being bossy didn't come naturally to me, but I used the voice that always got the twins to comply with my orders.

"I really don't want to bother him," she demurred as she dug out her phone from her knitted bag with trembling fingers. She tried to dial, but her fingers were shaking, so I took the phone.

"He's speed-dial number three," she said in a weak voice.

I hit the number without hesitation. Any issues I had with Evren were secondary to getting her help.

"Mira?" Evren's voice came on the line with the second ring.

"Evren? This is Brady from the People's Cup. Mira's not feeling very well." I spoke fast so that I could convey that the situation wasn't *dire* but still get his attention.

"Oh, thank you for calling, Brady. I'll be right there."

I sat with Mira, and Evren popped in five minutes later, all out of breath. "Mira! I told you to wait for me to take your lunch break." He crouched next to her chair.

"Yes, aşkim. But you turned down People's Cup and I so wanted their soup."

I looked away. I knew exactly why he'd wanted to avoid us, and it made my stomach bubble like the nasty kombucha health-food drink we kept on tap. "Well, I'll let you take it from here. Let me know if I can help." I pushed up from the table.

Evren grabbed my sleeve as I rose. "Thank you for calling me, Brady. Very much." His voice was more uncertain than I'd heard it, and a faint pink blush stained his cheeks.

"Any time," I said and meant it. I should have taken pleasure in his discomfort, but I couldn't. I shared his concern over Mira and watched as he shepherded her out of the store, letting her lean heavily on his arm.

* * * *

About an hour later, as I was finishing up my shift, a customer came to the counter and held out of a bundle of knitted fabric. "I found this under one of the tables," she said.

Mira's shawl. "Thanks. I know whose it is. I'll see it gets returned." I'd opened that morning, so it was only a little before two when I got off work. Audrey had the evening shift, so I signed out and headed up the street. I had time before the kids got out of school, and I wanted to check on Mira anyway, see how she was doing.

Iplik was two blocks down from People's Cup, past the garden store that sold no plants, the pet store with the bulk organic "cookie" bins that looked tastier than the snacks I had for the kids, and the neighboring gift stores. Whatever awkwardness currently existed between Evren and me was nothing compared to those two competing store owners. Mira had been threatening to make them hug it out, which was something I'd pay good money to see.

When I entered Iplik, a young woman was working the counter and I couldn't see either Evren or Mira. My stomach dropped like one of the heavy balls of wool in the plate glass window. Maybe my motives were less pure than I'd thought. I shoved aside my irrational disappointment and surveyed the store because I'd never actually been inside, despite walking by almost daily. Iplik was less industrial than the building that housed the People's Cup and more like an oversize teal-colored house with little Craftsman details on the exterior and homey print curtains waving on the upstairs windows.

The store portion was bright and airy, three or four interconnected rooms displaying various fiber types and sample projects. I slowed down my trek to the counter to try to spot which sweaters and scarves might be Evren's handiwork. A thick one-piece scarf adorned a mannequin. It was a maze of heavy cables and interlocking knots. Attached to it was a copy of a magazine article: "Trendsetting Designer Evren Demir Wows at Knit Expo." A quick glance showed that Evren was indeed a Big Deal in the world of knitting designers. Yeah, no way would he be sticking around if Mira got well. Or if she...

Not going there. I quickened my steps and continued toward the front of the store. The young woman brushed her heavy dreadlocks out of her face as she helped a trio of women I recognized from Knit Night. As I waited for her to finish, heavy footsteps sounded on the stairs to the left of the counter. Evren appeared just as the customers departed.

"Brady! What are you doing here?" He greeted me with surprise and a bit of nervous suspicion, as evidenced by his narrowed eyes and fluttering hands, but not outright hostility, which I took as a good sign.

"Mira left her shawl behind." I held it out. "I knew she'd want it back. It's too pretty to lose."

"Ah. You are too kind. Would you like to give it to her? She is resting quietly with her TV, but she is embarrassed about earlier. I think a quick word from you might be just the thing."

"Of course." I followed him up the stairs to a heavy wooden door with a "Private Residence" sign hanging on the front. Evren entered and motioned for me to follow. After a short entry hallway, we came to a living room, where tiny Mira was almost swallowed up by a giant recliner, a knitted afghan draped over her, and one of those tables like they have in hospitals across her with a remote and a big glass of ice water.

"*Hala*, Brady has come by with your shawl." Evren went and knelt down to her.

"Oh, Brady dear. I'm so sorry. I left in such a rush...left my dishes out." She sounded very forlorn and I went to stand next to Evren so that she didn't have to stretch to see me.

"It's no problem," I said. My throat felt thick. "You're my favorite customer. I'll bus your dishes any day."

"I'm so embarrassed...thought I could handle a little outing."

"You'll get stronger again, *Hala*," Evren said firmly. "But next time, maybe I will go with you for the soup."

The look he gave me was difficult to decipher. There was apology there for sure, but also something else.

"Evren, offer Brady a piece of the revani cake you made." Mira's voice was thin but insistent.

"Oh, no, I'm good." I held up my hands. "I just wanted to return your shawl. I'll leave you to your rest now."

"I insist. Besides...there is something I've been wanting you to try." Evren's voice was a bit uncertain, and if I wasn't mistaken, the barest hint of a blush colored his cheeks.

"Oh?" I was intrigued enough to follow him to a galley-style kitchen.

"Have you ever had Turkish coffee?" Evren asked as he picked up a curiously shaped silver pot from the stove. "I just made some, but Mira was not in the mood."

"I haven't actually." I'd tried just about every other coffee variant out there.

"Come. Sit." He indicated a small table at one end of the kitchen with two wooden chairs. After fetching two small cups roughly the size of espresso cups, he poured the surprisingly thick brew from the pot. He added two small slices of a very moist-looking cake to two plates and brought them to the table. "Here. Enjoy. Sip slowly. Like brandy."

"Thank you." I was grateful for the advice as it was scorching hot and overpoweringly sweet and strong. "Wow, that's different."

"It's not just the taste. It's an experience. A ritual, if you will." Evren's elegant hands moved as he talked. I could have watched them for hours. Not to mention the things I wanted to have done by them. I was more than a little obsessed with his hands.

He paused for a few sips before he spoke again. "And in this case, a chance to apologize."

"Apologize?"

"I was…harsh the other night. Not kind." He looked down at the white wooden tabletop, tracing a crack in its surface with a broad fingertip.

I shrugged. "At least you're honest. But seriously, what do you have against bi guys?" I kept my voice at a near whisper.

Evren's lips quirked. "It is okay. Mira knows I'm gay. You don't have to whisper. And it is not so easy to explain."

"Try me." I took another little sip of coffee. Evren was right—there was something to the experience of a small sip of thick coffee in between bits of conversation and bites of cake.

"I've had two serious relationships. Both men were bisexual, and I knew it upfront. And both had…indiscretions. And one left me for a woman and the other for someone 'open-minded' enough to accept…dalliances." His fingers drummed against the white wooden tabletop.

"And so all bisexuals are now off-limits?" I shook my head. "Look, I've never had a real relationship for…reasons." I wasn't ready to tell him about my situation with the kids. "But whether it was with a girl or a guy, I'd have no issue with monogamy. Bisexual doesn't mean you have to be poly or something to be happy."

"Ah. You say that, Brady, but it is not that easy." He shook his head sadly. "Regardless, though, I squelched your kind offer of friendship. And for that I am truly sorry."

I leaned back in my chair. "So you're saying you're willing to be friends with the bisexual guy?" I wasn't sure whether to be flattered or insulted.

He frowned. "Willing is the wrong word. I know I am…overgeneralizing, maybe. My biases are…silly. But I see you being all casual about it." He waved his hand as if to indicate me flitting about. "And I remember someone else, equally blasé. And I am not such a thing, no matter how much I *should* be. And I am trying to work on that really. I don't know many people in Portland yet, but you are a true friend to Mira. I think I would be honored to make your acquaintance as well."

"But not hook up?" I just wanted to clarify what we were talking about. Friends were in fairly short supply for me as well, but that didn't negate the fact that I really wanted into Evren's designer skinny jeans.

"I hate that word: hook up. I can't promise not to...*forget myself,* but I think we are better suited as friends, yes?" he asked.

I interpreted *forget myself* to mean flirting, and I liked that he was honest about it because that's exactly what we'd both been doing from the first—him in his subtle, more refined way and me in my eager Oregonian obviousness. *No.* "I'm not promising not to flirt either." I grinned at him. "But I'll take being friends. Maybe show you around a bit if we both have time?"

My vast, vast amounts of spare time consisted of the occasional uninterrupted long shower, but a guy could dream. As if laughing at me, my phone buzzed. My alarm for picking up the kids. "Oops. I gotta head out, Evren. Thanks for the coffee. And the friendship." I stood and held out my hand.

He shook it, and a most unfriendlike jolt slid up my arm. I was right. His hand felt amazing—solid and strong and warm. No matter what each of us said, we had some freaky chemistry.

"My friends usually call me Ev. You can as well." He said this solemnly, like granting me some privilege. And dang if I didn't feel a little warm to be given it. Ev. I liked it. It suited him. And he suited me far, far more than I wanted to admit, but I still smiled all the way to the school to get the kids.

* * * *

Ev resumed his Americano habit, and most days if I wasn't swamped, we chatted a bit. I told him about parks near where Mira was getting her treatments where he could walk and places to get cheap takeout when they were both too tired for cooking, and I tried to send him home with soup and cookies for Mira as often as he'd let me. For my part, over the last few years my life had narrowed down to only the kids and the job. And I loved both, don't get me wrong, but it was blissful to get some adult conversation that didn't involve child-care schedules or coffee orders.

My shoulders seemed to be lifted by invisible strings when he reported getting a sandwich at the new little joint I knew about near the hospital or when he asked for a florist near there and I pointed him at an open-air market on Wednesdays. Playing tour guide by proxy for Ev gave me a weird sense of satisfaction—like I got to uncork a useful side of myself that hadn't seen very much air lately.

After about three weeks of this, one Friday I was working the tail end of lunch when Ev came in. He changed things up a bit, got a large chai for himself and a small one for Mira.

"So, are you on mornings or evenings today?" he asked as I worked on Mira's drink.

"Morning. I'm off around two."

"Excellent." He smiled widely, the hand that wasn't holding his chai fiddling with the keys in his pocket. "Do you have dinner plans?"

"Dinner?" *Fuck. Fuck.* I did indeed have plans. Renee had a friend's birthday party. That left me with the kids and no babysitter.

"Violet and some of the Knit Night ladies are taking Mira for a 'girls night.'" He made air quotes around the term. "I hope she is up for a little dinner and fun, but it leaves me at a bit of loose ends because no men are allowed. So I thought—as friends—we could get that beer. Maybe you could show me a brewery with decent food and good local ale?"

I knew *exactly* which brewery I'd love to take him to. And I also knew it wasn't happening. "Sorry, Ev. I've got plans."

"Ah. Well, it was an idea." He shrugged, but a shadow passed in his dark eyes, and I had a sinking feeling the offer wouldn't be repeated any time soon. He turned to leave.

"Wait. Ev." I took a deep breath. I'd been enjoying being Brady the fun barista with Ev, but he deserved to know the truth about my situation. "I don't have a date—not those kinds of plans. My sister does, however, and I've got to watch my younger brother and twin sisters."

"Ah." He brightened a bit. "Your parents must be grateful for your help."

I made a hacking sound that wasn't sure whether to be a laugh or a cough. "Nope. It's just me. I'm raising the kids. My mom and stepfather died in a car accident."

"Oh, Brady," he started, and I braced for the expression of pity sure to follow. "That is so sad of a loss, but how wonderful of a thing you are doing. You are keeping the family together, yes?"

"Trying," I said and looked at my shoes. "So that's why I can't go out. It's hard for me to get away." *Try impossible.* And nice as Ev was, I wasn't sure about subjecting him to the chaos of the kids until our tenuous friendship was a bit firmer. Most guys our age saw kids as a huge drag, and I didn't want to scare him away quite yet.

"Hmm. You have your phone, though, yes? Perhaps you will tell me where I can get a decent burger, and I will call or text you how it goes. See how your evening is progressing."

It was a sign of how starved I was for adult contact that that sounded as good as a plate of wings and an icy brew. I quickly exchanged numbers with him before the next customer arrived and went home smiling. I had a date. Sort of. A phone date. A friends-only phone date, but it was more excitement than my Fridays had held in a long time.

Chapter 4

Dear friends, spring has come to Portland, and I find my adjustment has similarly perked up. Today, I am craving some local flavor—some craft beer and an organic burger with the sorts of toppings you only find on this coast. My tip for you today is to look for the local flavors wherever you are, and let your designs reflect what you find. Myself, I think I'll be knitting something substantial with a hemp blend later. —Evren's Yarnings

"Brady! Morgan has more chicken nuggets." Madison swung her feet back and forth on the battered blue chair she'd long ago claimed as her spot at dinner.

"And you don't! Nyah!" Morgan completed her taunt with waggling fingers in her ears and tongue out.

"Madison. Morgan." I slapped the bowl with the prepackaged salad down on the table. "You have the same amount. Madison, maybe tomorrow I'll make you do the counting."

"Why does Madison get to count? I want to count!" Morgan's hair escaped the half-hearted ponytail Renee had done that morning. Where Renee and I had Mom's blue eyes and brown hair, the twins had Greg's deep espresso eyes and kinky hair that defied all our attempts to keep it neat. Not that the ketchup mustaches were exactly helping the neatness factor.

Lord deliver me. "We'll take turns, okay? Everyone can count at dinner. But we all get the same amount. *Please* don't argue about it."

"I wish we had like a zillion chicken nuggets." Jonas's dark eyes were wide with longing, too. At ten he was a bottomless pit, and my brain cramped just thinking about how expensive he was going to be to feed in the next few years. His feet were already almost the size of mine, and he'd have Greg's height for sure. I took two chicken pieces from my plate and put them on his.

"No fair!" Madison screeched, despite not having touched a piece herself.

I closed my eyes and took a deep breath. In another universe, in another life, I was out with Ev right now, showing him my favorite brew pub, settling in for a nice talk, leaning in closer, laughing, working on this silly prejudice he had about bisexuals....

But instead I was in reality, in a cramped 1970s apartment that hadn't been renovated since it was built and was notable only in the fact that it was off Alberta, walking distance to the kids' school and walking or skateboarding distance to the People's Cup. And they'd given us a lease, unlike Mom and Greg's place, which had refused to let me take over the rental after they passed. I tried not to think too much about the sunny rental house off Killingsworth with the huge herb garden Mom loved and the basketball hoop where Greg and I would play twenty-one.

Like Ev and Mira's apartment, this place had a narrow galley kitchen ending in a small eating area, but where Mira's was all white wood and homey cheer, ours was dark, with inadequate lighting and mismatched cabinetry. I did, however, do my best to put a hot meal on the table every night and get the kids to sit down with me and eat as a family on the nights when I didn't work late. Mom had always been huge on dinner together; even as Renee and I got older and busier, she'd made sure we sat down with the family, and I wanted to try to give that to the kids.

"You took my broccoli!" Morgan whined.

"Guys. Just eat." *Try* being the operative word.

I usually tried to model good behavior for the kids at the table and not check my phone, but they were sorely testing my patience, so I snuck a peek under the table when it vibrated. There was a new message.

You were right. The bison bacon burger is divine. It would be more delicious with a bit of conversation, though. And how is your dining?—Ev

I smiled and hit a quick reply.

Chicken nuggets with bickering siblings. Wouldn't mind conversation beyond SpongeBob either.

Later, while I was doing the dishes, another text came in.

Now I am home with my new beer purchases. Which is your favorite ale?

We texted back and forth a bit while I cleaned, talking beer and food. We had similar tastes in food—lots of meat with strong flavors, not into cheese-covered anything, and we were both picky about fries being done right. I liked finding out little details about him.

Hold on. Gotta read the next chapter in Harry Potter three to the kids. Back in bit, I texted.

Oh, I love that series. Do you do voices?

Of course. Gotta do it right, I sent back.

I wish a command performance, then.

Yup. We were totally flirting. And I loved it. I read the chapter to the girls and Jonas. The girls shared the larger bedroom with Renee, while I shared the smaller one with Jonas. It wasn't ideal, but the social worker had nixed the idea of anyone sleeping in the living room, even though a lot of nights, I ended up passed out on the couch anyway. If I won the barista contest, however, we could maybe get a three-bedroom apartment, so Renee could get her own room, or maybe even get a rental house so I could have privacy as well. That was the dream.

"Can we read more?" Madison asked sleepily.

"Tomorrow. I hope," I said, kissing her head and guiding Jonas over to our room.

It was always a toss-up whether we actually got the story time in, but I always felt a bit less like a fuck up when I put them to bed the way Mom had always tried to. After they were in bed and the kitchen was clean, I sorted laundry from the loads Renee had run at the coin-op in the basement of the buildings. I kept looking at my phone. Oh, screw it. I picked it up and hit Call.

"Brady! I was just thinking about calling. But I didn't want to wake the little ones." Ev's voice sounded sleepy and relaxed.

A warm buzz shot through me like I'd had two of his beers. "They're asleep now. And my phone's always on vibrate. Just, you know, for future reference."

"I will indeed file that away." I could almost hear him smiling over the phone. "And I'm enjoying a nice beer and some *Pawn Stars*—a pleasant break from Mira's dramas."

"Oh man, I love that show. That and *Storage Wars*." I flipped on the TV, lowered the volume. "Hey, it's the one with the sword."

"Yes. I'm waiting for the part where they find out it's a fake." Ev chuckled. "I've no idea why I like this show, but I do. And yes, I like *Storage Wars*, too. Anything with auctions or antiques."

"Ditto." I loved that we both liked the same crappy TV. "Mira get home safe?"

"Yes, thank you. She was a bit tired, but not too bad. I made her go straight to bed. She came back with pretty nails, though, and it was lovely to see her smiling."

"You're a good nephew," I said as I balled up socks. "Is anyone else helping with her care?"

Not that I knew a ton, but the few Turkish people I'd met all had large, involved extended families. Ev paused for a long time. "No. It is just us. It's been that way since I was fourteen."

"Oh. I'm sorry." I knew firsthand what a lousy expression that was, but I couldn't think of what else to say. "Did your folks die, too?"

"Not exactly." There was a scritching sound, like Ev was rubbing his jaw. "We immigrated to the United States when I was twelve. But even in America, the Turkish community can be a bit...conservative. Our family especially, as my parents are devout and very rigid about things like homosexuality."

"Ah." The picture became a lot clearer.

"I was found kissing a school friend. And when I refused to apologize for my actions and wouldn't accept...efforts to change my mind, I was sent to Mira."

"I'm glad you had her, then. She's not conservative like the rest of the family?"

Ev snorted. "Hardly. She was already the black sheep. She immigrated two decades before my parents. Did you know she had a lady friend for many, many years? It would have been before you were working at People's Cup. She died about eight years ago. Lovely, lovely woman, my *Hala* Tanya."

"So they sent you to them?" On the TV, the coworkers were bickering over who had slacked off, but my heart was heavy for Ev's younger self.

"Yes. My father wanted to turn me out altogether, but my mother pleaded for the Aunt Mira option."

"Oh my God. That's awful."

"Eh. It was what it was. How about you? Did your mother know of your...preferences before her passing?"

"You can say bisexual, Ev. And yes, she did. I dated a guy in high school for a while. Wasn't a big deal to her. I got a safe-sex lecture and that was pretty much it. She was more occupied with twin toddlers and Jonas. Me kissing boys was the least of her worries."

"And how old are your siblings now?"

"Renee is eighteen, almost nineteen. The twin girls are seven and Jonas is ten. Technically, I could leave him alone some, but he's got severe ADHD and impulsivity issues." Renee and I argued about that a lot. She wanted to try leaving the kids alone more, or at least Jonas, but I wasn't about to let that happen. He might be ten, but he had the rationality of a much younger kid.

"I understand," Ev said solemnly. "You take good care of them. And they know about you being bisexual, too?"

"Well, it's never come up much. I haven't dated at all in the two years since Mom died, but they know that boys can like both boys and girls, and I don't think it would come as a shock if I dated a guy."

I had never been one for fishing, but my stepfather had taken me out on the Columbia once. Talking to Ev felt a bit like fishing with Greg. Casting out a bit of line, hoping it didn't spook Ev.

"Too busy for dating?" Ev neatly sidestepped the bisexual thing. "I empathize. Right now, it feels like all I can focus on is *Hala* Mira and making her well. And before that was craziness with design deadlines. Let me think…nine months maybe? A year?"

"That's a heck of a dry spell for a guy like you. And you were in New York right? I'd think finding dates would be easy."

"Ah. You flatter me." Ev's voice was easy and relaxed, and I could listen to him all night. I had a serious hard-on just for his voice, especially when it got all languid like that. "And I'm picky…very picky. And apparently not the best when I *do* choose."

"I'm picky, too," I admitted. "Tell me about your wish list." *Please let scruffy guys with beards and earrings be on it.*

"You? Picky?" Ev sounded more surprised than the boss on the show when they discovered a genuine treasure amid all the crap.

"What? You think all bisexuals are automatically manwhores? No, I've got plenty of requirements for both genders. I'm not attracted to everything that moves." God. Why did I constantly feel like a PSA for bisexual marginalization? Ev wasn't the first to assume that bisexual meant I'd screw anything with legs.

"My mistake." Ev seemed genuinely apologetic. "Tell me about these…requirements."

"Posture, for one. It's all in how people carry themselves. Confident posture is essential. Tall is even better." Ev was three or four inches taller than me, which I loved. I liked women who were taller, too. "A take-charge attitude to go along with that gets me going."

"So tall, bossy people with straight spines?" Ev chuckled. "You seem so…take charge, as you say yourself. You're very…together."

I figured that might be his delicate way of asking if I was a top. "I have to be organized. Even when my mom was alive, her husband worked long hours on the graveyard shift, and she always needed my help with the younger kids. And now I have to stay on top of things, help keep us afloat. But when I'm with someone...I like letting go of details. I like someone who can take over and make it so I don't have to think."

There. If he could be delicate, so could I.

"Even with women?" Ev coughed.

"Yes, Ev, even with women." I could really blow his mind and talk about pegging and fem-domme porn, but I restrained myself. "I like...handing over the reins, regardless of gender."

"I'm sorry. That's more a cultural thing on my part. Turkish men...they do not usually like their women...take charge."

"I like take-charge Turkish men. A lot," I said cheekily. We'd definitely moved into the flirty part of this conversation and I was going to enjoy it. Which was where I'd gone wrong with Audrey, letting her pull me into the stockroom and all, but I wasn't mentioning that to Ev.

"Ah." Ev paused a long moment.

"Is that weird?" I finally asked.

"No, not weird...just unexpected."

"A good unexpected?"

"Perhaps." His voice said it was indeed welcome news but he wasn't going to give me the satisfaction of a full answer.

"So tell me your list. What does it for you?" Folding done, I lay back against the couch to let his voice wash over me.

"Hmm. I do not like needy. So as you say, confident is good. No drama."

Seeing as how my life tended to be one clusterfuck of drama, that pretty much ruled me out. "What else?"

Something in my tone must have given my disappointment away. "I do not mean no problems. I mean...no false problems. No mountains out of molehills because someone is ten minutes late or the dinner is a little past done. I like...low-maintenance looks, too. Natural."

"You? You're pretty much a walking menswear ad. You dig scruffy, though?" I was seriously fishing now.

"I do not need someone who can't be...rumpled," Ev said.

Rumple me. Please. I disguised a whimper as a little go-ahead noise.

"But it is not so much about looks with me. People are pleasing in many configurations. It's about...compatibility." The way he said the word took my mind straight past liking the same TV shows and into the bedroom.

"Oh? Tell me more?" I got comfortable against the cushions. Simply enjoying this banter and Ev's deep, musical voice was turning me on more than a little.

"It's personal," Ev hedged.

"I live for personal. Besides, we're friends right? I'll happily overshare whatever you want next."

"Hmm."

"Don't make me start guessing. You need someone with a scarf fetish? Wool allergies need not apply?"

His laugh this time was deep and true. "Allergies can be accommodated. And it's not so much that I have…special tastes as what I don't like."

"Ah. You don't bottom? Don't take this the wrong way, Ev, but I'm pretty sure both New York and Portland are filled with guys dying for you to top them." *Take me, for instance.*

"I do not. Or top. Much."

Now there was an interesting wrinkle. I sat up, hands on my knees. "So no bi guys, no drama, and no anal? That's quite the list, Ev."

"Like I said, I'm…hard to please."

"Just talking hypothetically here…but no anal isn't a deal breaker with me." I was stretching it a bit. I *loved* to get fucked—loved the head trip almost as much as the act itself—but it wasn't like Ev and I were talking a long-term thing. We were flirting. Something I hadn't done in a very long time, and Ev's dislike of anal wasn't reason to stop the fun.

"It's not?" Ev sounded surprised, and I could hear him shifting around, too.

"Yes. I know. It's hard to imagine, but being bisexual doesn't mean penetration's required with me. I love bottoming, sure, but there's plenty of ways to fuck and get fucked. As long as I get that whole not-thinking thing, I'm not choosy."

"Ah."

"You know, Ev, we've really got to broaden your perspective on bi people."

"Perhaps you are right."

I fist pumped the air. Now that was real progress. "Is the not liking anal a cultural thing, too? Like you think it's morally wrong?"

"I thought it was about to be your turn to overshare next?"

"Sure. You get the next two questions. But answer mine?"

"No. It's not a cultural thing per se—obviously the religion I grew up with condemns it, but it's more…I don't like it. Messy. Involved. Uncomfortable…"

Ev needed to never have kids and all the varieties of mess they brought into one's life if he thought anal sex was a distasteful amount of yuck. But to each their own and all that. "I get it. Fair enough. What *do* you like?"

"Nuh-uh. I get a question now. Have you been with more men or more women?"

I didn't have to think hard. "Three girls, four guys. Told you; I'm not exactly a slut."

"And if you could only have one…"

Why did people always want to ask this question? I groaned. "I'd choose the one I was in love with and wanted to spend the rest of my life with. I'm not picking an ice cream flavor. Not that it's going to happen any time soon, but I'd pick a partner. Not a gender."

"And why won't it be happening?" Ev swallowed. Heck, even his sipping beer was a sexy sound.

"The kids. My whole focus has to be on them right now. I don't have time for anything more, and I'm not going to have a parade of people in and out or do a lot of quick hookups."

"Yes. I hear you. My priority is Mira. And it appears we share a dislike of hooking up."

Oh, I'd hook up with Ev in a heartbeat, but I wasn't telling him that. I'd break an awful lot of my rules for him.

"But it's nice to have friends right? Can't have too many of those," I said instead.

"Certainly. Oh, look, another episode is starting. Do you have to go or shall we watch?"

I grabbed the blanket from the back of the couch. "I'm in for the long haul. Bring on the bogus collectible coins episode."

Chapter 5

Dear friends, I get so many questions about knitted gifts. These can be problematic, especially when you are gifting to someone who is not a crafter. Start simple: a quick little project, one that you can give from the heart and not feel put out if the praise isn't as abundant as you might like. Giving should always be its own pleasure.—Evren's Yarnings

Ev and I became regular text and phone buddies after that. We seemed to be in a very similar predicament on the evenings we didn't work. Renee had a new study group this spring term and was leaving me with the kids more and more in the evenings, while Mira's pain was often at its worst in the evenings, making Ev reluctant to leave her. Neither of us had a real way to leave the house, but we were both a little starved for adult contact. My phone would buzz shortly after I got the kids settled, and my pulse would speed up, mouth smiling even though I was alone in the room. I got in the habit of flipping on the TV as soon as I said hello. We worked our way through most of the auction reality shows together, him knitting and me doing laundry or other household stuff while we talked.

"I made something to celebrate spring," he said one day when he came into the shop for some soup as a late lunch. "Flowers."

"Flowers?" I readied his soup and chai as quickly as I could.

He withdrew three knitted blooms from his pocket. Each was affixed to a small clip. "These were my testers. For your girls?"

"Thank you." I smiled broadly. I put them in my apron pocket before the other baristas could notice.

"And for you...shall we have a beer together again tonight?" he asked, making the phone gesture as an older gentleman came in and got in line behind him.

"Absolutely. Working till nine. Call me after."

My phone buzzed around ten, right as I sat down with a microwave pasta dinner as a late snack. The kids and Renee had eaten all of dinner, as usual. That was okay. Coming in to a nice quiet home was its own kind of reward, even if Renee did leave the dishes for me. Oh, well. I'd get those done while I chatted with Ev.

"Hey," I said softly into the phone.

"I am having some baklava and thinking of you," Ev announced.

"Oh man, that sounds amazing. I think this frozen dinner is supposed to be lasagna, but don't quote me on it." I laughed.

"Ah. I made Mira a nice couscous pilaf and some skirt steak. She didn't eat much again. I wish I'd known your dinner was going to be so meager—I would have walked over some leftovers."

"And I would have kissed you," I said without thinking. "My kingdom for a steak."

"I do not generally require...payment for feeding my friends," Ev said carefully. "But I would enjoy cooking for you sometime. *Hala* Tanya and *Hala* Mira taught me to cook and I find it very relaxing."

"My mom's ancient *Betty Crocker Cookbook* and four starving siblings taught me to cook and I hate it. Come cook for me any time. I'll even do the dishes. That's what I'm doing now." I ran the hot water to start dishes. "Maybe the next apartment will have a dishwasher."

"Next apartment?"

"Yeah," I said, and strangely, I found myself telling Ev about the national barista contest and my dreams of a better place for all of us. Not even Renee knew how much the contest meant to me.

"That is indeed a good goal. So you want to stay a barista?" He said it so nonjudgmentally that my defenses didn't kick up like they usually did when people asked me that.

"I tried some community college classes before Mom died. School's just not my thing. After she died, taking on loans for classes I barely passed seemed almost...selfish. Renee's going to school now. She's majoring in environmental studies and has all sorts of save-the-world dreams. But me, I love being a barista. Love the work. Love my customers. But..."

"Yes? Tell me." Ev made me feel like even my wildest dreams weren't stupid.

"There's this barista I used to work with at People's Cup—Robby. He has a coffee cart of his own downtown now. That might be nice. Someday. It takes start-up cash, though, and I'm not sure I'll ever have that."

"Maybe you will win more contests. And it is always good to dream."

"You don't think I'm foolish for not wanting something more... professional?" I thought about that all the time—trying to get something better-paying for the sake of the kids. But being a barista was what I knew. I didn't exactly have a wealth of other employable skills.

"I think it's good honest work, *canim*. You are making the best life you can. That's all any of us can do." Ev's words washed over me like a benediction. It had been so *long* since someone had told me I was doing a good job. I didn't even need to know what the Turkish word meant—it felt good to my ears.

"I'm not exactly impressing people making a living out of knitting," Ev continued. "I had a great job for a bit with a big design house, doing their knitwear line, but I chose to quit to come be with Mira."

"You can always go back to that, get a job with another design place maybe?" My hands started to tense up, but I forced each finger to relax. I'd known all along that Ev might leave again and I couldn't get all invested in him staying. Even if I totally was.

"Perhaps. We will see. Mira talks nonsense about my taking over the shop if..."

"Will you?" Like him, I danced around the specter of the worst-case scenario.

"It is a moot point. She will beat this disease. Iplik is a part of her, not me so much."

I wasn't so sure about that, but I made an encouraging noise.

"But the work I am doing now feeds my soul. Ever since Mira gave me a stack of old *Interweave* magazines to sort, I've known I wanted to design knits. And I was fortunate to go to FIT and get a good education. And yes, I could make much more money doing other things. We all must make peace with the intersection of our dreams and reality."

"Yes. That." Dishes done, I leaned against the counter. "And sometimes reality sucks."

"Yes, yes, it does." Ev groaned and told me a bit about that day's treatment for Mira. I liked that we could be a sounding board for each other. Even when he was venting, I still loved his voice, and I could picture him gesturing with those long, elegant fingers.

Eventually, I migrated to the couch, stretching out. I groaned because it felt so good to finally be off my feet.

"Was that your spine popping?" Ev asked.

"Yes. Forget steak. My kingdom for a massage." Of course my mind went straight to his sexy hands and how much I wanted them on me.

Ev made a sound halfway between disgust and interest. "Massage is… nice. But I do not like oils. Nothing slippery on the hands."

"Just skin is fabulous." Fuck. The thought alone was enough to get me half-hard.

"Showered is nice," Ev mused.

"You're right. You are picky." I laughed. "But if it gets me a massage, I'll shower right the heck now."

"You." Ev made a tsking sound. "You are not angling for a massage. You want the happy ending part."

"Guilty. So guilty. Couldn't *you* use…a happy ending?"

"Perhaps." Ev yawned. "I do not like oils on me either. But touch is nice."

"You've never told me what you *are* in to," I prodded a bit. This cautious dance toward the sexy talk we were doing was the most thrilling thing I'd done in weeks.

"Hmm."

"Come on. You've had a long dry spell. What do you miss most?"

"Kissing. I miss kissing." Ev sighed. "I like…enthusiastic kissing."

"Is that code for you like tongue or is it your delicate way of saying you like the sort of kisses where you're practically devouring the other person?" Okay. Forget half-hard; I was all the way there now.

"Both." There was a shifting noise and I had a feeling Ev wasn't any more comfortable than I was.

"I'm an…enthusiastic kisser," I told him with no false modesty for me. I was good at my job, decent with the kids, but I was fucking fabulous in bed. Particularly with a guy who wanted to eat me alive. Even if he didn't quite want to admit that yet.

"Of that I have no doubt." Ev's voice went a bit deeper. "And apparently you like bossy kissers?"

"Yes. Please. Take control of my mouth. Fuck me with your tongue and I'm a happy man."

"What if I…the other person…wants to kiss a long time? With clothes on?"

"You mean grinding for forever and I don't get to come?" I groaned, pulse speeding up. "That sounds fucking fabulous. Don't mind my begging to come while you do that. Make me wait."

"Begging is…a bonus."

"Knowing you, though, no one gets to make a mess in their clothes right?"

Ev made the tsking sound. "Towels are nice. I'm not opposed to the grinding…concluding with skin to skin. I simply enjoy taking my time. Also, swallowing is a good way to minimize mess, I've found."

"Yeah? Want to hold me down and suck me off?"

Ev's next sound was far from a tsk and more like a rumble of approval. "You are dangerous, Brady, very dangerous."

"Why? Am I turning you on?" My hand wandered over my fly. Not stroking, just firm pressure. We'd danced past sexy talk, far out of the friend zone, now meandering into something dark and heady. I pressed hard against my aching erection as I waited to see how far Ev would let himself go.

"Perhaps. I told you some things, now you tell me. What is your favorite thing?"

"Uh. The long, slow grinding ending in oral that you just described sounds amazing and hits a lot of my buttons. For the record, I'm totally good with…mess. And I like giving oral. Love getting my throat fucked. Being pinned down while grinding or getting my throat fucked, that gets me going."

Ev was silent a long moment. Perhaps I'd pushed him too far. "Tell me about this throat fucking. How do you like it?"

Aw yes. I'd never had phone sex, but I had a feeling we were about to head in that direction. "Where are you right now?"

"In my bed. With a closed door. Are you going to ask me what I'm wearing next?"

"Knitted underwear?" I laughed as I headed for the bathroom— the one room with a lock. My usual jerk-off method was a locked door and a longer-than-necessary shower.

"Sorry to disappoint. Pajama bottoms. I worry *Hala* Mira could need me in the night."

"Hey, you don't have to apologize to me. I share a room with a ten-year-old. I'm going to the bathroom now, though. And locking the door."

"You require a locked door to tell me about giving head?"

"I require a locked door, a quiet house, and about three hours to show you," I countered. "Fuck, Ev. I want you to wear me out."

"Oh, I could. Do not doubt that, Brady. You want me to wear your throat out? Use you so much you need me to feed you some gelato after?"

"Fuck yes," I whispered. "I'd like it if you were on the bed or in a chair and I were kneeling in front of you. Or you were standing in front of me. Me on my knees is the key thing."

"You ever try with your head over the edge of the mattress? It happens that this bed is the perfect height for that..."

"Oh yes. Tell me more. I want to jerk off while you fuck my throat like that."

"Ah. But I don't want that. Perhaps we will need to find other occupation for your hands."

Oh man. Ev knew how to turn my crank big-time. "I'm good with having my hands tied."

I could tell from his inhalation that it worked for him, too. "How flexible are you?"

"Bendier than I look. I had to do yoga stretching exercises to rehab a skateboarding injury. Turns out I dig it."

"Nice. Very nice. I like your mouth very, very much."

"Like the beard? Because if you want my mouth more...exposed, I can work with that. Beard is pure Northwest laziness on my part."

"The beard is...part of the appeal. Your mouth is very full and your beard always seems like it's...teasing. I think I want your hair down, though, yes?"

"Go for it." Getting into it, I pulled my hair free of the ponytail, let it flop against my shoulders. Spit gathered in my mouth like I really was about to get a go at Ev's cock. Fuck. Just the thought had me throbbing. I unzipped to get a little more breathing room. "I want to—"

Knock. Knock. Knock. "Brady, are you in there? I don't feel so good," Jonas called through the door.

Fuck. I kept my curse to myself. "Just a minute, buddy," I called.

"You need to go?" Ev said in my ear. "I understand."

"Yeah, I'm sorry."

"Another time, Brady, another time."

Even if he just meant the phone-sex version of the fantasy, part of me thrilled to his words. And I was pulling hard for the in-person version. Somehow, some way, I was going to get my mouth—and other parts—on Ev.

Chapter 6

Teasing is an essential part of life and of design. As treatment zaps Hala Mira's strength, I find myself looking for new ways to surprise and delight her. I see this coming out in my latest designs, too, that element of the unexpected, the whimsical where one least expects it. And as for myself...yes, I do enjoy teasing as well, and that's all I'm going to say about that.—
Evren's Yarnings

My obsession with Ev's voice grew by leaps and bounds after our almost phone sex, but while our conversations stayed flirty the next few days, we didn't reenter the one-handed conversation territory again. Pity.

"Are you working tomorrow night?" Ev asked as that week's Knit Night wound down. Violet and the triplets were making Mira laugh, which was a great sight to see. The triplets this week were in matching fake fur vests with gaudy plastic buttons and glittery fringe.

"I'm not. I'll have the kids until eight or so, when Renee gets home. What were you thinking?"

"Beer. I was thinking about beer. Or wine. A glass, in person, I think? Maybe halfway between you and me?"

"Perfect. I know just the spot. I can't stay out *too* late, though. I open the next morning." And I couldn't leave the kids overnight. Not that I was leaping *that* far ahead, but my body sure wouldn't mind if we did jump straight from *we can drink in person* to *let's get naked.*

"Likewise. We will have a nice drink." Ev nodded solemnly, like he would will it so. I tried to have the same certainty.

* * * *

Unfortunately, right when I was staring at the fridge trying to decide what I could make the kids for dinner before I grabbed a fast shower, my phone buzzed with a message from Renee.

Home late. Studying with friends. Sorry :(

No, she wasn't sorry. She'd been pulling this a lot lately—going out with friends when she said she'd be home to help. I tried calling her, but it went straight to voice mail. *Fuck.*

Just one night. One beer. Maybe a little groping. Was that too much to ask the universe? Apparently so.

My phone buzzed a second time, but it was Ev, not Renee, on the line.

"I'm sorry," we both said at the same time.

"I need to cancel," I said.

"Rain check?" he said, and we both laughed.

"My sister won't be home to take the kids." I groaned. "So sorry."

"It is okay. Mira, her pain is not so good tonight. She's barely eaten anything all day. She keeps talking about ice cream. Not store ice cream. Some strange stuff with bacon." Ev said bacon the way I might say *pubic hair.*

"Oh, she wants Salt and Straw!"

"Where is that?" Ev sounded so weary and worried about her that I wished I could rub his neck.

I looked over at the kids doing their homework at the table and at the uninspiring contents of the fridge. "It's on Alberta. Not far. Could I bring you some? I can tell you don't want to leave her."

"I don't." Ev made a pained noise. "I shouldn't make you go out with the kids. However, I do have a whole pot of soup here that Mira doesn't want. Could we trade soup for the ice cream with bacon?"

"Absolutely. And trust me: the second I say *ice cream* these guys are going to be all over me. Shall we see you in about an hour or so?"

I made sure that everyone had their reflectors, helmets, and pads on, and then we took the side roads to Salt & Straw, home of some of the most bizarre ice cream flavors in America and a beloved Portland institution. Jonas and I had skateboards, while the twins had the bikes Renee and I had gotten them from Santa the year before. Finding matching bikes at a decent price was totally my best Craigslist find ever. As predicted, the kids were incredibly overjoyed about getting cones. The gourmet ice cream was a pricey treat, but it was nice to be able to indulge them for once.

Madison and Morgan got lavender and strawberry balsamic cones respectively and traded licks while Jonas went straight for the chocolate.

I got Mira the bourbon and bacon ice cream and Ev some artisanal olive oil ice cream I knew Mr. Quality over Quantity would enjoy. The kids finished their small cones before we even reached the store.

Ev met us at the backstairs of Iplik. "You will want to put the bikes in here, girls. And the skateboards too, yes? I have the soup set out for you upstairs."

We stowed our stuff in the storage room at the back of the store and then followed Ev up the rear stairs that came out in the back of the apartment.

"I got you a flavor, too—no bacon. You'll like it." I held out the cartons.

"I will put it in the freezer, but first: soup." He led us to a surprisingly large dining room. I'd assumed the kitchen nook was their only eating area, but this was a real family dining room, with a round table covered in a crisp floral-print cloth and bowls of steaming soup and bread set out. The chairs all matched and the space had terrific energy—like you could sense the joy the room had held. I could almost picture Ev and his aunts enjoying a lot of happy meals there when he was a teenager.

"Oh, I thought you'd just send us back home with plasticware," I said stupidly. The kids raced around, grabbing seats.

"Nonsense." Ev shook his head. "Mira is set with her show. We won't disturb her, but we can enjoy a meal together."

"Mira is not set with her show." A weak-voiced Mira came to the door of the dining room. "We have guests. I will sit at my table a bit, I think. You will bring my cushions?"

"Certainly, *Hala*." Ev scurried away and returned with two pillows. He arranged her like a queen, fussing with her shawl.

"And I think..." She winked at the kids. "I will be very naughty and have my ice cream instead of the soup."

"We had our ice cream first, too!" Madison announced. "Mine was lavender. Brady says it tastes like soap. But I love it."

"It is indeed good to have things you love," Mira said indulgently. Her voice was weak and a bit slurred.

"She's had her pain meds," Ev whispered in my ear. "She'll probably sleep soon, but it is good, I think, for her to see the children."

I wasn't so sure. My siblings were hardly low stress, attacking the soup and bread like they hadn't just had the ice cream treat. They bickered over whose bread had more butter and reached around each other to trade napkins based on color preferences. The soup was really good, though—an interesting mix of barley and spices and ground meat. It was hearty and fortifying and I shared Ev's disappointment that Mira couldn't enjoy it. She ate two or three small teaspoons of ice cream, then put her spoon down.

She mainly seemed to soak in our chaos. She kept smiling at Ev and me encouragingly. *She doesn't want Ev to be alone.* My gut twisted because I got what she wanted for him and I couldn't be that guy—my life was too much of a mess and I didn't have time to give him the focus he deserved. Even a quickie at some point seemed like a pipe dream.

The soup she couldn't eat was a heavy weight in my stomach. *She may not come back from this.* I'd known that of course, but this was the first time the reality of her situation really smacked me. Ev was always so positive on the phone—another treatment, another drug, anything to strive for. He really believed she could beat the odds. Even now, he hovered over her so sweetly. *What will happen to him if she goes?* I didn't want to think about that.

"And now, I think it's time for my TV. A movie perhaps? Would you children like to choose for me?" she asked in a thready voice.

"Oh, we don't need to stay. You need your rest." I shot the twins a look so they wouldn't contradict me.

"Nonsense. I will doze better in the company of these young spirits. And they can choose me something uplifting. Evren will settle me nicely. And you can both have a visit."

The kids were already racing ahead of her to the living room on the promise of TV. I sighed. "I'll help with the dishes. And you'll tell us if they tire you out?"

"We will watch about princesses. It will be lovely. Do not worry." She patted my cheek as she slowly made her way after the kids.

"She sleeps most nights in the recliner now," Ev said, following to settle her in the chair. "Says she can't get comfortable."

"I'm right here, Evren *aşkim*. My ears still work. And I'm an old lady now. I've earned my right to sleep where I wish…" she trailed off sleepily.

"Absolutely, *Hala*." Ev kissed her cheek as he drew the covers over her. "You are warm?"

"Go, enjoy your friend." She made a shooing motion.

"Lead me to your dishes," I said to Ev.

We made quick work of clearing the table. Ev whisked off the cloth and replaced it with a sunny yellow one from a sideboard.

"Sorry the kids ruined the cloth with soup spills."

"Nonsense." His dismissive noise sounded exactly like Mira. "That's why we have a cloth. And it has brightened Mira so much to have them here. Better than a pain pill."

We headed to the kitchen, and doing dishes with Ev was miles better than doing them on my own. For one, he had a dishwasher; for another,

I got to watch his hands and experience a lot of accidental brushes and bumps as we worked. Or not so accidental. We were definitely wandering away from strictly friends territory, but I didn't want to spook him until we reached the destination.

Ev kept checking on Mira and the kids every few minutes. Finally, he leaned against the counter next to me as I washed the last big pot.

"This is so fucking hard." He almost never cursed, so he must have been worn thin by worry over Mira. "She's lost thirty pounds. Withering away. And the chemo…Sorry. I don't mean to vent."

"Vent away." I rubbed his back. Not an I-want-to-seduce-you gesture. Two friends. He needed touch and I needed to give it. "I get it. This would overwhelm anyone."

"How do you do it? With the kids, I mean? Taking care of her feels a bit like parenting in a way. Like our roles are reversed now."

"Oh man." I groaned. I'd never voiced this before. "I went from asking for permission to be out all night to having three kids who needed me for *everything* and a fourth who had to grow up way too fast. I barely slept the first year. Terrified the social workers would take them. Terrified I wasn't up to it."

"I worry about that every night…" Ev relaxed into my touch more, stretching like a cat. God, it had been so *long* since I'd touched anyone like this. "I worry I can't do this. But I am. And I have to."

"One day at time," I said. "That's what gets me through. I can't think of the future. Just until the next school pickup, the next dinner."

"One doctor's appointment to the next. That's the space I'm living in right now," Ev said quietly. "There's not room for anything else."

There was heavy subtext in both our words. There was a huge gap between what we wanted and what we could have. And that gap did nothing to diminish the heat arcing between our bodies. We stood there in quiet commiseration for several long moments, me rubbing his back. I gradually became aware of him staring at my mouth.

I glanced at the doorway. No kids. Happy singing coming from the living room. Glanced back. Ev was still staring. Fine. Two could play at that. I looked at his lips and his hands and all points in between.

You need? Go ahead and take, I said with my eyes. I wasn't going to make the first move. That wasn't the dynamic I wanted between us. I could push, sure, but I wanted him to do the leaping on his own.

He turned so that he was trapping me against the counter. *Yes.* My exhalation echoed through the small kitchen.

"I find I keep thinking of our phone conversation the other night," he said, his breath close enough to ghost across my face.

"Yeah?"

"Enthusiasm...it is maybe missing from both our lives, yes?"

"Absolutely." *Let me show you how enthusiastic I can be.*

"And it is not so...casual to want just a taste?"

"We're friends. Not a bar hookup. Friends. And maybe we both need a friend right now." *An enthusiastic, kiss-me-senseless friend.*

"I think so." Ev's hands bracketed either side of me on the counter, and he leaned in, body a firm pressure against mine, lips against my ear. "Show me."

And then he was kissing me, deep sips of lips and tongue. He worshipped my lips as if he'd been dreaming about them for weeks, and I was no better, inhaling him. I was usually good at taking my time, ramping up slowly, toying with who had control of the kiss, but with Ev, the kiss started in a desperate place and only got more frantic.

"That's very...enthusiastic," he said, pulling back for air. "But you can do better."

Oh fuck yes. Give me directions. I nipped at his lips, inviting him to do the same to me. I opened for his tongue and sucked hard until he started the sort of tongue fucking that had me arching against him, dick straining to get closer.

Heck, enough of this and I could come, no problem. My hands clung to his shoulders, trying to pull him tighter. And it didn't feel like simple relief and release either—it felt an awful lot like comfort despite the roughness of our actions, and I wanted to sink into it.

A loud laugh from the other room—one of the girls—wormed its way into my head. My hands relaxed their hold and my lips slowed, sanity returning in sips and gulps.

"Brady, come watch," Jonas called.

Fuck. I slumped against Ev, my forehead to his chin.

"That was not just a taste—it was a meal," Ev mused, his breath ruffling my hair.

"No, it wasn't." I groaned. "Fuck, that was *good*, Ev. Let's do that again sometime?"

"Without an audience would be ideal." He still hadn't released me.

"Six hours with a locked door is now item one on my life goals list."

"Mine too, and I might add tying you to the bed for half of it," Ev said lightly.

"You're killing me, Ev. You really are."

He finally let go of me and removed two bowls from a nearby cupboard. "But right now, we have ice cream."

"That is absolutely no consolation," I grumbled, but I accepted the serving he dished up and followed him into the living room, brain still foggy from the kissing. The kids had taken over the couch, so I took the floor in front of them. To my surprise, Ev took a seat next to me.

As the movie progressed, our feet bumped. At first it was accidental, then more deliberate contact, little reminders of what we'd shared in the kitchen. We smiled at each other, the best kind of secret between us. Across from us, Mira dozed in her recliner, breathing slow and steady. It was... homey. Made me sleepy, so much niceness.

The twins were starting to nod off, too..."Oh crap." I nudged them with my foot. "We still need to ride back, sleepyheads."

"Do not worry," Ev said. "Mira is resting peacefully. I can take you in her Subaru. We'll put their bikes in back."

"Will you carry me?" Madison stretched her arms out like she was four, not seven.

"Me too." Morgan repeated the gesture.

And so I ended up carrying one twin and Ev, the best sport in the whole world, took the other, Jonas trailing behind us. Mira's Subaru was peppered with knitting-inspired bumper stickers and was at least ten years old, but I was profoundly grateful not to have to herd sleepy kids home.

It was a short drive, but all three kids were asleep in the backseat when we pulled into the apartment complex. Ev spent a long time looking in the rearview mirror at them, contemplating.

"Yes, we can risk it," I said and leaned in for a quick kiss. I was careful not to ramp things up like in the kitchen, but even this quick contact felt full of promise, and it made me want all sorts of things I couldn't have.

Chapter 7

Dear friends, I find I am obsessed with blue and brown
combinations lately. And not just any blue—a crisp ocean blue,
more turquoise than pastel. The brown is a deep, tweedy nut
brown, shot through with reds and caramel hints. Thus was
born my newest project on the needles…—Evren's Yarnings

We kissed in the car. We kissed on my front step as I walked him out after we deposited the kids in their beds. We snuck a quick kiss in the back hallway of People's Cup after Knit Night. We were the kings of sneaky looks and weighted pauses and lightning-fast kisses in this…friendship that neither of us paused to redefine as something else. We were friends. Now we were friends who kissed, which clearly was outside the boundaries Ev had set for us, but I wasn't about to remind him of that. He still didn't date casually or date bisexuals; I still didn't have time for serious. But kissing? Everyone had time for a bit of kissing.

What we lacked was time for more than kissing.

"I don't have to be in until two tomorrow," I said to Ev on the phone one night. "Weird short shift. But it's Knit Night, so I'll see you there right?"

"Of course. Violet and Mira and the triplets would come after me if I didn't show." He'd picked up on my nicknames for a number of the knitters, which was cute. Similarly, I occasionally found myself doing his habit of phrasing statements as questions. We were rubbing off on each other. But not the kind of rubbing I *really* wanted.

"Yeah, they would. All the ladies want to adopt you."

Ev made a dismissive noise. He didn't believe me that he had a huge fan club—attendance numbers were up at Knit Night and despite what

Ev thought, he was the primary reason. And with Knit Night getting even more popular, a trickle-over effect had started with knitters showing up in clumps on other nights of the week and coming by to grab their morning coffee from us. Business was up for the first time since Chris left, and that had Randy doling out more hours to me and me grateful to Knit Night for a whole variety of reasons.

"But why not come here for lunch?" he asked. "I will take my lunch break and cook for you. Mira is having a good week—it's a rest week from chemo, and she will be downstairs in the shop. I have moved a rocking chair there for her to sit and knit while Adele works the counter. Mira is too social to spend all day with the TV. She takes her energy from others—"

"Back up. You mean we could be alone? Like alone-alone?" A hot spark chased its way up my spine.

"I do believe that is what I said, yes. My bedroom, it is over the stockrooms. Very private," he continued conversationally. "But tell me, are you a screamer? Because we may have to entice you to be quiet…"

I swallowed hard. I loved the little bit of kinky, pushy edge Ev showed from time to time. "I can be quiet. Give me something to bite if I'm not. I'm not crazy about being gagged."

"Something to bite? Oh, Brady, we may need more than a lunch hour."

"Tell me about it."

Ev met me at the back entrance of Iplik, where we snuck upstairs like a couple of teenagers. He was older than me, twenty-eight to my twenty-three, but I liked how much more settled he was in his skin than most guys my age. Still, for all our comparable maturity, we laughed and pushed at each other on the stairs.

I could have entered through the front of the store—I knew Ev had told Mira where he'd be and she was nothing if not supportive of Ev's and my friendship, but something about having a secret lunch date had me kissing him before we even reached the top of the stairs.

"Why do I feel like we're getting away with something?" Ev mused as he broke away from the kiss to open the door.

"Because we are." I chased him into the apartment, trying to capture him for another kiss. Actually, to be more accurate, I wanted him to capture *me*. Push me up against the wall…However, to my dismay, he led me to the kitchen.

"I want to show you what I made for lunch—"

"Ev. Really? There's food?" I groaned. "I thought—"

"Dolma, köfte, and cacik. I thought you would like to try."

"I would." I was trying desperately to be a good sport and not be disappointed that I wasn't getting intimately acquainted with his bed.

"Ah! See?" He opened the refrigerator to reveal a neat row of glass jars. "For you to take. After. And here is a lunch sack for you." He picked up a small knitted cotton tote from the counter.

"You made this?" I fingered the thick spongy yarn. Blocks of blue and brown formed the sort of mosaic pattern I was starting to associate with Ev's signature look.

"Yes. The blue reminded me of your eyes."

Pile of goo, party of one. He noticed little things about me, like when I changed my earrings out or whether my hair was back or up on a given day. "You mean it's for me? Not just to borrow?"

"Of course it is for you. Who else did I make a takeaway lunch for?" Ev bristled a bit. "But it is for after. Don't forget to grab it if you are... pressed for time."

"After." I leaned against the counter, content to let him orchestrate this show. "And I'm going to be pressed for time?"

"Very." And then he was *finally* on me, pressing me against the cabinets with a hard kiss. He tasted like strong coffee and sugar and a whole lot of pent-up lust. Breathing hard, he pulled away to tug me down a side hall I hadn't seen before. "Someday I'm going to do very improper things to you in that kitchen."

"Promises, Ev, promises. Show me this room with a door."

"And a lock." He raised one dark eyebrow as he opened a doorway. "After you."

The bedroom was a very Ev space—lots of browns and grays held together with unexpected splashes of color like a teal pillow and a terracotta knit throw draped over the chair in the corner. A full-size bed sat against one wall, and I didn't care that it wasn't bigger. We didn't need a lot of room because I planned for us to be mashed together soon enough. It was higher than normal beds, with drawers under it for extra storage and a thick wooden headboard and footboard.

Because time was of the essence, I toed off my shoes and started to pull off my shirt, but Ev made that disapproving noise of his again.

"Oh, right. Clothing on." I laughed at him. "I forgot. You are a man of particular tastes."

"Yes, yes, I am. And right now, my favorite flavor is you."

Ev kissed me like we had all the time in the world, which was strangely relaxing. He slid his lips over mine with whisper-soft precision—light but expertly angled for maximum tease. I exhaled around the kisses, the rush-

rush of my everyday life falling away. We stood next to the bed, but it seemed less urgent now, like it would wait patiently for Ev's fantasy to unspool. I'd had a lot of kisses over the years from both genders, but Ev was the first to kiss me like I was precious, worth savoring. Ev kissed like I *mattered*.

His eyes were closed as his tongue finally slipped inside and dominated my mouth, but I felt more *seen* than I had in years. Every time I tried to start grinding, Ev's hands stilled my hips. He nuzzled my beard, kissed my ears, licked my neck, blessed my eyebrows and nose with feathery kisses, and still no grinding.

"Please. Ev." My voice was already lower and needier than usual.

Ignoring my pleas, he expertly fended off my own roving hands as he let down my hair, briefly burying his face in it like he wanted to memorize my shampoo. Pushing the neck of my shirt down, he sucked along my collarbone.

"Killing me here, Ev." My voice sounded shaky even to my own ears. "I need your skin."

"You said you like me taking over?"

"Yes—" My answer was edging close to a whine.

"And overwhelmed? Are you not sufficiently overwhelmed?" His voice washed over me, stronger and more erotic than any rope.

"Well—" I started, but he cut me off, tumbling us onto the bed, him on top. "Yes. That. Push me into the bed."

"You like being held down?" He peered down at me, body already moving to pin me in place before his mouth attacked me again.

"Love it." I arched against him, just to test the hold he had on me. Delightfully, he pushed me down hard with his pelvis. Not grinding, but his cock was a thick, solid weight against my own, anchoring me.

Ev took my hands and placed them on the headboard. "Good. Now I'm going to have some fun."

"Awesome. Use me." I stretched against him. I *needed* this, and every cell hummed with awareness.

Ev moved my shirt again to kiss my neck and collarbones. "Keep holding on."

Then he pushed up the sleeves to kiss and lick at each wrist in turn, kissing each bit of skin he uncovered. I wore two bracelets on my left wrist that the twins had made, and Ev gently moved those aside to lick at my pulse point. It was a simple cotton long-sleeved shirt, but I resolved to wear something with buttons next time we did this.

"Should I be wearing a cardigan for this?" I laughed, trying to distract myself from the very real possibility of coming in my pants at some point.

"Shh." Ev moved so that he could lick my waist, uncovering a narrow strip of skin, and my next laugh died in my throat. He raised the shirt millimeters at a time, and when his lips finally found one of my pierced nipples, I almost shot on the spot.

"Ev. Seriously. I didn't bring spare pants."

"You have very little self-control." He made a little chiding noise that went straight to my dick before he went back to teasing my nipples with little licks and flicks. I'd gotten them pierced on a whim when I was nineteen, but Ev played them like a finely tuned instrument and made my impulse seem like genius.

And I wasn't kidding—my balls tightened and I had to start making complicated drinks in my head to keep from exploding. Eventually, mercifully, Ev returned to my waistband and unzipped me, but his microscopic removal technique had me cursing softly and clutching the headboard hard. He kissed everywhere *but* my aching dick—tops of my thighs, all around my patch of hair, over the arch of my hip bone—until finally my pants were around my lower thighs and my shirt was around my neck. He sat back on his heels, surveying his work like he was very pleased with himself for trapping me with my own clothes and driving me out of my mind.

Then, wordlessly and in one smooth motion, he swallowed my dick down. I arched up, but his strong forearms locked me in place.

"Wait. Want to get you off, too," I panted. My body was used to very efficient orgasms—five-minute shower specials. On very rare occasions, though, I got a chance to practice edging, and Ev made me feel both like I'd been edging for hours and like I was on the express train to quick and dirty. His nimble tongue danced through whatever restraint I had.

Ev lifted his head long enough to say, "You are."

"Want to touch you." I groaned, but my hands didn't leave the headboard.

My cock still in his mouth, Ev grinned up at me wickedly. He let it slide out of his mouth with a loud *plop*, a lewd sound that made my balls tighten up. "I have fantasized about this for *weeks*. You at my mercy. Touching and tasting you until I've had my fill. Next time, I will allow you to touch. But right now, I am going to live out my fantasy, thank you very much."

"When you put it that way…"

"There is much I want to do to you, but if you don't be quiet…" he trailed off ominously.

"Shutting up now."

He gave a dark laugh before swallowing me down again. He didn't deep throat, but that was okay—his dexterous hands teased the base of my shaft and my balls, working in concert with his generous mouth to make me pant and moan. Remembering what Ev had said about noise, I turned my head to bite one of Ev's fluffy pillows.

"Yes. Bite the pillow. Such a beautiful picture," Ev praised in between more sucks and licks. I wasn't touching him and we weren't even all the way naked yet, but I still felt closer to him than I had anyone in years.

"Fuck, Ev...gonna..." The bastard slowed it down, keeping me riding the edge for what felt like decades, until without warning, he tightened his grip, fingers just this side of too rough on my balls, and that was it. I buried a scream in the pillow as I came. He swallowed greedily around my cock, and the sensation was enough to milk out a few more spurts. The orgasm made my whole body shudder and my hands dropped away from the headboard.

"So beautiful." Ev sat up, kneeling next to me. He wiped his face delicately with a towel at the foot of the bed.

"You planned ahead." I laughed. I patted my chest and shoved a pillow behind my head. I wasn't moving, but I *needed* his cock. "Your turn now."

Ev considered my offer like it was a choice of entrees, head tilting to one side. "In my...fantasy, I shot on your stomach. Because you are good with being made a mess."

Hot as the image of Ev jerking off was, I was desperate to taste him. "Fuck. That's hot. Let me suck you until you're close, then you can make all the mess you want on me."

I liked his curious bundle of quirks—hating wet mess and stuff on his hands but wanting to paint me with his cum. The unwrapping me bit by bit had been kinky and sweet and dirty all at the same time. My cock stirred at the memory, waking up a bit more as Ev unzipped and unveiled a thick, uncut cock with a plump head.

"Fuck. Ev, you're delicious. Get up here."

Straddling my chest, he fed me his cock with the same slow deliberateness he'd explored my body, first giving me only the heavy head. My hands bracketed his hips, but there was no question who was driving this show. In my fairly limited experience, some cock-heads were perfectly round, while others were ovals, but Ev's had an interesting elongated angle to it, giving it an almost elegant flair before the thick crown and ridge of foreskin.

He kept a hand on his dick, controlling how much I could suck, and that bit of bossiness got my motor humming again big-time. It also motivated me to do my best work with my lips and tongue, teasing and dancing over his tip, lapping up the copious pre-cum from his slit. The salty tang of pre-cum had always turned me on, and I loved guys like Ev, who made lots for me to lick up and tease out. Finally, he slid his hand back a bit and gave me more to play with. I groaned as the thick length of him slid over my tongue. He was wide enough that I had to do some oral gymnastics to keep my teeth at bay, but not so long as to tax my ability to take all he wanted to give me.

He found a rhythm of slowly fucking my mouth in long, fluid strokes punctuated by soft curses. If I hadn't come minutes earlier, his husky whispers combined with the taste of his cock might have been enough to tip me over. He didn't speed up, but his breathing hitched, and I could tell by the tension in his thighs that he was getting closer. He started going deeper, little jerks of his hips now, not pulling all the way back. My eyes watered and my throat stung and the sensations washed over me in a perfect wave as my focus narrowed to only him and his cock fucking my mouth, him owning me so thoroughly that I needed him for my next breath.

"*Siktir.*" Ev moaned the word. I didn't have to speak Turkish to know he was almost there. I loosened my grip on his hips so he could slide backward, jerking himself with a surprisingly loose grip over my bare stomach. Less than five strokes and he was covering me with thick ropes of cum that pooled on my belly.

"My imagination is clearly not good enough," Ev panted, staring at his handiwork for a long moment. Eyes locked on his, I dragged a finger through the puddle, then brought it to my mouth, licked it clean.

"Dirty man." Ev laughed approvingly as he fumbled for the towel, first gently dabbing at his dick, then cleaning me up with a tender thoroughness before collapsing next to me.

"Mine either." I touched his face, pulling him closer. He smiled at me for a long moment, and I had a feeling he was trying to decide if he was okay with tasting himself on my lips. Just when I was about to roll away, he surprised me by capturing my mouth in a soft kiss. We made out like that for several long minutes, trading little kisses and touches.

"Oh, Brady, I want—"

Beep. Beep. Beep. The alarm clock on Ev's nightstand beeped angrily. I glanced at the time and winced. "Fuck. I'm going to be late!"

"Hence the alarm." Ev sat up and rubbed his face. I scrambled to rearrange my clothes and get my shoes on. "Don't forget your lunch!"

As I hurried down the stairs, lunch tote in hand, I realized Ev had never finished his thought. All the possibilities made my stomach flop around. Over at the People's Cup, I got my hands washed and my apron on with two minutes to spare. I had to simply hope that what Ev wanted was what I wanted, and that for once in our lives, we might actually get it.

Chapter 8

Dear friends, longtime reader Reba writes, "You have so many gorgeous sweater patterns for men. Which do you suggest I knit for my new boyfriend?" No, dear Reba, no. Unfortunately, I'm here to tell you that the curse of the boyfriend sweater is real. I listen carefully to the ladies in the shop and at Knit Night, and everyone, including yours truly, has a horror story of the sweater gifted too soon. May I gently suggest limiting the number of skeins required for your gift to the number of years you have been together? And for goodness' sake, put a ring on him before you gift him a sweater. —Evren's Yarnings

Given Renee's general stubbornness lately, I shouldn't have been surprised when she showed up at six on a Knit Night with Jonas in tow.

"I tried to see if Carlos's mother would take him," she said, bypassing any attempt at a greeting. Carlos was Jonas's best friend, and his mother was already doing me a huge large by taking him the weekend I had the barista contest. The twins were going to their best friend's house that weekend as well. Not that Renee couldn't handle the kids for a weekend in theory, but she had a geology overnight field trip that weekend. And even if she didn't…Renee couldn't be trusted not to pull stunts like this.

That night the twins were going on a birthday dinner and kid movie date with their best friend, and Renee and I had had an argument the night before about how Jonas could not be home alone while she went on a study date. She'd asked if he could come hang out at People's Cup, something we'd had to do once in an extreme emergency, but I couldn't have that on Knit Night, when we got so crowded.

"Look, I can give you guys some soup and bread for dinner before you head home, but Renee, I told you to break the study date." I kept my voice firm, but I knew my parental tone didn't work on Renee. Neither of us had signed up for this, but we were a team. And our team had rules—like no boys over while she had the kids. We'd had some issues early on with her friends distracting her from the kids' needs. "Look, I'll hurry home. You can do a late-night study date. And I'll do the getting ready for school by myself tomorrow."

"Why don't you want me to be happy?" Tears filled Renee's eyes. "This is the nicest guy I've *ever* met, and I keep needing to put him off to take care of the kids."

Join the fucking club. But of course I couldn't say that in front of Jonas. I'd planned to be even later than usual by sneaking in some quality Ev groping. *That* so wasn't happening now. It didn't matter if Ev was the nicest guy or the sexiest or the sweetest—the kids came first, something Renee just couldn't seem to grasp. In the two weeks since our lunch date, Ev and I had managed exactly one other quickie, a lot of nonsexy phone calls, one furtive sext session, and another whispered late night of phone sex. Renee needed to take a number in the I'm-entitled-to-see-my-friends sweepstakes.

Her tears spilled over and my chest squeezed tight. She was still so much a kid herself. I knew I'd regret it, but I rubbed her arm. "Fine. This *one* time, Renee. This can't become a habit. If someone complains, I could get fired."

"You won't!" She waved, already backing out of the store before I could change my mind. Eventually, we needed to have a long, painful chat about this new behavior of hers. I was barely functional as a caregiver for the little kids. I had no clue how to parent a teenager. I tried. I laid down rules, but lately she just blew through everything, like today.

I didn't allow myself the luxury of missing Mom very often, but right then, I missed her so much my eyes squished shut and my hands clenched. She would know the right thing to say to Renee. But me? I had no clue.

I set Jonas up in the very rear of the shop at a tiny table almost no one used, with strict instructions not to leave his chair.

However, I underestimated Violet and her furniture rearranging crew, who came in a few minutes early. The triplets were wearing what appeared to be purses masquerading as tank tops—thick, bulky yarn in a weird tapestry pattern with leather straps. Even Portland's penchant for the weird couldn't make those acceptable fashion choices, but I was more concerned with their looks and clucking.

"Who lets a *child* come to a coffee shop on his own?"

"Do you see a parent, Violet?"

"We *always* use that as the head table." The triplet in the fuzzy olive-green tank shook her head sadly. "Maybe someone should report he's here on his own."

Oh, for fuck's sake. I was going to have to confess he was with me and that was *not* going to go well—

"Ah! Young Jonas! You were dropped off early? How kind of you to wait for me." Ev breezed past the triplets and Violet. I wasn't sure how much of their judgy conversation he'd heard, but he sent me a smile as he effortlessly bailed me out. "You will sit next to me, yes?"

Jonas studied his iPod, chewing on his lower lip. *Please say yes*, I tried to beam at him. If he balked, this wasn't going to work. Finally, he nodded. "Can I have a hot chocolate?"

Way to negotiate, kid. "Of course. Let me go order." Ev smiled at him.

Because Ev the almighty had spoken, the women transformed into the other type of hens—coddling Jonas and making sure he was all set next to Ev's usual seat.

"Everything okay?" Ev asked in a low voice as he came up to the counter.

"Yeah—" I started, then stopped. This was Ev, the one person who might get it. "No, it isn't. Renee couldn't watch him. He can't be home alone—"

"Of course not." Ev nodded. He'd heard enough Jonas stories from me on the phone that he understood Jonas's special needs in a way Renee didn't seem capable of. "You should have called me. I am thinking about doing some children's classes and projects at the store."

"You're a lifesaver." My chest expanded at how ready he was to help me. Ever since Mom died, it had been only me and Renee, with no one to call for backup. Hadn't even occurred to me that Ev and I were that kind of friends—the hey-I'm-in-a-jam kind—but I guessed we were. It felt weird. I'd spent so many hours trying desperately *not* to need help, to prove to the social workers and the doubters that I was up for the task. But every time I vented to Ev, it felt like a crane knocking away another chunk of concrete from my shoulders.

"It is nothing." He waved the praise away.

"It's not. And I'm sure Mira agrees—bet she's thrilled you're doing more with the store. Everything okay?" I wasn't sure exactly how to ask how Mira's treatments were going. Ev never wanted to talk about them on the phone. I hoped eventually he'd let me reciprocate his willingness to help and open up about his worries about Mira like he had that night in the kitchen.

"I will be around a bit longer. It is okay, though—only some minor setbacks. It is not like I am in a rush, and I've thought about doing classes for a while. In fact, I'm going to run back over, get him some big needles and thick yarn—"

"I'll pay," I said, my throat all thick and tight.

"Don't be ridiculous." Ev waved the offer away. "He is my test case. We must see if I am capable of teaching any young people to knit before I start charging for it. He is doing me a favor. You will see."

Fifteen minutes later, Ev was back with a large ball of yellow yarn—Jonas's favorite color—and some thick wooden needles that looked pricey even from a distance and a sign-up sheet for Knit Night members who would be interested in a children's class. Leave it to Ev to turn my misfortune into an opportunity and further sell the Knit Night ladies on his brilliance. In fact, not a single person complained about Jonas, and Violet and the triplets doted on him. To my surprise, Jonas preened under all the attention. He was a typical middle kid at home—quietly enduring the chaos of the twins as they demanded all the energy Renee and I had to give. But here, he was laughing and actually talking as Mira slipped him pieces of the cookie she was supposed to be eating.

She looked tired and frail, and I felt bad that Ev was distracted with teaching Jonas instead of focusing on her. I said as much when he came up for more hot chocolate for Jonas.

"He is the best medicine for her. Not much I can do anymore." Ev shrugged helplessly. It was the most he'd admitted about her condition, and my teeth clenched hard around expressions of pity he neither needed nor wanted.

He turned back toward the table, and we both watched as Mira praised Jonas's efforts, straightening his grip with her own trembling hands. Ev's eyes flickered with heavy shadows, and I longed to rub his shoulders, get some of the tension out, maybe gift him with a nap to relieve some of the circles under his gorgeous dark eyes.

Ev turned back to face me, making an obvious effort to smile. "Now, what should I order for me?"

"Decaf latte," I said with a grin. I might not be able to give him a nap with a happy ending like I wanted, but I could make him smile.

The initial drink rush was over, so I could take my time, and I did a careful latte art just for him—a little sweater and two knitting needles.

"I love it." Ev's smile made me want to make him dozens of lattes.

"We are not *quite* to the sweater gifting stage, though." He said the last bit like the punch line to a joke I should know.

"Knitting humor?" I asked.

"Something like that." He winked at me as he collected the drinks and headed back to the table.

As the evening wound to a close, I came out from behind the counter to help put the tables back.

"So, what's the verdict? Is Ev a good teacher?" I asked Jonas.

"The best. See what I made?" Jonas held out a scrap of lumpy knitted fabric. "It's going to be a blanket for my guinea pig."

"You're not getting a guinea pig." All three kids were desperate for a pet, but with my hours and their schedules, it so wasn't happening. Jonas looked at me like I stole the last chocolate bar and I sighed. "Sorry, buddy. Maybe someday."

"It would make a lovely coaster for a pot of tea," Mira said faintly.

"Can I *at least* have a teapot? One that plugs in?" Jonas asked. Kid didn't even *drink* tea, but that was how his brain worked—an errant comment from Mira and he was off to the races. All that boiling water and the kid with no impulse control? My insides went all wobbly at the thought. "How about a water pitcher?"

"I think I'll take Mira home, get her settled while you close up," Ev said, touching my shoulder. Even that small contact had me wanting to sink into him. "But then I can come and give you a ride home?"

"You don't have to." It would be a long trudge without a skateboard for Jonas, but we'd done it before.

"I want to." Ev looked right at my mouth as he said the words. "And you do not work Sunday night right? I want to cook for you again."

My whole body went hot at the memory of the last time Ev had cooked for me. When I'd finally eaten the food on my break, each bite had been laced with the memory of his kisses. I wasn't sure whether he meant cook or *cook*, but I had to shake my head.

"It's Brady's birthday!" Jonas fairly trembled with excitement. "And we're going to the zoo in the morning. Like last year. And then we'll help him make the cake!"

"It's your birthday?" Ev made a tsking sound, like I should have told him sooner.

"Yeah." Truth was, I didn't need a big fuss. Last year, Mom's death had been fresher, and my birthday had been more about giving the kids something to get excited over and feel connected as a family about than something for me. But as I'd found out, kids love making traditions out of things. So zoo and a cake it was.

"Jonas? Do you think your plans could include dinner at my house?" Ev spoke directly to Jonas. Manipulative, brilliant bastard. "If you want help making the cake, you could come early. Or you can bring the cake and I will do dinner."

Jonas considered his options with a very adultlike furrowed brow. "We'll bring the cake. Do you know how to make whipped cream?"

"I do indeed," Ev said solemnly. "Now, what is Brady's favorite food?"

"*Brady* loves all the Turkish stuff you've made me," I interjected before Jonas could request pizza or spaghetti, both of which were *his* favorites.

Jonas thought for a minute. "Nothing *too* weird. And lots of bread. The floppy kind you had with the soup."

"Consider it done. Lots of bread. Maybe kebab? That's meat on sticks?"

Jonas nodded. "We'll bring him to you at dinnertime. He doesn't want presents unless we make them ourselves."

"That I can most certainly do." Ev's eyes sparkled.

Later, as he drove us home, I said quietly, "You don't have to make me something. And the kids are going to exhaust Mira. And it's not like we'll be able to—"

"One more *and* and I'm going to make you barley water and knit you something unmentionable out of fake fur," Ev grumbled. "It's your birthday. People want to do nice things for you. Your job is to let them."

"All right. Although I'm intrigued by the fake fur—"

"Hush. We do not speak of such atrocities." Ev did an exaggerated shudder as he pulled up by the apartment building.

"Thanks for the ride," I said, checking my phone to see a message that the twins were on their way home as well.

"Any time." Ev spent a long moment looking right at my mouth, his eyes furrowed, like he was doing some complicated calculus about whether or not to kiss me good night.

I solved the issue for him by leaning in to brush a quick kiss across his lips. Damn. Even the briefest contact with Ev's mouth had all the sizzle.

"Call me later." I gave him a heated look promising all the whispered dirty talk he could stand. And yes, that was totally what my game was reduced to these days.

"Is Ev like your boyfriend?" Jonas asked as I grabbed my skateboard from the back of the car.

I waited until we were on the path to the apartment to answer. "Not exactly."

"But you both like kissing boys right?" Jonas pressed.

"Yes. We both like kissing boys." Oh, if only Ev saw it as simply as a ten-year-old.

"I don't want to kiss a boy." Jonas made a sour face as he considered the prospect.

"When you're older, you can kiss whomever you'd like, as long as they want to kiss you back," I said carefully, ruffling his hair.

"Ev kissed you back." Jonas gave me a sly smile. "I think you guys should be boyfriends. I like him."

"I like him too." I sighed as I opened the door to the apartment. *I like him far, far too much.*

Chapter 9

Because we have spent so much time on gift knits the last few months, dear friends, I wanted to share my latest design with you. And I know I'm going to have a hundred comments, all asking me about the recipient, and all I can say is: no comment. Not yet at least... —Evren's Yarnings

The day of my birthday was the sort of perfect Portland spring day that makes all the rainy months worth it—gorgeous blue skies, mild temperatures, and green everywhere we looked. People too. The buses and sidewalks were crammed with people soaking up the change in seasons. The zoo was packed, but the kids had a great time. We didn't have the money to do many outings like this, so it was nice to indulge them a bit. The girls wore the flowers Ev had knit them, and I posed them by a statue and sent him the picture. He replied back quickly.

Happy birthday, tatlim. I am looking forward to later ;)

Ha. I sincerely doubted there would be anything to wink over tonight, not with the kids and Mira around and Renee glued to her phone like it was a needy infant, responding to the slightest beep with a little excited "oh!" Yeah, no way was I getting her to watch the kids long enough for us to sneak off. And I also really needed to download a Turkish translator app. I knew he liked sneaking the little Turkish pet names in, but I really wanted some sort of hierarchy to them that could magically reveal how he felt about me. Was he over the bisexual bias enough to see me as more than a friend with benefits? Did I *want* to be seen that way? I studied the flamingo exhibit, like the gaudy birds might have a clue about my twisted feelings.

"Come on, Brady! Snakes are next!" Jonas bounced on his feet. Slimy reptiles. That was more like it. No mooning over fanciful creatures and even more unrealistic thoughts. I might love—

Wait. Where did that thought come from? I most certainly was *not* falling in love with Ev. Even I wasn't *that* stupid.

"Wait up, buddy! We're coming, too." *Stop thinking impossible things. Focus on the kids.*

My thoughts were still jumbled when we arrived at Ev and Mira's that night, lumpy cake in tow. It was supposed to be vanilla with chocolate frosting and sprinkles, but it looked more landslide than layer cake. The twins had taken a very rare nap when we'd come home, leaving me and Jonas to make the cake while Renee murmured sweet nothings into her phone.

Balancing the cake on the bus ride up Alberta didn't help its appearance any. Ev let us in the back entrance, and he was exceedingly polite to Renee, whom he was meeting for the first time. When we reached the top of the stairs, he did that thing again where he kept looking at my mouth. I might not know exactly how we felt about each other, but I knew what that signal meant.

I brushed a quick kiss across his mouth, reveling in how his whole body seemed to light up from the contact.

"Eww." Renee rolled her eyes. "If you get to make out with your boyfriend, does that mean I can bring Indigo over when I have the kids tomorrow?"

"Absolutely not." I had rules with her about having friends over when she was watching the kids for good reason. I did, however, notice that neither Ev nor I corrected her about the boyfriend label.

"What can I help you with?" I asked him in the kitchen a few minutes later, once we got the kids settled in the living room with a TV program and a dozing Mira.

"This." Ev pushed me against the fridge, kissing me hungrily. He licked at my lips before spearing me with his talented tongue. I loved when he took charge like this, and I was grateful the cold press of the fridge held me upright and kept me from combusting.

"Happy birthday," Ev said as he pulled away. "Now you may help me plate things."

"No fair." I laughed. "You turn me into goo and then you put me to work?"

"Exactly." He winked at me.

"Sorry Renee's being pissy," I said as I held a platter for Ev to arrange skewers of meat on. "She's all hung up on this boy."

"I know the feeling." He gave me a long, searching look that made me shift from foot to foot. "Waiting for the next text."

My laugh was tinged with the relief that I wasn't alone in the craziness. "Counting down the hours until the house is quiet enough to call."

"Trying to figure out how much kissing you can get away with on the clock." He dumped a bunch of rice into a bowl.

I cast a glance back toward the living room. "Or with small people around."

"At least one more." Ev set the rice down and pulled me into the corner for another scorching kiss.

"Okay. Maybe I can't be too hard on her," I said, panting hard as we finally came up for air. "Does it bug you when the kids call you my boyfriend?"

"Should it?" Ev raised an eyebrow.

"No! I mean, I'm not *encouraging* it, but I wouldn't mind…" I trailed off, not sure how much of my inner wants to reveal.

"Yes, you wouldn't mind?" Ev encouraged, still all crowded into my space, not giving me room to regroup.

"I wouldn't mind if it was…accurate."

"Well, I *am* a male. And we are very good friends, yes?"

"Yeah…" I drew the word out. "If you want to get technical. But there are other definitions…"

"And you are going to let the kebabs get cold while you figure out which is most accurate?" Ev raised both eyebrows this time, his expression pure mirth. He had me on the ropes and he knew it.

"You're enjoying this far too much," I grumbled.

"The Knit Night ladies keep calling you my boyfriend, too," Ev mused. "And as with the children, I strangely do not mind. Do we need a specific definition? Isn't it enough to just enjoy this…whatever? For however long I'm still needed here?"

I need you here always. I realized with the sharp clarity of a perfect espresso shot that I didn't want a *whatever* with Ev. I wanted the standard definition—the not seeing other people, cuddling up at the end of the day, putting each other first....

And there the fantasy fell apart because that wasn't happening for either of us. We barely had time for discreet kissing, let alone a real relationship.

But damned if I didn't want one.

"No phone at the table," I said to Renee for the third time. She'd been hiding it in her palm and under the tablecloth, but I knew what she was up to.

"You texted Ev during dinner the other night," she accused. She wasn't wrong, and I resolved to crack down on both of us, even during quick meals.

"I had a good reason," I lied. "And we are *guests*. Put the phone away."

"It is fine." Mira smiled indulgently at us. Her smile wasn't quite worth the awkward family argument, though, and I needed Renee not to be rude.

"Fine. I think I'm taking off after dinner anyway. I've got a huge test tomorrow."

"So you're going home to study?" I couldn't keep the skepticism from my voice.

"Library." She studied her flat bread intently, refusing to meet my eyes. "There're too many distractions at home."

I had a feeling there was a six-foot distraction named Indigo at the library, but I leveled a glare at her instead.

"I can take you and the children home later," Ev said to me.

"Wonderful." Renee gave him a gold-medal smile. "See, Brady? It'll all work out. You get to hang out with your boyfriend and I get to…study."

I coughed. "Invite Indigo to get a coffee with you at People's Cup this week. I think I need to lay eyeballs on this kid."

"No!" Her eyes went wide. "You'll scare him off. Besides, I haven't exactly told him about…you."

I had no idea whether she meant telling him about me being a bisexual and kind-of/sort-of having a boyfriend or telling him about me and the kids and her home responsibilities, but we couldn't have this conversation in front of Ev and Mira. Ev got twitchy whenever the word *bi* came up, and besides, we didn't need to air our family business in front of them when they had way more serious problems to confront.

"Bring him by," I said sternly. "And we'll talk more later."

"You know, *tatlim*, it is always better to be honest," Ev said to Renee. Wait. She was *tatlim*, too? I was back to feeling muddled about what Ev felt about me and what *whatever* meant.

Renee rolled her eyes at both of us and wasted no time in escaping as soon as her plate was empty. She didn't even stick around for cake, which honestly was probably for the best. Her negative attitude had spread toxic vibes over the whole evening. She and I were going to have a long heart-to-heart very soon.

She gave me an IOU card for an evening off bedtime duty on her way out and my frustration softened a bit. She knew me better than anyone. No way could I raise these kids without her help.

Jonah shyly offered up the lumpy knit square he'd been working on all week. "It's kind of a cross between a coaster and a towel and a scarf," he said.

"I love it," I said and ruffled his hair.

The twins both made me books with stick-figure pictures and uneven writing, and my throat burned as I thought about how much Mom had loved gifts like that. "Can I take these to work? Show them off?" I asked, my voice a bit gruffer than usual.

"You should frame them," Madison said confidently.

"I don't want people looking at mine," Morgan said. "I made it just for you."

"Fair enough," I said and turned my attention to the last package on the table. It was wrapped in shiny silver paper with a brown fabric ribbon with crisp corners and a perfect tape job worthy of a high-end department store. And it was exactly the wrong setting for Ev's attention to detail to be turning me on, but then he glanced at the ribbon, and oh so subtly at my wrists, and I had to shift in the chair.

"This is from Mira and me," Ev said, clearing his throat as he glanced away from my wrists.

"Oh, aşkim, you did most of the work," she demurred. "I did a bit of finishing and blocking, that's all."

I opened the package to reveal a pair of hand-knit socks—and unlike the muted earth tone palate Ev preferred for himself, these were a sensuous ocean of undulating blue and green stripes. They reminded me of the trip to Seaside I'd taken with some friends senior year—back before everything had gotten complicated. They seemed to radiate peacefulness and were so soft I had to resist the urge to put them to my face.

"There is too much black in your wardrobe," Ev said. "I would dress you in all blues if I could."

"Uh. Thanks." I knew I was blushing. Ev seemed to have a thing for my eyes, which I swore were a normal, average shade of blue but which Ev called "arrestingly bright." He liked to make me look at him while we were making out. And there I went, thinking about sex at the dinner table again.

"I love the socks," I said. I knew better than to ask how he'd guessed my foot size—knowing how sneaky he could be, he'd probably looked at my shoes last time they'd been on his floor, which was not something I needed the kids knowing.

"They are not a sweater," he said with far more gravity than necessary. "But I confess to having shared the pattern on my blog last night. I call it 'Barista Blues.'"

"You blogged about me?" *Oh Ev, you marvelous bundle of contradictions.*

"I blogged about *socks*." Ev looked away, cheeks turning pink.

"Evren, you should show him the blog," Mira urged. "My Evren is one of the most popular knitting bloggers. His fans all love the new pattern—"

"Who would like to help me bring out the cake?" he asked the kids, effectively ending the discussion of his blog. That was fine. I might not have Renee or Jonah's computer skills, but I could work some Google-fu on his name later. And I planned to tease the heck out of him about his fans, too.

"I want to help!" Jonah said.

"Most certainly," Ev said, smiling at him. Silly guy. I could have predicted what happened next.

"No, me!" Morgan made the sound of the mortally wounded.

"No fair!" Madison tried to beat the other two around the table.

All three chased after Ev into the kitchen.

"I am so happy you and Evren are friends," Mira said, shifting in her chair. She had barely eaten dinner, managing a bit of bread and a bit of yogurt sauce and a tiny dab of the warm hummuslike dish. "He needs someone like you in his life."

Someone with three kids and more baggage than PDX could hold? I didn't think so, but I smiled politely. "He's a great guy."

"And so are you." She smiled expectantly at me, and I didn't know what she wanted me to say. Did she want me to declare feelings for Ev that I wasn't certain he returned? A future commitment? A *whatever* didn't exactly bode well for the longevity of our friendship. I fingered the soft, fine yarn of the socks. Surely the care in them reflected *something* of Ev's feelings right?

Luckily, I was saved from answering Mira by the return of the kids and Ev. He was hovering over Jonas and Morgan, who were balancing the cake platter between them.

"Hey, why does Jonas get to hold more?" Madison bumped Morgan, who jostled the platter.

"Watch out!" Ev called as the platter tipped precariously. Next thing I knew, I was wearing the cake—icing in my hair, cake down my shirt, in my lap, and the rest landing on the pretty sky-blue tablecloth.

"Ugh." I groaned.

"Oops." Madison's eyes went wider than the now empty cake plate.

"Does this mean no dessert?" Jonas sounded close to tears.

"I have some cookies. And a towel," Ev said, way more pragmatically than I could have. I was surprised he didn't get mad or scold the kids for not listening to him. Lord knew, *I* was still taking deep breaths and counting to fifty before I spoke.

"I need a shower," I said, finally finding my voice and an even tone as Ev handed me a faded towel to brush off the crumbs. Getting the worst of the cake mess off, though, did nothing about all the frosting in my hair.

"You already had one. A crumb shower." Ev laughed, and once he started laughing, we all joined in. It was pretty hilarious once you got over the whole no-cake-to-eat thing.

"Chocolate-covered Brady," Jonas said and set us all off laughing anew.

"Evren, you will take young Brady and the children home," Mira said, coughing between weak laughs. "And take your time, *aşkim*. Stay and help your friend out."

"You will be okay, *Hala*?" Ev asked.

"I plan to take my medications, put on my show, and doze until tomorrow. I will be fine. You will see your friend home."

"All right." Ev nodded, then gave me a smile that started both of us laughing again. It was a good, cleansing laugh, a balm against the awkwardness of Renee's leaving in a huff, a buffer against the realities of Mira's illness. Our eyes met and the laughter shifted to something hotter, the latent heat between us rising again. I gave him a sly smile as I started scheming how I could get my lips on him again. Screw cake—it was Ev I'd been craving all along.

Chapter 10

As a new knitter, it is easy to fall into certain comfort zones as you become proficient at a certain type of project, neat piles of scarves or hats or socks waiting to be blocked and gifted. And this is lovely, but, friends, you must occasionally push past your comfort zone. Try a new yarn, a new colorway, a new technique or stitch pattern. Pushing yourself carries its own sense of satisfaction and reward.—Evren's Yarnings

Ev brought towels down to the Subaru to minimize the amount of chocolate I smeared around. The kids were appeased by some Turkish cookies, and they all seemed tired from their big day.

"Pajamas," I ordered as soon as we got home, pointing toward their rooms at the back of the apartment.

"Shower." Ev pointed at me.

"I should probably read to them quickly so they start trying to go to sleep—"

"I will do the reading. You go get clean." Stern Ev was sexy Ev, and I shivered a bit at his commanding tone. I grabbed a pair of flannel pants and a T-shirt before heading to the shower.

It took three rounds of shampoo before I felt my hair was clean again, and even then I was totally rethinking the long-hair-is-less-maintenance thing. I heard laughter coming from the twins' room, so I took my time, trimmed up the beard. It was a luxury these days having another adult around, not having to take a three-minute shower out of worry about what the kids might get up to. Usually, I go barefoot around the house, but I slid on the new socks. They were every bit as soft as they looked and fit me perfectly.

When I came out of the bathroom, the giggles of Jonas greeted me. Ev did a spot-on Hagrid and had Jonas rolling with laughter next to Ev on the floor of the twins' room. The girls were already dozing in their beds. My heart did a weird flip at the picture they all made in the dimly lit room. Ev shut the book when he spotted me.

"I think we will let Brady finish this chapter tomorrow," Ev said with a fake yawn.

Jonas totally fell for the yawn, though, letting loose one of his own. "Okay," he said sleepily and let me usher him across the hall to his bed, where I tucked him in. He was snoring softly by the time I shut the door.

I found Ev in the kitchen, washing up the last of the dishes from the cake making.

"Hey. You didn't have to do that," I said, wrapping my arm around him from behind.

"It is just a mixing bowl. But I will accept the hug." He leaned into my embrace. "You like the socks?" He glanced down at my feet.

"Love them." I kissed his neck. "Do you have to go right home or do you think you could stick around a bit? Maybe watch some *Storage Wars* with me?"

Ev looked at the couch and back at me, specifically right at my mouth. "I can watch some TV."

While Ev got the show queued up with the remote, I flipped off the living room lights and grabbed the blanket from the back of the couch before patting the spot next to me on the couch. Ev studied me for a long second, a little smile tugging his lips.

"You have no intention of watching the show, do you?" he asked.

"None. But it's excellent background noise." I gave him a smile that I hoped was more seductive than the bone-tired I suddenly felt.

"How deeply do the kids sleep?" Ev asked as he settled himself next to me, a bit farther away than I was hoping for.

"Pretty soundly. And that's part of my evil plan: dark room, TV noise, blanket. Now, stop worrying and make out with me a bit."

"If I come over there, then you will have to be very, very quiet indeed." Ev's voice took on that commanding edge that never failed to make me sprout wood. And I could tell from his wolfish grin that I had him—he was just going to make me work for it a bit.

"I'll be quiet. You might go home with teeth marks, though." I smiled back at him.

"I am counting on it." Ev slid closer and I threw the blanket over us. "You smell nice."

"I just grabbed Renee's conditioner, but I'm glad you approve."

"And your hair is almost curly freshly washed. Very, very nice." He fisted his hands in my hair, pulling me close enough to kiss.

It didn't matter whether it was a sneaky, fast kiss or a more lingering one like this, the first brush of Ev's tongue against mine always made gooseflesh break out at the small of my back. And when he held my head firmly in place and took charge, I got electric tingles all over, my whole body charged and waiting for whatever he had planned next.

He pressed me back into the couch and my whole body exhaled, every cell welcoming his warm weight. The towel I'd had around my neck fluttered to the floor and a whole stack of worries followed it down.

We kissed long and slow, legs tangling, hands languidly stroking. No one was getting naked, which totally played into Ev's whole thing for clothed sex. "This is totally your kink, isn't it?" I whispered.

"I don't have a kink." Ev lavished kisses all along my neck, paying particular attention to the line where my beard met bare flesh.

I snorted. "Ha."

"Do not inspire me to get a kink for gags," he said sternly before kissing me thoroughly.

Mr. I'm Not Kinky usually had me put my hands against the bed frame, so the freedom to explore him, even clothed, made me a little giddy. His back muscles were lean and ropy, flesh warm under my hand when I slipped it under his shirt, reveling in his inhalation. But he didn't stop me, only kissed me harder, so I got bolder with my hands, cupping his firm ass and pulling him against me. His slim-fitting pants were too tight for me to get a hand far inside, but it didn't stop me from teasing all along his waistline.

Apparently, I'd found some new Ev magic erogenous zone because the touch made him gasp and buck against me. I kept my nails blunt and short because of my job, but I did the best I could to tease his waist and sides, dragging my fingertips against him.

"Be good," he said against my lips.

"I am."

He snaked a hand under my shirt and pinched a nipple hard enough I had to stifle a moan.

"Fuck. Ev. Do that again."

He pushed my shirt up, torturing my nipples with his talented fingers while his mouth worked mine over.

I rocked against him, our hard cocks rubbing through our pants. I fumbled for his zipper as he shoved my pants just low enough to free my cock. I snorted again. Ev had a major thing for trapping me with my own clothes. But no, he wasn't kinky. Except he totally was, and I loved it.

We'd done oral again on our second lunch date, so our bare cocks touching and rubbing was novel and intense. Much as I loved Ev's cock in my mouth, kissing him while we ground together made more than simply my dick overheat—I felt his presence deep in my chest. It felt like he was owning me with his possessive mouth and demanding hips.

"I know you're very anti-mess, but I really want to come just like this," I whispered. "Need it."

"For you, I am totally making a mess exception," he panted. I loved knowing I'd affected his composure so much.

"Fuck me," I whispered, pulling him closer against me.

His hips stuttered and his kiss slowed.

"Not literally. Just want you to get me off." I kind of hated having to clarify. This was enough. This was everything. And I wanted him to feel that way, too.

"You have a filthy mouth." Ev kissed at the edges of my lips, regaining a bit of his swagger after my reassurance.

"And you love it." My kiss turned more demanding, trying to get him back to that toppy zone where he completely overwhelmed me.

"I do." His hand tightened in my hair, tipping my head back so he could nip at my neck, hitting all the spots that made me need to stick my fist in my mouth to avoid moaning out loud.

Ev pried my hand loose and replaced it with his forearm. My teeth grazed the sensitive flesh on the underside of his arm and he hissed in pleasure. I buried a moan against his skin. He hit *all* my buttons.

Fuck. I loved this. Loved him.

No. Not that.

But my body didn't listen to my brain, hurtling toward orgasm on that thought. This wasn't some fumbling with a near stranger in the dark—this was Ev and me and knitted gifts and him reading to my kids and secret smiles over soapy dishes. This was everything I'd never had but always wanted, and it was scary as fuck because like the fleeting rush to orgasm, there was no way it could last.

"Come on," I muttered, trying to outrun my thoughts by flooding my senses with Ev.

"I want you so much," he whispered and our eyes met in the dark, illuminated by only the glow from the TV. A potent current passed between us, and all the thoughts I was trying to avoid were right there, free for the taking, in his eyes.

This meant something. For both of us. Every thrust, every gasp, every inch of skin our fingers uncovered—it all meant something.

He shifted so that his shoulder was level with my mouth, his dick riding hard against my abs, shaft and balls dragging against me. His next thrust perfectly scraped my cockhead and I bit his shoulder to keep the moan in.

"Yes, *aşkim*, bite me. That's it," Ev urged.

As I complied, my body arched up, balls tightening, muscles tensing. *Now. Right now.* Every neuron waited, poised for the fall. Ev muttered something else in Turkish, another string of endearments, but the praise and affection were clear and it pushed me over. My whole body shuddered as he bucked against me, flooding my belly with warmth.

Ev captured my mouth in a long, slow, sloppy kiss as he slid back down my body. In a second, I'd have to grab the towel, mop us off. In a second, there would be feet on the stairs outside and we'd have to untangle ourselves in a hurry. In a second, we'd both have to go back to being responsible adults. In a second, I'd go back to wondering about what he felt for me. But right then, all I wanted was to hold him a little longer, squeeze him a little tighter, pretend that all those other seconds and minutes and confusing hours weren't bearing down hard on this perfect moment in time.

Chapter 11

All right, dear readers, the time has come for an apology. For years, I have resisted doing children's patterns. I have been firmly against cutesy pastel yarns and novelty patterns, and I've politely declined to do kid versions of my sweaters. And some of you have teased me relentlessly about this stance, and so it is cautiously that I admit that over the last few months my opinion on small people has...evolved. There are some special young people in our lives right now, and I see daily how their joy enriches Hala Mira so much. And if I am honest, my own life benefits from their presence as well, which is not something I would have said a year ago. But I find I very much enjoy their company and the welcome distraction they provide. And Saturday, I'm teaching a class especially for those pint-size new knitters, and thus, I offer you three new patterns to enjoy with or for the children in your lives.—Evren's Yarnings

After my birthday, Mira's health took a sharp decline and I didn't see Ev more than a few stolen moments for the next week, but as always we had the phone and our late-night conversations, few of which were actually sexual and most of which were venting about our respective charges. But Mira was rallying a bit with another week off chemo and I had big plans to see Ev after work the next night—I was going to redeem the IOU from Renee.

I found her on the couch with a pile of homework spread out, some reality show about teen virgins desperate to hook up on mute.

"Hey, sweetheart, I wanted to ask you—"

"Me first!" She bounced in place like one of the twins. "I was waiting for you to finish the story time with the kids. I need a huge favor tomorrow and I know you're going to say no—"

"Renee." I settled down heavily next to her, the IOU fluttering from my hand to the floor. I didn't bother retrieving it. "If you know I'm going to have an issue..."

"Hear me out, okay? Our environmental studies class has a visiting lecture and reception we can attend tomorrow. It's extra credit and I really need it because I had to miss class last week when you got called in to work for Audrey."

I rubbed the bridge of my nose. "You did us a huge favor and I owe you big-time, but unfortunately, I've got to work and I can't change it. I already had to ask for a schedule change for the twins' teacher conference."

"I know. But I've had the best idea—"

"No." I already knew where this was headed. "They can't be home alone."

"Jonas can handle two hours. I'll lay out snacks before I go and I'll use my money to buy them a new movie on the Xbox, and Jonas has a phone now, so he can call one of us—"

"Nope." I'd given Jonas my old phone for the sole purpose of having a backup to Renee's in case of an emergency, and to give him access to the game he was always swiping mine to play. "The phone is not a babysitter."

"What if I find them a playdate?" She looked up at me with big eyes.

"We're calling in too many favors with their friends." I tugged my hair loose from the bun and flipped the TV to Discovery. "But okay. Make some calls."

She took her phone into the kitchen area, but she was back less than ten minutes later, shaking her head. "Brady, I *need* to go."

"Is Indigo in this class?"

"What does it matter?" Her indignant tone told me everything I wanted to know. "I can't risk my GPA. And Indigo gets that. He's tutoring me in stats. Or at least he would be if you'd let him come over here."

"Bring him by the coffee shop. I need to meet him before he spends time around the kids, and we'll need some rules in place," I relented. Maybe her having Indigo around would be preferable to her trying to ditch the kids all the time. "But I can't have you leaving the kids home tomorrow. Call Indigo and ask him to take good notes for you."

"Why are you so *mean*?" Tears ran down her cheeks as she pushed away from the couch. "I'm going and that's final." She stalked away to her room, where the twins were already asleep. I couldn't follow without risking a double cranky wake-up and Renee knew it.

Hell. Lord save me from entitled teenagers. I flopped back on the couch. Now I got to spend the next twenty-four hours waiting to see if she carried through on her threat. Most likely she'd still show up on time to get the kids and just whine at me later, but if she didn't...

Buzz. My phone rang in my pocket.

I fished out my phone, but I really wasn't in the mood for my nightly phone call with Ev and was dreading telling him that our plans would have to wait yet again.

"Hey, babe."

"What is wrong?" Ev asked immediately.

"Nothing," I said automatically. I thumped my feet against the couch, wishing it was true.

"Do not *nothing* me. Do we not have the kind of friendship where we can share unhappy days? Tell me and you will feel better."

"Fine." I explained about Renee's tantrum, finishing up with, "And now I get to either call in sick or wait for a frantic call from Jonas."

"*Tatlim.*" Ev made a clucking noise. "Why did you not call me? I can help you."

"You're busy with Mira and your new classes and—"

"And the children are good for Mira. My first children's class is Saturday afternoon. We'll test out my projects together down in the classroom of the shop while Mira rests; then, when she awakens, I will give them a little dinner, yes? And save some for you?"

"That sounds great," I said weakly, hating needing him this much. I hadn't signed the kids up for his Saturday class because I simply couldn't afford the fee, and I wasn't about to ask Ev for charity.

"Now, will the school need a phone call from you that I'm picking them up or can Renee bring them to me at the shop?" Ev sounded so matter-of-fact that I wanted to weep, and I wasn't even sure why my eyes were burning.

"I'll work it out with her," I said. "And I'll pick them up the minute we close and—"

"*Tatlim.* You are going to exhaust yourself with *and* again," Ev chided. "This will be fine."

I didn't really believe him, but I had no choice but to murmur my agreement.

Around four thirty the next afternoon my phone buzzed, but I wasn't able to check it until closer to five thirty, at which point there were three pictures and a text informing me that Renee had dropped them off on time. The pictures were two of the kids knitting in the sunny backroom at Iplik, goofy grins on all three faces, then a picture of the twins cooking something that appeared to be made with dough.

Save some for me! I texted back, hoping that whatever it was would be edible after the kids finished.

Ev's reply was almost instantaneous. *Always, tatlim. Things are fine. Do not trouble yourself.*

However, when I arrived to pick up the kids, the normally perfectly put-together Ev was looking decidedly rough around the edges—flour on his designer pants, hair all messed up like he'd been dragging a hand through it, shirt half untucked, and the sort of glassy expression around his eyes that I knew only too well.

"They break you?" I asked as he let me in the back entrance.

"No, of course not." Ev greeted me with a weary kiss.

"Liar." I inhaled his scent, suddenly more turned on than hungry and tired.

"There is food for you." He started to lead me up the stairs, but I pulled on his hand, stopping him. I tugged him into the shadows on the landing, giving him a proper kiss, one that left us both panting.

"Need you more than food." I chuckled against his neck.

"Well, lahmacun is what we have—it's like a Turkish version of pizza. Your kids approved. The other will have to wait."

"I know." I still didn't release him. "Doesn't stop me from wishing I could blow you right here."

Ev made a clucking sound that wasn't entirely disinterested. "Now I must walk around with that image in my head. Thank you."

"Come on. I can be fast, and I know you can, too...." I reached for his belt and he didn't shove my hands away.

"Brady! Ev! Come see my drawing!" Madison's voice echoed down the stairwell, and we pulled apart.

"Hold that thought." Ev kissed the top of my head. "Because it was indeed a...compelling idea."

Lahmacun was indeed delicious—flat bread topped with a ground-meat sauce—but eating with the overtired kids bouncing around wanting to tell me about their adventures with Ev made me feel every minute of the long day. The kids went to go collect their belongings and I sagged against Ev as soon as they left the room.

"Why does Renee get to have all the fun?" I voiced the petty thought that had been rattling around my head all day. "I just don't get why she's stopped pulling her weight and left it all on me."

"Because she's eighteen." Ev tangled his hands in my hair, pulling it loose from the sloppy bun I had it in. "And at a certain point, *tatlim*, you have to let her be eighteen."

"I'm not sure I can do this without her." Something about Ev's soothing hands had me voicing my deepest doubts.

"You're not." Ev kissed my neck. "You don't have to do this on your own."

"Yeah, I kind of do. I'm always worried about using other people too much. The social workers didn't think I could do this on my own and I... don't want them to be right." I still remembered the first awful months after Mom and Greg died, the endless meetings with social workers, the implication that foster care might be preferable to me. I'd never really lost that fear and sense of inadequacy and Renee's behavior the last few weeks had brought all those worries bubbling to the surface.

"Getting help doesn't prove them right. It proves you smart." Ev kissed my forehead again. "Let people help you."

"Ev? I think you need to come here." A very frightened Jonas cut my pity party short. Ev and I rushed into the living room. Jonas was standing next to Mira's recliner, a frown on his face. "We were talking to Mira and then she just went to sleep! In the middle of talking!"

Oh, no. My heart beat double-time as Ev put his fingers on Mira's wrist and gently kissed her head.

"*Aşkim?*" she muttered.

"Shh. Sleep now," he soothed. To us, he said, "She does that now sometimes. Drifts off without warning. She must conserve her strength for her fight."

Her turban had slid to one side, revealing her bald scalp, and her color was pale grayish pink, nothing like the healthy, dark-haired, rosy-cheeked lady she'd been even six months ago. She wheezed a bit as she dozed, a dull rattle shaking her slight frame.

I herded up the kids as quietly as I could and we made our way down to the car. Before Ev could get in, I pulled him aside.

"What do the doctors say?" I asked. It was the first time I'd seen Mira since my birthday, and the rapid decline made my lungs fill with frigid air.

"Eh." Ev made a dismissive gesture. "We do not listen to them. She simply needs to recover some strength. They are saying nonsense about hospice and we are not to that point yet. She has much fight left."

"Yeah." I wasn't so sure, but I rubbed his arm anyway.

He shrugged away from the touch. "Enough about that. Let's get you home."

"Ev." I stayed him with a hand on his shoulder, and thankfully, he didn't throw this touch off, too. "Remember what you said? It's okay to need help with this."

"But we don't." Ev's face was stony as he slid into the driver's seat, and the chill in my lungs reached arctic proportions. He might be there for me when I needed him, but if he couldn't let me help *him*, this wasn't much of a partnership.

Chapter 12

Summer is approaching with long, sunny days filled with a riot of color. I try to bring as many of those colors into the shop and our home as possible, filling Hala Mira's world with color. So many of you have asked how we are. And the truth is, I'm not sure. Talking about it... it is hard, dear friends, and so I don't. The days are growing longer all around us, while here at home, the hours grow shorter, the doctor's voices less bright, their handshakes turning to sympathetic pats, the nurses full of false cheer. Everyone knows us there now, and at Knit Night, too, our friends are full of the big smiles and hushed tones. And I do the only thing I can do. I knit. This pattern is slipper socks in the softest cashmere and silk blend I could find.—Evren's Yarnings

The sicker Mira got, the more Ev pulled away from me, canceling dates and keeping phone calls to a minimum. Strangely, he was only too happy to hear about my troubles with Renee or to offer to have the kids come by the shop. We brought him and Mira ice cream a few times, but the kids and I did most of the eating and the best Ev and I got were some stolen stairway kisses.

The week of my barista championship trip finally came, and I was busy double- and triple-checking the arrangements for the kids when Renee bounded over to the kitchen table, where I had my to-do lists spread out.

"So when you win—"

"If," I corrected her, even as I smiled at her. I loved her faith in me.

"Maybe you won't need me around as much?" She had a strange, sly look on her face.

"What do you mean?" My stomach got the same floppy feeling it always did when one of the twins said they didn't feel so well.

"See, Indigo and Sierra and Ray are all looking at getting a place near campus—"

"You are *not* moving in with your boyfriend at eighteen. No way, no how." I used my firmest tone possible, but she just rolled her eyes. Her hair was done in two French braids and her tiny pink shirt only made her look that much younger. She might not like it, but she still needed me in her life, every bit as much as I needed her help. Maybe I was a piss-poor substitute for Mom's guidance, but I wasn't going to let her ruin her life either.

"I wouldn't be moving in with *him*. It would be a group of us. The college is asking for theme houses in the campus apartments. They're going to apply for an environmental one and they asked me to join them. I'd be sharing a room with Sierra. The financial aid office says I could get more aid to cover it, and there are some scholarships for housing, too."

"*Renee.*" I clunked my head on the table. "You are not moving out. I need you too much. The whole *family* needs you."

"Yeah? Well, maybe I'm tired of being needed all the time, okay?" Her eyes welled up.

For once her tears didn't have me rushing to reassure her. Instead, I felt weary. Bone-weary with worry over why Ev was shoving me away and with all the details for my trip and with picking up the slack as Renee did less and less around the house. So many times in the last month I'd had to cancel plans with Ev or rush to make sure the kids had someone to watch them. She really wanted to talk about being tired? I was fucking exhausted.

"You think I like this, Renee? You think I like calculating how much groceries the Social Security survivor's benefit check will cover this month? You think I like turning down meals with my boyfriend to supervise showers and read stories?"

"You like bossing me around." Her eyes narrowed. "You think you can guilt me into staying home."

"No. I think I haven't been guilting you *enough*. We had an agreement this year right? For you going to school and not having to work? But you keep canceling—"

"I have *reasons*." She stamped her foot exactly like the twins. "Classes are hard. And I have a life—"

"And so do I." It was the first time I'd ever asserted that with her and it made my hands shake. "Like tomorrow. I need you to be home on time and take the kids *on time*." It was the last night before my trip and some Ev time was exactly what I needed to ease the raw feeling in my insides.

"And if I don't?"

I played one of the few trump cards I still had with her. "I'm not paying for your phone next month. You need to step it up, Renee."

"I hate you." She stormed off and I heard the shower click on a few minutes later, a sure sign that she was sobbing in the bathroom.

Fuck. I needed to talk to Ev. Right the fuck then. I grabbed the phone and hit his number. The call rang so long that I was rehearsing a voice-mail message in my head when Ev picked up at the last minute.

"Hello, Brady. Is everything all right?" Ev's voice was too formal, weighed down with something I couldn't identify, each word seeming to require great effort from him.

"Yeah. Especially now that I'm talking to you." Any thought I'd had of confessing the stressful chat with Renee fled. He didn't need my petty worries, just the one bit of good news I could offer. "Actually, I'm unexpectedly free tomorrow night after I get off work. I was thinking I could come over, help you get Mira settled for the night, then you and I could spend some time together."

"I do not think so." More of that plodding tone from Ev. It killed me to hear him so burdened, and I longed to wrap my arms around him. "You are still leaving Thursday evening for your contest, yes?"

"Yeah. I'll be gone until Sunday evening, which is why I'd really like to see you before I go."

A very long pause had me checking the phone to make sure we were still connected. "It's not a good time for me. There is...much to do."

"So let me help," I wheedled. "You've helped me with the kids a bunch, Ev. Why can't you let me help you when you need it?"

"We...I...do not need help. All is fine. Mira is...fine. It is just...work things." His voice couldn't sound more strained than if he were balancing on a tightrope over the Grand Canyon. "Focus on your trip."

"It isn't all fine." I used the tone I did when I caught the kids in a lie. "You're struggling. I've seen it all week. I thought we were the kind of... friends who helped each other when the going gets rough. Isn't that what you said?"

"Friends does not mean you can make...demands," Ev snapped. There was a thumping sound, as if he'd just whacked his pillow. "I said I am too busy. What are you not understanding? Pack for your trip. Have a most excellent weekend. Please." He said the last bit as a half curse and half plea.

"Ev. Are we boyfriends or not? Because if we're boyfriends, you can't keep shoving me away just because you're having a bad week that you don't want to talk about. You don't have to talk—let me rub your shoulders. Let me help you cook. *Let me help.*"

Another pause long enough to fit the entire Columbia River in. "We are not *that* kind of boyfriends."

"Oh? What kind of boyfriends are we, then? Fuck buddies? There doesn't seem to be any of that happening lately—"

"Is everything with you about sex? Are you upset that we are not having backroom fumbles tonight?" Ev's voice was more condescending than I'd ever heard it. Suddenly, I knew *exactly* what this was about. I pushed away from the table, pacing the length of the narrow kitchen.

"It's because I'm bisexual, isn't it? I'm good enough for casual friends, but not good enough to be a real boyfriend who you trust with your feelings and problems?"

"I did not say that."

"You didn't have to. You don't want a real relationship with me. You *still* don't trust me not to go chasing after some girl instead of standing by you."

"It is not about…trust." Rustling noises muffed Ev's words, like he was shifting around in bed.

"Prove it. Let me come over and help you tomorrow. Let me see you when you're down, not just when you're available to be my rescuer."

"I cannot. Enjoy your trip, Brady," Ev said with a firm finality that pierced my heart.

"So what? We're through?" I tore my hair loose from the bun.

"I did not say that. We will talk when you return."

"Fuck that. I want to talk *now*. And I want to know if you're *ever* going to get over my being bisexual." I couldn't shake the feeling that was what was really happening here—he wouldn't let me get closer because of an inability to trust me. "Can we have a real relationship or not?"

It wasn't until I asked the question that I realized how much I wanted that with him—as complicated and uncertain as it was, I wanted it. I wanted the logistics issues and the missing him and the late-night phone calls and the stolen kisses, and I wanted us each wrapped up in the other's life. I hadn't wanted that a few months ago, but Ev had changed me. Changed what I was willing to reach for, changed what I dreamed about.

"Brady. You are blowing things out of proportion and I cannot…deal with the…drama right now. Go win your contest and call me when you return." Each of Ev's words was stiffer than the last, little pieces of shrapnel that hit every insecure spot on my body.

"I won't." My retort was worthy of a back-talking kid, but I couldn't keep it back and couldn't stop myself from hanging up by hitting the Power button instead of End Call. I'd turn it back on in a bit of course, but right then I wanted to be as juvenile as Renee having a tiff with her girlfriends. I wanted to stomp around and loudly declare that no way was I taking *his* calls. And maybe I kept the phone off out of the more realistic fear that he wouldn't call, that he was every bit as done with me as I was him. *Liar. Liar. Liar.* Keeping to the teen-drama theme, I flopped on the couch. I wasn't ever going to be done with Ev.

And speaking of Renee, I opened my eyes a while later to find her hovering above the couch, eyes puffy and swollen.

"I hate fighting with you. You're..." Her lower lip wobbled. "You're all I've got, and I *hate* that."

"I hate it, too," I said, pulling her to me. She landed next to me in an ungraceful heap. I pushed all thoughts of Ev and our fight from my head. Renee was right. We were all each other had and I needed to focus on that. I needed to focus on what I could do for *my* family, not what I couldn't do for Ev's.

"None of us chose this life, Renee. *None* of us." I reached into the deep pocket of my cargo pants and pulled out a folded sheet. I shouldn't have grabbed it when I was skateboarding home but hadn't been able to resist. "Look. I get it. You need more privacy. If we get enough money together, we could get something like this."

She stopped scrubbing at her eyes long enough to consider the flyer. It was for a rental house; still our neighborhood, but closer to the People's Cup without being too far from the school for the kids. "Three bedrooms and...a partially finished basement." She looked up at me with such hope that my hands shook on the paper.

"Yeah. See, you could have the basement. Your own little apartment, kind of?"

"Can I have a minifridge?"

"Yeah, princess, you can have a minifridge." I rubbed her head.

"And I could help with the kids some, but mainly hang out there in my own space?"

"Yeah." I wanted that future for her so much it hurt. She deserved something of a normal teenage experience.

"And Indigo could come over?"

I sighed heavily. We'd had an exceedingly awkward chat about birth control two weeks earlier. I was losing this battle. She had a boyfriend, and no amount of my going all caveman brother was going to change that fact. "Indigo can *visit*. With rules. No overnights."

"Maybe." She chewed her lower lip. "The whole basement would really be all mine? And I could decorate however I wanted?" Her creased face showed the strain of living with the princess-obsessed seven-year-olds.

"Yes." I squeezed her hand. "Promise me you won't do something like telling your friends yes yet. Let me see if I can make this happen for us."

"Okay." She squeezed back, but her cloudy eyes said she was still tempted by the idea of the group housing. And honestly, what eighteen-year-old wouldn't be? My gut felt like an angry beaver was gnawing at it—like maybe my best effort wouldn't be enough to keep us together.

"I love you, Re-Re, you know that right?"

"I know." Her laugh was a girlish tinkle as she headed off to bed, a perfect counterbalance to my misery.

I flipped my phone back on, finally. No messages. Not even the "sleep well, *canim*" that Ev had sent me every night for a month straight. Whatever. The ache in my stomach was just going to have to deal because I couldn't afford to focus on someone who didn't even want me.

* * * *

Here's the thing about having small children depending on you: You get really good in a hurry at plodding through even the deepest of heartaches, still slapping peanut butter on sandwiches and packing overnight bags and working one last shift before leaving—because calling in heartbroken to life isn't an option. So outwardly, I was the same—kissing the kids good-bye, accepting the good wishes of my coworkers and customers, and lecturing Renee about no overnight guests or parties—but inside I was a wreck. I missed Ev, but I didn't want to be *that* guy and bombard him with texts, and I also knew he was having a superhard time even without our argument. It made my rib cage ache to think of our friendship being one more stressor in his life. Despite his obvious bias against bisexuals and his stubbornness, I still lo—liked the guy tremendously.

But then he surprised me by texting when I was on the MAX on the way to PDX Airport.

Godspeed on your flight. Go win.

I immediately tried to call him, but it went right to voice mail. I settled for texting, *I'll call you Sunday night, okay?*

I wanted to believe this thing between us might be salvageable. I *had* to believe it.

Because you love him. Oh, how I wanted that not to be true. I didn't want to feel like I'd lost the best part of my day, the sun break in the monsoon that was currently my life. I didn't want to *need* him this much, to care this much about his stupid prejudices.

Once I was through security, I took my phone out again, trying to find any hidden subtext in his message.

Buzz.

Another text. My heart sped up. Maybe we could work this out—

Oh, wait. The message was from Audrey of all people.

So, so, so sad about your friend! :(:(All the ladies here at Knit Night are crying.

I immediately called Audrey on the shop number, not wanting to risk her not picking up her cell. "People's Cup," she chirped.

"What about my friend? What happened to Ev?" I demanded, no time for niceties.

"Ev?" I could practically hear her bow-shaped mouth crease into a frown. "Not him. Mira. Violet said she's in the hospital—has been there a few days now—and they say she's going to…" Audrey lowered her voice like words could be contagious. "*Die* soon."

"Oh, fuck."

"Well, don't let it depress you too much, okay? We're all rooting for you to go win big." She put a lot of deliberate chipper in her voice, like I was supposed to ignore the bombshell she'd dropped.

Go win. I made some bland excuse to end the call with Audrey while she was still spitting out platitudes about doing People's Cup proud. *Go win. Just worry about your trip.* Ev's words rang in my ears.

Oh, Ev, you beautiful bastard.

He'd let me hang myself in a noose of my own insecurities. Maybe it wasn't about my bisexuality—maybe it never had been, but he'd let me use that pretext rather than tell me the fucking truth. Mira was dying and he was all alone, and he'd *lied* to me to get me to go on this trip.

Because he loved me. That was the only explanation. Right?

"Flight 987 Service to Los Angeles will begin boarding shortly…" The loudspeaker crackled.

I stuck a finger in my ear, dialed Ev. As I'd expected, it went straight to voice mail.

Fuck. I shoved the phone in my pocket but hit a weirdly folded piece of paper. I pulled it out and saw it had my name in block printing. It was Morgan's handwriting because the *R* was too tall and the *D* drooped. I unfolded it.

"AR FAMLY SAYS GO WIN!" read the misspelled banner at the top, and below it were the five—no, *six* of us. She'd drawn Ev in, too, right next to me, holding my stick figure's hand. Off to the side stood Renee, her crayon smile just as brittle as the real ones these days. She and the kids needed me to board that plane, go try to win, get that house on the flyer. We *needed* that money.

But money wasn't family. And Ev—he was family, even if he didn't want to be. There would be other chances, other ways to make the money. I would find a way somehow. But there was only one chance to help Ev. And it didn't matter if he didn't want me—I knew what I was going to do, even as every logical cell in my body screamed for me to get in line for the plane.

Chapter 13

I haven't posted all week. I am sorry, friends. I am not knitting right now.—Evren's Yarnings

I knew which hospital Mira would be in thanks to playing tour guide for Ev and finding him restaurants and parks in the area to spend time at while she had treatments. And the hospital was off the MAX train line, so it wasn't that hard to get to from the airport, but it wasn't logistics that had my chest pounding. I was, unfortunately, well acquainted with this particular ICU, part of the nightmare that was the aftermath of Mom and Greg's accident. I wasn't sure if Mira would be there or on the oncology floor, but confronting my own demons first seemed like a good idea, even if I had to take several deep breaths as I got off the elevator, familiar scents and sounds hitting me.

Here. Right here was where I stood, holding a sobbing Renee after we got the bad news that there was no hope. Over there was the small room where we'd met with the organ donor coordinator. And over there was…

Ev.

He sat alone in a small waiting area tucked behind some ferns and out of sight of the elevator and main thoroughfare. I knew it well. It might as well have a sign over it saying "Cry Here" because it was that sort of place, well stocked with tissues and a muted television no one watched. He hadn't spotted me yet. Instead, his head was bowed forward, studying his phone with an expression that could only be described as utterly broken.

Not wanting to startle him, I circled around, took the seat next to him, and waited for him to look up.

"Brady! What are you doing here?" His eyes went wide as he registered my appearance. "You are *not* supposed to be here."

"Yeah, actually, I am." I knew that all the way to my lug soles. This was where I *needed* to be.

"There is nothing you can do here." He spoke with brutal honesty. "No one can. There is only waiting."

"Then I'll wait with you. As long as it takes. I'm here."

"She would not want you here. She would want you to go, win your contest, get the money for your family." His words should have sliced me clean open, but I knew in my gut he was lying.

"Liar," I said gently. "She'd be sad I had to skip the contest, sure, but she'd want me here for you, Ev."

He didn't reply, just stared at the medication ad on the television as if it held all the answers.

"The real question, though, is what do *you* really want? No guilt over me missing the contest—can you let yourself admit you need...someone here?"

Ev shook his head sadly. "I should be able to do this on my own. She took care of me so many years, just her and *Hala* Tanya. And look at me; I can't even give her...the end she wanted. She's not lucid right now, but she'd hate being here. I resisted the hospice when I knew she wanted to be home, and now she's here. I thought it was just a cold and took her to the ER...."

"Hey." I wrapped an arm around him. "You are *not* failing. You've done the best you can. And sometimes we *all* need someone to prop us up."

He gave me a pointed look, and I had to crack a smile. "Okay, okay, I suck at that, too. But you've shown me that it's not so bad to ask for help now and again. You've taught me how nice it is to have someone to complain to at the end of the day."

"It is...hard for me to do the same." Ev sagged in my arms. "This is the hardest thing I've ever done, Brady. It really is. I had to leave the room for a bit...I just...."

"I know." I rubbed his shoulders. "I've been there. Renee couldn't stay in the room more than a few seconds."

"I just wish there was something I could do besides just sit there and... wait. She signed all the advanced directive papers weeks ago, so there are no big decisions, but the waiting is *horrible*."

"Then we'll sit there together. You don't have to wait alone."

He glanced at his phone again, a pained expression crossing his face. "I tried calling my parents. She asked me to call in a rare moment of lucidity, and I thought they might want to know...Might want to come, even after...."

"But they didn't?"

"They said they trusted me to handle it. And then they hung up. Not even a sympathetic word..."

"Screw them. They don't deserve either of you. And you don't need them." I thought of my own mother, so completely blasé about my bisexuality, and how she would have liked Ev. Would have loved how he was around the kids. My throat got tight.

Ev sighed heavily. "I do not like her so alone. A woman like her deserves a family with her."

"She's not alone. She has you. Ev, tell the truth: How many messages do you have from the Knit Night ladies wanting to know about Mira? You're surrounded by love and you're not really letting yourself feel it."

"Dozens." He shrugged helplessly. "But I don't know what to tell them."

"When you have an update for them, I'll handle that." Sending dozens of text messages and making phone calls was the least of what I was willing to do for Ev.

"You're not going to go to LA, are you?" Ev sighed.

"Nope." I squeezed his hand. I had so much I wanted to say to him and things we needed to work out, but right now, the only thing that mattered was being here for him.

"If..." Ev struggled to speak. "If she wakes up enough to ask...do I tell her that the family did not even care?"

"You lie," I said with utmost tenderness. "And is that why you're out here? Not knowing what to say?"

"No...maybe," he muttered, kicking at the speckled carpet. "You are right to lie to her about my parents. But...I do not know how to say good-bye."

"So don't." I stood up, reaching for his hands. "Let's just go sit with her while she sleeps, and you can tell me about when you came to live with her and *Hala* Tanya. I want to know how you learned to knit."

"I can do that," he said shakily.

And so we went into the little room where Mira lay, and we sat side by side in hard plastic chairs that were in no way designed for this sort of vigil. Ten years ago, I'd been fourteen when my only living grandmother passed away from cancer at home with hospice, and my mother had sat with her on the last days, calling me in to say good-bye. That had been a slow, mysterious, almost peaceful thing. With my mother, things had been both rushed, in some ways a blurry nightmare, but also a slow, carefully scripted final dance with the organ transplant team waiting. There was neither a rush nor a script here. We sat, Ev holding her hand, me holding Ev's hand, and Ev told stories and she slept fitfully, breathing getting shallower all the time. I laughed at the right places, asked questions, held his hand, and wished like heck there was any way to avoid this.

Something changed—the air in the room, a hitch in her breathing, an errant beep from a monitor—I couldn't have said what, but suddenly I *knew*.

"Ev." I squeezed his hand hard. "Ev. Tell her now."

"Is it now?" He looked at me with wide eyes.

"Soon." I nodded, a certainty born out not by the monitors but by the chill at the base of my neck.

"*Hala* Mira…" He moved so that he could kiss her hand, then her papery forehead. His voice broke before he lapsed into Turkish as the peaks on the monitor grew shallower and shallower. At a certain point, a nurse came into the room, then another, and Ev stopped speaking, and then it was just me holding him in the hallway, him trying so hard not to cry, me not trying at all to keep it in, tears running down my cheeks.

"I told her…" Ev tried to speak, then trailed off.

"It's okay. You don't have to tell me."

"I told her she was the mother of my soul, but I do not think she heard."

"She knew."

"And I told her I'd do it…I'd keep the shop for her."

"Oh, Ev…" My eyes got all itchy again. "That's a huge promise."

"It's one I was ready to make."

"She wouldn't fault you if you changed—"

"I would," he said, firmer now. "I can do this, Brady. I *need* to do this."

"I love you." It was the exact wrong time to make such a declaration, but I couldn't hold it in any longer in the face of his tremendous courage.

Ev's darkening face told me he wasn't crazy about the timing either, but he lightly sidestepped the issue. "Mira loved you a lot, too. And the children."

"I mean I love *you*, Ev. Not Mira—although I really did love her, too, but not like I love you. And I'm proud of you."

He opened his mouth, then closed it.

"It's okay. You don't have to say anything. We're going to make us work, okay?" I stroked his arms. That was all that mattered right now, that he knew I wasn't angry about his well-meaning lies and that we were going to figure out how to be together. "Let's get you home, get you some food and sleep."

"No food." He rubbed his stomach, which had to be roiling.

"We'll see about that." I kept up the slow, steady strokes on his arms. "Now give me your keys and let's get you home."

After Ev handled the necessary paperwork, I trundled him off to the car, awash in emotion for him. It didn't even matter if he couldn't fully return my feelings. What mattered was how good it felt that he was letting me in, even a little, letting me help.

It was well after two a.m. by the time we got back to Ev's place. It was eerily quiet, the air stale and oppressive, like it hadn't circulated in days. Like most of the buildings in the neighborhood, Ev's didn't have air conditioning, so I set about opening windows even as Ev stood there, not moving beyond the hallway. It rattled me worse than any skateboard fall to see tall, strong Ev so gutted. I tried to wrap my arms around him, but he shoved me away.

"Not now, aşkim. I can't." His voice was ragged and his hands were clenched, as if he were working double hard not to cry in front of me.

"Shower," I said in the same firm tone he used with me. I steered him toward the large white tile bathroom off the hall, starting the water for him while he stripped.

Ev was the cook, not me, but after I pushed him in the shower, I found a carton of chicken broth and heated up a mug of it and made Ev a toasted English muffin with butter. I remembered how Ev added parsley to just about everything, so I chopped a bit and sprinkled it over the broth. I brought both to his room to wait for him to come out of the shower, but I found him facedown in the bed, towel askew, covers not even pulled back, snoring softly. Not about to disturb him, I pulled the extra blanket he kept at the foot of the bed up around him and returned the food to the kitchen.

I was too wired to either eat or sleep myself. I pulled my phone out, dreading the call I had to make. I'd already called the families that were looking after Jonas and the twins from the hospital, letting them know I was in town and occupied with a crisis but that I'd pick up the kids tomorrow. They'd been nothing but understanding, but I wasn't sure whether to expect that same compassion from Renee.

She picked up on the first ring, despite the late hour. "Brady! How is LA?" She sounded as perky as if she'd had a double shot of espresso, and I could hear the murmur of voices in the background. Home she definitely was not.

"Not there." I took a deep breath. "I'm with Ev. Mira died this evening. I'm sorry, sweetheart, because I know you were counting on me—"

Her sobs cut me off, but not for the reason I was thinking. "Poor Ev," she choked out. "That's terrible."

"I know you were counting on the contest—"

"I don't care about that *now*," she sobbed. Someone behind her made soothing noises. For the first time, I was grateful for the infamous Indigo.

"He shouldn't be alone, Brady. Don't let him be alone." Her voice was muffled now, like she was leaning into someone.

"I won't." My throat felt like I'd inhaled one of Ev's sweaters. I knew that, like me, she was flashing back to those first awful days after the accident.

"Should I skip the trip tomorrow? Come help?"

"You go. Get an A in the class. You can help out Sunday when you're back." I honestly wasn't sure I could deal with her grief issues, my own, and still hold Ev up.

"I will. I promise." She hung up, promising to help more next week and full of apologies for her recent behavior which I gently brushed aside. Now wasn't the time to dwell on our struggles.

Pocketing my phone, I surveyed the apartment, cleaning up the little things that indicated that Ev had left for the hospital in a rush—dishes in the sink, magazines spread out in the living room, tea still in a cup by Mira's chair. Eyes burning, I cleaned up that area with a sort of reverence. I carefully folded her shawl and knit blankets, then cleaned up the lines of medicine bottles and water glasses on her special table before moving the table to the side of the room. It didn't really help—the room still seemed to weep for Mira's absence, every object seeming stark and lonely.

Finally, the hours awake caught up with me and I returned to Ev's room. He'd cuddled up to his wall, hunkering under the main comforter at some point. His form looked far smaller than normal, wide shoulders folded inward. Stripping down, I climbed in behind him. How long had it been since I'd slept next to another adult? Watching Ev sleep, I couldn't get my fuzzy brain to do the math, but it was years. And never with Ev. We'd had this…thing for months now and this was the first time I'd gotten to hear the soft rumble of his snores or see the perfect fan of his eyelashes.

I needed to shut off the light, but I gave myself a moment to memorize this version of Ev. As I flicked the antique bedside lamp off, he rolled into me, arms coming around me to hold me close. My heart literally stuttered in my chest—I felt my muscles contract with the force of the emotion I was struggling to keep in. Ev nuzzled my neck, arranging us like I was his personal furry body pillow.

I sighed, all tension leaving my body. Didn't matter how crappy my day had been, this was damn nice. Still mainly asleep, Ev's lips clumsily trailed from my neck to find my mouth. I met him readily, eagerly, and his clumsy kiss became something more urgent, more raw—and more awake.

Blinking, he pulled away. "You're actually here."

"Yeah." I yanked him back, dick more engaged than brain. But I wasn't so far gone that I missed the moment he came more fully awake, everything hitting him again. He flopped back onto the pillow, a muttered stream of Turkish curses coming from his mouth.

"Hey." I ran a hand down his chest.

"I am sorry." He didn't move my hand, so I continued making long, soothing strokes. "Why are you here? Don't the children require you?"

You require me. I didn't say that, though, because I knew he'd protest. "Everyone thinks I'm in LA. I've got my cell if there's an emergency. Tomorrow I'll straighten everything out."

"Tomorrow. The arrangements. I should start some lists...." Ev sat up.

And oh no, we were *not* having any of that. I shoved him back, straddling his waist to keep him down. "Tomorrow, Ev. Tomorrow is soon enough for everything we've both got to do. Right now, we're going to sleep."

"This is not sleeping," Ev pointed out, looking straight down at our dicks, neither of which was the least bit asleep.

"Nope." I let him pull me down for a long, searching kiss. Right when I could feel the doubts gathering in his brain again, I kissed my way south, mouthing a tender trail down his lightly furred chest and stomach. I loved the softness of his stomach—for all Ev was slim and polished, his stomach retained an endearing realness that I enjoyed far more than any six-pack abs.

"It is wrong," Ev whispered. "To want you so much...now." His hand sifted through my hair, pulling it loose from the ponytail.

"No, it's absolutely, perfectly *right*." I dropped two kisses near his belly button. "This is what we both need right now."

"Perhaps, but it still feels...off."

I gave his stomach a little lick before answering him. I knew exactly what he meant. The air felt sharper, my senses magnified, like someone had stripped away the top layer of my skin, and I knew whatever he was feeling was a thousand times worse. But I could also tell from the tension in Ev's muscles that he wasn't falling back to sleep any time soon. I couldn't care less about coming myself, but I wanted Ev to rest, and orgasm was the surest way I knew to make him boneless and sleepy and get him out of his head for a bit. He needed that.

"Do you want me to stop?" I gave him another kiss before he could answer. He yawned. One hand came to rest on my bare shoulder. "Yes. No. Yes. How have I never seen you fully naked before now?"

I laughed. "Because you're a kinky devil." I didn't mention how we'd both been too busy with life for happy naked time to happen very often. "How about you think of me as your human-size sleeping pill and just let me do this for you?"

"Fuck." Another, very rare Ev curse. "I do not wish to think right now."

"Then don't." I scooted backward and swallowed his dick all the way to the root.

"Fuck." His voice was more guttural. "I love your mouth."

I knew he did and I exploited that knowledge, working him with my tongue as I held him deep. Ev was usually in charge of whatever fucking we did. He would set the pace and depth for me, controlling how much I got to taste in that bossy way of his I loved so very much, but this freedom to go as deep as I wanted was rather heady, too. I loved the way his foreskin slid against my tongue, loved the tang of his pre-cum, loved the thick weight of him on my tongue.

Doing this for him was better than a shower, washing away the yuck of the last few days—the stupid argument with him, the hospital, the helplessness over not being able to do more for him. I could do this; I could remind him how wonderful our bodies could be, even on days that our hearts broke. He *did* need this, even if he didn't want to admit it. He needed the deep, cleansing power of orgasm, and I could give him that.

He panted and gasped—he wasn't a loud moaner, even freed of the need for quiet, but the hitch in his breath, the tension in his thighs, the clench of his hand in my hair all told me that he was getting close.

"Turn around," he commanded. It was so good to hear the firmness back in his voice that I complied, moving so that we were both on our sides. Sixty-nine wasn't one of my favorite things—I preferred to go into a zenlike state giving oral, where everything shrank to my mouth and what I could make it do for another person—but Ev latched onto my dick with an almost feverish enthusiasm, and I reconsidered my stance.

Energy flowed between us. It wasn't just about dicks and mouths, it was about what we could give to each other, even in the darkest hours of the night, what we could be for each other. And it didn't matter who came first or second, or that my own orgasm felt warm and soft, not the usual tidal wave of gasping moans as I got thrown up onto some rocky shore. No, this was a fluid ballet, let by Ev's quiet murmurs and graceful hands on my body, and it gently deposited me on a featherbed of good feelings. As I came back to earth, I scooted back around, wrapping myself around him.

"Sleep," I whispered, only to discover that he already was.

Please let me be enough for him, I prayed instead. I wanted more than to be here for Ev in his grief. I wanted a real future together, and for the first time, I was 100 percent ready to fight for that.

Chapter 14

Dearest friends, I am going to share a beloved memory, one I keep close to my heart. When I was fourteen and my Hala Mira didn't know what to do with this tall, gangly kid eating her out of house and home, she put me to work on the yarn swift, making balls with the ball winder for her and customers. She had me putting price tags on merchandise and keeping the store well swept, but I grumbled. Oh, how I grumbled, friends. Knitting was women's work. Fanciful women's work at that. I was surrounded by a king's buffet of fibers, but all I could think was that real men didn't knit. And they certainly didn't fondle the yarn when they thought no one was looking. You see, I was already a bit sensitive about what real men did and did not do. Being gay had already gotten me rejected from the only family I'd ever known. Here I was in a strange city with two eccentric women and no friends. Knitting? I scoffed every time she offered to teach me, instead going outside to kick a soccer ball against the house or for a run in the park. Manly things, I thought. I turned her down over and over, but she never stopped offering to teach me.

"I see you," she teased me. "I see you touching that merino. It wants to be a hat."

"It does not," I retorted, shocking myself. "It wants to be a pair of gloves."

"Oh my, aşkim, that's ambitious. No one does gloves as their first project."

"I will draw you a picture. You will knit them for me," I said

*with all the imperiousness of my father commanding his tea.
"I will not." Hala Mira laughed at me. She laughed in the face
of thousands of years of gender norms in our culture a lot. My
father and uncles didn't intimidate her in the least, so it was
no wonder my attempt at a commanding tone failed miserably.
"But you are right to be afraid. Gloves are too hard for even
some longtime knitters. I dislike them immensely. A lot of fiddly
bits. You probably couldn't manage a scarf out of that chunky
blend over there."
She had me. She knew it of course. A little bit of reverse
psychology and a little bit of dare, and I finally took her bait
and let her show me how to cast on. And thus, dear friends,
when you write and ask me what someone's very first project
should be, let me be clear that I speak from experience when I
say: anything but gloves.
Today I send Hala Mira on her final journey—the one I can't
accompany her on—and I put those gloves in her pocket, even
though they are old and moth-eaten, with more dropped stitches
than I'd ever admit to you, dear friends. You see, my Hala Mira
didn't just show me how to knit—she taught me how to embrace
life. How to love it, stitch by stitch, as we made something
beautiful from the broken ruins of childhood. And now, friends,
I must figure out how to do that alone. I do not know if I can.—*
Evren's Yarnings

Early in the morning, I went with Ev to the funeral home to make the sort
of arrangements no one wants to think about. I was far less shell-shocked
than I had been with Mom and Greg, far more able to help Ev make choices.
It's funny how life forces us to make a series of trivial decisions at a time
when we are faced with some of our biggest dilemmas. I'd been reeling
from social worker visits and an officious man in a bad suit wanted me
to pick a color of urn? Hah. I tried to shield Ev from the silly stuff, but
mainly I just held his hand and dared anyone to object to that.

And then, even as it wrings us out, life grants us some of its greatest
kindnesses at the same time. When we returned to the store after the funeral
home, Ev went in through the front because he wanted to tell Adele, the
clerk, about the arrangements and to make sure she was coping okay. He'd
offered her the day off and to close the store that day, but she'd insisted
on coming in to open it.

"Ev." She ran across the store to give him a huge hug. And then she had one for me, too, despite our barely being acquainted. Her dreadlocks bounced with her movements and her long, elegant pink nails fussed with our collars. Luckily, I'd had a dress shirt in the bag I'd packed for LA. The day seemed to demand more than a People's Cup T-shirt.

"Things are going okay, yes?" Ev asked Adele.

"I tried texting, but uh, Ev, where do you want all the food?" Adele made a gesture toward the rear of the store.

"Food?" Ev's eyebrows wrinkled.

"It's been a steady of stream of casseroles since we opened at nine. I think I've seen all our regular customers and it's not even eleven yet." She led us to the classroom at the rear of the store, where all three tables were covered with flowers and food. In true Northwest fashion, most were labeled with their ingredients, proudly proclaiming which allergens they'd managed to leave out.

"But..." Ev stuttered. "It is just me."

My heart winced that he hadn't said *us*. But I didn't correct him on that front right then. "Ev, you said how Mira deserved to be surrounded by family—she was. This was her family. Her village. And look how loved she was."

Ev's voice had broken a lot last night and his hands had trembled and there had been a fair amount of face scrubbing, but I hadn't actually seen him cry until that moment. Tears spilled down his face and I shoved him into a nearby chair, crouching in front of him, not saying anything, just holding his hands and letting him grieve.

"I grew up here," he said shakily. "But I didn't see it as *home* until it was too late. I stayed gone in New York too long. Lost track—"

"You never lost her. Never. Not when it counted."

"But I didn't see this...family before."

"Maybe you weren't ready." My own voice was none too steady. I thought of the little gifts Mira had given me for the girls. Thought how hard I'd worked not to tell many people about what I went through to keep custody of the kids. Maybe I'd been oblivious to this community, too. Maybe, like Ev, I'd been scared to embrace it fully.

Ev and I sat there a long time until finally he blinked and looked around, like he'd finally gotten recentered in his body. "Brady? What *are* we going to do with this food?"

"I have an idea," I said and got up to summon Adele to make it happen. Then I did what I always tried to avoid doing and called my boss to ask for a favor.

They started trickling into People's Cup at five thirty. First Violet, with flowers for the tables and a huge hug for Ev. She set me to rearranging tables and chairs. Because of course whatever arrangement Audrey and I had done thirty minutes earlier wasn't good enough. A few minutes later the triplets trailed in after Adele, helping her carry the casseroles over. Behind her, Jonas pulled our old wagon, loaded down with more of the food. Slowly, the rest of the Knit Night family showed up, most a little dressier than usual, many in unseasonal cardigans and knit socks. Rarely seen spouses and children made appearances, too, something the twins and Jonas celebrated by claiming a back table for their new friends. Randy was there, helping to arrange the food along the coffee bar. To my surprise, he'd readily agreed to my plan to close for usual business. I hadn't even told him or Chris when Mom died because I'd been so afraid of losing the job. Maybe that had been a mistake. A few other business owners had also shut early and shown up with food and condolences for Ev, including both stationery store owners, who were managing to stand near each other without flames darting from their eyes. Perhaps Mira's legacy could bring them some peace as well.

It was an impromptu wake for the heart and soul of our neighborhood and community, and it was more heartfelt than anything formal could have been. People shared Mira stories and showed off projects she'd helped with. Ev was surrounded by love—and he wasn't the only one who'd insisted on being an island of self-reliance for far too long. He hadn't needed to go through Mira's end by himself and I hadn't needed to be so alone with the kids. This community had always been here and we'd both refused to see it for our own silly reasons. Two years I'd trudged alone, and maybe I didn't have to any longer. Maybe it was okay to wrap myself in the fabric of community and to knit my life to Ev's.

Despite my newfound resolve, I wasn't sure if Ev really felt the same way, and I had to work hard not to let doubts ruin this nice, fuzzy feeling.

He was mobbed by a constant stream of people, so I went and fixed him a plate, being careful to avoid anything that might have had pork, and then I made him a coffee, extra sweet, and brought both over to him.

"Ev needs to eat," I told the ladies surrounding him, pushing in so I could hand him the plate.

"I am not hungry," Ev said wearily.

"And you've been on your feet too long." I ignored his protests and steered him into a chair near Violet and the triplets. "Now eat."

Ev's sigh was weightier than our weekly delivery of coffee beans. "She would have loved this." He gestured at the gathering around us.

"And she would have loved you eating, too," I urged.

"She couldn't taste anything at the end." Ev ignored my pleas.

"You did so good by her," Violet butted in. "You need to keep up your strength."

"You'll need it," added the pink triplet, who had brought a quinoa and edamame casserole. "Did I hear you're taking over the store? Not going back to New York?"

Ev paused, swallowing hard, and I found myself holding my breath. This was a moment of truth. Whatever he'd told me in the throes of grief at the hospital, no one could hold him to that. But what did Ev *really* want? Finally, he spoke.

"Yes. Iplik will continue as she would have wanted. My life is here now." He glanced at me, and sunshine spiked me straight through the heart. It should have been the most somber of days, yet that one look had me ready to dance.

A potent murmur swept through the room as news of Ev's pronouncement spread, and then there was a ripple of applause that culminated in backslapping by the other business owners. Randy and the rest welcomed Ev to their ranks, and the knitters celebrated even as they mourned.

"Now eat," I said as the clamor died down.

"You are going to be the most insufferable of boyfriends, aren't you?" He smiled at me, a weak one, but genuine affection was still there, too.

I waited until Violet and the triplets were back to talking stitch patterns before I answered, lowering my voice. "Depends. Exactly what type did you have in mind? The friend-who-is-indeed-male?"

"That is true." His voice was a whisper, but his eyes sparkled for the first time all day. "But I also want the exclusive kind. The you-and-me-forever kind. The you-are-sleeping-with-me-tonight kind."

"I can't." Regret laced my words. Forever was going to be tempered by the weight of my responsibilities, and that was the truth. "I've got the kids. Renee's at her geology field trip still. She sends her love."

To her credit, she'd sent a half-dozen texts throughout the day. I knew she was taking it hard, and when she got back, we'd have a long talk, work out a new arrangement, one that let us *both* have lives. And maybe, eventually, down the road, I'd lean on Ev, not her. Because that was okay and right.

"They have sleeping bags, yes? I saw them getting dropped off from their sleepovers." As usual, Ev had the solution. "They can have a slumber party in the living room. Fill that space with a few movies and popcorn. We'll move the chair so they have room to spread out."

"You make it sound so easy."

"Because it is." He gave me an indulgent smile.

"The kids and I…we're a package deal, you know? This isn't a temporary thing—I'm going to be their guardian forever, and whomever I'm with has to understand—"

"I do." He silenced me with a brief, soft kiss. "I am not talking about rearranging for a night. They are a part of your life, and I want them—and *you*—in mine."

"Okay," I said, a bit shaky.

Another step forward, another step, not away from Mira but toward a life where we could grieve and love together.

Ev's smile turned to something hotter, something almost feral, and I shivered a bit. Yeah, I could compromise and go along with the sleepover plan if it meant more smiles like that.

Chapter 15

Dear friends, I am absolutely awestruck at the outpouring of love and comments. Yesterday was the darkest day of my life, but today there are small rays of sunshine—one for each of you and all our local friends—breaking through the gray skies. A little while ago my friend, the barista, and I moved Hala's chair from the living room. We made room for giggles and stories and popcorn fights. And that was right and good. Her house will not stay quiet long, I think, and that is exactly what she would have wanted. This place will ring with laughter and footsteps, and her dearest wish that it be filled with the sort of love she shared with Hala Tanya will also come true. I think. I hope. I pray. I see this shimmering image that I hope is the future and not a mirage. To that end, for the first time in almost a week, I picked up needles. My barista needs another pair of socks.—Evren's Yarnings

When I packed up the kids for the impromptu sleepover, I grabbed two items from the secret box I kept far underneath my bed. Hopeful planning, you could say. Truth was, sex was the one area I was still a bit uncertain about. Not only had we had precious little of it, but I wasn't sure Ev completely trusted he was everything I'd ever need. And while I was being honest, maybe I had a few doubts, too. We'd had quickies and we'd had grief-filled comfort sex, but it still felt like maybe we hadn't made love yet.

Something I fully intended to rectify. I made sure all the kids were sound asleep after the movie and story, then said a prayer of gratitude that Ev's room was the farthest one from the living room, down the long, narrow hallway that also housed Mira's room, the bathroom, and a small office. And his door locked. I pushed aside any twinges of guilt over uprooting the kids for this evening. This was a grand adventure for them, and I was slowly figuring out that sometimes it was okay to put my own needs or Ev's first. When I opened the door, Ev sat cross-legged on the bed, laptop in front of him, knitting needles in his hands.

"Oh, hello." He looked up, giving me a wide smile. "I was just finishing my blog for the day."

"You ever going to let me see this mystery knitting blog of yours?" I scooted in behind him, draping myself over his back. I'd jokingly threatened to Google it a few times, but in the end I hadn't, wanting him to have his privacy until he was ready to share.

"Of course." Ev hit a key and Evren's Yarnings flashed on the screen. The blog was every bit as elegant as one might expect from Ev—classy fonts, simple layout, and the most gorgeous, artful photographs of knitted items. But it was his prose that struck me the deepest.

"I'm getting socks?" I asked, kissing his neck.

Ev held up the ball of multicolored yarn. "Yes. It has not escaped my notice how often you wear the others. These will be colorful stripes. We both need a little color."

"Yes." I kissed the spot right below his ear. In truth, he could knit me something in puke green and I'd still wear it proudly. Whatever made him happy to knit, I was completely in favor of.

Ev made his ruffled chicken noise as I paid more attention to his ear. "Let me save the laptop, yes?"

"Good idea. We don't want anyone getting impaled by needles either." I gestured at his knitting.

He set his stuff aside, then gave me a long, considering look. "Now what shall I do with you?"

"If we're taking votes, I'd like to grind with you for a long, long time until my lips are raw from kissing and my dick's about to explode."

"Do I get to hold you down?" The sparkles in Ev's dark eyes told me this wasn't really a negotiation.

"Of course. We've got *hours*." Luxurious, beautiful hours. "You can tie me up like you keep threatening."

"Perhaps. But first, strip for me."

"What's this? I get to be naked?" I laughed as I bounded off the bed, only too happy to give him a bit of a show.

"I find I did not get to see my fill last night. Also it amuses me."

"Well, then." I unbuttoned my shirt slowly, teasing him with glimpses of my T-shirt rather than my chest, then removed the T-shirt with equal deliberation. I paused as I got to my pants, loving the look of rapt attention on his face. My hand brushed the items in my deep pocket. There wasn't going to be a better time than now to bring it up.

"How much show would you like?" I asked, fingering the pocket's edge.

"What do you have in mind?"

Taking a deep breath, I withdrew the lube and slim plug I'd stashed there. "Would you like to watch me finger myself and put this in before we grind?"

In typical Ev fashion, he didn't answer right away, thinking. Eyes narrowing.

"We don't have to fuck. Ever. But sometimes I do like a little penetration. And I thought this might be a sexy compromise."

"I am not entirely opposed to fucking you." A small smile tugged at the corners of Ev's mouth.

"But you don't have to." I reached out for his hand. "I meant what I said yesterday, Ev. I love you. You're everything I've ever wanted. Everything. And I know you don't trust bisexuals—"

"Pssh." Ev gave a dismissive wave of his hand. "My past is done now. I trust *you*. Completely. That's all that really matters."

"Yes," I said. His words warmed me more than the early summer air on my skin. "You're it for me, Ev. You really are."

"I believe you." Ev licked at his lower lip. "Now, about your request. . . Is it wrong that you fingering yourself for my eyes only turns me on far more than the idea of me fingering you?"

"Nothing is wrong between us." I leaned down and kissed him.

He carefully folded the covers back on the bed, then patted a spot at the bottom. "Come, then; show me."

He made quick, efficient work of his own clothes before climbing back into the bed, legs folded under him.

I gave a little shimmy as I shed my pants, then sat back against the footboard, legs spread. I knew better than to bring up past partners with Ev, but this wasn't the first time I'd played like this in front of a partner. I had an ex-girlfriend who had loved ordering me to do her bidding while she watched, and I'd discovered I had a real kink for being watched by commanding eyes.

Flicking my nipple rings, I gasped, letting Ev see how much I liked this.

"Those are mine," Ev said in his most imperial tone. "You focus on your...task."

Fuck. A little moan escaped my mouth. He knew exactly how to turn my crank.

I dipped my hand lower, trailing over my stomach. I fisted my cock but barely got a stroke out before Ev made a tsk noise. "None of that either. I will handle that. Your hands have better things to do, yes?"

"Killing me, Ev." I groaned.

"Slowly," he agreed with a sly smile. "That is the point. Now show me your ass."

Oh, a dirty-talking Ev never failed to make my cock throb and leak pre-cum even without a hand on it. I squeezed out a bit of lube, then swirled my fingers around my rim, lightly but still enough to make me hiss.

"Feels good?" Ev asked. "Tell me."

"So good." I gasped as I worked a finger in. The muscle was almost painfully tight—other than quick play in the shower, I almost never had the chance to indulge in this.

"Deeper," Ev commanded, his eyes never leaving mine. Fuck; that was sexy—he was reading my pleasure in my face, not my hands.

A guttural sound rumbled from my chest as I grazed my gland.

"That's it. Two now."

Either Ev had done this play before or he was a studious watcher of porn, but my dick didn't really care how he got these mad skills, only that he kept talking. I drew my knees up to get better access and worked a second finger in, hissing a bit at the burn.

"So beautiful, *tatlim*. So perfect. A little harder now, just for me."

"Fuck. Fuck. Fuck." My eyes squished shut and I had to work not to come just from his words.

"Now your toy. Put it nice and deep." Ev's hot gaze almost singed my beard hair.

The plug was my favorite one—slim, with the perfect curve to rest right against my gland and a wide, flared base that put delicious pressure on my rim. I worked it in slowly, giving Ev as much show as I could, moaning softly as it found its mark.

His lips found my neck as my head fell back, and he pushed me back down on the mattress, maneuvering me until his long body covered mine.

"Hands up," he murmured, stroking my arms until I complied, wedging them under a slat in the footboard. "Perfect."

And it was. He kissed me, using his tongue to attack mine hungrily, his cock rubbing against my own leaking dick. His thrusts were far more aggressive than before, hips snapping into mine and making me gasp. Our motions made the plug wiggle inside me, and pleasure, thick and heady, coursed through my body.

"Gonna come," I whispered. It was simply too good—the plug, his mouth, his body on mine, the dirty whispers of encouragement spilling from his mouth.

"Not yet," he commanded. He dipped his head to nip at my piercings, growling slightly.

"Not helping." I gasped.

"Mine," he said as he captured my mouth again.

"Yours," I agreed. I hooked my legs around his waist, both to hold him impossibly close and because the angle put terrific pressure on the plug.

Ev shifted, and then the most amazing thing happened—he tapped the base of the plug. Not fucking me with it, only tapping lightly as he continued to rock. "This is what you like?" he whispered against my ear.

"This is perfect," I gasped, and it was.

"I think…someday I may let you prep yourself like this…then I will pull it out…and fuck you." Ev punctuated his words with taps on the plug, and when he got to *fuck*, my whole body started shaking. I tensed my thigh muscles, body bowing as the orgasm hit me like a rush-hour MAX train—swift, urgent, and loud.

Ev swallowed my moans with a kiss. A few more hard thrusts against my belly and he, too, was coming, alternating American curses and Turkish endearments. He kissed me for a long time as we both drifted back down, and the freedom not to rush was almost sweeter than the sex.

"Will you shower with me before we sleep?" Ev asked with a kiss to my temple.

"Of course." I turned, met his mouth, tried to tell him with my kiss that it didn't matter what little quirks he had—his thing about sticky fingers or cleanliness or whether or not we ever actually had anal sex—none of that mattered as long as I had him.

In the shower, we made out as the water coursed over us, and I decided that I didn't love Ev despite quirks; I loved him because of them. Because of all the unique textures and patterns that made up my Evren.

"I want a life with you," I whispered against his chest. "I don't care how hard it is to make that happen. It's what I want."

"We will make it happen, *aşkim*. You will see. Have faith."

Faith. It was such a funny, strange thing. For so long, I'd had none, and he'd almost had too much, but now we'd both found the one thing worth going all in on: us. What started as a small thread, the skinny yarn Ev used for socks, was now a hefty ball of hopes and dreams and a future we were going to make happen.

Chapter 16

All right, friends, I have heard the questions for a year now: when does my barista get a sweater? After all, I have kept the man so well shod with socks that my new book of sock patterns, out next month, is dedicated to him. When does he get a sweater? I have no idea why this has become an obsession among you all and my Knit Night group, but the answer, my friends, is today. Today he gets a sweater. Or, more precisely, today he gets a Fair Isle wedding vest with custom wooden buttons. As he would say, I went all in *on this particular project, and the pattern is my gift to you on this most joyous of days. Today, I am not only gaining a husband but a family, the biggest of life's blessings—one that I did not anticipate ever receiving, but one I am grateful for every day.* —Evren's Yarnings

"The book is dedicated to me?" I asked as I leaned over Ev's shoulder. He was typing at the dining room table.

"But of course." He stretched back to kiss me. "The shawl book coming out next year, that one is for Mira, but this one...it's you."

"Thank you." The kiss turned deeper until I was forced to remember where we had to be in half an hour.

I broke away and did a spin for him. "So, am I modeling it sufficiently well? Did you get enough pictures for the blog last night?" My suit was a great vintage find from a place off Hawthorne, the tie a gift from Renee, but the vest was the real star. It had a ridiculous number of shades in it and a complex pattern, showcasing Ev's signature masculine style with little hints of unexpected hues here and there in the mosaic patterns, too.

"Yes, but I am still not used to the new look." He gestured at my clean-shaven face. I knew the beard would be back in a matter of weeks, but I'd wanted something different for the wedding. Fresh start and all that.

"Almost forgot. I have something for you, too." I fumbled in my pocket, withdrew a lumpy square. You'd never know this was actually lumpy square try number four. I would have gone for a fifth try, but we ran out of that ball of yarn, and Jonas sagely noted I wasn't exactly improving. "It's a pocket square. I think."

"It is lovely." Ev held it up like he held up the knitting efforts of the kids. "Jonas taught you?"

"That obvious?" I rubbed my chin. "And in his defense, I think I'm a really poor learner."

"No, you're an incredibly sweet—"

"*Ev!* Madison *touched* my hair!" Morgan came shrieking into the room, followed quickly by a protesting Madison. Both girls had complicated braids that looped around their heads with flowers woven in. Three guesses which adult in the house was responsible for *that* bit of whimsy.

"Indoor voice, *aşkim*. Indoor voice. And I will fix it." Ev did some bit of magic that tucked the errant strand back into place. "Is your room picked up? We will leave for the courthouse in a moment."

"We'll go check!"

No need to guess who had the girls and Jonas on a new cleaning kick. Complete with color-coded chore charts that looked suspiciously like knitting patterns. A few weeks earlier, we'd painted Mira's old room a shade of dusky rose that reminded all of us of Mira, then moved in the twins' bunk bed. Jonas had the small room that had once been an office. It was tiny, but he was thrilled at the privacy.

"Jonas? Are you ready?" I yelled down the hall.

"Let me lock Fluffy's cage and I'll be right there." Fluffy was the male guinea pig Jonas had received for his birthday last month. The creature was already awash in knitted blankets and balls.

I checked my phone before turning back to Ev. "Renee and Indigo are on their way, too."

Renee didn't have a room in the apartment. She had, much to her delight and my eternal worry, gotten a new grant for housing and moved into the group house with her friends. But as Ev said, it was time to let her be nineteen. And it turned out that doing that actually brought us closer together, smoothed over a lot of the tension of the previous year. We were meeting her and Indigo at the courthouse. He, too, had become a fixture in our lives, and I credited his placid nature with balancing out some of Renee's more…dramatic tendencies.

This was to be a simple affair—a trip to the courthouse with the kids and Renee, then, afterward, Violet and the rest of Knit Night had organized a big party at People's Cup. Thanks in large part to the knitters and their friends, business was back up at our location. And after five years of working there, I had a new title: I wasn't just Brady the barista anymore, I was Brady the manager of the Alberta branch. Apparently *someone* had told Randy that I was investigating coffee carts, and next thing I knew, I had a nifty new title and paperwork I'd rather not do. Ev swore it wasn't him, as did Audrey and Violet. Someone had meddled, though, and for once, all I felt was gratitude. I was grateful to have a life filled with all these people—Ev, the kids, our Knit Night family, and the rest of the community.

"Thank you." Ev kissed my temple.

"For what?" I asked. "The square was nothing—"

"For being you. For filling my life at a time when it seemed to be emptying." He glanced at the picture of Mira we had on the wall, along with the kids' most recent school pictures.

"I didn't think I had any room for you," I admitted.

"Nor I you. But I'm so happy with what we spliced together. You. The children. This life." He kissed me again, another of those kisses that made me wish we had hours and a locked door.

As we pulled apart, I laughed. "I freaking love Knit Night."

Wrapped Together
Portland Heat

Annabeth Albert

LYRICAL SHINE PRESS
Kensington Publishing Corp.
www.kensingtonbooks.com

Chapter 1

"Don't forget the holiday decorating contest begins next week."

Even my piping-hot mint tea wasn't enough to warm me at Ron Atkinson's words. Holiday. Decorating. Contest. Dear lord, what was the business association thinking?

"Are there guidelines?" someone closer to the head of the table blessedly asked so I didn't have to. The Alberta Street business owners were meeting at the People's Cup coffee house on the Thursday evening before Thanksgiving. This was our monthly meeting, ostensibly to discuss making our tiny business district more welcoming to customers, but usually more of a social hour except when, like today, a special event was in the offing. I hated the special events.

"No guidelines this year other than the theme 'Magic of the Holidays! ' so you can have fun decorating your windows and storefronts in whatever way that theme speaks to you." Ron had a bushy mustache and a booming voice better suited for a minister or a politician than the owner of an upscale pet supply store. He was our unofficial leader—sent out reminder emails about the meetings and set the agendas and worked tirelessly on the special events.

The holiday season held no magic for me, especially not for the past two years, and I doubted "crushing grief" made a good decorating scheme, so I didn't join in the excited murmurs that started up as people shared their plans, many of which sounded months in that making.

"Does anyone have a pen? I want to write some of this down." Ah. Sawyer Murphy had come late and unprepared as usual. He'd squeezed in between Mary Anne, the florist, and Ev, the yarn shop owner, balancing his coffee drink and agenda in one hand. He wore a hoodie advertising some video game. His unruly brown hair and several days' worth of stubble made him look more like a student at the nearby community college than part owner of a chain of gift stores, including the one in our neighborhood.

Ev passed him a simple ballpoint, one with his store's logo on it. Good. Saved me having to offer the Kaweco Sport in my jacket pocket. I carried it not for advertising my stationery store but because it was a damn fine portable fountain pen, one of my personal favorites.

"Anything else we need to discuss?" Ron asked.

This was my chance, the reason I'd come to the meeting in the first place, and I pulled out the thick stationery-stock note card where I'd jotted down my thoughts on retailers encroaching onto sidewalk space. Namely *Sawyer* sprawling out of the front of his store with all manner of trinkets. But in the time it took me to get my card out, people were murmuring "no" and already starting the gossip hour part of the meeting, talking in small groups, no longer paying attention to the agenda or Ron.

Just like that, there went my chance. I didn't have the bravery required to lift my voice above the din. Indeed, my hand shook getting the card out of my jacket's breast pocket. *Not today.*

I took a sip of my now tepid, almost-gone tea. Ugh. The good barista was on duty, the one who went with Ev from the knitting store and who always happily made my tea with the same care he did the fancy coffee drinks. I left the group, happy to have the excuse of needing a refill, but as I stood in line, Mary Anne joined me.

"Hollis Alcott, we almost *never* see you at these things!" Her voice seemed to ring out above the din. "Will you be participating in the contest this year?"

"I doubt it. My fall display is already set." I tried not to sound too dour—she always had the best houseplants and had custom-ordered the rare fern I'd wanted.

"Ah, well, that's too bad. You let me know if you change your mind. I'd be happy to lend you some poinsettias or other decor. I know you could do a splendid, *tasteful* window."

It was my turn to order, so I gave her a smile as a reply before handing Brady my stainless-steel tumbler for tea and ordering a scone to go. I had to wait down at the other end of the bar for my order, and as I was waiting, Sawyer came loping over, a smile on his boyish face. His wide shoulders stretched the hoodie in distracting ways.

"Hollis! Did I hear you say you're not decorating?"

"You did."

He frowned. "I know how much you hate the holidays, but I bet you'd get an uptick in sales if you decorated. I heard Mary Anne offer to help. I could, too. I've got gobs of lights."

"Thank you but no." Truth be told, I could use the increase in sales, but it wasn't enough of a motivator to get me ready for the onslaught of red and green.

Sawyer's head tilted, considering. Oh no. I knew that look too well. A Sawyer who was scheming was downright dangerous. "We should bet, you and I."

"No," I said firmly. I stepped away from the coffee bar to let Mary Anne and others wait for their orders, but Sawyer kept step with me, effectively pinning me in between two tables on my path to the door. I sighed and repeated my objection. "No. The last time we bet, I believe you cracked a wrist."

Sawyer waved a hand, dismissing my concern. "We were fifteen. We've had other bets since then."

We had, but there was one in particular I was determined not to remember right at that moment. This was the peril of having known someone for almost two decades. "How precisely would one even bet on this?"

I let my inner musings escape before I could rein them in, and Sawyer smiled. He knew he had me. Whatever nervousness and shyness captured my tongue around large groups did not, unfortunately, extend to Sawyer. "Well, I was thinking whichever of us makes it into the top three is the winner of our bet, and then the loser has to do whatever the winner wants for an evening."

Oh, I did *not* like this. *"Anything?"*

"That wasn't a no." Sawyer's grin showed the sort of charm that made him so darn popular. "And I wasn't thinking of something kinky. Trust me here, Hols."

"Don't call me that." And I most certainly did not trust him. I was pretty sure the always-affable Sawyer didn't have a kinky bone in his body, but that didn't mean he wasn't up to *something*. "But I could get you to do any task of my choosing?"

See, the thing about me that Sawyer knew was that I have a very hard time resisting a bet. Always have, hence the aforementioned bet freshman year of high school about jumping over auditorium seats during drama class. I'm also notoriously cheap. And as it turned out, I *did* have a job for him.

He nodded. "Anything."

"I have a bathroom I want painted at my store. Including the trim."

Sawyer, to his credit, didn't look remotely pained. "That's fine. I'm good at painting."

"And you? What would you want?" I had no idea why I was asking. I certainly wasn't planning on agreeing to this ridiculous plan.

"A surprise." He winked at me.

"I don't like those."

"I *know*. Which is why you need one. But if it makes you feel better, I'll specify no sex or nudity involved." Sawyer had mercifully dropped his deep, clear voice to softer tones. I still bristled at the thought of anyone overhearing this.

"Or humiliation, public or otherwise."

"Oh, Hollis, you know me better than that." He held up his hands. They were big, capable hands, and I had to blink to get my eyes to look away. "Now, come on. I dare you. Bet me."

"I suppose I could muster some sort of decor. Something simple. Tasteful."

"I wouldn't expect anything less." He put out a hand for me to shake.

I took it, reluctantly, knowing that his firm clasp would send the same jolt up my arm it always did. "All right. I suppose I'll call you if I win."

"But I'll see you before that, right?" Sawyer didn't seem in any hurry to part, lounging against an empty table. I knew exactly what was coming next, but good manners kept me from rushing out the door. "Aren't you coming to Thanksgiving? My mom's looking forward to seeing you."

"I sent her my regrets the other day. I have plans."

"You do?" Sawyer blinked.

"I do." It didn't matter if those plans were a movie marathon for me and a turkey breast for Benedict and me, they were my own.

"More than just hanging out with your cat?" Oh, Sawyer knew me a bit too well, which was one of the many reasons I strove to avoid him as much as possible.

"Yes," I lied with absolute confidence. Rewatching *Sherlock* totally counted as *more*.

"Char and Tucker will be disappointed, too, I'm sure. And Aria." Sawyer threw out the three cards most likely to get me to waver, but I stood firm.

"Just because my sister married your brother doesn't mean I need adopting by your family really. I'm quite content with my life." It had been bad enough that Char had been best friends with Sawyer all through high school. Then she had to go and marry Tucker, who was Sawyer's twin, making Sawyer practically *family*, something I still wasn't reconciled with.

"Oh, Hollis," Sawyer groaned. "I swear to God, I'm going to find you some holiday spirit this year if it kills me."

Whatever small modicum of holiday spirit I had had died almost three years ago and we both knew it. All I really wanted from the holidays was a quietly forgettable month—it was the most I could hope for really. "Now, if you'll excuse me, I need to get going."

"Okay. Just don't forget our bet!"

As if I could. I cursed my impetuousness the whole walk back to my place, pulling my coat tighter against the late November chill.

Chapter 2

"That is the most Charlie Brown–looking Christmas tree I've ever seen." Char's voice interrupted my work in the front window of Paper, my store. It was an old-fashioned space with a large front window—the building had been a haberdashery in a previous life and I'd kept the bare wood floors, classic glass cases, and large display window with a raised platform.

"That's because it's not a Christmas tree." I crawled out of the window to give my sister a perfunctory kiss on the cheek. She had Aria with her in her bright orange stroller. Her I gave a big smile to and a high five. She loved handing those out.

"It's not?" Char's nose wrinkled up.

"This is a seasonal branch," I explained, gesturing to the bare stick. "It symbolizes the austereness of winter, while the red ball is merely a touch of whimsy."

"Whimsy." She didn't look convinced. "And the single candle is for solstice, then? Is that your theme?"

"Not really. Just giving a nod to the season really."

My sister had celebrated solstice since her hippie college days at Reed. And ever since they'd had Aria, she was firmly in the all-holidays-matter camp and celebrated from Thanksgiving through the Epiphany, hitting Hanukkah, Christmas, with a nod to Kwanzaa, too. Not all of us reacted to the sheer awfulness of December in the same way. I hunkered down and hibernated. Char celebrated like they might be handing out medals for it. Indeed, today she had on a tunic stretched across her pregnant belly with turkeys made out of handprints, and Aria had a matching T-shirt with the year on it. They also had matching riotous mops of curly dark brown hair.

"Well, it's more than you have the last few years." She chewed the corner of her glossy lip—no doubt there was homemade beeswax balm coming in the holiday presents this year. "So you're coming for Thanksgiving tomorrow, then?"

"No. I sent my regrets, as I'm sure you heard."

"Oh." Her face fell, and I had to look away, concentrating on untangling the single strand of white lights that would be the final touch for my window. "It's not healthy for you and that cat to be alone so much."

"Bun—Benedict and I get along just fine. We'll have a nice day," I assured her, patting her arm before I climbed back into the window area.

"*Bunny* and you. It's okay to admit that your cat only comes to the name Bunny." Char's laugh removed most of her disappointed look. Her usually pale skin had a rosy glow to it. We had the same coloring—dark hair, light blue eyes, skin that refused to tan—but Char was so…*animated* that it was often challenging to remember that we'd once shared a womb.

"Regardless, I'll get along fine." I busied myself artfully draping the strand of lights.

"But I'm making a mince pie. Could I drop a slice or two off for you after?" she asked.

"If there's any left. Don't hold some back on my account." I crawled back out and dusted off my pant legs before returning to her and Aria.

"Hollis. You're my brother. You *matter.*" She leaned in and gave me an awkward hug. "For what it's worth, I miss them, too. I know my pie's not as good as Mom's, and Christine's turkey isn't like Dad's, but they're good people, Hollis. They'd love to have you."

My throat got thick as it always did when she mentioned our parents, gone three years in December. She could talk so much more easily about memories than I could. Just thinking about Dad's turkey had me resolving to do a Cornish hen instead for Benedict and me. "I know Christine and Phillip mean well. I'm just not up to the full family right now."

Sawyer's family—now Char's in-laws—was huge. Christine and Phillip had separated a decade ago, yet somehow they managed to spend holidays together with their new partners, as if it was no big deal that their family was more blended than a French Impressionist watercolor with stepparents and stepsiblings along with the usual assortment of grandparents and aunts and uncles. A forty-person holiday meal wasn't out of the ordinary.

"Mama! Out!" Aria demanded, kicking her heels against the stroller.

"No, no, darling. Uncle Hollis has too many pretties for you to break." To me, she said, "You know, you could let me set up a little corner of the store with a few playthings for those customers who have kids—that way they can browse while the kids play and—"

"No," I said with a shudder. "Few of my customers have kids anyway." Finishing with the lights, I went behind the register to dig around in the low shelves beneath it. "Ah, here it is."

I came back around the register to kneel in front of Aria. "Here, sweetheart, Uncle Hollis has something for you." I held out the small paper parcel.

"No s-u-g-a-r," Char spelled out as Aria tore open the wrapper.

"Trust," I told her in exactly the same tone Sawyer had used on me the night before. Aria revealed a little board book I'd picked up down the street for her, one of those wordless books with imaginative drawings. I'd been drawn to it instantly.

"Her birthday's in a few weeks," Char chided. "You spoil her so."

"She's my only niece."

"For now." She patted her round belly. "Can't wait until February gets here and we find out what these two are."

"Healthy babies, we hope." I stayed at stroller height, turning pages for Aria. As a twin who'd married a twin, Char had been convinced she'd have twins, too, the first time around. Trust Char to get her way eventually, though. I really wasn't one to speculate on genders or names with her, but I was unmistakably besotted with Aria and had no doubt this new duo would similarly make me way mushier than I was comfortable with.

"Did I tell you my friend Jeannie's having twins, too? Later next year. It'll be just like the Murphy and Alcott twins, growing up together," she crowed, and I winced.

"Congrats to her." Much as I could enjoy the quieter company of Tucker, the extroverted pair of Char and Sawyer had made my high school experience very...*loud*. And I hadn't exactly enjoyed going through school as "the twins," something made much more...*challenging* when Sawyer had exuberantly come out our junior year of high school. More than ten years later, I'd finally worked up some forgiveness for Char's blurting to Tucker, "Now we both have a gay twin!" *Some* of us preferred not to have our private lives be the subject of public speculation. There were *reasons* I'd gone east for college. Not that I'd ever tell any of them that.

"All done!" Aria threw the book to the polished concrete floor, and I retrieved it.

"We're going to walk and look at all the new windows. Won't you join us?" Char made a begging face. "You can hang your 'Back in Ten Minutes' sign."

I mainly used that sign for my lunch break, but I could tell Char and Aria would have a big pout if I declined, so I sighed and went in the back to grab my coat, scarf, and gloves.

"Goodness, Hollis. We're just going down the street. Not to the arctic."

"I run cold," I said testily. "Always have. And this cold snap is no joke right, Aria?" I reached out and tweaked her furry hat so that it protected her little ears better.

"Brrr, Unca Holly!" She laughed as we headed out.

"Oh, it's gorgeous," Char said when we were outside, indicating my window, which did look very nice, if one asked me. The lights gave off just a hint of twinkle, accenting the bare wood of the tree branch with the single red ornament. The electronic candle wasn't as nice as a real one would be, but it still created a suitable effect.

We headed down the street, admiring windows with frost and snowy murals and windows full of wrapped presents or good things to eat. For Aria's sake I tried to be upbeat and not too sarcastic in my commentary. We came back up the block, and at last we reached Sawyer's store, which if I hadn't been so absorbed in my window, I would have noticed earlier. His place practically glowed. In fact, on closer inspection, it *did* glow, lights dripping from the awning, lights even around the metal table and chairs in front of his place. And in the window…

Well, I'd never seen such clutter.

"Oh, it's *magic*." Char's breath was visible in the chilly air.

"Magic," Aria echoed.

Mess, Uncle Hollis added, but in my own head, of course. But really, it was much too much. Christmas tree hung with all manner of ornaments— and some things *not* ornaments, like comic books and bobbleheads and other novelties Sawyer sold. Around the base of the tree was a train track, meandering through a snowy village, but this wasn't just any village—no, it was populated with the sort of commercialized stuff I associated most closely with Sawyer's family's stores. Disney characters caroling, *Star Wars* figurines in the town square, anime-looking dolls skating. Boxes of cards made smaller "trees" on the sides of the display, a reminder that this was ostensibly a "card" store.

If Cards & More had started out as a card store, it had quickly been taken over by gifts and licensed merchandise to the point that one was hard-pressed to find the paper goods. Sawyer and his father did love their collectibles, and apparently they sold well. They might as well just call it More and be done with it.

"Hollis! Char! What do you think?" Sawyer came bustling out wearing a holiday sweatshirt emblazoned with the store logo. "And check out our new shirts! I've got one in your size, half-pint." He knelt to give Aria a high five.

"It's magnificent," Char said.

"And you, Hollis? What do you think?"

"It's…I'm speechless. Really," I said truthfully.

"Thanks." Sawyer grinned. "I peeked at your window a few minutes ago. It's gorgeous in its simplicity."

I was surprised Sawyer knew the concept of simplicity, but I charitably bit my tongue and nodded.

"I heard about your little bet," Char said, because of course she had. Nothing stayed a secret around the Murphy family. "May the best man win."

"Hey, we were *both* the best men," Sawyer joked. "No, seriously, Hols is giving me a run for my money. Can't wait to see what Ron and the committee think."

"Be prepared to be covered in Proper Gray next weekend," I said. Char snickered, and only too late, I realized how that sounded. "It's *paint* color."

"Bring it on." Sawyer's eyes sparkled, not a hint of nervousness in them, which didn't explain why *I* was suddenly feeling a bit unsteady.

* * * *

Both Black Friday and Small Business Saturday were steadily busy—not crazy crowds, but then, I attracted a more discerning level of patron, which was something I aspired to. The masses were never going to clamor for fountain pens and handmade paper, and that was okay. These things made *me* happy, and it seemed increasingly important to offer simple, beautiful alternatives to the crowded, digital age of quick convenience and zero aesthetic appeal.

The sidewalks were crowded, though, and the buzz among the other business owners was that it was a good year. After Cyber Monday, though—and lord, did I hate these names for otherwise perfectly respectable business days—things were back to usual for early December.

I was straightening a display of handmade papers when the door chimed. I turned to find Sawyer there, holding a sign.

"See what Ron and the committee just brought for my front window?" He beamed. Sawyer did happy the same way a Labrador did—all smiles and wags and bouncy energy that had no idea what to do with itself.

"'Winner of this year's window display contest,'" I read. The sign was adorned with cheery little snowmen. I hated it. "Congratulations."

"I'm sorry your bathroom will go unpainted," he said with an impish smile, not sorry one bit.

"I think you hypnotized the committee. Your window was so...*busy.*"

"Oh, come on, Hollis. You know you loved it. I put some hobbits in there just for you. Representing your favorite fandom and all."

"I'm not fifteen anymore. I don't have a fandom," I lied.

Sawyer snorted. Fine. Let him not believe me. "So, are you free Friday night?"

"This Friday?" I walked to the register area and pulled out my paper planner even though I knew perfectly well I was free.

"Whoa. You still use one of those? You know you can get Google to—"

"Yes, but I don't sell Google. And I happen to like paper things."

"I've noticed." Sawyer made a show of looking around the store.

"All right. I'm free. So what hideous thing are you having me do?"

"So little trust, Hols, so little trust." He grinned at me. Today was apparently one of his shaving days, and he had only the lightest dusting of stubble. He'd missed a spot on his left cheek, which I found both endearing and irritating. "And I'm not telling you yet. Dress warmly and be prepared to take transit. I'll pick you up right as you close up, and don't worry, I'll be feeding you, too."

"Meals are the least of my worries."

Sawyer gave me the sort of once-over that made me profoundly uncomfortable, especially coming from him, when it was very clearly a joke. "If you ask me, you could use a few more meals."

"I eat." He was taller than my six feet by a good two inches and outweighed my lean build by a fair bit, but none of that stopped me from looking down my nose at him with a glare designed to shrink him down to the size of one of my pens.

"Good. You should enjoy Friday, then." He started to head toward the door.

A thought suddenly occurred to me. "Sawyer, exactly how many people are involved in this little excursion?"

A strange look flitted across his face, one I hadn't seen before. "Just us. I mean, I'm sure the city will be crowded as usual, but I'm not bringing the family, if that's what you're worried about."

"All right. See you a little after seven on Friday, then."

"It's a date," he said with a little wave on his way out the door.

Oh no, it wasn't. I simply refused to consider that this...*obligation* to Sawyer Murphy was a date. Dates meant trouble, and trouble was all Sawyer was.

Chapter 3

Friday night I turned the sign to closed, locked the till in the safe, then grabbed my warmest wool coat. The cold snap had continued, with it dipping down past thirty each evening. Not that cold elsewhere, but I was a native Oregonian by way of British parents—my blood objected to anything below fifty on principle. I'd purchased another new scarf from Ev at Iplik, this one a sample from one of his newest patterns. Long, with a soft, thick cashmere blend, it had a subtle texture to it. I loved it immensely and thought it brought out the gray in my eyes. *Not* that I was dressing up in the slightest for Sawyer. I'd worn a light blue button-down shirt with a pair of wool pants because that's what I wore to work most winter days. If it happened it was my favorite oxford shirt, well, that was because tomorrow was the day to take everything to the dry cleaners. It was one of my rare days off. I had a very occasional clerk—a mother friend of Char's who worked two Saturdays a month and the odd evening so I wasn't working seven days a week continuously.

And so I had a chance to do things like get a haircut. My hair was getting altogether too long again, the curl obvious despite a healthy application of hair product and combing. I checked my planner while I waited for Sawyer, verifying that yes, I had the haircut prior to Aria's birthday party at three. *That* I'd rather forget, but Char had promised me a small gathering. Aria had had her big kidcentric thing today, so tomorrow was just for the family.

Which wasn't exactly reassuring, but I'd missed Thanksgiving. No way could I miss this, too.

Rap. Rap. A noise came from the door, and a bundled-up Sawyer stuck his head in. "Ready to lock up?"

"Yes. Did you know about Aria's party tomorrow?" I asked. *Please say you have plans.*

"Are you kidding? Uncle Sawyer's coming prepared. I have to knock you out of the uncle-of-the-year sweepstakes and I've got just the present to do it."

"I ordered her gift from France," I shared, keeping my tone conversational, even if I was every bit as competitive as Sawyer.

"France, huh? Mine has sounds, lights, and takes three kinds of batteries."

"Clearly being on your brother's best-uncle list isn't as important." I locked the door and led him to the rear of the store.

"What? He'll love it, too." Sawyer clapped me on the shoulder. "Besides, their house is about to get way louder than just one toy."

I shuddered to think of the decibels the coming twins would add. "So, do I get to find out where we're headed now?"

"We're going downtown," Sawyer said as we headed out into the frosty air. "Got a bus to catch, so step it up a notch."

We caught the bus, which seemed to have an awful lot of passengers clad in black and red.

"*Please* tell me we're not headed to a Blazers game." We were squashed together because space was at a premium.

"Now, Hols, you know soccer is my game." This I did know, as I had vivid memories of being dragged to games by Char and Tucker.

"And football." I gestured, indicating his green-and-yellow Oregon Ducks scarf. Tucker joked that Sawyer had gone to U of O just for the chance to go to the football games at student prices.

"Yup. And I know better than to drag you to a sporting event."

"Good." I still expected he had something equally hideous lined up for us. We got off the bus at Pioneer Square, and Sawyer set off at a fast clip for the center of the large brick plaza rimmed by tall downtown buildings and many shops.

"There it is." Apparently satisfied with his vantage point, Sawyer pulled up short to gaze up at the huge Christmas tree in the center of the square. And it truly was a giant, seventy feet tall at least, and lit up with a lavish amount of multicolored lights. All at once, a memory from elementary school hit me: my parents bringing Char and me to the tree-lighting ceremony the day after Thanksgiving, me cringing at the packed crowd, Char chattering excitedly, carols wafting over the air until...

"*Magic*," I whispered, voice barely more than a breath.

"Exactly," Sawyer said happily. "Isn't it magnificent?"

"Look, Dad, it's the biggest tree ever. It probably came from the North Pole."

"Not the North Pole. Right here in Oregon. But isn't it magic?"

Magic. I could still hear my father's deep timbre in my ears, his British accent more pronounced with excitement. Regret and loss mingled with a sort of wistfulness that made my sternum ache and my voice feel like sandpaper scraping against my throat. "Is this what we came to see?"

"This is stop number one." Sawyer nodded.

I groaned. "Stop one? Sawyer, are you really using your night to try to...*infuse* me with some sort of holiday spirit? Don't you have something I could...I don't know, alphabetize instead?"

"You'd enjoy that too much." Sawyer bumped arms with me, still much too close despite the fact that we were no longer on the bus. "And so what if I am?"

"It's not going to work," I warned.

"It could. I remember in high school how you used to wrap presents with military precision. You haven't always been a Scrooge."

The truth of his statement hit me like a punch. I hadn't been anti-Christmas prior to my parents' death. True, I'd always been reserved, not heading out to the bevy of parties and events like Sawyer and Char, but I'd loved picking out beautiful things for the people important to me, and my love of unusual wrapping paper led me to my love of stationery. I'd loved my mother's cooking and the quiet holiday evenings spent doing a puzzle with the two of them.

"I am *not* Scrooge. I already ordered Aria's gift. Just because I don't like any of the...trappings, does not mean I'm anti-holidays or whatever."

Sawyer turned so he was looking into my eyes. Oh no. Not the scheming look again. "What if it worked?"

"Your plan to make me holly and jolly?"

He laughed at that. "Even the Grinch finds his heart. I have faith in you, Hols. What if I make you find your holiday spirit this month? Will you come to Christmas dinner?"

"Another bet?"

"Another bet." He nodded. "Your bathroom isn't going to paint itself. I help you find some holiday joy, you come to Christmas dinner with the family. If my grand plan fails, I'll paint your bathroom by New Year's."

"Deal." I held out a gloved hand, telling myself that I really did want that bathroom painted.

"Great!" Sawyer's grin rivaled the tree's lights in front of us for sheer wattage. "Now on to stop number two."

"Which is?" I followed him across the square and up a few blocks.

"We've got a reservation at the Palm Court in the Benson."

"This is hardly torture for me." We walked briskly toward the historic hotel. I liked nice hotel food, something I'd shared with my father, but unlike so many memories, this one didn't make me melancholy. Just hungry and wishing I'd decided to travel this month. Then I could be spared everyone's efforts to perk me up.

"But first we're going to admire their gingerbread city." Sawyer held the door open for me, and sure enough, there was a crowd around the huge display in the lobby. As we got closer, I couldn't help my intake of breath. "Careful now. Wouldn't want any of that holiday spirit infecting you already."

"It's stunning. I forgot…" I'd been here before. Many years ago, probably the same year we'd attended the tree lighting ceremony, my parents had brought us to see the huge gingerbread house village the Benson did each year. We'd probably eaten here, too. Suddenly I was less than hungry. "Did you talk to Char?" I demanded.

"What?" Sawyer's eyes went wide. "No. I just wanted to see some of my favorite places. We always came here to see the gingerbread house when Tucker and I were little. And I always go see the tree a few times each year—mainly while doing my shopping in Pioneer Square, but I figured making you shop might be too cruel."

"You figured right." It was crazy for a store owner to hate shopping; I knew that. But the truth was that I hated crowds, especially holiday crowds. The Pioneer Square and Lloyd Center holiday crowds were the worst—a constant crush of other people all looking for the perfect gift. I tried to frequent smaller, online merchants as much as possible this time of year.

"Isn't it spectacular, though?" Sawyer gestured at the creation spread before us. It was like one of the seek-and-find puzzles I'd loved as a boy—little details piled on little details. Snow on the top of buildings, bicycle tracks in the snowy roads, clusters of people here and there. A thought occurred to me, and I couldn't hold it back. "This is where you got the inspiration for your window, isn't it?"

"Absolutely. I love all the tiny surprises." He crouched to get a better view of the street level. I saw his display in a new light, then, an homage to the classic displays and an ode to the things he loved. I wouldn't say I fell in love with it right then, but I certainly…softened.

And I softened a bit toward him, too, the awkwardness of the last few years fading away as I remembered how he'd been as a teen, hy-perinterested in whatever his latest obsession was, absolutely unafraid to show his passion for whatever the interest of the week was. I'd hung back, my usual default, content to watch him and Char emote.

The live jazz filtering in from the restaurant also went a fair way to relaxing me, and by the time my soup came, we were chatting aimlessly about Aria and the coming babies and other easy topics. After dinner, however, Sawyer had another of his stops in store.

"Get ready to catch the MAX," he said after a little tussle over the check, with him insisting on paying because the bet was his idea.

"More ghost of Christmas present?" I asked as we walked to the Blue MAX stop. I had a feeling where we were headed.

"This is me wanting to see the ZooLights and Char insisting that Aria is too little and she's too pregnant to enjoy it."

I refrained from pointing out that he had dozens of other friends he could have called on. Literally. Oodles. Sawyer delighted in being the entire world's gay best friend, not just Char's. He shopped. He watched romantic movies. He gossiped incessantly. And he was simply so utterly charming; he knew how to deliver compliments that make both genders swoon, a talent I've *never* had. Besides, I refused to embrace that—or any other—stereotype. And I'd spent two decades refusing to be another member of his entourage, another person with a hopeless crush on him.

We got off at the Washington Park MAX stop, taking the big escalator up to street level, Sawyer grinning like a little kid who had never been up so high before. And damn if I didn't smile a bit, too. He was just that infectious. *No crushes. Not even a small one*, I reminded myself sternly.

The line to get into the zoo on a Friday night in December was insane. It felt like every family in the metropolitan area had come to see the lit-up zoo displays and animals made out of thousands of lights.

"When was the last time you did the ZooLights?" Sawyer asked as we waited in line.

"I never have," I admitted.

"Oh wow. I can't wait to watch your face." Sawyer peered much too intently into my eyes. "I come every year. But then, I've got a zoo membership so I come to all the special events."

"I remember the year your parents got everyone memberships to different places. That was the year Char and Tucker were married right? They got me one to the Art Museum. I've kept it up ever since."

"Mom would be delighted to know that. You could tell her yourself on—"

"Ah-ah." I made a warning noise. "You promised. I have to feel sufficient holiday spirit first."

"Just you wait. Just you wait." He totally looked like a lion waiting to pounce on me before it was our turn to pay. We got in free with Sawyer's membership. Once in, there was a lit pathway proclaiming "ZooLights" and a volunteer handing out programs and maps.

"I'm buying you a coffee or *something* inside," I grumbled. His doing all the paying and the steering me from place to place was starting to feel decidedly datelike, something we couldn't have.

"See, I waited until later in the evening to bring you," Sawyer explained as we walked down the main path. "Less crowded."

"This is less?" We were being jostled along by a steady stream of visitors, most of whom were families with young children.

"Trust me. This is less." He grabbed my arm. "Stick close, though."

"Not that close." I took my arm back.

"Oh, Hols—"

"*Wow.*" I came to a dead stop, interrupting him and causing him to bump into me at the same instant, and I cared not one whit. All of a sudden the pathway had become illuminated with thousands of red lights lining the walls, red, blue, and purple trees looming over.

"Is that a hint of wonder in your voice, Hollis?"

"Oh hush." I meandered in a haze, as the walls shifted from red to blue and creatures were revealed along the walkway—a stunning peacock in blues and pinks, a menacing alligator, and a flock of happy hippos. We picked up steaming cups of hot chocolate from a vendor and I barely paid her any mind as I marveled at the animals made of lights behind her.

"Dragons are *not* zoo creatures," I observed at a yellow and red fire-breathing display that was easily longer than my entire store.

"Look at the lit-up train coming through." Sawyer pointed to the zoo train pulling into the station. He pulled out his cell phone and checked the time. "Oh hey, we'd better hurry!"

"Are we riding the train?" I couldn't keep the excitement from my voice. I knew Sawyer's love of trains, and while I wasn't thrilled with the crowd on the platform, I quietly shared his love. While I hadn't come during ZooLights before, few children grow up in Portland without riding the zoo train at least once. And even as an adult, nothing was more relaxing to me than the train ride up to Seattle or Vancouver for a weekend away.

"Yup. I got our tickets online." Sawyer bounced on the balls of his feet.

"Sawyer...you..." I trailed off, unsure how to express my gratitude. "You went through a lot of trouble for this bet."

"It was worth it. You should have seen your face as we came down the path."

My chest went strangely tight and I had no idea what to reply to that. We slid into the last compartment together, him on the outside, me on the inside. It was a tight squeeze for two grown men, but the conductor was packing everyone in.

"All aboard!" the conductor yelled, and my pulse raced like a little kid's as the small engine let out a piercing whistle.

"Here we go," Sawyer said excitedly.

And lo, what magic unfolded as we chugged through those lights. I still...I lack the words for the splendor of the colors and shapes and imagery we saw. There were many lights we hadn't seen on our walk through the grounds—special displays only visible from the trains. And during it all, Sawyer was pressed against me. He smelled like chocolate and fir and, like he had at Char and Tucker's wedding, he also smelled vaguely of the ocean.

"Come on, Hols. I dare you. Dance with me."

"Right here?" I gestured to the balcony where I'd escaped from the party only to be discovered by Sawyer.

"Right here. Because you won't inside."

He wasn't wrong. "It's not you, Sawyer. It's...there are so many people and..."

"Shh." He took me in his arms, then, music from the DJ wafting out onto the balcony, providing a little pretext for the contact we'd been dancing toward all weekend at the resort. He'd volunteered to pick me up, sharing the long drive to the resort together, and something indefinable had shifted between us. All my stern lectures to myself not to fall for his charms went ignored. We were flirtier. Snarking less. Talking more, everything leading up to this moment of inevitability. He smelled like the ocean, like champagne and something woodsy, and it was all I could do to follow his lead.

On the train the lights sped by, excited squeals from the children in the cars ahead of us. "Oh Sawyer," I breathed. *"Thank you."*

"You're welcome." He touched my face, cold, bare thumb scraping along my smooth cheek. I'd shaved that morning—*not* for him, but because I always did. Still, though, it brought me strange pleasure, knowing he could probably smell my aftershave, feel my skin. He'd removed his fuzzy glove for a *reason*, one that was boldly apparent when he turned his gaze toward me.

His lips lowered to mine, right there on the zoo train, as we headed around a curve. And it was like kissing a memory—a soft whisper of something that had almost been.

We were kissing against the ferns on the balcony. It hadn't really been about dancing, and I'd known that. Champagne and too little food sloshed in my veins, making me giddy at his touch. We swayed gently, the barest nod toward the music, but Sawyer's mouth plundered mine. All wedding weekend he'd flirted and I'd parried, and we'd been building to something big, he and I. And it was scary and it was wrong and I needed to stop it, but right then all I could do was kiss him.

"Dare you to come up to my room." Sawyer pulled away slightly, eyes twinkling in the darkness.

The train lurched, pulling me back to awareness of Sawyer's mouth on mine, warm and hungry. He tasted like chocolate and temptation.

"Coming into the station," the intercom boomed and I jerked away, sloshing my now-cool hot chocolate on my leg.

"I—"

"Ohmigod! There you guys are!" A very tipsy Char made her way onto the patio, right as I'd been figuring out my reply. She slung an arm around both of us. "You guys are totally next!"

And just like that my answer had become crystal clear. There was no next, not where Sawyer was concerned. I was just a weekend diversion, nothing more. I shook my head at Sawyer and escaped the wedding reception as soon as I could.

"Sorry," Sawyer mumbled.

"We can't do this," I whispered.

"Not here?"

"Not at all and you know why."

"Hols, we're *not* actually related. You get that right?" Sawyer shook his head at me as we disembarked. "And despite how you like to act, we're not actually archenemies. We can kiss."

"Shh," I hissed, aware a few people had glanced in our direction at the word *kiss*. "Keep your voice down. I should have said *I* can't do this. I can't." And with that I fled, past the lights, past the crowds, past the sound of Sawyer's voice, memories and regrets dogging my steps.

Chapter 4

By the time I reached the birthday party for Aria the next day, I was itchy from the haircut and tired from the walk to the cleaners and then to Char and Tucker's Craftsman, which was located in the same artsy neighborhood as my store and my condo but tucked on a quieter residential street. Like always, I had to take a moment on the wide front porch. Three years, almost, and I still wasn't used to Tucker's bike, not Dad's, chained to the porch, the stroller in front of the porch swing instead of the low table with Mom's gardening magazines. The redwood porch rails were new, too, part of the spruce-up job Tucker had undertaken. Gone was the rail where I'd etched my name with a homemade pen, but I still rested my hands in that space and breathed. In. Out.

It had been natural for Char and Tucker to get the house. They needed a bigger place, and this was always meant to be a family home. I'd gotten more of the liquid investments and life insurance money, which allowed me to start my store, and she'd gotten the house. After all, I'd gotten my long-time dream of a carefully curated store. She should get her dream, too. I didn't begrudge her wanting it, nor modernizing it for the needs of her growing family, but damn if I didn't *hurt* every time I went in. The door swung open and there was Tucker, who was smaller and leaner than Sawyer but with the same boyish grin.

"Hollis, come in, come in!" Once upon a time we'd been best friends, united by our more flamboyant siblings, quietly watching from the sidelines together. Then, slowly, he'd joined in their exploits and I'd stayed behind, still watching. The last few years we'd talked some, but it wasn't the same as those early years. Still, though, I accepted his back-slapping hug and tried to match his smile.

"The birthday girl has been asking for Uncle Holly."

"Has she, now?" I put a smile on my face, straightened my shoulders and back. "Lead me to her! Oh, I see the living room is turquoise now. How...lovely."

"Your sister has been on a nesting tear lately. She had Sawyer and me in here last two weekends getting everything set for the holidays and the birthdays."

Yes, he really did mean birthdays plural—he and Sawyer had a birthday coming up on December 18. As if this month wasn't crowded enough. And speaking of crowds, the living and dining rooms held Tucker and Sawyer's parents—both sets—their biological sister and two stepbrothers along with Sawyer, who was sitting on the floor playing blocks with Aria and two other small children. Char was busy with something in the kitchen, but I could hear her humming holiday music as she worked.

"Char, do you need a hand?" I called. *Please need a hand.*

"Not at all," she called back.

Of course Sawyer chose that moment to look up and our eyes met, the memory of last night passing between us.

I didn't forget, his raised eyebrow said.

I didn't expect you to, my glare replied.

"Hollis, are you nursing a grudge that Sawyer won the decorating contest?" Tucker asked, concerned professional voice firmly in place. He worked as a psychiatric nurse practitioner over at Legacy Health, and if I heard the suggestion of grief counseling from him one more time, I might throw one of my sister's colorful tapestry pillows.

"No, sorry, just a bit of a long walk today. Must be a bit fatigued."

"Sit, sit," Phillip, Sawyer and Tucker's father, urged, giving up his place on the couch, so of course I *had* to sit, right near where Sawyer was playing on the floor.

"Unca Holly! Prezzie!" Aria squealed when she saw what I had in my hand and ran over.

"Yes, darling, a present for you. Happy birthday." I picked her up and gave her a kiss on the cheek before handing over the box. She smelled like baby shampoo and cake, but it was the nearby scent of Sawyer's aftershave that clung to my nostrils.

She toddled over to the stack of other presents and dropped mine in the mix. "Now? Now?"

I would have said yes, but of course Char had an order for these things. Snack food. Mingling. Cake. Then, finally, presents. I waited through the block sets, board books, trains, little creatures, and dollhouse from the other aunts and uncles before it was my turn.

"Babies!" Aria shredded the wrapping paper as I knew she would. Toddlers do *not* share my affinity for artisanal papers, as two years of uncledom had shown me. She revealed the two twin baby dolls nestled in their wicker carrier.

"From France," Sawyer added. I might have kicked him. I'm not proud.

"Mine own babyeeeeee," Aria sang and danced around. It was the best reaction she'd had to a gift all afternoon, and I was feeling awfully smug until Sawyer said, "One more gift, half-pint."

He disappeared with Tucker into the hall and wheeled in a car. *A car? You're joking right?* I tried to catch his eye as the two of them situated the giant plastic monstrosity in the middle of the room. It lit up. It made sounds. It had seat belts.

"Baby! Baby!" Aria dragged the babies by their arms over to the car, dropped them in the trunk, and pedaled away. "Mine own car!"

Sawyer got a best-uncle-ever high five from Tucker and the stepbrothers, and I drifted away to the kitchen, which was mercifully empty. Char was sitting with her feet up in the other room, and I didn't want her to have to face a messy room when she got up. Lord knew I couldn't cope with this level of chaos. I got the counters clear first, then sponged them down, becoming calmer and less homicidal toward Sawyer the more I worked.

I was filling the sink with hot water for the dishes when I heard someone else come in. I could tell it was Sawyer without turning around because the air always seemed to crackle when he was nearby. Maybe it was his scent or the heaviness of his tread, but regardless, I'd always been able to sense his presence that way.

"Here, move over," he said, coming to stand next to me at the sink. "I'll wash and you can dry."

"I'm fine. You go mingle with your family."

"Oh, they can spare me." Sawyer laughed. "And you hate the washing part. So let me, and we can be done doubly quick."

"Fine. I'll empty the dishwasher while you get started."

"You know where everything goes." Sawyer rolled his sleeves up. His forearms were a thing of beauty, but for once his words distracted me more.

"That I do."

There must have been something in my voice that tipped Sawyer off. "Oh, Hols, I wasn't thinking."

"Nothing to think of," I said and stacked the bowls neatly in the same cupboard my mother had put them my whole childhood.

"You got a haircut," Sawyer observed. I didn't think he'd ever noticed my hair before. Or anyone's hair really.

"I did." I carefully slid Grandma Rose's cake platter into the cupboard above the fridge.

"Are we going to talk about last night?" Sawyer asked as I finished up the silverware.

"Nothing to talk about," I said. "I am sorry for running off, though. You...went to a surprising amount of effort."

"*Hollis.* I don't want an A for effort here."

"Yes, well, what *do* you want?" I regretted the question almost as soon as I said it.

"Right this minute I'm debating between throttling you and kissing you. Can I have both?"

"Neither."

Sawyer moved, trapping me against the cupboards. This was an old house, with the kitchen tucked in the rear of the place. From where we were standing, no one in the dining room or living room could see us. I still shivered.

"If I kissed you right now, you wouldn't scream, and we both know it." Sawyer's voice was full of challenge.

I blinked. "I never scream. I might bite you, though."

"Yeah?" He came in alarmingly close. "Prove it." He glided his lips over mine. He tasted like chocolate and Char's strong coffee and like the worst kind of temptation.

I didn't scream. I didn't bite. I didn't quietly endure. Instead, some alien impulse took over my body and I kissed him back like I'd seldom kissed *anyone.* Kissing always seemed like such a messy, intimate business, but with Sawyer it was different. His tongue was less invasion and more welcome invitation, and he seemed to know how to keep things from getting too moist and sloppy—a big bonus. Actually, Sawyer seemed to know a lot more about kissing than I, and he used that knowledge—and teeth, tongue, and lips—to tease and torture and work me up until I was rocking into his embrace.

I was painfully hard and he was pressed close enough that I could feel the thick length of him through his jeans.

He pulled away slightly. "Now would be a good time to remind you that I live—"

"Sawyer? Can you bring me a coffee?" Christine called from the living room.

Sawyer groaned softly, then raised his voice. "Just a sec, Mom. You want anything in it?"

"With coconut creamer and stevia. Thanks, sweetie!"

"I'd better get back out there, too," I said, still breathing hard. I straightened my shirt and adjusted my pants and willed my body to return to normal.

"Hollis?" Sawyer stopped me with a hand on my arm.

"Yes?"

"We're not done with this. Not hardly."

That was exactly what I was afraid of.

* * * *

All week I felt on edge, waiting for Sawyer to spring something new on me. And truth be told, I was a bit disappointed when Friday morning arrived and I hadn't seen the man. I'd expected him to press me for…well, *something* after the kiss, but he hadn't. Friday, though, I had weightier concerns on my mind. I'd actually considered closing the store; the first two years I had, taking a rare personal day, but this year, it felt like the world had well and truly moved on, and I didn't quite know what to do with myself.

Thus, I was already out of sorts when Sawyer came loping in at around one. Unlike mine, their store had regular employees, and his schedule was more flexible. My post-lunch traffic was light—okay, nonexistent—and I'd been busy arranging the next year's planner display. I'd selected a beautiful one to carry: vellum overlays and library-quality binding. Being surrounded by lovely things like these had always soothed me, ever since I was gifted my first journal and fountain pen by a British uncle I'd never met. My hand absently stroked one of the planner covers as Sawyer approached.

"We're going out tonight," Sawyer announced with no preamble.

"We are not. I have plans. And if Char sent you—"

"She didn't. But I know what today is, and I'm not letting you be alone tonight."

"You do?" Sawyer didn't seem to keep close track of much. I wouldn't have thought he'd remember the exact date of my parents' deaths.

"Of course." Sawyer shook his head, as if he was disappointed in me. A strange feeling bloomed in my gut. "Hollis, I know it's nothing compared to what you're going through, but I miss them, too. They were great people to me. And you shouldn't have to grieve alone. Not tonight."

"So you're taking me drinking or some such?" Drowning my sorrows with Sawyer wasn't without its appeal, but Char's wedding had taught me well the hazards of being even slightly drunk around the man.

"No, although we can drink after if you really want. I have two tickets to the Gay Men's Chorus's Seasonal Show tonight, and you have a much greater appreciation of the arts than me. I need you to come."

"You do not." Any other night the invitation to the show would have been much more tempting than a pub crawl or something more typically Sawyer.

"Come on. I might applaud in the wrong place or something." Sawyer gave me his most beseeching smile, one that almost worked. "Ernesto Garcia is with the choir now and he gave me the tickets. We should really support him."

"Ernesto gave them to you?" He was an old friend from high school; more Char and Sawyer's than mine, of course, but he was an exceedingly nice man who'd had a very rough road of it.

"Said he didn't have anyone else to give his comp tickets to. Guess his family situation is still awful. I really feel obligated to use both tickets and he really perked up when I said I might bring you."

"You could have asked me first," I groused, but we both knew he'd won the war at that point. Maybe I didn't *really* want to be alone. Maybe I felt guilty for not keeping up more with Ernesto. Maybe it was the sheer power of Sawyer's smile. Regardless, I nodded and said, "Would closing at my usual time give us enough time to get over to the theater?"

"It's at the Newmark this year, and yes, I can meet you at your place about seven fifteen or so if you want to spruce up a bit."

"Spruce up?" I looked at his Portland Timbers sweatshirt and faded jeans and several days' worth of beard. In contrast, I was in gray wool pants and a heather dress shirt. I might add a tie for this event.

"Hey, I'm dressing up, too." He winked at me. "Got something new."

Well, now I pretty much had to go, didn't I? Curiosity along with knowing just how well Sawyer *could* clean up edged past my black mood, made me say, "I'll see you, then."

"Excellent. Gotta win my bet, you know."

Oh heck. I'd almost forgotten about his plan to make me show up for Christmas dinner. Something told me I'd have to work extra-hard that evening not to succumb to the season's charms—or Sawyer's.

Chapter 5

Sawyer, as it turned out, did clean up nicely. As usual, his jacket was much too thin for December, but he had changed into dress pants, a gray vest, and a red, black, and gray bow tie.

"I didn't know you wore bow ties," I said as I locked my front door, really meaning *I didn't know I had a fetish for bow ties.* I joined him on the steps of my condo, busying myself with keys and coat to cover how devastating the combo was on him—hot, intellectual, sweet, and charming. In a word: Sawyer.

"I'm trying a new look. Going to be thirty next year. I figure this and a walking stick would fit my advanced age."

"Oh hush. I'll reach thirty in March. I'm sure I can reassure you that you don't join AARP or start needing bran."

A wide grin split Sawyer's freshly shaved face. "Why, Hollis, was that a...*joke*? I'd almost lost hope of you remembering what one is."

"I have a fine sense of humor." Had I really lost so much the last few years? I'd always been quiet, but I used to make Sawyer, Tucker, and Char laugh on occasion, something that always filled me with quiet pride when they got one of my sarcastic barbs. And maybe I was more reserved, but I always used to laugh at Sawyer's more obvious clowning. God, I missed laughing.

"That you do." He grabbed my arm. "Car's this way."

"Car? We're not taking transit in?"

"Nah. I felt like driving, and I wasn't sure the buses would get us there in time. There's parking nearby."

"I'll pay for the parking," I said.

"I'll pay for your drink afterward." He winked at me, and I had to work triple hard to remember that this wasn't a date. It wasn't. I didn't date.

I wasn't a virgin, despite what I had a feeling Sawyer and Char assumed. I was just...*discreet* in my liaisons. Back in college I'd had a long-running affair with an older man that had ended badly enough to have me swearing off long-term entanglements. But there had been a few encounters since him. Not many and not recently, but I wasn't celibate—I just didn't date, especially not the last few years. I knew it was irrational of me, but it felt disloyal somehow, seeking out pleasure when the emptiness inside me was an ever-present reminder of what I'd lost.

Sawyer, however, did date. Openly. Publicly. With much affection. Friends with benefits. Benefits with friends. Boyfriend auditions. Whatever you wanted to call it, he always seemed to have someone around. Which, come to think of it, made his more recent *lack* of attachment noteworthy.

"Are you seeing someone these days?" I asked after we parked and were walking to the theater.

There was an edge to Sawyer's laugh that I hadn't heard before. "No, not at the moment. Why? You volunteering?"

I made an inelegant snort. As if he wanted more than to bang me to say he had. Sex was Sawyer's handshake—he'd made it clear on Sunday that he wanted more kissing, but this was Sawyer. He loved a challenge, but date me? No.

"Hardly. I was just having trouble remembering the last time I saw you with someone, and you're usually so..."

"Slutty? Such a manwhore?"

"That was *not* what I was going to say. Friendly. You're always so... *friendly* with your circle."

Sawyer laughed at that. "That's one way to put it. But maybe I'm turning over a new leaf. Less sleeping around."

I didn't really believe he was capable of that, but I didn't want to argue. The night was cool and crisp but not rainy, and the theatergoers around us as we got close to the Newmark provided a sort of anticipation to my steps. Despite myself, I really was looking forward to what was in store. I'd been to other productions at the Newmark and it was truly a special place; the main floor plus two balconies were angled so that one felt very close to the stage, despite the theater's capacity. It was all warm woods and cushy seats.

We had decent seats on the main floor—a bit crowded with people on either side of us, but I could cope. And the show was all I'd hoped—large ensemble numbers mixed with smaller group pieces and a few solos. The chorus was outfitted in snazzy black and red tuxedos. The orchestra was superb, the harmonies complex and pleasing. I even laughed at some of the region-specific spoofs like "A Gluten-free Holiday." Somewhere midway through, Sawyer stretched and his arm came around me.

"Sorry. Seats are cramped," he said in a low voice between numbers.

That excuse might have floated in high school, but I didn't buy it now. I let it slide anyway, because his getting cuddly wasn't entirely out of character. He was the most touchy-feely guy I knew, and given our company, I couldn't really tell him it wasn't the place. All around us couples of all sorts of gender combinations were holding hands and snuggling up.

The entire ensemble—easily a hundred singers—gathered for "I'll Be Home for Christmas." My spine went as stiff as my new LAMY studio pen. My hand unconsciously tightened on my thigh, digging into the flesh, until Sawyer grabbed it.

"It's okay," he whispered. "Look. Others are crying." Indeed, in the audience many were tearing up, but I didn't realize I was one of them until moisture hit my lip, salty and bitter.

"It was her favorite," I said quietly. Mom had always missed London more than Dad, and never more than at the holidays.

"I know."

He held my hand the whole song, a tight, firm grip that helped me rein in my emotions. There were other numbers after that one, but the chorus of "I'll be Home for Christmas" lingered in my ears.

"I'm sorry," Sawyer said on the way out of the theater after the program ended. "I didn't know they'd do that song."

"Not your fault," I said crisply. "I enjoyed the lighter numbers immensely. We need to get Char to watch a clip of the gluten-free holiday number."

We'd parked in a smaller, underground garage a few blocks from the theater and the dim lights flickered as we made our way to Sawyer's Charger at the back corner of the garage.

"Hols." Sawyer turned to me as we got into the car. "You do know it's not *your* fault, too, right? I mean, you don't talk about what happened—"

"For good reason." The thick feeling was back in my throat.

"But you have to know it's not your fault."

"I know," I said, because that was the answer he and Tucker and even Char demanded. But the truth was I'd blame myself until my dying day. It was a skiing accident—we'd been on a ski weekend, the three of us, a chance to see the new powder. I'd gotten too cold, as I always did, and headed back to the lodge for a cup of tea. They'd gotten trapped by a freak avalanche. Rescuers had been too late.

Sawyer apparently didn't believe me, putting both hands on my face and making me look at him. His hands were bare, but I shuddered from emotion, not cold. "Not. Your. Fault."

"I should have made them come with me to the lodge. Or stayed out with them," I whispered. I rarely said even that much.

"Then what? The three of you gone?"

I was quiet because that was something I thought about more than I should have.

"Hols. *No*." There was so much anguish in his voice that I couldn't help myself. I leaned into his hands and did the least sensible thing I could—I kissed him, pouring all my mixed-up grief into the most mixed-up action I could think of.

It was raw, not sweet like at the zoo or controlled like in the kitchen. This was the sort of messy passion I always shied away from.

"Oh fuck yes," Sawyer groaned, coming half across the gearshift, pressing me back against the passenger door, tongue thrusting in my mouth in an unmistakable rhythm.

His hands pushed my coat open, pulling my shirt free of my pants at the same time. His questing hand against my bare stomach made me hiss. His touch was warm now, and our breath had fogged up the windows.

"God, you make me crazy." Sawyer's mouth found my neck, a spot most lovers were content to ignore but Sawyer exploited to its fullest.

I moaned and gasped, little needy sounds I couldn't seem to hold back. His hand was rubbing me through my pants now. I had never, not once, climaxed in my pants, but Sawyer presented the very real possibility of that happening.

"Not yet. Not. Yet." I started to pant, my body tensing. Just saying the words ratcheted my pleasure higher. "Can't."

"So responsive." Sawyer licked where my neck and shoulder joined. "Like this, do you?"

"Don't stop." I'd never felt like this before, slightly drunk on desire. His mouth on my neck was like touching jumper cables that went straight to my groin. I sometimes touched my neck when pleasuring myself, but it was nothing like this.

In the back of my head I was aware that Sawyer was probably leaving a mark, but at that moment I would have begged him for a neon sign as long as it kept his mouth right there.

Sawyer grappled for my zipper, and suddenly it wasn't enough to have his hands on me. I wanted—*needed*—to touch, too. I worked my hands between us, losing my gloves in the process. It was tight and awkward and the struggle simply made the victory of finding his fly that much sweeter.

"Yeah. Keep making those sounds," Sawyer growled. "Fuck, you are so sexy when you let go. Gonna come for me?"

"Unnh," I moaned as he found my cock and pulled it out. "You. First."

I got his fly open finally and grasped his cock, giving it a firm stroke for emphasis. Good lord, the man was big all over. I was no size princess for sure, but even I had to admit Sawyer was impressive.

"Oh no, no." He lightly bit that live-wire spot on my neck. "We're not playing that game right now. Sometime—*soon*—I'll make you wait, but right now, Hols, I want to see you fly."

I wasn't used to so much...*talk* with sexual encounters, and Sawyer's words did indeed launch me into orbit as his mouth attacked my neck again.

"Not yet, not yet, need to...oh God," I babbled as the pressure built.

"That's right. Work for it. Come on." He found a spot below my ear that made me cry out.

"Please, Sawyer, please. Oh. Oh."

"I got you. Come now." His teeth met my flesh and there was no doubt about a mark now. He was claiming me, and part of me thrilled to it, relished the slight edge of discomfort until it was all too much and I was falling, thrown over the cliff with reckless abandon, straight into an intense orgasm that left my whole body shaking.

My fist had reflexively tightened on Sawyer's cock and he made a desperate noise, hips snapping up to meet my hand. I stroked more deliberately as I came down from the high.

"Yes. God, Hols. Needed this so long. Hols." Sawyer chanted my name as he lost control, spurting all over my fist, catching my coat and chest in the process, too.

He collapsed back into his own seat. "That was—"

"Messy." I swabbed at the mess with the lone napkin in Sawyer's glove box.

"I was going for incredible." Sawyer sighed. "But, yes, messy. I love mess." He licked a finger, probably just to see if I'd cringe, which I didn't. I also didn't let on that it made my pulse leap a bit, the hint of that pink tongue laving at his finger like that. I also had absolutely no clue what we should talk about, so I busied myself fussing over my clothes until he'd started the car.

He didn't seem to have any more idea than I did about what to talk about so it was a blessed relief when he flipped on the stereo. I even forgave him the One Republic. What the heck had I been thinking? A public parking garage? Sloppy hand jobs? Absolutely no restraint whatsoever?

"Your place?" he asked as we headed back to the northeast part of town. "Or...mine?"

"Mine, thank you." Then, prim as a Wild West schoolmarm, I added, "No need to see me up."

"Hollis—"

"I need to *think*, Sawyer, and thoughts are in short supply when you're around."

"Fine." He sounded so resigned, and why that made me sad I really couldn't say. The words to counter him, to tell him to come up rose in my throat and died on my tongue.

"See you Sunday, I guess." His voice was still so strangely flat. I wanted the usual Sawyer back.

"Wait. What's Sunday?"

"We really do need to get you a Google calendar with reminders on your phone." He laughed, some of his usual humor coming back. "Sunday evening is the annual business association holiday party. It's at People's Cup after we all close up for the evening. Potluck."

"I skipped it last year—"

"All the more reason to come this year."

"I hate potluck."

"Bring something you want to eat yourself. That's what I'm doing." He grinned as he pulled up on my street. I lived just around the corner from my shop in a newer condo development.

"You cook?" I couldn't keep the skepticism out of my voice.

"I bake." His smug grin made him look like the kid I once knew, way back when everything was silly bets and bad pop music. "You'll have to come to find out what. Or to witness my downfall."

That last bit was surely tempting, but it was the vulnerability in his eyes that had me saying, "I'll see."

Chapter 6

I worked Saturday and Sunday with steady business, the kind my bottom line liked to see. Thanks to the money from my parents, I wasn't solely dependent on the business, but I did need to turn a profit. I knew Char—and Sawyer, for that matter—thought the solution was to carry more stock, but that wasn't the vision I had for the store. A well-curated boutique is better than an emporium of odds and ends. I actually did a fair amount of online business—people who shared my obsession for pens mainly, and those who trusted me to put together the right sort of gift for a graduation or corporate milestone.

Milestones deserved recognition—and not the loud, cheering kind. I felt something tangible was increasingly important to help make sense of the chaos of hundreds of social media likes and no real sense of accomplishment on a visceral level. I was working on one such gift Sunday afternoon, packaging a Leuchtturm 1917 notebook with an Edison Beamount, one of my personal favorite pens for its understated beauty. I used a handmade paper presentation box and had put everything just so when my phone buzzed.

It was a message from Ev, the yarn shop owner. *Are you coming tonight? Sawyer said he thought you were, and I am ready to sell the ecru silk and angora blend sample. I can bring it tonight for you?*

Oh, that Sawyer. He knew if the prospect of him baking—or failing at baking—wasn't enough the new scarf would tempt me into coming. And I *needed* the scarf. I wore my gray one at the moment, my vanilla colored cables yesterday. Sawyer had done a number on my neck, and seeing as I'd pretty much egged him on, I couldn't be too mad about it. But still, I'd be wearing my scarves all week thanks to him.

And each glimpse in the mirror was a reminder of what a fool I'd been.

I'll be there with cash for you, I typed quickly before I could think twice about it. At least I could be a fool with a nice scarf.

At seven I entered the People's Cup with a large kale salad—something I'd quickly tossed together. I still had my gray scarf firmly in place, and I hoped to God that Sawyer could manage to withhold any innuendo. I'd told him I needed time to think, but my thoughts were still a jumbled mess, no conclusion forthcoming. It wasn't just who Sawyer was—or wasn't—and it certainly wasn't just his penchant for the casual. I wasn't *that* much of a prude. No, it was something deeper, a sharp, shameful tug of guilt, a reminder that maybe I shouldn't be feeling this good right now. Resolving that mess of thoughts was more than I'd been able to do.

I placed my offering with the other food, then looked around the room. People's Cup had frosted their plate-glass front windows with winter scenes. A small tree was set up to the side of the counter with the register, and even the tip jar sported a jaunty red bow. The place was closed for outside business but full of the same crowd that attended the monthly meetings, some of whom appeared to have brought family and significant others. Just my luck, Sawyer was standing with Ev and Brady near the couches. If I wanted my scarf, I'd have to brave his presence, and I couldn't exactly snub Ev after saying I'd be there with money. Still, though, my feet felt trapped in thick, gluey, old ink as I made my way to them.

"Ah! Hollis! Here is your scarf." Ev held out a small brown bag with the Iplik logo on it.

"Thanks." I gave him the cash, which I'd placed in a small envelope with the amount and purchase information for him.

"You're always so organized," Brady observed.

"He is." A smile tugged at Sawyer's mouth.

"I wanted to make it easier on your bookkeeping." I took the scarf out, petted its impossibly soft yarn blend, and admired the nubbly texture of the knit pattern.

"Put the scarf on," Brady urged. "I almost made him keep that one back for me when it came back from the test knitter."

"No, thank you. I'm saving it for a special occasion." *Like Tuesday.* I quickly put it back in the bag.

Sawyer looked like he was fighting an attack of the giggles. He knew darn well why I wouldn't be showing off my neck right then. "You do that."

"I'm starving," Brady said, tugging on Ev's hand. "We'll catch back up with you guys."

"Me too," Sawyer said, but he didn't follow closely behind Ev and Brady, instead hanging back with me. "So, Hollis…any interesting thoughts lately?"

"Not many." I kept my voice light. "Trying to figure out what three-quarters of the dishes are, though."

Sawyer grabbed a plate and handed one to me as well. "What did you bring? The kale?"

"Yes."

"Thought I recognized your silver bowl." He smiled up at me. "You feel free to take as much of that as you want to fill your plate, but be sure to leave room for dessert."

"Oh?" I followed his suggestion, taking a large portion of my salad and a small amount of some roasted chicken, leaving the casseroles for braver folk. "What did you bring?"

"The spice cake." He pointed to a homely square that was a bit squashed with some lumps to the icing. "I know it's a bit sad-looking, but I got the recipe from Char."

"Mother's spice cake?" I couldn't keep the hope from my voice as I helped myself to a small piece.

"That's the one." Hollis looked a bit uncomfortable, worrying the edge of his lip with his teeth. "Char said you'd been missing it, and that she still couldn't figure out how to duplicate it. I thought I'd give it a try and I hope that's all right. It turned out okay, but…well, you taste it and tell me what you think."

Moving away from the table, we found chairs near Ev and Brady. I took a bite of cake first because Sawyer's eyes were so eager. "It's…not bad." It wasn't Mom's—she'd gotten the recipe from her own mother back in England—but it wasn't terrible either.

"See, something's off with the texture. I just can't pinpoint what." Sawyer took a bite from his own serving.

"Hmm." I took another bite, considering. The flavors were there, but he was right about the texture. "Mom always used a Bundt pan. Try one next time."

"I'll have to get one. I want to make this again for the big family Christmas dinner. I've been really into baking lately." His smile was a bit more sheepish than usual.

Something about that smile totally disarmed me and loosened my tongue. "I have one. If you walk me back after this, I can lend it to you."

"Really?" Sawyer's eyebrows went skyward. The man had the most expressive eyebrows. Bunched together, they could show disappointment or anger better than any of my well-honed looks, and flaring up and out, they did surprise as well as a TV hostess. "That would be…*cool.*"

Oh dear. He assumed I was asking him back for sex. I shook my head slightly, but he only grinned wider.

Aren't you? a devilish little voice in my head prodded me. I could have just as easily pointed him to Char for a pan or dropped one off at the shop.

Ev turned to ask me a question about business and I made my reply on autopilot, carrying on small talk while my head raced. What was I doing? What *would* we do?

Sawyer knocked ankles with me under the table, further increasing my distractibility. I shot him a look.

We are not playing footsie here, I said with a glare.

We already are, his quirked eyebrow replied with a sly smile. He knew I couldn't jerk away without giving something away, which left quietly enduring as my best option.

"We have to get back to the kids," Brady said as they cleared their plates. "Sorry."

"No need to apologize," I said.

"I was just about to head out as well." Sawyer grinned at me. Damn, confounding man. "Want to walk out with me, Hollis?"

He knew I had few choices, seeing as I'd already made the invite. I didn't really *want* to walk out with him though—more than a few of our fellow business owners were terrible gossips.

"I suppose." I gathered my things and my nearly full salad bowl. And then I attempted to gather my wits. We were *not* having sex. But one look at Sawyer's twinkling eyes told me I was going to have to work to cling to that resolution.

* * * *

My condo was a short walk away and the evening was warmer than it had been, which should have pleased me. However, I was too busy being a nervous wreck about Sawyer coming over.

"You know, I haven't seen your place since Tucker and I helped you move in." That had been right before the wedding, after I'd returned from graduate school, back when this development had been new with a fabulous financing deal my parents had helped me secure. Watching Sawyer carry boxes all afternoon had certainly played a role in my foolishness over the wedding weekend. As had driving together to the resort—something had been different that summer as Tucker and Char became a family, leaving Sawyer and me with each other's not-unwelcome company. At least it hadn't been unwelcome right up until the wedding, when I'd realized what we'd been creeping toward and put on the brakes before I could be Sawyer's flavor of the summer.

"I don't entertain much." I led him up the steps to my unit.

"No kidding." Sawyer laughed. Benedict was waiting just inside the door for me. "And there's Bunny!"

"Benedict." I picked him up. He'd been with me since I'd adopted him as a kitten my final year of graduate school. And unfortunately, he had a tendency to dart toward doors, which meant Sawyer had heard me and Char try to stop him by calling the only name he responded to. Darn Humane Society and their cutesy names.

"It's neat to see the place all put together." Sawyer wandered into the living room as if he were about to give himself a guided tour. Not that there was much to tour: one big living/kitchen/dining/work area with a bedroom and a bath tucked behind the kitchen. Sawyer tossed his coat on the couch. I picked it up and placed it on the hook by the door next to mine before toeing my shoes off and placing them on their rack.

"Ah. No shoes rule?" Sawyer kicked off his like he was planning on staying a while and pushed them toward the door with his foot. He looked around more. "No tree?"

"For only me and the cat to pull off ornaments?" I shook my head. Char had all the family ornaments, and as for me, I hadn't even put up the cards I received in three years.

"You've got a fern, though. You could toss some lights on the planter. It's not...is that the same kind they had all over at Char's wedding?"

"I wouldn't know," I lied, pretending the memory of being pressed into that foliage wasn't imprinted on me. "And I don't need lights."

Sawyer looked unduly sad on my account as he shook his head. "Nice treadmill, though."

"Thanks." I liked walking briskly or jogging while watching TV. So much better than joining a crowded gym.

"And dude! Is that Mordor?"

"I thought you came for the pan?" I tried to steer him away from my bookshelf wall, which meant my hands on his broad shoulders, which led to him spinning around to face me. I dropped my hands and stepped back before he could make good on the dark intent in his eyes.

"Pan can wait." Sawyer made a dismissive gesture. "You've got a whole *Lord of the Rings* section here. Framed map and everything."

"I also have an art history section—"

"I'm sure you do, but that section doesn't have three—or wait, *four*—different editions of the series. And collectibles!" Sawyer chortled as if he'd discovered my porn stash. "You have collectibles. *Why* have I never seen you buy from me?"

"Most of them were gifts," I said frostily.

"An ex-boyfriend?" Sawyer frowned.

The back of my neck itched. It would be easy to let him think that. "No, my father."

"Oh. That's right. He took all four of us to see the first movie." Sawyer grinned at the memory, which was a good one, even if he and Char had chattered in line incessantly.

"Hollis, you sit next to Sawyer," Char hissed.

"Why?"

"He talks during movies." She blushed. That wasn't it at all.

"But then you'll be next to Tucker," I whispered.

"I know." More blushing.

It was dark out, the line for the movie wrapped around the front of the theater, and I was glad for the chill in the air that might disguise my own blush.

"I don't want a talker," I mumbled. "I want to enjoy the movie."

My protest was no more real than hers. I didn't want to sit next to Sawyer because he smelled too good, talked too loud, and just last week had confessed to kissing Jimmy Ingles behind the school. I was not jealous. I refused to be jealous. So what if he was out? So what if he ran around handing out kisses like trading cards? So what if Jimmy Ingles got to find out what he tasted like—

Stop it. *It was going to be a long movie and I was* not *going to let Sawyer ruin it.*

"He was as big a geek as you for that fandom."

"I am not in any fandom." I removed my Aragorn action figure from his grasp. "I merely share an appreciation for some of the greatest fantasy literature of all time. That's all."

"That's all? Hollis, you even own the Risk and Trivial Pursuit *Lord of the Rings* editions."

"Unopened." I tried to keep my voice disinterested.

"Well, they could *be* opened if you'd invite some of us for a game night." Sawyer clearly had me mistaken for one of his many friends who had such things as game nights. Dinner parties. *People* in my space. I thought not. A brief image of Sawyer and me playing, just the two of us, popped into my head, but I quickly dismissed it. Never happening.

"Would you like some Scotch?" I offered, still trying to get his attention away from the board game.

"Sure." Sawyer followed me over to the small bar area at the end of my shelves.

My hands shook as I brought down two tumblers. I knew full well what I was doing, prolonging his time in my apartment. "Ice or neat?"

"Neither." Sawyer removed the glasses from my hand and set them back on the shelf. "We don't need a drink."

Chapter 7

I didn't step away. I knew what was coming next, but I didn't step away. Instead, I met his heated gaze. He raked his eyes over me, intention clear as he moved forward and closed the gap between our bodies. But rather than kissing me, his hands went to my neck, gently unwinding my scarf until it hung open, draped across the back of my neck and down the front of my shirt.

"Fuck. Look at your neck." His hazel eyes went even greener than usual.

"I *know*. You did a number on me."

"You let me." He traced one mark with his thumb. "Fuck. That's the sexiest thing I've seen in a long time."

"Perhaps you need to up your porn intake," I suggested dryly.

Sawyer laughed. "God, I love it when you joke."

He ducked his head, kissing the worst of the marks, the one where my neck and shoulder met, a big, blooming love bite that had turned lurid colors over the past few days. I shivered, hands instinctively seeking the warmth of his body. The spot where his sweater met his jeans made the perfect hand warmer, and my next shudder was pure pleasure.

Grasping either side of the scarf, Sawyer used it to tug me forward until we were kissing, him locking me in place with the scarf. His mouth was more confident tonight, as if he'd figured out some essential truths about my reactions on Friday and intended to exploit them. And indeed he did, lips and tongue claiming my mouth. He sucked on my lower lip and I moaned. He was simply too good at this.

He shifted, hands still on the scarf but pulling it lower so it dropped across my shoulder blades, another tug and our chests were mashed together. He chuckled softly, obviously pleased with himself.

"Someday I want to tie your hands with this scarf." His voice was a dirty promise in my ear.

I made a noncommittal noise as *someday* implied a future of repeats that I refused to think about right then. One act of insanity at a time. But his words also thrilled me, made my pulse flutter. I hadn't let anyone do that since Yuto. Hadn't *wanted* to do that since Yuto, truth be told. But affable Sawyer, the last person I would have thought, made those old longings hum.

"You'd let me," he said, wonder in his voice. My eyes must have given me away. "Hols…"

He dropped to his knees, a surprisingly graceful movement from a six-foot-two guy built like a soccer defender. His hands immediately went to my belt, but I stayed his touch. "Not that."

"You don't like being blown?" Sawyer looked up at me like I'd confessed to not liking birthday cake.

"I'm not *entirely* opposed, just…*context*…" My hand fluttered as I struggled to explain. This position in particular didn't work for me, for reasons I really didn't understand.

"Context." Sawyer raised an all-knowing eyebrow, then stood, eyeing past the kitchen to my bedroom door as if trying to decide how far he could push me before I'd bolt. Evidentially not very far as he tugged me toward my couch. It was a nice, long midcentury-styled gray number, one I'd dozed on during more than one insomniac movie marathon. I silently praised its sturdy build as Sawyer none too gently toppled me back into the cushions. "You'll tell me when I find the right…*context* for touching your dick?"

"This isn't terrible," I admitted, luxuriating in the heavy press of his body against mine as he stretched out. Two tall men was a tight fit, even with the generous proportions of my couch. Truth be told, I kind of liked being a bit squashed by Sawyer. He propped himself up with one arm, using the other to work at my shirt buttons. One-handed was more than a bit fiddly, and after two buttons I pushed him up.

"Oh here, I'll do it." I shed my shirt and T-shirt in short order while he did the same, his green and yellow Ducks sweatshirt hitting my white rug.

"Swear to God, if you need to stop and fold, Hollis, we're going to have an issue." He half-growled, half-laughed.

"No." I pulled him down for a kiss for the sheer luxury of feeling his fuzzy chest against mine. He had far more chest hair than I, a contrast that made me hum with approval. And whereas I was fair, he was still tanned from a summer and fall of outdoor sports.

We lay there making out until I lost all track of time and reason. The wide expanse of his back muscles called to my hands, which roamed up and down as he continued to plunder my mouth. I'd been the one to initiate the kiss, but he'd been the one to master it.

His lips drifted to my jaw. "You good with wearing one of your hipster scarves tomorrow?"

"Yeah." My head fell back against the arm of the couch, exposing my neck to his eager mouth.

"Christ. I just can't get over how sensitive you are," he said as I writhed under his attack. I was rocking against him, and it was like rubbing up against a solid oak tree. We were both hard, but he made it clear he wasn't about rushing. The more he limited my range of motion, the more I moved and moaned.

"So fucking hot, Hols, the way you let go..." He laved my collarbones, sucking lightly. He shifted, giving me a hard thigh to ride as his mouth made its way down past my light sprinkling of chest hair to my nipple.

"Here?" He raised his head slightly. "Sensitive here, too?"

I made an inarticulate noise.

"Guess we'll find out." He laughed before sucking hard on the little nub.

"*Fuck.*" My back bowed and my legs tightened around his thigh.

"Oh yeah." He exploited his new knowledge, toying with the free nipple while sucking the first, experimenting to see how much teeth I could handle, how much suction made me moan his name.

"Sawyer. S...not yet, not yet," I started to chant. "Can't. Not yet."

"You going to come?" He chortled, like this was the best news he'd ever heard. "Please, Hols, do it. Don't worry about me. Come while I play with your nipples and neck. You're so fucking sexy."

A frustrated noise escaped from my chest. "No. Can't."

My hips kept rocking restlessly, seeking something just out of reach. His eyes widened—his I've-had-a-brainstorm face that usually made me nervous. "Hols? Do you need *me* to say the words? Tell you to wait to come? Is that what gets you off, babe?"

Oh, he was a cunning one for sure. The casual hookups since Yuto hadn't really bothered to figure out that my mutterings got me *more* excited, not less. It was like grinding against Sawyer—something hard and immovable only made everything sweeter for me. I didn't nod, though; that was a level of vulnerability I wasn't sure I had in me.

Sawyer moved so his lips were right near my ear. "It is, isn't it? Gets you off if I tell you I'm going to come first, make you wait."

My hips convulsed under him.

"Yeah. It is. I got you, Hols." His lips were tender against my skin, even as his voice went harder. "I don't want you to come yet. But I'm going to suck your neck and nipples until you beg me."

"Please." The word was a broken sound torn from my lungs.

He was good as his word, too, sucking and nipping, licking and teasing. My nipples ached and I might need a scarf all week and I couldn't care less. I flew.

"No, not yet, not yet." His voice was a stern growl that came straight from my dearest fantasies.

I made a keening noise in the back of my throat, rutting hard against his thigh. "Please."

"No." Sawyer sat up slightly, unzipped. "Think I'm going to jerk off on you first."

The sound that came out of me next was a half sob.

"How good are you, Hols?" Instead of following his words, his hand went to my fly next. He shoved my pants and boxers down. "Good enough at waiting so I can touch you? Still can't come."

"I'm good." I would have promised him a symphony if it got his hand on my dick.

"This good?" He shifted again, pushing his pants out of the way before wrapping one of his meaty hands around both of our dicks. His mouth found my neck, and despite my promises, I almost came on the spot.

"Want to come like this. Your dick against mine. Kissing you. But not you, not yet." Sawyer's breath was ragged. Sweat beaded up along his forehead. His eyes locked onto mine, even as his breath and hand sped up.

"Can't...oh...*Sawyer*. Can't."

"Yes, you can. You can wait. I'll tell you when."

"*Yes.*" I had a strong feeling he hadn't played like this before, but he knew all the right buttons to push to make my body sing.

"I'm close, Hols. Can you feel it?" His big body shuddered, thighs tensing against mine.

"Yes." My hands gripped his shoulders hard enough that I wouldn't be the only one with marks. The slide of his dick against mine was almost too much, and when I looked down at his hand working, I had to close my eyes quickly and use every trick I knew to clamp down on the rising pleasure.

"I'm going to jerk you after...messy...and you're going to love it."

"God, yes."

"Oh, Hols. Here it comes." His hand jerked harder and I moaned, my whole body tightening, balls lifting. But holding back was its own kind of intense pleasure-pain. His mouth found mine right as the first spurt hit my belly. He moaned into my mouth as his body shook and came.

"Fuck. You are so good. So good." He let go of his dick, slippery hand working only on me now. "You ready?"

"Yes. Please. Yes."

"Good." He stroked faster. "Now, Hols, now. Come for me."

"Unnh." After all that waiting my orgasm was right there, but I hung on the edge.

"You were perfect," he whispered. "So good for me." Then his mouth found my neck and I let go of the edge, falling softly into the waves of an orgasm so powerful that tears were rolling down my cheeks as I cried out and clung to Sawyer.

I called his name and he made little soothing sounds as it felt like my entire body turned inside out. Somehow we ended up with Sawyer on the floor, sitting with his side to the couch, his head resting on my chest. I wove my fingers through his soft, bushy hair.

"That feels nice," he said sleepily. He'd lost his pants at some point, and Sawyer naked on my rug was something even my wildest fantasies hadn't conjured up.

"I should get us a towel," I said, but my muscles refused to move.

"I'll do it." Sawyer didn't get dressed. Not even his boxers. He simply loped naked across the living area to the bathroom. Water ran, then he was back with a warm cloth. Instead of handing it to me, he sponged off my stomach. "You were incredible, Hols. I had no idea…"

"Neither did I." I managed a little laugh.

"You're kinky," he said, unexpected affection lacing his words. He pushed my pants the rest of the way off, then grabbed the cashmere throw I kept on the back of the couch and spread it over me. "I love it."

"You're the one who suggested tying my hands." I didn't bother denying his words as I pulled the cover tighter around me.

"Hey, however kinky you need, I'm game." He winked at me before settling back down on the rug. Still didn't make a move for his clothes. "Never tried much before, but it's fun."

"Fun," I echoed, then groaned. "Sawyer, what are we doing here?"

He patted my hand. "Having fun. Does it have to have a name? We're two horny guys who just came gangbusters together and who wouldn't mind doing that a time or ten more."

"Repeating this would *not* be sane," I lectured myself every bit as much as him.

"But it sure would be fun." He gave a happy little sigh. "If keeping it quiet is what you need, I can keep it on the down low—"

"Sawyer. You have never kept *anything* discreet. Ever. You told me and Char *minutes* after you lost your virginity."

"I won't tell her, if that's what you're worried about." He sounded a bit hurt. "You were my friend back then. I wanted to share.... Never mind."

"Hollis. Char. It finally happened!" Sawyer collapsed on our leather couch, looking even more out of breath and disheveled than usual. He'd even turned down my mom's offer of food when he first came in, waiting until she was back in the kitchen to speak.

"You did it? For reals?" Char leaned forward. When—not if, but when—Sawyer would lose his virginity had been the topic for weeks.

"Yes." Sawyer sighed happily, snuggling into the cushions like a content puppy.

My world stopped revolving with that single syllable. I hurt, muscles aching, teeth clenching. Was this jealousy? I didn't know, only knew that I had to get out of there. Right then.

"I've got homework," I said stiffly and headed for the stairs, but not before I heard Sawyer call it "magical."

Magical. The word instantly lost all its sparkle for me.

My gut twisted a bit at the memory, making words slip out of my mouth I otherwise would have held back. "We're friends now."

"We are?" He smiled broadly at this, like I'd handed him some sort of present. "Then see, we can be the sort of friends who bang for the holidays. No worries."

"Sawyer," I groaned. "Is this part of the holiday cheer package? Use sex to win your bet?"

"Would it work?" He peered intently at me. "Because it could be."

"No." I pushed at his shoulder. "You might be good in bed—"

"Thank you."

"—But you're not getting me singing carols just because you have a magic cock."

"You haven't even seen half of what I can do." His pride was almost adorable. "Tuesday's my birthday. You should come over after the dinner."

"I don't usually hand out sexual favors as *gifts*." I didn't bother trying to get out of the dinner; Char would roast me if I didn't come, and something about Sawyer's eyes told me he cared about my showing up. That made me both warm and queasy at the same time.

"Maybe you should start." He leered at me, the vulnerability of a few moments ago all but gone. "And we're going to my place because your cat has been staring at us the last twenty minutes and it's starting to freak me out."

I looked over, and sure enough, Benedict was on the side chair, a strange expression on his Siamese face, as if he wasn't sure exactly what he'd witnessed. I felt much the same way.

Chapter 8

By Tuesday I'd worked myself up into a low-grade panic attack over the dinner that night. I wished I could cancel, but it was a tradition, and upsetting my very-pregnant sister wasn't something I was willing to do. It was bad enough that I was still planning on being a no-show to Christmas dinner. I couldn't miss this, too.

Char had started the birthday dinner tradition our junior year of high school. When we were all in the same city, we did a dinner for the Murphy twins in December and then one for us in March. It was all very twinsy and cute and totally not my idea. The duo having a birthday got to pick the restaurant, which meant beer and burgers in December and Japanese in March because it was the one thing Char and I could agree on.

She'd called earlier in the day, leaning on me about Christmas plans. Between her and the bet with Sawyer, my resolve to pretend the season didn't exist was…well, weakening wasn't a word I wanted to be associated with, but it was under fire. The silly bet with Sawyer had me seeing details I hadn't let myself notice in years: the decorated windows walking up Alberta, the wreaths on the doors to the other condos in my building, the goodies at my favorite gourmet grocery store. Maybe this was what people meant when they said grief lessened with time. Or maybe it was that Sawyer and all his distractions were more pressing. And that made me sad in ways I couldn't really verbalize.

I was still mulling over my melancholy or lack thereof when my phone buzzed. I had no one in the shop so I pulled it out to check.

It was from Sawyer, and it wasn't the first text since Sunday either. He'd texted when he'd gotten home on Sunday and he'd sent a few innuendo-laced texts yesterday, the most notable being, *Been Googling rope. I blame you.* He seemed to love getting me all flustered.

Tucker picked Hopworks because they have the play area for Aria. Need a ride?

I did actually, as I didn't have a car, and squeezing in Char's minivan to head to the brewery in the southeastern part of the city had limited appeal, but what I typed was, *This is all part of your ploy to make me go home with you.*

His reply was almost instantaneous. *Guilty. Pick you up at the close of business?*

Fine. I do need to get home to feed Benedict after, though.

Ha. I'll pick you up at your place instead, give you a chance to lay out extra kibble ;)

For a brief moment I wished for one of those discerning Siamese cats who would only eat fresh food proffered at the exact right moment. No, I had the composter version that ate everything from corn to off-brand kibble with equal enthusiasm. *He* wouldn't mind if I were out late, but the prospect still gave me shivers.

All right. Just typing that felt like a huge leap, the sort we'd made as kids into the deep end at the neighborhood pool. Then, because that was a bit curt, I added, *Happy Birthday btw.*

*Thanks. Oh, and don't worry about getting me anything, Hols. Really. I'm in more of a *giving* mood this year ;)*

Oh damn, Mr. Winky Smiley Face. Now he had me shifting about uncomfortably behind the counter. And I didn't care what he said about no presents, no way could I show up empty-handed. The last few years, I'd gotten him and Tucker exactly the same thing, usually a gift card to Powell's Books or perhaps to the restaurant where we were dining. Our tastes were so vastly different that the gift cards made the most sense. I'd exhausted belts and wallets as gift options, but I wasn't sure what else to get them. I did, however, take pride in packaging the cards nicely.

Regardless of what I did, it had to be near identical or Char would be on to Sawyer and me before the dessert was served. I wandered around my store, considering options, until finally my eyes landed on an idea.

* * * *

When Sawyer picked me up, I had two gift boxes tucked into my bag, both done in my store's signature style of handmade paper boxes with silver flourishes and bows. For Sawyer alone I might have gone a bit more.

whimsical. And I didn't want to think about why that was, why I suddenly had this urge to treat him...*differently*. But as it was, I was taking a chance not going the gift-card route.

After feeding Benedict I had stared at my toothbrush for several long minutes. Way longer than I needed to. Throwing it in my bag seemed to be a tacit admission that I was spending the night at Sawyer's. Not throwing it in seemed like something I'd regret later. After all, I was already planning on ordering the pear and blue cheese salad. Hygiene was only kind right?

Oh, screw it. You're kissing Sawyer and you know it.

Fine.

Tired of arguing with myself, I put it and a travel-size toothpaste in my bag, but I steadfastly refused to add anything from my dresser to the bag. Better the walk of shame than packing for a sleepover. Not that there would be a walk of shame—

Buzz. My phone jangled with a text from Sawyer that he was out front but double-parked. I grabbed my bag and hurried out.

"Hey, nice scarf." He gave me a wink as I got into the car.

"Thanks." It was my new scarf, the one from Ev, and I'd paired it with a slim-fitting jacket and a light blue shirt with slim-fitting pants. And boots: totally frivolous things I'd seen online and been unable to resist. A bit dressy for a Tuesday at the brewery, but they suited me. And I wasn't the only one who'd dressed up. Sawyer had on his bow tie, sans vest this time. "You dressed up?"

"Told you. I'm trying some new stuff lately." The look he gave me was downright filthy as he pulled out.

"Yes, I do believe you told me your browser is getting a workout." I gave him a look in return. "But you know what they say about curiosity..."

"YOLO." He laughed.

"You are *such* a dude, bro."

"Says the hipster who definitely knows what nonwhite color that scarf is."

"Ecru."

"My point." He smirked, but he was driving so the most I could do was sigh heavily. "And you even own moisturizer. I saw it in your bathroom. The other night when we..."

"I know when," I said tartly. "And you try having parched British skin and not wanting to look fifty before you're even thirty yet."

"Next year, man. I can't wait for the big bash Tucker and I are throwing. We're even talking about having a band."

"Goody."

"Oh, come on. You'll come right? I'll make sure there's something leafy and green on the menu for you. And wine, not just beer."

"I'm the only one of us who drinks wine." I didn't let on how it made my hands tingle that he'd planned for me.

"More for you, then. Char's love of champagne doesn't count?"

"No." And just like that, the wedding weekend hung between us again, what had almost happened. What tipsy Char had curtailed. A memory from earlier in the wedding weekend popped into my head: him bringing me a glass of good chardonnay at the rehearsal dinner.

"They seem happy," Sawyer said, passing me a glass as I stood near the entrance to the dining room. Across the room, Tucker and Char posed for pictures with both sets of parents.

"They are." I took a deep sip, expecting something close to boxed wine, surprised at the heady taste of a quality vintage. "Is this their house white?"

"No. I asked the bartender for something good." Sawyer winked at me. Knowing him, the wink meant he'd gotten a phone number from the admittedly very attractive bartender. But somehow I doubted it as, for once, all Sawyer's charm seemed meant only for me.

Dangerous, foolish thinking, that. I took another sip anyway.

"You like me sauced, don't you?" I asked, still warm from the memory.

We pulled into the Hopworks lot and he grinned. "You *are* awfully fun lit. I know you don't do beer, but the sour cherry cider here is really good. You should try it."

"I'll see."

"Damn. I really wish I hadn't had to double-park back at your place. There's no chance of you letting me kiss you before we go in, is there?" The turn of his eyebrows was so beseeching that I had to laugh.

I scanned the parking lot thoroughly for Char and Tucker's van. Not seeing it, I leaned in and gave him the world's fastest cheek kiss. "Happy Birthday."

"You can do better than that—" He leaned in, then, at the last moment, pulled away. "Fuck. There they are."

Sure enough, there was Char's van pulling in a few spaces away.

"Oh, Hollis, I *love* your scarf," Char said once we were inside and waiting for a table. "Let me try it on? Pretty please. I need something like that to go with my red sweater?"

She reached for it and I batted her hands away. Sawyer coughed into his hand as I put on my sternest tone. "We're not fifteen. I'll order you one from the woman who knits samples for Ev."

Luckily, she got distracted by Aria, who wanted to head straight for the play area. We got a table near where she was happily playing with a train set. Somehow we ended up with Char and Tucker opposite Sawyer and me, despite my maneuvering to try to get seated next to Tucker. The Murphy twins each ordered tasting flights of beer.

"And you?" The waitress turned to me.

"Tea," Char said, gesturing across the table to encompass both her and me.

"That and I'd like a sour cherry cider." I still hadn't quite forgiven her for messing with my scarf.

Sawyer gave me a happy little kick under the table. He ordered the Huba Nero spicy burger, so maybe we weren't going to be kissing after all. I kicked him back.

The hard cider came and was surprisingly not bad, especially when paired with my salad. About halfway through eating, Sawyer deposited a few fries on my plate. "What's this?" I asked in a low voice. Char was busy with Aria.

"You keep looking at my plate like you haven't eaten in a month."

It wasn't his plate I was looking at, but I didn't share that, only raised an eyebrow.

"Oh." He smiled warmly, giving me a few more fries. "Just saving you from stealing Char's fries. She needs all her strength."

Ha. Sawyer wasn't wrong, though. I never ordered fries myself and yet inevitably I ended up stealing others'.

When Char turned her attention back to us, she put on her most winning smile. "Sawyer? Could you babysit on the twenty-first? Tucker and I want to go to this solstice concert. Might be one of our last chances to have a date night before the babies come."

Sawyer consulted his phone for a second. "Sure." He nodded, but his thinking face had my fingers drumming against the table. "Hollis will come, too."

"Hollis will what?" I speared him with a look.

"I'm just saying that you need to be familiar with the bedtime routine and stuff before the babies come, Hols. If you want to help out, that is."

"I do." I had already made a reservation with an organic meal service for Char's family for after the babies came. But babysitting wasn't exactly my strong suit. I'd only watched Aria for a few moments while Char got ready to go out, things like that.

"That's a brilliant idea," Char enthused.

"No, it's not." Tucker laughed. He'd had more beer than Sawyer, who'd stopped after his tasting flight. "I don't want our kid to witness bloodshed. Those two are barely civil anymore."

Sawyer's foot met mine midnudge. Barely civil; yes, that was us. Barely civil with Sawyer's tongue halfway down my throat two nights prior.

"I suppose I can check my calendar when I get back to work," I said for reasons that had nothing to do with wanting to spend another evening with Sawyer. Really.

"Yay!" Char gave a little cheer. "Now presents!"

"Prezzies!" Aria added.

Char gave Sawyer a cookbook on baking and Tucker gave him a certificate for baking classes.

"We need more edible experiments," Tucker said, and we all laughed.

"His offering for the business group's holiday party wasn't half bad," I said absently.

"I just need the right pan." Sawyer didn't wink at me, but he didn't need to. And as it turned out, I hadn't given him the darn pan the other night. Which meant he had an excuse for another visit to my place. And why that thrilled me, I really couldn't say.

Sawyer gave Tucker golfing lessons.

"Golfing lessons? But that will take you away from the kids!" Char moaned.

"Exactly," the three of us said in unison, and everyone laughed.

Then, feeling exceedingly foolish, I brought out my gifts.

"Oh, something from the store!" Tucker's enthusiasm sounded more than a little forced.

They opened them at the same time, opening the lid to reveal well-packaged presentations of notebook, ink, and Kaweco AL Sport pens.

"Because I never have a pen?" Sawyer smiled so broadly I thought he might pull something.

"And that one never has paper." I gestured at Tucker, trying to cover how pleased I was that Sawyer liked the gift. And no one but me would ever know that his pen was the exact shade of the jeans Sawyer wore the most, the ones that hugged him just so, and the mottled leather of the notebook cover reminded me of the infinite shades of his hair. And the jaunty green ink I'd chosen? That was Sawyer's eyes. He'd never know any of that, but it made me hum a bit, having put it all together.

"Hey, dude, my ink's cooler than yours," Sawyer said to Tucker, who had received the same brown notebook but a black pen and black ink. Reasons.

"Thanks, man." Sawyer's eyes caught mine and something passed between us—not the secret heat that had been simmering all evening and not the rekindled friendship I'd promised him the other night. Something stronger and warmer than either of those and infinitely scarier. I looked away before he could see too much.

Later, after Char and I got the check, Sawyer made a show of popping some mints. Ha. As if that would be enough to tempt me into kissing his habañero-infused mouth.

Of course twenty minutes later that's exactly what I was doing, not caring one whit about lingering spiciness as Sawyer pinned me against his entry wall.

"God, I've wanted to do that all evening," he said, coming up for air. With surprisingly careful hands, he unwound my scarf.

"Is this becoming a thing for you?" I asked.

"Yes." There wasn't a hint of apology in his voice as he unbuttoned my collar, licking at the skin he exposed. He turned me slightly so that he could kiss the back of my neck.

"Hell." I went limp and pliant in his arms, shivers racing through me.

"What do you want, Hols?" his voice licked at my eardrums, all wicked suggestion.

Chapter 9

Hell if I had an answer to Sawyer's question. It was hard to think with his lips right below my ear. I had a feeling what *he* wanted and I wasn't opposed to giving it, but asking for it wasn't something I did easily.

"It's your birthday," I said.

"It is." He bit my neck lightly. "And I want you to tell me what you want. You're the one with...*exacting* tastes. I'm just a guy who's happy getting off. Want a rerun of Sunday? I'd be happy with any variation of that. Not into oral? I can cope. You want to fuck me? I'm good. You want me to fuck you? Excellent. So you're going to have to give me a clue here."

"You'd let me fuck you?"

"Happily." He pushed me a few paces forward when I snort-laughed. I didn't doubt Sawyer had tried bottoming—he was nothing if not agreeable—but the guy had had a toppy vibe even as a teenager. He flipped on a light. Sawyer had an older upstairs condo off Broadway in a fourplex his family owned. Big and airy with lots of crown molding and original details, its sunny colors and open spaces totally suited Sawyer's outgoing personality.

"Bedroom's this way. So that's what you'd like, then? Me to ride you—"

I laughed again, cutting him off. The image wasn't without its appeal, but in a distant sort of way. And I knew perfectly well where the bedroom was, having been in the mirror unit many times when Tucker and Char lived there. "You know it's not."

"I love it when you laugh." He folded me in a hug from behind, seeming unable to let me walk down the long hall without touching me. "And yes, I *think* I know."

"But you're going to make me say the words." I turned in his arms, looping my arms around his neck.

"Absolutely." He nodded against my head. "It *is* my birthday and all."

Maybe it was the cider still humming pleasantly in my veins. Maybe it was the fact that it was his birthday. Maybe it was simply *him*. Regardless, I stretched to put my lips against his ear and uttered words I usually reserved for very drunken requests. "Fuck me."

"You have no idea how long I've waited to hear that." He kissed me and we stumbled the last few feet to his bedroom. Sawyer had, predictably, a monster king bed. A big sprawling affair with puffy comforters and huge pillows. I moved to take off my jacket and Sawyer shook his head. "Let me."

He undressed me the way he kissed me: slowly and thoroughly and joyfully, as if he were unwrapping chocolate truffles and savoring them one by one. My jacket hit his hardwood floor, then my shirt. He knelt to unzip my boots, then motioned for me to step out of them. Still on his knees, he removed my belt, then unzipped so I could wriggle free of the pants.

"I love that you wear silky briefs." Sawyer stroked the fabric with his fingers, skirting the outline of my cock. "It's so you."

I laughed. "I didn't even notice yours the other night, but I'm betting cotton. I'll get you some good ones. You'll never go back."

"Still wrong context?" He mouthed my length through the slippery fabric. I nodded.

"Damn." He shook his head, then brightened. "Can I suck you after I fuck you senseless? That sounds like fun."

"Do you need to choreograph everything?" I extended a hand to help him stand. "I'm not used to so much…talking."

"Tough." He tweaked one of my nipples before pulling off his tie and shirt. In contrast to his slow, deliberate moves when undressing me, he was fast and clumsy as he stripped himself. I twitched a little at the mess of our clothes, but I knew he'd laugh if I stopped to straighten. Pushing his pants and boxers—black cotton—off, he gave me a feral grin before he pressed me back into the bed. "Want to grind against your pretty underwear a bit."

"Less narrating, more doing," I ordered.

"Sorry, Hols. We'll get you earplugs for next time."

"You will not." I shoved at his shoulder. All this talk of *next time* and *someday* made me nervous, so I channeled all that into kissing him desperately.

"Yeah," he murmured, moving so that his big body covered mine, hard cock dragging against mine through my briefs. Like the other night, he was surprisingly unhurried as we made out for long moments, kissing and stroking, a slow blaze as opposed to a fast inferno.

"Sometime I want to get off like this," he murmured. "Come all over your expensive underwear and make you wait and wait."

Okay, maybe all his narrating *was* sexy because his words made me shiver.

"But tonight I'm going to fuck you." He rolled away to riffle through a nightstand drawer. "Happy Birthday to me," he said almost under his breath.

He returned with condom and lube, and a thought I'd rather not have floated through my head. "Sawyer, I hate to ask—"

"Yeah, I'm tested." He kissed my neck. "I know you think I'm a big old manwhore, but I do play safe."

He kissed his way down my front. "Is rimming one of those needs-the-right-context things for you?"

"It's a 'I'd rather shower first, please and thank you.'" I laughed, both to cover my nerves and because I couldn't *not* laugh. God, I *never* laughed like this in bed. Ever.

"Oooh. Adding showering with you to my list." He licked the line of hair on my stomach. "And just for the record, I'm not so picky. And I'm *very* oral."

"Noted." I deliberately made my voice dry simply to hear his laugh. I might be developing a fetish for his deep chuckle, but I'd never tell him that.

Pushing my underwear off, he grabbed the lube, intent clear in his eyes.

"I can do it," I said, holding out my hand.

"Noted." He imitated me but didn't surrender the tube. "And it's not about *can.*"

He captured my mouth, showing off his impressive wingspan as he folded me up so that he could finger me while we kissed. I wasn't so sure about this until his lips drifted to my neck; then, once he had me pliant and moaning, he latched onto a nipple, slick fingers continuing to quest. He lit me up in ways I hadn't been in years.

"Now." I shoved at his shoulder. "Now."

He released the nipple with a lewd smacking sound that wrenched another soft moan from me. "Oh, we both know you're not about the now."

Withdrawing his fingers, he considered me. "Hands behind your head. Lace your fingers." Wordlessly, I complied and his breath hissed in. "You just...*do* it. Oh, Hols..."

Apparently my quick compliance did something to him because it earned me another plundering kiss before he took care of the condom. I stretched regularly after running on my treadmill, and I was grateful for every bit of flexibility as he bent my legs up, getting his thighs underneath me. I wanted to say something about not being a pretzel or how he didn't have to show off his sexual gymnastics, but he took away my very breath when he started to push in.

"Keep your hands there." His eyes weren't on my hands, however; instead, they were locked on where we joined. He wasn't the only one with tricks, and I willed my body to relax, let him press in with a smooth stroke.

"Holy fuck." Eyes rolling back in his head, he groaned. "So. So. Glad... that your kink isn't...my waiting."

"Don't tempt me," I said darkly.

"Fuck, I I—" Whatever he was going to say was lost in another moan as his second stroke brought him even deeper. He knew precisely how to angle his hips and mine to maximize the pressure on my gland, and soon I was the one crying out.

He pinched my sensitive nipple and my arms jerked.

"Nuh-uh. Keep your hands there."

"Want to touch...myself," I panted.

"I know you do." His voice soothed, then hardened most deliciously. "But you're not going to."

My cock leaped at this, drooling clear fluid against my belly. Hissing a little, he released my nipple and swept his thumb across the head of my cock, gathering up the slick before sucking his thumb into his mouth.

"You play dirty," I accused as my dick got all sorts of ideas about what it might like.

"You love it." He laughed as he thrust, a talent I wouldn't have thought he had. "God, I want to suck you, Hols. Want to swallow you down and finger your freshly fucked ass."

"You've got a filthy mouth."

"Guilty." He bent forward to lick at my mouth. "And that wasn't a no."

"That was a please, for the love of God, let me come. Now." I strained against my linked hands and his heavy body.

"You don't *really* want that." He pumped harder, his voice getting breathier. "And it doesn't matter. I'm not letting you come yet."

"Please," I moaned as he hammered my spot—short, hard strokes that pushed my body to the edge even without a hand on my dick. My arms jerked again, hands almost coming apart as I *needed*...more.

"Keep your hands there." His hand went to my wrist, not pinning me to the bed but enough pressure to remind me why my hands were up. Because it pleased him. Because he'd ordered and I'd complied and something in that dynamic made my body sing, made me feel like I'd left behind every worry and anxiety and could simply exist from request to request, reduced to little more than a hungry vessel for pleasure, begging for relief even as I wanted never to leave this moment. "Gonna research safe knots," he muttered.

"What...think I'm going to let you?" I tried to sound arch and ended up only sounding desperate.

"I know you will." His body shuddered at his words. "Fuck. Hols. You'll let me."

"Come," I said because I could tell he was close, and I was close to sobbing for release. "I need it, Sawyer," I babbled. "Need to come."

"You will. But...not...yet." His hips sped up. "Not yet."

"*Sawyer.*" My whole body tensed.

"Don't you dare come yet." His thrusts were growing more erratic, which tossed me ever closer to orgasm.

"Please."

"No. You have to wait." He moaned, deep and low. "Watch me now, Hols. Watch me come."

"Yes, yes," I cried out. He fucked deeper, strokes losing all their earlier finesse, his big body convulsing and coming apart. My balls tightened and my chest flushed. I had to clamp down hard to keep from joining him, especially at the pinch of pleasure-pain when he pulled out.

He took a minute to breathe heavily next to me, then launched himself at me, breath a warm mist against my cock. "Tell me this is the right context. You did good, babe. So good. Waited perfectly."

"Yes." It was entirely possible I could come on his command alone. I was that tense.

He didn't tease with his tongue, instead swallowing me all the way to the root, moaning happily as he did so. He hadn't said yet, so I trembled and shook as he sucked. I started keening as he added fingers to the mix.

"Now." He lifted his head the barest of seconds before returning to sucking, fingers working my spot as I came, crying out. I was sobbing with relief, curling up into a ball as I was powerless to do anything else but simply let pleasure have its way with me. Sawyer's large, capable hands stroked and soothed me as he murmured in my ear about how perfect I'd been.

Gradually I uncurled, clinging to him as aftershocks continued to rack my body.

"Fuck, you're incredible." He kissed my forehead before sitting up long enough to clean us both up with a cloth from the basket next to the bed. I guessed there were advantages to not putting laundry right away.

He flopped back next to me, pulling me into his arms. "Hols...I've had a lot of sex—"

"*We know.*"

"But nothing like that. I mean *nothing*. I didn't even know sex could feel like that. Shit. I'm not even making sense. But I had no clue..." He kissed the side of my face. "Felt so close to you, too. Like I could feel your...I don't know...*pulse*."

I felt exactly the same way but couldn't let on. This was just Sawyer taking the training wheels off his kinky side for the first time. This was Sawyer who seldom got serious about anything or anyone. No way could I let on that the sex had undone me as well. "Do you always *talk* after sex?" I asked instead.

"Yep." He didn't sound put out at all and pulled up the covers around us. " 'Specially when it rocked my world."

"I should get—"

"It's going to be a bit before I can drive. And no way am I letting you walk a couple of miles this time of night."

"It's not *that* far—"

"How is it that you only take orders when you're turned on?" He laughed. "No, Hols. You're not leaving. Go to sleep."

He effectively pinned me with his snuggling so that his arm and leg encircled me. He breathed deep, nuzzled my head a few times, and then was asleep. I wished desperately that it was as easy for me, but instead I lay there, heavy with the knowledge that *everything* was changing, and probably not for the better.

Chapter 10

"You're gripping it too tightly," I said, a bit too chiding for that early in the morning. "It'll splatter if you're not careful."

"Geez. So sensitive." Sawyer corrected his grip. "How do you manage to do this all the time?"

"Oh, you get used to the idiosyncrasies. Especially when you're...*committed.*"

"Hey, I'm plenty committed. I'm the one who asked for a pen lesson before I run you home."

"Indeed you are." I sipped the tea of indeterminate age and origin Sawyer had had in his cabinet. Somehow I'd slept all night next to Sawyer; I had no idea when my worrying had given way to sleep, but I'd woken up with Sawyer wrapped around me. I'd gently extracted myself and gone in search of tea, but he'd found me before the tea finished steeping and requested that I show him how to use his new pen before he ran me back to my place.

I really did need to shower and change before I opened the store at ten but get me talking pens and I lose all track of time. We were sitting at the cherry table in his little dining nook, me with my tea and him with some coffee that looked like it could double as airplane fuel. I'd shown him how to fill the pen and how to clean it and now he was practicing making some notes in his notebook.

I want to see you tonight, he wrote in his blocky script, passing me the notebook.

I plucked the pen from his grasp. *We'll see.* Don't waste your notebook paper on trifles.

He took the pen back the moment I finished. *You calling this a trifle?* He leaned in and kissed me soundly before I realized what he was about.

"It's an indulgence," I said. "One that's going to lead to regret and awkwardness once you get this out of your system."

"What makes you think that's going to happen?" He kissed along my jaw, which was in need of a shave, but he didn't seem to care.

"Sawyer. Other than soccer, you've never had a hobby last—you took one semester of choir, gave up trumpet before you even needed a valve replacement, quit photography before Aria's first birthday, tried knitting when Ev first came to town and lost interest as soon as he and Brady became a thing, and left Spanish before that series of classes ended. You'll move on from baking eventually, too—and me."

"So this is just a diversion, that's what you're saying? Something I'm going to quit on?" For this early in the morning, his voice had plenty of challenge in it.

"We are *not* betting on this," I said firmly before he could propose something.

"I am." He kissed me again, almost toppling me out of my chair with his intensity. "And I don't believe in doom and gloom, Hollis. Especially at this time of year."

I didn't tell him that was *all* I believed in, or rather, all I would let myself believe in with him. The morning outside his window was a stark gray contrast to the sunshine Sawyer kept trying to blow my way. Everyone in Oregon knew better than to trust December sun. The rain always came back. I knew with absolute certainty that by January he'd be on to something else. Instead, I kissed him back with desperate intensity.

"Shower here." His eyes gleamed. "I've got a nice one."

"I'm not—"

"I am." He kissed me again, lips working far better than words to turn me inside out, make me forget the boundaries I was supposed to be erecting. And when he dragged me toward his bathroom, all I could think about was how filthy Sawyer made getting clean sound.

"Better not make me late."

* * * *

As it turned out, I had barely enough time to take a second lightning-fast shower and shave at my place, feed Benedict, and rush to open the shop. As I pulled my keys out of my bag, I discovered a note written in green ink by the scratchy hand of someone still getting used to a fountain pen.

Thank you for the birthday gift! I can tell I'm going to have fun

with this…
And I was serious about seeing you tonight.
There once was a hot guy named Hollis
Whose phallus was totally flawless
Whene'er he got blown
His lover would moan
Until he was totally jawless

I laughed, tucking the note back away. The store was empty so I grabbed my phone and sent a fast text.

You're incorrigible. And you might want to stick to store management.

The reply came faster than I would have expected. *Aww, Hollis, that's the first compliment you've given me on our store.*

Oh, that man. I wasn't sure whether to strangle him or count the hours until I could kiss him again. I smiled to myself as I straightened displays and waited for my midmorning traffic to arrive.

To my surprise, my first customer was looking for thank-you cards. "The clerk across the street said you'd probably have just the thing," the older woman in a trench coat said.

Sawyer sending me business? Either he'd snuck a look at my bottom line—not *that* one—or sex had addled his brain. His store had thank-you cards, too—albeit most with licensed characters, whereas mine were thick, embossed card stock.

I got that customer all squared away with thank-you cards, a nice micro gel pen, and some small-batch stickers for her planner, then had a nice stream of lunchtime traffic. Around two thirty, when the store was dead and I was working on the books on my laptop, Sawyer came in juggling a white envelope and two steaming coffee cups from People's Cup.

"What's this?" I asked, coming out from behind the counter to take a cup before he could spill on my floor.

"Gingerbread lattes. I dare you to taste one, Mr. Grinch. Guaranteed instant holiday spirit."

"I don't usually drink coffee," I reminded him, even though these did smell exquisite.

"Just try it," Sawyer urged. He was so cute when he was eager that I had to laugh before blowing on the coffee and taking a sip. It tasted spicy and sweet, heavy with notes of ginger and brown sugar. It reminded me of Mom's holiday baking, but in a way that left me comforted, not sad.

"Not bad," I allowed. "I'm not feeling the urge for huge gatherings, but not bad at all." I took a second sip.

"And here." Hollis handed me the envelope, which had a card in it.

I withdrew the card, which proclaimed, "I'd walk to Mordor for you." It was one of a four-pack that Sawyer's shop sold, all with corny Tolkien-referencing slogans.

The inside had another limerick,

> *Hollis, you're just so damn hot*
> *You tie all my thoughts up in knots*
> *Which was inconvenient*
> *Because I was too lenient*
> *But now I would knot you a lot!*

Underneath, he'd written, *Tonight? My mouth, your dick, my place again?* I laughed because I simply couldn't not. "You *are* rather oral-obsessed, aren't you?"

"Yup." He grinned shamelessly. "You're...er...*not*, right?"

"Tie my hands, get me on my knees, and you'll see."

Sawyer's breath hissed in. Oh, I did love shocking him. "I think I like your poetry better than mine."

"I'm not into swallowing, but I trust you to get...creative." I couldn't believe we were really standing here flirting like this. Or that I was enjoying it so much. I blamed the latte.

Sawyer's eyes went to the slate-gray tie I was wearing that day. "Put up your 'Back in Five Minutes' sign and show me this bathroom that needs painting."

"You're not ruining a perfectly nice Hugo Boss tie."

"I own some cheap ones," he said quickly. God, his eagerness to go there really was adorable. "And I was reading up on the right kind of rope—"

"I might own some," I admitted.

"What time should I come over?"

"There are poodles at the dog park less eager to hump something than you."

He snort-laughed until he had tears at the corners of his eyes. "I'll bring pho."

Oh, the man knew just how to be tempting, with one of my favorite foods. "I suppose I do still owe you that pan. But I want to get a run in, so let's say eight."

"I might die of a hard-on by then," he whined.

"Good. More pho for me." I looked at the door; no foot traffic seemed imminent. It was a rainy day with a heavy drizzle coming down. "Do you want a quick glance at the bathroom you'll be painting one of these bets?"

"God yes." He followed me around the corner behind the register.

"Note that I'm not flipping my sign," I said as I turned on the bathroom light. "I'm just showing—"

He stopped me with firm hands on my shoulders and soft lips against my own. He plundered my mouth until I sagged bonelessly against him.

"God, I needed that, Hols." He rested his forehead against mine. "You make me crazy."

"You make me reckless," I countered. "And—"

"See you at eight," he said, backing away before I could continue a lecture.

* * * *

I fretted the remainder of the afternoon. I'd apparently created a monster by introducing Sawyer to the shallow end of the kink pool and I was torn between wanting to show him more and wanting to slam a lid on that part of myself. I hadn't indulged in any of this since Yuto, and because all that trusting him had gotten me was a badly bruised heart, I'd always assumed I wouldn't go down that path again, no matter how much I craved it. It simply wasn't worth the risk. And Sawyer? Sawyer was all kinds of risks—and a total newbie to these things to boot.

Also, inviting Sawyer over for the express purpose of having sexual relations felt...momentous somehow. So momentous that I took shower number three of the day. A very *thorough* shower, the likes of which I hadn't done since Yuto. When Sawyer rang the bell I was just toweling off, and I pulled on a pair of pants but left off a shirt. No need to play coy. We both knew where this evening was headed.

Sawyer carried in steaming containers from Pho Jasmine, a no-frills noodle joint with heady broth. He gave me an appreciative look as he set down the food, one that made me nervous I was about to be his main course. My pulse gave a little thrum. Okay, maybe more excited than nervous, not that I'd ever let on to the excitement. Yuto had trained me out of such impulses if I'd ever had them to begin with—showing too much anticipation with him had inevitably resulted in my getting the opposite of what I'd hoped for.

"Can I ask you something?" Sawyer said as we dished up the food into my wide white bowls, which were perfect for pho.

I had a feeling what his line of questioning was going to be, but I still nodded.

"You weren't a virgin last night. But I've never seen—or heard—about you with anyone. Who was he?"

"Who was who?" The condiments came in a plastic bag, which was a bit unhygienic for sharing, so I arranged the bean sprouts and herbs and such on a platter.

"The guy who taught you what you like in bed? The…kink master?"

"The kink master?" I laughed as I finally was satisfied with the arrangement of the food and took a seat next to him at my breakfast bar. "There was an older gentleman. An adviser to the museum sciences program—"

"Your professor?" Sawyer's jaw dropped open.

"No, not a professor. An administrator at…a local museum. I did an internship there and he took…an interest."

"And he was kinky?"

"I'm not a fan of that word, but yes, he had…interests that he shared with me."

"Were you…" Sawyer made a vague gesture with his chopsticks. "I don't know…in love or whatever with him?"

"In love," I scoffed, even though I very much had been infatuated, with a stupid kind of devotion. "It wasn't that type of arrangement. It was simply advantageous while I finished my education for us to…associate."

"Associate. That's going to be my new high-class way of saying fucking from now on."

"You must not want to kiss me very badly," I observed as I watched him douse his food with chili sauce.

"I brought mints." He winked at me. "So this guy, was he into dungeons and shibari and the whole BDSM thing?"

"Slow down," I ordered. "You really need to curate your Internet searching more. Yes, he was into the local BDSM scene in Baltimore, but *I* am not into any such trappings as parties or sex rooms or the like."

"God forbid you go to a party." Another devious wink from Sawyer. "So your main kink, then, is the orgasm denial? And maybe being tied up?" He looked so hopeful on the last bit that I had to laugh.

"A better question, Sawyer, is what *your* kinks are. Do you *want* to tie someone up?"

"I didn't think I did before you seemed open to the idea. I think I have a Hollis kink. You mention something and I instantly want to do it…with you."

My cheeks heated at his words. He was sweet. Too sweet. And I hadn't ever talked this frankly with someone about my desires. Yuto had always seemed to have the road map to our encounters, and anyone since him hadn't been around long enough to sniff out my true desires. Somehow putting a label on things made them extra dirty. Still, though, I needed to teach Sawyer how to play safe for the next time he tried this on.

An image of Sawyer binding the hands of some faceless young thing on his knees made me near homicidal. *This* was why us sleeping together was such a bad idea. Never again would I be able to be civil to any new friends he brought around without also wondering if he was fucking them.

"Well, that's a good starting point, to want to do what turns the other person on." I nodded, keeping my tone academic. "*Always* ask, especially before you tie them up. Don't just guess what the other person's limits are—"

"Hols. I don't want a lecture on kink. Tell me about *you*."

"I like being tied up," I said softly to my soup bowl. "There are different ways to be restrained—but yes, shibari is one that...interests me."

"Handcuffs?" Sawyer looked ready to run out for some if I nodded.

"I'm not into handcuffs or metal restraints as much."

"Why am I not surprised to hear that you have a natural fibers fetish?" Sawyer laughed. "So silk, cotton, that sort of thing? What about leather?"

I nodded. "Leather has its appeal."

"Tell me what you like when you're tied up. Or, knowing you, you've got a list of things you *don't* like."

"Hey, I'm not *that* picky."

"Yes, you are, Hols, and we all love you for it. So tell me what stuff pisses you off or takes you out of the happy zone?"

"Extreme pain is a hard limit for me," I admitted, although it was a limit Yuto had leaned up against fairly often. "I like...being teased. I don't like being humiliated."

"I would never humiliate you." Sawyer looked so earnest that I had to reach over and pat his knee.

"I know you wouldn't." I realized as I said it how true it was. I did trust him, more than I had even thought.

"What else?" Sawyer's eyes narrowed, as if he was mentally taking notes on all this. He was concentrating so hard that his whipping out his notebook wouldn't have surprised me at all.

There was one more limit, one that I hated to bring up for fear it could—and it had been—used as punishment and control, but somehow I knew with him it would be honored. "When I'm bound I hate being left."

"Oh, Hols, *no*. I wouldn't just leave you there." Sawyer's eyes went wide and he grabbed my hand. "I want to have *fun* with you. That's what this is all about right? A new way to have fun together."

My laugh this time was a creaky thing, little used in this context. God, he was a treasure. Too bad he wasn't mine to keep. "I think a lot of people take it a lot more seriously than that."

"Yeah, well, a lot of people take *life* too seriously." Finished eating, Sawyer stood to help me take the bowls and plate to the dishwasher. "So can we?"

"YOLO," I said, in my best dude-bro voice, which got peals of laughter from Sawyer. I led him to the bedroom that had scarcely seen anyone other than Benedict and me. My heart sped up; again that feeling of climbing a mountain that was a little too big for me. Whatever came next, I had a feeling things—*I*—would never be the same.

Chapter 11

With Sawyer watching, I withdrew a slim box from the top shelf of my closet. I removed a few items and returned the box to its place before Sawyer could poke around and get all curious.

"This is cotton silk bondage rope." Dropping the condoms and lube to the mattress, I held up the hank of black rope. "And these"—I held out the gold scissors—"are for cutting me loose if you can't untie fast enough. Always have scissors or a knife nearby."

"Hols. I read tips online. Less lecture, more doing. Lose your pants and get on there." Sawyer gestured to the bed, which was a low, modern-designed platform.

My stomach wobbled precipitously as I took off my pants. "Just my hands tonight, if you please."

"Relax." Sawyer came up behind me and wrapped his arms around me. "I've got you, Hols. You're safe."

That's what I'm worried about. I didn't want to feel safe with Sawyer. I didn't want to trust him this much.

"Kneel on the bed." Sawyer took off his shirt and shoes but left his pants on. I knelt on the edge of the bed, clasping my hands behind my back.

"Oh, Hols, you are...*perfect.*" Sawyer breathed against my ear.

Instead of uncoiling the rope right away, as I'd expected, he brushed the hank over my shoulders, then my chest, teasing my nipples with little flicks before giving attention to my neck and back. It was extraordinarily soft rope, which was why I'd kept it. Sawyer kept his touch light as butterfly wings caressing my skin. He carried on for so long that my sudden attack of nerves fled, replaced by the quiet hypnotism of wondering where he'd touch next. He brushed the rope up and down my arms while whispering filthy little nothings in my ear about how perfect I was and how hard I was going to come for him.

"God, the things I want to do to you."

"Yes." My voice shook.

Slowly he wound the rope around one wrist, then the other, stroking with his fingers as well, a sensuous unfolding the likes of which I hadn't experienced since my first few times. He used his nimble fingers to check tension as he made his way up my forearms a bit. I couldn't see, but I could tell from his sharp intake of breath that he was pleased by what he saw.

"You make me want to take a class in this, do it right," he whispered. My heart sank a bit because taking a class was usually the death knell of whatever new hobby had gripped Sawyer. "I want to learn to make you look like the pictures on Tumblr."

"Yes, well, most of those are far more flexible than me, and you're not suspending me from anything."

"Oooh. I may need a trip to the hardware store." Sawyer ignored my warning, his hands soothing my back muscles, quieting this new tension. "Can you bend forward comfortably?" Sawyer arranged the pillows in front of me so my head and shoulders were supported.

"Yes," I said. He moved back behind me, fingers tracing the ropes again. I wasn't crazy about how the position pushed my ass in the air, but I was already starting to float on the endorphins of giving up control to Sawyer, letting him bind me. I tested the bindings, pulling a bit, but whatever Internet research Sawyer had done had paid off with secure knots that didn't dig in or cut off circulation.

He licked his way down my spine, then proceeded to lick and kiss the exposed skin in between the bindings. I'd had no idea that my wrists were erogenous zones, but Sawyer's attentions had me softly moaning. He gently raised my arms so he could lick at the small of my back before letting my arms fall. His tongue slid lower.

"I've never..." The bindings on my wrists loosened my tongue, made me admit things I'd usually keep quiet about. "That is..."

"The fancy ex-boyfriend didn't eat your ass, Hols?" Sawyer's breath was a warm tease against my skin. "That's a shame."

The sound I made next didn't seem human as he licked his way down to my rim. The man wasn't kidding about being seriously orally inclined. All the dexterity he'd shown on my neck and my nipples came out to play as he quickly had me moaning into the pillow. My hips rocked up into him, my dick getting nothing but air. This was the most intimate act I'd shared with anyone, the most exposed I'd been for another person, and my whole body trembled, coalescing into a single raw nerve.

I floated on sensations, losing all track of time, of everything other than the rope around my wrists and that maddening tongue. My muscles softened for him, but it wasn't the deliberate relaxing I had to do for sex; this was an unconscious unwinding. At some point Sawyer worked a thumb in, then more, licking and fingering until I was an incoherent mess.

"Fuck me, please fuck me. Sawyer. Oh God, Sawyer, I need you."

"Right here, babe, right here." He rubbed his face against my thighs, bristly cheeks abrading the sensitive skin there. His hands went to my arms again, fingers tracing along the bonds, probably checking circulation, but it also seemed like some deeply held need he had to continually touch where he'd bound me.

There was the *snick* of the lube opening, then a soft, "Hey, this is *nice* stuff. I'm getting this brand next time."

I laughed, which had never, ever happened with my arms bound before. Laughing did something to my chest, made it both tighter and looser at the same time—tight with emotions I didn't know what to do with and loose with a giddy sort of pleasure I'd never known before.

"I'll put some in your stocking," I said, rocking my hips back to meet his fingers. A few thrusts and he had me back to begging.

"Now. Please now. I need to come."

"You know I'm not going to let you. Not yet." There was a quaver to his voice, a sexy sort of strain, and his thighs brushed mine as he teased me with the head of his dick a bit. He'd taken care of the condom at some point, but I'd been too floaty to notice the crinkle of the wrapper.

Sawyer pushed in slowly, my already sensitive tissues resisting the intrusion even as I hissed with the pleasure of it. Hands bound. Nothing to do but take this, open myself up to the sensations.

"That's it." Sawyer's hands were back on my bonds, gently pulling me back. I wanted to make a quip about how I wasn't a yogi, but I was too far gone, pleasure licking every nerve ending, the tightness in my arms only magnifying it.

His thumbs caressed my bonds and he moaned softly. "Can't believe you let me...so fucking hot," he muttered.

Each thrust dragged me closer to the edge, especially when his hands moved to my hips, finding the perfect angle to nail my gland.

"Please touch me," I begged.

"Not yet." His hips snapped faster and his breathing started to sound like the whoosh of a MAX train. "Not yet."

One of his hands crept around to my stomach, maddeningly close to my dick but not touching it. "Please."

"I'll tell you when," he ground out, panting between each word.

I tightened my internal muscles, milking him hard. "Oh, holy fuck, Hols. Do that again."

I obliged, working more deliberately now, determined to see him unravel as much as I was, but the action was also getting me perilously close to orgasm. "Please, Sawyer. Please."

"Now." His hand found my dick. "Now. Fuck. Now, Hols. Do it now. With me." His hips jerked and his voice devolved into a shout as he came. A single tug on my dick and I was joining him, my body spasming and shaking, continuing long after he pulled out. Without him to hold me up, I collapsed onto the mattress, scarcely aware of him untying me until he was rubbing circulation back into my tired muscles. He kissed my shoulder blades, then my wrists.

"Not much marking. It'll fade by morning." He sounded like he couldn't decide if that was a good thing or not.

I gave a shaky chuckle. "Denser rope like hemp marks more. If you're into that."

"I might be." He sighed happily. "Damn, Hols, I had no idea I was into *this*, but you…you make me want more."

That was precisely the problem. He made me want more, too. More of him, more of this blissful surrender, more time before he moved on to whatever—or whoever—caught his fancy next. He made my December funk fade, made me want more than fleeting pleasure, made me feel worthy of feeling good for the first time in a long time, but I knew in my bones that such feelings couldn't last.

* * * *

I wasn't sure exactly what one wore to babysit, but I was pretty sure my wool pants and H&M shirt were *not* it, so I hurried home from the shop to change. It was bitingly cold with the possibility of snow on Christmas, another cold snap that had me hunkering in my thickest coat and drinking vats of tea and craving my blankets. Of course my blankets weren't as much in demand these last few days, not with Sawyer-the-space-heater sleeping over and chasing even the most persistent chill away. I knew I should have put a stop to things after our *lesson* in bondage, but somehow the words never made it past my throat—not when there was early morning sex to be had.

And in the evenings, when I should be putting my foot down, Sawyer kept plying me with all my cold-weather favorites—soup from the soup bar place that kept winning awards, udon from the Japanese restaurant downtown that we'd been to with Tucker and Char last year, and a seemingly endless supply of seasonal drinks from People's Cup in the afternoons, most accompanied by more bad limericks and shockingly awful haikus.

Which I, fool that I was, was coming to look forward to. I grabbed a rarely worn pair of jeans from the back of my closet and paired it with a charcoal Johns Hopkins sweater advertising my alma mater's crest.

Buzz. I was just pulling on my boots when Sawyer texted that he was down front. I could have walked to Char's place, but Sawyer's car was much warmer, and I wouldn't have turned down a ride even if we weren't... whatever we were doing. Or so I told myself as I rushed down my steps, much too eager to see a man I'd seen only hours earlier.

"Wow, Hols, you look..." Sawyer shook his head slightly. He wasn't double-parked this time and didn't seem in a hurry to pull away. "I haven't seen you this casual since school. I like it. Love how that sweater makes your eyes gray."

I did, too, actually, but Sawyer wasn't supposed to notice tiny details like that. It disarmed me, made me all twitchy. "Aren't we going to be late?"

"We've got a minute." Sawyer used the lapels of my coat to drag me closer. "And you won't let me kiss you at Char's house, I'm sure, and you had customers this afternoon so all I could do was drop off your latte."

"I'm having to tack on extra miles to my runs," I grumbled. "All these sweets."

"You love it and you know it. Speaking of, I brought cookie dough to bake after dinner. Aria can help roll it out." He looked so supremely proud of himself that for once I was the one to move first, kissing him lightly, if only to knock that look off his face.

"Missed you, Hols." He pulled me back for a second kiss, this one longer, with him firmly in charge. He tasted like the mints he always carried and coffee and something achingly familiar. "Guess what?"

"What?" I said cautiously.

"I found a rope workshop in January. It's a small group thing so it shouldn't be too crowded for you, but the guy also does private lessons if you really don't want a class with other people."

"But you do? Want a class, I mean?" He'd mentioned it before, during sex mainly, and each time it filled me with dread for when this thing between us ended.

"Well, yeah. I learn best hands-on, and YouTube is only so helpful." He gave a rueful laugh. "And as patient as you are with me, I still think it would be fun to get better at the fancy stuff."

"Is it a couples-only class?" I asked.

"Well, no, but I'm taking it for *you*. For us really."

That didn't reassure me at all. Sawyer's résumé of dropped hobbies were often externally motivated: the baby pictures he wanted to snap for Char, the trumpet player he'd wanted to blow, the knitter he'd crushed on. His wanting to do this for me was sweet, but it was also yet another sign that his fascination was temporary and would likely be over before the class even finished.

"Come on, just say you'll check your calendar and think about it." His tone was his most wheedling one, the one I found hardest to turn down.

"I'll see," I said at last.

"Thanks." The kiss he gave me was worth the discomfort of agreeing to think about this outing. But then, lately *all* Sawyer's kisses felt worth it, and that scared me enough to have me pulling away from him and straightening my coat.

"Did you feed Bunny extra before you left?" he asked as he finally pulled out into traffic. "I wanted to spend the night at my place. I put some lights up in the windows and on the balconies to show you."

We'd been at my place all week so I supposed it was only fair, but what was I doing thinking about *fair* like we were in some sort of relationship. *Now. End this tonight.* But I didn't. "He won't starve," I conceded.

"Good. Now I've got something to look forward to." The streetlights had nothing on the force of his grin.

"You better not be planning on wrapping *me* in lights," I warned.

"Don't give me ideas, Hols." He laughed. It was funny; we seemed to slip effortlessly between sex that was more free-flowing and that which was more...adventurous. I'd never had that before. With Yuto nearly every encounter had been a scene, and with my few hookups fast was really the only appropriate adjective. But with Sawyer, as impatient as he was to try new things, he also seemed equally happy to lie together under a pile of covers and make out while grinding off together.

My breathing did a funny hitch as we entered Char and Sawyer's neighborhood. A lot of the neighbors had lights up, as always, and my chest ached to see such old familiar sights. Sawyer gave me a concerned look. "Everything okay?"

"Of course."

"Tucker's not as good with lights as your dad was."

"That's true." It was funny how I dreaded talking about them and yet how at the same time Sawyer's easy reference to them helped ease the tension in my chest. Dad *had* had a knack for lights, and it was. . . reassuring that I wasn't the only one who remembered. Somehow having Sawyer with me during this darkest part of the year made my grief more manageable. And lord, I did *not* want to depend on him this way. Needing Sawyer would be the height of foolishness.

"Ready to go play superuncles or do you need a minute?" He parked on the street so that Char and Tucker would be able to back out of the driveway.

"Bring it on." I tried to channel his usual enthusiasm, even if inside I had no such confidence.

Chapter 12

"I'm sorry; we had a really late nap so I'm just now trying to find her some dinner," Char apologized as soon as we came in the door.

The living room was decorated for the holidays now—probably had been since fifteen minutes after Aria's birthday party ended. Tree in the same corner Mom always put it, real because Dad wouldn't let us get anything else. The felt menorah was new, as were a set of solstice-themed candles on the mantel. Also new were all the toddler holiday crafts everywhere, and somehow that saddened me, too. Aria wasn't a baby now—time just kept right on marching forward.

"Hey, we can feed the munchkin, no problem," Sawyer said as he added his coat to the pile on the hooks by the door. "Aria, do you eat pizza yet? Uncle Sawyer—"

"Is *not* feeding her Bellagios," Char said firmly. "She has some gluten-free meatless nuggets and potato wedges in the freezer."

"Are potato wedges the same as fries?" Sawyer asked, scooping Aria up and flying her around.

"No junk food, Sawyer. You know the rules." Char turned to me. "You'll be a good influence right?"

"Not sure." I shrugged. "Uncle Hollis is hungry, too. Maybe she eats sushi? That's healthy."

Char, Tucker, and Sawyer stared at me.

Tucker broke the silence at last. "Hollis, did you just make a *joke*?"

"What? I have been known to make them." I shrugged out of my coat and hung it on the rack. "And what good is a babysitter if he or she doesn't eat your best leftovers and fill the child with junk food?"

"We had the Murphy family for that growing up." Char laughed. "And now I've got *two* of them trying to corrupt my kid! And you're not helping!"

"We'd better get going," Tucker said before he clapped me on the shoulder. "It's wonderful to see you be...well, *you*."

"Don't kill Sawyer," Char said as she put on a velvet-lined cape.

"At least not in front of our kid," Tucker added. "And hide the body."

"*Tucker*." Char followed him out to their car.

Tucker popped his head back in thirty seconds later. "Save me the last piece of pizza."

"We aren't ordering pizza," I said once they were finally in the car and on their way for real.

"Just because you're the one—"

"Second—" Char and I might not share much else in common, but neither of us had the stomach for pizza.

"*Second* person on the planet who doesn't like pizza doesn't mean the rest of us have to suffer." Sawyer still had Aria under one arm, and she squealed as he tickled her.

"No pizza!" she said, laughing uproariously at her own decree. "No pizza!"

"Unca Holly is a terrible influence." Sawyer shook his head and set her down. "What do you want, sweet pea? Your nuggets?"

"Pancakes." She clapped and twirled. "Baby pancakes!"

And thus Sawyer and I ended up making silver dollar pancakes together on my mother's old griddle, the one where you had to jiggle the plug just right. I knew all the tricks for making little pancakes on it, having watched her, then later Char, through the years. The memory hurt a little less, pain muted by Aria's boundless enthusiasm. And Sawyer knew how to make the batter, adding cinnamon and pumpkin pie spice "for fun."

"Make a snowman," Aria ordered.

"Just pour your circles closer together," Sawyer said, looking up from the bacon he was supervising on the stove. He'd found a package, probably Tucker's, in the back of the freezer. "We can use blueberries for the buttons and eyes."

"I get!" Aria went to the fridge and got a box from the lowest shelf. The three of us didn't make a half-bad team.

Of course I was singing a different tune not fifteen minutes later when I was cleaning spilled syrup from the floor, dusting flour off my jeans, and extracting blueberries from my hair.

"Unca Holly need a bath!" Aria giggled as Sawyer carried her from the room in search of her own cleanup.

As they passed, Sawyer whispered in my ear, "I'm totally going to run you a bath at my place. Scrub you *all* up."

"Behave," I said, even as I blushed.

The next two hours were two of the longest of my life.

"Why won't she sleep?" I asked as she bounced on her toddler bed in the room that had been Char's as a kid. Her footed pajamas made her look like a little elf as she hopped from flat surface to flat surface in the room.

"I don't know." Sawyer slumped on the floor. He'd done the lion's share of the work—the cleanup and pajamas and the first five stories and the rocking in the rocking chair to see if that tired her out. I'd done the next five stories, and as scintillating as *Santa Duck* was, I didn't think I had another read-through in me.

"When she was little I'd walk the halls with her, but she's too big for that now," Sawyer said. "And it's too cold and late to load her in the stroller. That works, too."

"How does Mommy get you to sleep?" I asked. It still felt weird to think of my sister as *mommy*. To me she was still fifteen and bossy with a bad haircut and a love for trashy TV, not someone's *mother*.

"Sing!" Aria laughed as she kept jumping. We'd tried leaving the room, but she'd followed us out every time.

"Will you lie down if we sing?" Sawyer asked.

"Yes." She *finally* snuggled under her covers. "You sing."

Sawyer launched into a show tune from a musical he and Char were in back in high school. I started to creep from the room so that I could clean more downstairs, but Aria let out a bellow.

"Unca Holly stay, too!"

Sawyer sent me a look that said we were escaping together or not at all. He continued the song, which was a bit too upbeat for bedtime, but he'd always had a very pleasing baritone voice.

"Sing about Santa!" the tiny dictator ordered.

Switching gears, Sawyer launched into a Christmas carol, one the chorus had done at the concert the week before—and had it really only been a week? It felt like a lifetime from our kiss in the parking garage.

"Unca Holly sing, too!" Aria did *finally* sound a bit sleepy.

"Uncle Holly doesn't sing." I yawned. At least one of us was going to fall asleep before nine.

"Please." She looked over at us with beseeching eyes.

And so I did the only reasonable thing and joined in, which made Sawyer grin widely and lose his place in the song. He recovered nicely, though, and there we sat on the floor of that little pink room for the next twenty minutes, singing until we were hoarse. Something changed in me in those minutes as memories of singing the songs with my parents flooded me not with grief but with warmth. And a new memory was cemented into place, one almost more sweet and tender than I could bear. Out of view of Aria, Sawyer held my hand until we could finally creep out of the room and fall in a heap on the couch downstairs.

"Never having kids," Sawyer said as he flipped on the TV to some Christmas special.

"You don't have to convince me." I laughed. "I'm perfectly fine being the bachelor uncle for perpetuity."

"Hey, you don't have to be the *lonely* uncle." Sawyer tugged me closer. His eyes were wide and serious. If I weren't so damn tired, I'd tell him that I was perfectly happy being alone, thank you very much, but I was exhausted both from running after Aria and from a week of not enough sleep, and Sawyer was so warm as he wrapped his arms around me.

We both yawned at the exact same moment and I burrowed in closer to him. It said something that I knew his almost-asleep noises so well now that they were as soothing as a cup of herbal tea to my senses. The low notes of a pop star singing in the background and Sawyer's steady heartbeat up closer lulled me until I, too, drifted off.

The next thing I knew the door was creaking.

"Oh my God, they fell asleep *together*," Char said in a whisper that was anything but. "This is the most adorable thing ever."

"You take a picture and they'll both kill you," Tucker said sharply, and at the mention of a picture, my body came back online and I jerked upright.

"You're home?" I slid away from Sawyer, who was also waking up and stretching. I carefully didn't look over at him as I adjusted my sleep-wrinkled clothes.

"Yes, and the concert was lovely." Char settled into one of the side chairs. "You know, I've always said you guys would make the *cutest* couple."

"Char. Leave them alone," Tucker said before I could object. "Aria probably just ran them ragged."

"She was a handful." I seized that excuse like it was a life preserver tossed out to me in the churning river that my life had suddenly become.

"Very," Sawyer added. "I'm not sure when I fell asleep, but it was probably because she had us singing endless Christmas carols."

"Wait. 'Us'? Hollis sang?" Char laughed.

"I don't know why everyone seems to think I'm some bitter character in a holiday drama." I stood and got my coat off the rack.

"The last few years you've been the epitome of Scrooge," Char said. "But you singing carols…come on, Sawyer, what *have* you done to my brother?"

"Nothing." Sawyer's voice was strained and he looked like he was suppressing a smile. He'd always had the *worst* poker face.

"Except give me a ride home," I added sharply. We needed to get out of there fast.

"Yeah, we should get going." Sawyer finally stood and got his jacket. That didn't stop Char from giving us both a knowing smile. Even Tucker was looking at us strangely.

"You know, it would totally be the coolest thing—"

"Never happening." I cut off whatever twin fantasies she'd been about to spin and headed for the door, hoping Sawyer would follow. I needed out of there quick.

* * * *

"You can take me home." I shivered against the bite of the night air, waiting for his car to warm up as he pulled away from Char and Tucker's house.

"What? No way." Sawyer turned in the direction of his apartment, not mine back on Alberta. "I get that you're embarrassed that Char and Tucker found us asleep, but it's not like they found us fucking—"

"Thank God." The mere thought of that gave me hives.

"I don't see what the problem is." Sawyer shrugged. He wasn't shivering at all. "They'll probably guess next week at Christmas, and if not then, then soon. I can't keep my hands off you and you keep going all indignant and looking guilty every other minute."

"I do not. You're the one with no poker face." I ignored the part about not keeping his hands off me and definitely ignored the warm flush his words gave me.

"How about we just tell everyone at Christmas?" Sawyer made this sound like the most reasonable suggestion ever, with a heavy dose of why-don't-we-get-a-puppy level enthusiasm.

I made a strangled sound as he pulled into his apartment's parking lot behind the building. True to his word, he did have festive lights hanging from his balconies, but to me they looked more like spotlights waiting to uncover my personal failings. I *wished* I could share his unbridled enthusiasm for this terrible idea.

"You can't be serious."

"Why?" Sawyer got out of the car, which left me no choice but to follow him up the stairs to his place.

However, I waited until we were in the apartment to answer. Last thing I needed was more airing of our dirty laundry. "I'm not going to Christmas."

"Yes, you are." Sawyer's face wrinkled up, his eyes narrowing. "I've won the bet right? You sang Christmas songs tonight. You've…softened to the season. I can tell. Even Tucker and Char could see that you're…different."

It wasn't Christmas that had turned me soft and gooey—it was *him*. He was the one who had shown me what I'd lost. If I did have holiday feelings that weren't morose, he was the one who had given them back to me. I needed him—needed his joy for the season, his prodding and cajoling and good humor. Needing him to get through this month was beyond foolish. Where would I be next year, when he moved on and I was alone once again with my grief? And that, even more than some newfound appreciation for the season, made terror fill my veins. My hands shook and I shoved them in my coat pockets so he wouldn't see.

"I haven't changed. And even if I was to show up, one does not usually announce casual…*liaisons* to one's *family*."

"Oh come on. You know that's not what this is." Sawyer kicked off his shoes, sending them skittering in opposite directions. "We're…*something*. Something that apparently scares you, but we're something."

"I'm not afraid," I lied. "But what do you want? To go to Char and Tucker and say, 'Hey, I've got *something* with Hollis. Not sure what, but it's something.'" I imitated his deeper voice.

"Yes, okay, *yes*. Because it is *something*. Something real. And you know that. And letting people know that we're seeing each other or boyfriends or however you want to put it, seems to make a lot more sense than skulking around, acting like there's something to be ashamed of."

"We are not boyfriends." My voice shook. "I don't do boyfriends. Never have."

"Yeah, well, maybe you should start."

"You're one to talk—you're the king of casual. Maybe you call them boyfriends, but we both know they never stick around long enough to justify the label."

Sawyer recoiled as if I'd punched him. I regretted my harsh words almost instantly. I started toward him, but he held up a hand.

"Look, I'm sorry that that guy—the kink master, whatever his name was—broke your heart. But I'm serious about us having something. And I've told you, I'm not nearly the manwhore you seem to think I am."

"He didn't break my heart," I said firmly. "And I've never once called you that."

"You didn't have to. But Hols, it's clear you think I'm a flake when it comes to stuff like a relationship. Is that why you can't trust me when I tell you I want something real with you? Tell you that we already *have* something real?" Sawyer sounded so hurt that I had to look away. I wanted to believe him....I just couldn't.

"You *think* you're serious." I tried to soften my voice. "But you're not. This is just a lark, a little preholiday diversion—"

"I'm already making plans for January," he shot back. "That class? What more do I need to do to show you that this isn't just a fuck for me?"

"Your track record—"

"Seriously? You're going to hold me to who I was fifteen years ago? I'm willing to believe that you're no longer a judgmental introvert—"

"Sawyer, I have *always* been a judgmental introvert, as you put it. I've never pretended to be anything less."

He grabbed me then, kissing me fiercely. "You're scared, Hols. And I get it, but you've been scared of what's between us for *years*, and I'm done waiting for you to come to your senses. And I'm not going to keep sneaking around when I want to celebrate that we're *finally* doing this thing, and it feels so damn right—"

"Don't you get it?" My voice broke. "That's the last thing I want. The celebrating. The people saying *I told you so* and *isn't it so cute* and *oh, how perfect* and *here, let me get a picture*. Other people's plans for us snowballing. Being noticed. I want *privacy* for my feelings. How I feel about you isn't something I want to go wave around."

"Wow. Okay, then." Hollis stepped back.

"Call me an introverted asshole if you must, but Sawyer, I can't be what you want here. I just can't."

"Can you at least come to Christmas? I promised Char—"

"What? Has this whole month been a promise to my *sister*?" My chest felt torn open. "You wonder why I can't take you seriously? Sawyer, the whole world is just one big bet to you. You didn't really care about me. You just wanted to prove you could get me to show for Christmas and you weren't above using sex to do that—"

"What? No, Hols. That's not how it went down at all." Sawyer's voice was sharp. "I just meant that even if you can't...be with me, I just don't want you alone for the holidays. If we can't be friends, Hols, at least let us be family."

"Family is the last thing I want right now," I said sharply. "And I *like* being alone. You say you want to be with me, but all you really want to do is to change me into the guy you think I should have been all along."

"You'd be happier, that's for sure," Sawyer muttered. "And we wouldn't have spent *years* in this stupid limbo."

"Allow me to cast you free, then." I strode to the door, trying hard not to show how much his admission shook me. I'd had no idea—*none*—that he'd been as twisted up as me. I simply couldn't process that thought and all it meant right then. "No more limbo. No more ambiguity. We simply wouldn't work as a relationship. I can't be what you need—what you *deserve*." My voice broke on that last bit and I headed to the door before my emotions could betray me even more.

I headed out of the apartment and down the steps, but a shoeless Sawyer headed after me. "Hols. Wait. Let's talk some more—"

"No, thank you." My back muscles were so rigid from trying to keep my voice even that it was a wonder the drizzle coming down didn't bounce off me.

"At least let me drive you home."

"I need the walk." I headed across the parking lot.

"Hols." Sawyer started after me, but he must have hit a puddle at the end of the stairs. "Fuck. Hell. It's cold. *Hollis*."

I knew if I turned around, he'd see me cry, and I couldn't do that. I hunkered down deep in my coat and started the long, cold, wet slog home.

Chapter 13

I made it home, wool coat soaked and me chilled through. I cranked the tub as hot as I could stand, started it filling while I stripped, and poured myself a Scotch to sip in the bath.

I'll scrub you all over. Sawyer's sexy tease from earlier in the evening haunted me as I slid into the water. How had things gone so poorly so fast? The Scotch burned my throat as I took a thoughtful sip. Logic said that this was for the best—there never had been any future in this dalliance with Sawyer—but logic wasn't what had my sinuses clogged at the thought of the sort of nightcap I was supposed to be having right then with Sawyer.

Damn it. Just one more night…

And didn't I of all people know just how faulty that dinosaur prayer was? *Just a little more time, Lord, just a little more time.*

More time with my parents.

More time with Aria as a baby before she went and turned into a little person on us.

More time with Sawyer and Tucker and Char as kids before things went and got all complicated.

In my head Sawyer's voice went from the squawky fifteen-year-old's voice to the excited college guy drunk dialing me to the deep timbre of an adult.

"So I kissed a guy, Hollis, and it was amazing…"

"Char! Char! Hollis! It finally happened!"

"I think Char likes Tucker. And not just as friends."

"Tucker's going to pop the question this weekend. He talked to your dad and everything."

"Are you coming home for the wedding, Hollis? What time does your flight get in?"

"So neither of us have dates this weekend. We should get drunk together."
"Dance with me. I dare you."

He'd said he'd changed, like I didn't know that—I'd blinked and here we all were, staring down thirty, the kid who used to copy my chemistry notes because he'd been out late necking with Jimmy Ingles was in my bed and my life all twisted up. I *knew* he'd changed. I sipped deeply of the Scotch and it was my own voice that I heard next.

"I think I might...like guys, Char. Don't tell anyone."
"Char. Stop telling me about Sawyer's sex life."
"Stay, Yuto. Don't take the New York job. Stay while I finish school."
"What do you mean, we're not a couple? Yuto, I don't understand."
"Sure, Sawyer, you can pick me up for the wedding."
"I'll take more champagne."

I wasn't like Sawyer, who had plunged into his sexuality with both feet, embracing who he was loudly and openly. I didn't do anything loudly. Never had. I was the one tentatively dipping my toes in the shallow end of the social pool while the three of them frolicked in the deep end. I was the weird one home ironing and reading Proust while Sawyer was doing God knew what with the Jimmy Ingleses of the world. I was the one who lived for Sawyer's updates on his life, but who could never see a way to join that life—and I still couldn't.

Sawyer said I couldn't see he'd changed, couldn't trust that, and maybe he was right. But the problem was that *I* hadn't changed—the world had changed around me, Sawyer was becoming a responsible adult, Tucker and Char becoming parents, but I was still who I'd always been, and who I'd always been wasn't enough for Sawyer, no matter how much he'd changed, no matter if he wasn't the same guy who flitted from interest to interest. I was still me. And damned if that didn't *hurt.*

* * * *

I didn't sleep much the next few days. I'd been ripped loose from an essential mooring in my life, similar to the way I'd felt after my parents died. And like then, I curled up on my couch to watch *Lord of the Rings* over and over in the dark hours of the night when sleep wouldn't come. And every single time I teared up when Gandalf spoke of time and how fleeting and precious it is. And in *The Fellowship of the Ring*, Arwen's impassioned plea to Aragorn made my chest feel flayed by feelings, and still I watched, both numb and drowning in feelings.

My occasional clerk had asked for more hours the week of Christmas, trying to pay off some presents, so Christmas Eve I found myself at loose ends, craving a gingerbread latte and not sure I could stomach one without Sawyer there to tease me while I drank it. At People's Cup there was a line anyway, so I kept walking. I found myself in front of Iplik, the yarn store, hypnotized by a new scarf in the window. This one was an ethereal white, probably some sort of mohair blend, and looked like a cloud adorning the bust in the window. The subtle openness to the texture only called to me more. It was long and billowy and seemed like the perfect antidote to the permanent chill I seemed to walk around in lately.

And I was having trouble wearing my favorite scarves without remembering Sawyer unwinding them, without remembering his lips on my neck, and the way he'd traced the fading marks with his fingers. I'd never be able to look at a scarf without feeling an erotic charge again.

In a rarity, Ev was working the counter. "Oh, Hollis, I am just about to close up for the afternoon, but please, how can I help you?"

"I want the scarf in the window," I said.

"I'm sorry. I just sold that this morning. The buyer hasn't stopped by for it yet." I must have looked utterly crushed because Ev came out from behind the counter and took my arm. "Please, let me show you a few other samples that came in. There's an alpaca you'd love."

"That's okay." I *was* crushed, no two ways about it. I'd wanted something, some little piece of this week to go my way. The other scarves he showed me were nice, but they didn't call to me the same way.

"Do you have holiday plans?" Ev asked as we walked around the store with him pointing out various sample garments he thought I might be interested in.

"Oh, just the usual." I'd learned several years ago to never say no to that question. "You and Brady have big plans for the kids?"

Ev and Brady were raising Brady's siblings, and I imagined their living room would be even louder than Char's come tomorrow morning. "Of course." Ev laughed. "We overspent as usual, but they grow so fast, it almost doesn't seem like enough."

"I know what you mean," I said, thinking of my gift for Aria.

"It is bittersweet," Ev mused. "Not knowing how many more Christmases you have left."

I knew he meant how long kids stayed children, but his words burrowed deep into my soul, lingering far after I'd bought the indigo alpaca number and headed on my way. *You don't know how many more Christmases you have left.*

Deep in my thoughts, I settled at one of the cold metal tables out front of People's Cup. Hadn't I thought I'd be celebrating our quiet little Christmases with my parents forever? A memory crept in: us enjoying some tea that weekend, them making plans for changing things a bit to accommodate Tucker and Char now having to do two holidays.

"You should go to the Murphys, too," Mom had said. "You know you're invited. And Sawyer will be there."

For the first time I wondered if she'd known. If the whole *world* but me had known what a hopeless crush I'd had for *decades*. Then my memory shifted and I was ten or eleven, my father trying to talk me into trying a harder ski run for the first time. I'd argued that I was much less likely to fall on the bunny slope.

"Some risks are worth it, Hollis. You'll see someday."

But I hadn't, not really. I'd grown from a risk-adverse kid to a risk-abhorring adult. My business was my big risk of the decade and even then, I had made sure I had a safety net. Risk meant falling and falling meant people noticing. People laughing. People *gossiping*.

"Are you really so afraid of a little gossip, Hollis?" I heard my mother's voice, plain as day in my ear, so startling that I actually glanced around. Inside the People's Cup, Brady was finishing up his shift, already looking up the street toward Iplik. Like me, he'd lost his parents too young, but he'd fearlessly crafted a life for himself after tragedy.

Live, Hollis, the wind seemed to whistle at me. This wasn't the life my parents would have wanted for me. They'd want me to go to Char's tonight, go to the Murphy family tomorrow. They'd want me to do the hard thing, to expand my comfort zone. If she'd known how little time she had, would my mother have come out and confronted me about Sawyer? It had been there in her eyes that day and I was only now seeing it.

They'd want me to be happy. I knew that deep down. They'd want me to stop punishing myself. The problem was that before Sawyer loped back into my life I hadn't seen a way past the mountain of grief and guilt. And now I could see past, could see what happiness looked like, what it felt like to have memories comfort instead of stab.

You don't know how many more Christmases you have left. Not this year, but maybe next, Sawyer would move on. There would be someone new at his family's gathering, someone folded up into the family for years to come. Was I really so worried about Sawyer's staying power? Or was it more that I was invested in the Sawyer who couldn't settle down? Because he would. I knew that in my bones, even if I didn't want to admit it.

He'd find some adventurous man to bring home, someone who let him bring out the side that only I had uncovered. He'd string lights with someone else, bring them lattes, bask in their gratitude and affection. He'd take them to the kink workshops that caught his fancy. He wouldn't be chasing after the prickly shopkeeper forever. He'd find someone who loved the season, someone who admired his window without caustic wit. Someone worthy of him and his boundless enthusiasm and his limitless heart.

He'd said he couldn't live in the limbo we'd been in for years, and I'd tried, I'd really tried to find a part of me that could be happy for him moving on. He was a lovable guy. He *deserved* love, deep and true. He deserved not to be bound up in the weird dance we'd done for years. After all, it was me who liked having my hands tied, not him.

We overspent, but it doesn't feel like enough, Ev had said, and I understood some of his urgency. This was my Christmas. It was the one Sawyer had tried to give to *me*. Not the faceless man who would get him forever but *me*. This was the last Christmas before the twins came, before things changed yet again. Who knew, with the growing family, maybe even Char would stop trying so hard. Maybe I'd finally get the quietly forgettable holiday I'd wanted so badly.

Somewhere my mother and father frowned. *You don't have to live life on the bunny slope, Hollis.*

Down the street, Ev was greeting Brady now, a hug in the middle of the sidewalk, before they left, arm in arm to do whatever joyful things one did on Christmas Eve with a partner in tow. What would that be like?

I'd focused so much on what I didn't like—the crowds, the noise, the huge gatherings, the endless questions and prodding—that I'd never once visualized a moment like Ev and Brady's quiet companionship heading off to handle the holiday together. And suddenly, fiercely, I wanted that. I didn't want Sawyer having those quiet moments with someone else, selfish though it was of me. I didn't want someday to look down the street and see him greeting a partner.

I'd rejected what Sawyer had tried to give me, but maybe, just maybe, it wasn't too late. Maybe we could still have this Christmas. Maybe we could have *all* the holidays, if only I could take a risk and head down the steep slope of uncertainty.

Chapter 14

I had found some courage, but Lloyd Center Mall on Christmas Eve remained a special kind of torture. Even the buses were packed. Still, though, I found what I wanted. Shopping bags bulging, I paused on the second floor right above the ice skating rink. Holiday music blared and coffee and cinnamon pastries scented the chilly air. The ice skating rink was full of families and couples. I was about to look away when I spotted two teen guys skating together, hand in hand. The taller, blonder one pulled the shorter guy into a spin and they both laughed. They had that young love glow to them—the sort of way of looking at each other that you knew they might not make it out of the parking garage before they were necking....

Don't kiss Jimmy Ingles, Sawyer. Kiss me instead. How different might my life have been if I'd found my courage back then? Or if I'd followed him up to his hotel room at the wedding? How much time had I frittered away because I couldn't get out of my own way? All I'd known was that Char was laughing and I'd felt so *visible.* And I'd run. As usual.

When I got back to my apartment I did something I hadn't done in three years, probably more, and voluntarily turned on a holiday movie. *White Christmas* was always Mom's favorite, but while I felt nostalgic watching it, I didn't feel the crushing weight of grief I would have even a few weeks ago. And when "Sisters" came on, I laughed out loud, because there had *always* been a sister between me and my mister.

I was still laughing, in fact, when the door buzzed. Damn it. If Char had sent Tucker to fetch me for Christmas Eve, I was going to—

"Sawyer?" I opened the door to find Sawyer standing outside my condo, holding the world's tiniest Christmas tree, a can of paint, and a little bag.

"Hollis? You okay?" Sawyer's forehead creased as I held the door for him to enter. "You alone?"

"Why wouldn't I be?"

"You were...*laughing*, and is that *White Christmas* on? Hols, have you been drinking?"

"I'm having some wine." I gestured to my glass next to a finished stack of presents.

"You're wrapping..." Sawyer's eyes narrowed and then the widest grin split his face. "You're coming tomorrow?"

I nodded, not sure I could speak in the face of that much joy.

"Hollis." The look of wonder on Sawyer's face as he crossed to me was something I'd remember my whole life. "You were going to *come*."

"I was going to try." *For you.* I had to pinch the bridge of my nose to keep my eyes from stinging. "What are you doing here? You always spend Christmas Eve with your family—services with your dad and helping your mom with the food for tomorrow. Won't they miss you?"

"They'll survive without me." Sawyer set down his things. "I brought you a tree."

"I see." I rescued the poor spindly thing before its little pot could tip over, put it by my stack of gifts for tomorrow. "And the paint?"

"Proper Gray. You won the bet. I figured we could get a good start tonight, finish it up tomorrow so it'll be ready for customers with your big after-holidays sale."

"I didn't mean you had to give up your Christmas!" *Why are you really here, Sawyer?* was what I most wanted to ask but couldn't.

"I'm not. I'm bringing it to *you*." Sawyer took another step toward me, all big eyes and open hands. "I've been doing a lot of thinking, and you were right."

"I was?"

He nodded. "You said that I wanted to turn you into something you're not. This whole month I just wanted to give you the kind of holiday *I* love, wanted you to open up and see how much fun it could be, but I forgot to consider what *you'd* like, who *you* are."

"It was fun," I whispered. "More than I let on. But you're right—I'm not, I can't be like you and Char. I'm not wired all social."

"I know." Sawyer stroked my jaw. "I know. And so I'm bringing you a quiet little Christmas, because that's what you deserve. I thought we'd paint a bit, then walk back here and scare up some lights for scrawny and maybe roll out the cookie dough I brought. Figured maybe I could talk you into a funny Christmas movie, but you're already on that—" He gestured at the screen. "I've got eggnog in the bag, too. Maybe we'll crack open your liquor cabinet, go a little crazy."

"That sounds...lovely." I leaned into his touch, much the same way Benedict leaned into mine when I'd ignored him too long. "But I don't want you to give up your family Christmas for me. All your traditions —"

"Are meaningless without you. That's what I was trying to say the other night and doing a horrible job at. I love you, Hollis." He said it so easily, so confidently, that I inhaled sharply, oxygen in short supply.

"You do? But why? I'm the introverted asshole, remember?" My voice was far shakier than I would have liked.

"Yeah, but you're *my* introvert. And you're not an asshole. See, that's what I've been thinking about a lot—why you make me so crazy. And I think it's because you're always so...selective. You're choosy about your clothes and your books and your pens and your food. And for years now, I've just wanted you to choose *me*."

"I do," I managed to choke out. "And I was coming for you. I was. I had a whole plan—"

"You taking on all the Murphys for me?"

"I wanted you to win," I whispered, my voice thinner than an extrafine line, the barest trail of sound. "I wanted to see your face when you won."

"This isn't a game." Sawyer cupped my face with both hands. "It never was."

"But it was, see. I was so afraid of losing—of proving every gossip who ever bet on us right, on letting you win the bets—that I forgot to see what I was gaining, too." I couldn't look him in the eye for the next part, but he wouldn't let me look away so I shut my eyes. "I let myself call you a rival for so long, let that be my truth, when in fact..." I trailed off, my voice failing me.

"In fact?" Sawyer's voice sounded like he scarcely dared to hope.

"You're my best friend."

"Me? Not Char? Not Tucker?"

"I never looked forward to their emails and calls when I was at college like I did yours. Seeing him never...lit me up the way you do."

"I light you up?"

I nodded and his lips claimed mine. I met him eagerly, trying to tell him with my mouth the words I couldn't seem to push out of my throat, not yet. *I love you. I've loved you since the moment you plunked yourself down next to me in drama class freshman year. I loved you drunk dialing and I loved your dares. I loved you so much that I built a wall around those feelings, hoping they could hurt me, hoping I could hide them. But I love that you smashed through those walls. I love that you didn't give up on me.*

I pressed myself against him, desperate for more of him, desperate to let him know how much he meant to me. We ended up on my couch, a frantic heap of mouths and searching hands and straining bodies. Gone was my usual fetish for delay—every cell screamed now, now, now. And when Sawyer's hand found my cock I was climaxing within three heady pulls. I trembled and shook as I tried to reciprocate and Sawyer was equally hurried, mouth latching onto my neck as he came all over my fist with a shout.

"Hi," Sawyer said as we both floated back to earth. "That was...*wow.*"

"Yeah."

"So...painting?" He grinned at me and I grinned back, facial muscles straining at the unfamiliar joy splitting my face in two.

* * * *

"You have paint on your nose." Sawyer laughed, which jostled me because we were pressed so close together and made me spill a bit of my Scotch. My tub was huge—a big selling point when I bought the condo—but even so, two tall guys in it was a very tight fit. Not that I was complaining. Being squished by Sawyer was fast becoming one of my favorite things.

Sawyer had set his phone up with my speakers to stream his holiday playlist, which gently filtered in through the open bathroom door. I had a well-earned Scotch after all the painting prep while he had a beer we'd picked up with pizza for him and a salad for me on the walk back here. Bubbles danced across the surface of the steaming water.

"This is my favorite Christmas Eve ever," I whispered, more than half to myself.

"Mine too." Sawyer laughed.

"I *am* coming with you tomorrow," I said, my voice stronger now than it had been earlier.

"You don't have to." Sawyer licked my neck and made it hard to think.

"I want to." I took a deep breath. "If we're going to do this thing—"

"We *are*." Sawyer pulled me even tighter against him, making the water slosh.

"Then compromise is important. I can handle a short visit with the family—"

"If it helps, I'll stay right with you. Won't leave you to the gossip hounds or uncomfortable small talk."

"Please." I wasn't above asking for the fortification.

"And we can leave as soon as the presents are done—before even, if you've had enough."

"You're pretty wonderful, you know that?" I leaned back to kiss him, long and slow. "Why do you put up with me?"

"Hmmm." For once Sawyer didn't make a quick joke. "I think it's because no one my whole life has ever *listened* like you do. Everyone else is always *oh that's Sawyer just joking around* or *Sawyer's the funny one*, but you've always listened. Always cared. You...*think* about what I say. And even when you don't agree, you *hear* me like no one else does."

"I made you wait," I said ruefully, hand trailing through the sudsy water.

"I wasn't ready before. I thought I was at the wedding, but I was still trying too hard to make you something you're not. And you deserve something serious—I wasn't quite ready."

"I'm not sure I do," I whispered, revealing the deepest of my fears. "I'm too—"

"You're perfect." Sawyer kissed me soundly. "And you're like...a swan."

"A swan?" I snorted.

"Hey, those fuckers can be *mean*. I once got chased by one. But they say they mate for life. And they're deeply loyal to their little families. And pretty sweet to look at, too." He gave me another, longer kiss. He pulled away, blinking. "Does Bunny always watch you take a bath?"

"*Benedict*." I looked over to find the cat perched on the toilet lid. He did seem rather...amused by us, head tilted to one side.

"I don't know, man—I really want to touch you right now, but I'm worried about getting my eyes scratched out."

"*Bunny*. Scram." I tossed a sprinkle of water in his direction, which sent him fleeing from the room.

"There. Touch away." Setting my drink aside, I leaned back, luxuriating in the hard press of his muscles behind me. I expected Sawyer to go straight for my cock, but instead he rubbed my neck and shoulders, big soapy hands massaging me until I was limp against him. He was anything but limp, though. I could feel him hard against the small of my back. Eventually his hands dipped to toy with my nipples.

I made a noise that was half whine, half moan.

"You're so responsive you make me wish nipple clamps were one of your presents." Sawyer laughed darkly. "But my fingers are more fun."

He tweaked and pinched until my ragged moans filled the small space.

"I know you're all about the waiting, but tonight you're *mine*, and I want to play with you like this." His hand snaked down lower, over my belly to my cock, which bobbed below the surface of the water. "Want to make you come."

"We're going to need a shower after our bath," I said breathlessly.

"That's the whole plan." He started to stroke in earnest now, one hand on my nipple, one on my cock, both holding me tight against him. I leaned my head back so that we could kiss while he worked me. Deliciously luxurious sensations swept over me. It was heady being the center of all his attention like this. He was turned on for sure, but he didn't seem all that close to orgasm himself. He was doing this for me and that made all my muscles hum for him.

I arched up to meet his stroke, but his hands and arms kept me locked in place. "No, let me. Just let it come," he whispered. "I've got you."

"Yes." I gave myself over to the sensations, let him toy with me, speeding up and slowing down as he wished until finally I felt my body start to tense. "Right there. Oh fuck. Right there."

"Yeah, I've got you. Come now." His fingers pinched my nipple right as his grip tightened on my cock, stroking faster now.

"Sawyer. God. Sawyer." I came in a series of full-body shudders. "Love you."

"Love you, too, babe." Sawyer laughed. "We're going to work on you saying that when you're not drunk on sex, though, okay?"

"It's a deal." Giddy laughter swept through me, too.

"Water's getting cold. Shower now?" He helped me stand up. I set the tub draining while Sawyer got the shower turned on. He was still erect and he leered at me as I joined him.

"What would you like?" I looped my arms around his neck, pressing a kiss to his lips before sinking to my knees in the tiled shower stall.

"That. That's pretty much it." Sawyer's chuckle seemed to bounce off the glass shower door. "But you don't have to."

"I want to." I wasn't entirely unfamiliar with the appeal of this act. It wasn't my absolute favorite, but there were times like right then when it was what I most wanted to be doing. I licked all around his crown, making him gasp.

"Only thing hotter is if we'd tied your hands first." Sawyer moaned, his head falling back to rest on the shower wall.

"Life goals," I said right before I swallowed him as far as I could. I worked the base of his shaft with my fist, keeping him from going too deep too fast.

His breath hitched as I sped up my mouth and hand. "Hols...put your hands behind your back." There was a heavy dose of *please* in Sawyer's command.

Still, though, it took me a second to comply. This was a new level of trust; trusting that he wouldn't go too deep and choke me, giving up this last piece of control to him. Slowly I let go of his shaft and clasped my hands behind my back. From his swift intake, I could tell he liked this very much. And I needn't have worried—his hand replaced mine at the base of his cock, controlling the depth of his thrusts. His other hand cradled my face. Never had I surrendered like this.

"Can I—fuck, I want to come on you. Keep your hands like that. Fuck." I could tell by the salty tang against my tongue that he was close.

"Do it." I closed my eyes and gave myself over to the sensations of being used like this by Sawyer. My cock gave an ambitious throb, but this was a different sort of pleasure—a diffuse one that made my whole body thrum with joy.

"Here it comes." Sawyer pulled out of my mouth. *Thwap. Thwap.* His hand made obscene noises as he jerked himself the rest of the way there.

"Oh fuck. Hols. You look…so sexy. Fuck." The first warm spurt hit my shoulders, the rest my neck and chest.

"Hols…" Sawyer hauled me to my feet, pressing his front to my back. "You're incredible."

I was entirely certain he'd had far better blow jobs, but I basked in the praise nonetheless. He soaped me up, washing away the last of his come.

"I love you." He lightly bit my ear.

"What's this? I thought you just said not to trust after-sex declarations?"

"How about you tell me again anyway?" He spun me around so he could look me in the eye.

"I love you." I met his gaze, tried to tell him with my eyes that this wasn't just a sex thing for me.

"Love you, too, and I bet it's after midnight now. Merry Christmas."

"This really is the best Christmas Eve ever." I pulled him down for a kiss.

Chapter 15

Christmas morning Sawyer brought me tea in bed before getting back under the covers with me. He had his phone in hand and was reading a text.

"See? Char sent a picture of their Christmas morning. Wrapping paper everywhere." He held out the phone so I, too, could see pure, unadulterated two-year-old joy. A second pic was a group shot of a tired Tucker, grinning Aria, and squashed-in Char. *My family.* My chest loosened, fewer of the thoughts of what we were missing creeping in. This was what I had now and it was more than enough.

"And this one's from my mom. I didn't tell her where I was last night— *promise*—just that I couldn't come over. She sent a pic of all the food in the oven." His mom had used some sort of app that let her add a holiday border to the picture.

A little idea crept into my head. "Hey, give me your phone for a second?"

"Sure." He let me take it and I flipped it to the camera app.

"Come here." I gestured. "I want a selfie."

"You, Hollis Alcott, want a selfie?" His eyes looked ready to spring from his head. "I didn't even know you knew that word."

"Yes, well, it seems the whole world is documenting their Christmas morning and I want to as well. Smile."

He leaned in and I took a picture of our faces. My smile looked a bit unused. Like new sneakers or stiff jeans, it was going to take a bit before it eased up. But Sawyer's joyful face was more than worth the effort to capture the memory of our first holiday.

"Want me to show you how to add a border?" Sawyer offered.

"No. I think it's perfect just like this," I said. Then I took a deep breath so that I could say the next part really fast. "And-send-it-to-Char-and-your-mom."

Sawyer blinked. "Seriously?"

"Just say *Merry Christmas from us* or something." My hand shook. "But this way they'll know before we head over for dinner and they can get their squealing out of the way before we arrive." *Hopefully.*

"I really am okay with easing into this." Sawyer rubbed my shoulder. "I shouldn't have pressured you about that. We can just wait and let them guess—"

"That's far *more* gossip." I shuddered. "No, *you* were right. We shouldn't slink around. We should celebrate this."

"I do." He gave me a quick kiss, then returned his attention to his phone. "Okay, sending in three-two—"

"Oh, just hit Send already, drama queen."

"Okay, sent."

And predictably, twenty seconds later, Sawyer's phone—and mine—started blowing up with messages from the family.

"How about we shut the phones off and do our presents?" Sawyer suggested. "They'll still be flipping out later, I'm sure. And you're going to need one of your presents before we head over there."

"Now I'm intrigued." I wrapped myself in the blanket and carried my tea into the living area. This really was the nicest of Christmas mornings—slow, sleepy sex, tea in bed, and now gifts.

"I have one for you, too." I dug the box out from the pile of gifts for Aria, Char and Tucker, and Sawyer's parents.

"Hey, Hols, look out the window!" Sawyer motioned. "Snow."

"A dusting," I corrected. It wasn't a Christmas blizzard, not even close. But by Portland standards it was absolutely the rare "white" Christmas.

"This one first." Sawyer handed me a flat box. I recognized the wrapping job.

"Iplik?" I asked.

"Open it and see." Sawyer bounced a bit from his seat on the couch.

"Oh my." I opened it to reveal the scarf that had so called to me. White and billowy, it felt even nicer against my skin than I'd imagined.

"I kind of did a number on your neck again." Sawyer gave me a sheepish smile. "Thought you could use more camouflage."

"Always." I gave him a quick kiss before he was shoving the other present at me.

"And this one is for us for tonight."

"After the family gathering?"

"Yup." He grinned. "It can be our reward."

I opened the large box, expecting to find some sort of bondage gear, but instead laughed out loud. "*Lord of the Rings* Legos? The Tower of Orthanc? Really?"

"I figured we could build it together tonight."

"We could." I looked over at my Tolkien shelf.

"I know it was kind of your thing with your dad, but I thought maybe it could be our thing, too. A new tradition of building something together on Christmas evening."

"We are building something." I leaned in and kissed him, and it was a while before we came back up for air and I handed him his present. "I'm feeling a bit guilty now because your gift isn't quite as—"

"Let me open it first." He opened the box to reveal a neat row of bow ties. "Ties!"

"I know it's kind of a cliché gift, but…" I struggled to explain what had drawn me to this gift for him. "You said you were changing. Trying new things. And this is me believing you."

"Thank you." He kissed me tenderly and the paper I'd tucked in among the ties fluttered to the floor. He picked it up and opened it. "And a receipt for the shibari workshop?"

"I believe you when you say this isn't a whim for you, too." I pulled him close.

"You're my last, best hobby, Hols. I promise." He grinned down at the paper and never had I so anticipated a January in Portland.

* * * *

That anticipation carried me through the family gathering—and the flood of *Finally! You guys! Finally!* jokes and comments. Sawyer hadn't been lying when he said they'd still be flipping out. But I endured, with more good humor than I'd thought. Having Sawyer right next to me helped. We'd baked Mother's spice cake together—Bundt pan and all—before heading over, and I nibbled on that as we watched the kids open their gifts. It wasn't exactly my mom's cake, and I'd miss them both forever, but this was, as Sawyer put it, *something.* Something real. Something enduring. Something I'd almost let slip away.

Aria laughed at something Sawyer said and her crinkled-up eyes looked so much like Mom's that my breath caught.

"You know who you look like?" I said, scooping her up. "Your grandma Rose. She would have loved you."

"I wuv you." She kissed my nose. Sawyer fed her bits of cake and I told her about the recipe. She was much too little, but someday she'd be old enough for my stories about them, for me to bring my memories to life, and I was finally ready to share, to open myself up instead of bottling it all inside.

Eventually, Sawyer's dad made his way to the piano, and his mom herded up all the little ones to sing along to some carols. Char and Sawyer joined in first of course, but I was surprised to find myself humming along with the second song, and by the third, I'd softly joined in.

Sawyer squeezed my hand as across the room Char gave me a knowing look. Sawyer *had* won the bet after all—he'd given me reason to look forward to this season again. Reason to look forward to *all* the seasons with him by my side.

ONE YEAR LATER

"Come on, Uncle Holly!" Aria squealed from atop Sawyer's shoulders as we pushed through the moderate weeknight crowd at ZooLights. We'd timed our excursion well, but it still felt like half of Portland had turned out for the crisp, clear night without a trace of rain.

"Is your tree up?" Char asked. She trailed behind us, waiting for Tucker, who was pushing the double stroller with the sleeping twins in it.

"Yup. We went down to Sleighbells to cut our tree and get our first ornaments last weekend," Sawyer said.

"You cut a tree?" Char bumped my shoulder.

"*Sawyer* cut a tree. I drank cocoa and plotted how to keep the cat off the tree."

"We put baby gates all around ours," Tucker said. "You could try that."

I shuddered at the idea of the plastic monstrosities that had been all over Char's house ever since the twins had started crawling, taking over our nice, clean condo. We both loved being uncles, we really did, but we were in solemn agreement that Char and Tucker were doing all the child-rearing for this next generation.

"Has the cat forgiven you for moving in yet, Sawyer?" Tucker asked.

"I think so," Sawyer said cautiously. "He hasn't puked in my shoe for two weeks now, but he still watches me while I shower like he's plotting my doom."

"He likes you," I said loyally. As I kept telling Sawyer, the fact that he regularly practiced his shibari on me and the cat never once jumped to defend me was proof enough that he wasn't *that* upset with Sawyer's new presence in our home.

And it truly was a home now. A tree in the front window, graphic novels on the shelves next to my Tolkien collection, baked goods in my kitchen as Sawyer's *other* classes yielded tasty dividends, and a warm man in my bed every night.

"Can we see the windows 'gain tomorrow?" Aria asked. The neighborhood business association had held its contest again this year, and I supposed they were rotating the prizes through the different stores because somehow Sawyer didn't win despite having singing Jedi knights and a replica of Pioneer Square, tree and all.

"Uncle Holly would love to show you his certificate again." Sawyer laughed. Really, I still didn't know why they'd picked my window as the winner, which still stood in stark contrast to Sawyer's. But I'd built trees out of handmade paper and pencils and created roads of ink. Miniature lights illuminated everything. It was all very fanciful and far too much work to be practical.

And speaking of fanciful, I'd finally given in and created a small corner with only the best paper goods for children, and yes, a bucket with books to be looked at in the store. Business was up. I couldn't complain.

Sawyer passed Aria off to Char as we came through a lighted tunnel. Tucker, Char, and the kids headed off to the petting zoo area, leaving Sawyer and me to explore on our own a bit. Grabbing my hand, he pulled me close. "You're sitting next to me on the train right?"

"Of course." I smiled dopily at him as we headed over to the station.

"Good because I've waited all year for a do-over."

"I promise not to run this time." Deep meaning laced my words. I'd focused so much on my being able to trust *him*, when in truth, he'd had to extend the same trust to me, make sure that I wasn't going to bolt again at the first sign of adversity.

"Better not." Sawyer pulled me close as we boarded the train. "Then I'd just have to tie you down."

"On second thought—"

"Okay, maybe I'm going to tie you down regardless." Sawyer's breath was warm in my ear. And when he kissed me this time, my whole body lit up like the sights around us. I'd been hunting for the perfect present for him for weeks, but nothing could compete with the gift of the last year together—of the joy of having him by my side. Sure, my life was much louder these days—no one in the world was better at driving me crazy—but I was also filling it up with memories I wanted to keep forever. Just like Sawyer.

Danced Close
Portland Heat

Annabeth Albert

LYRICAL SHINE PRESS
Kensington Publishing Corp.
www.kensingtonbooks.com

Chapter 1
Kendall

"Are we ready to have our cake and eat it too?" I joked as my clients, Maria and Leah, walked up the sidewalk in front of the bakery. Both of them laughed, which was my intent.

"I'm so nervous," Maria confessed, tossing her long, black hair over one shoulder. "I've never ordered something so fancy."

They were both prone to attacks of nerves about their wedding, and it was my job to reassure them and keep everything running smoothly. I prided myself on taking good care of my clients, so I put on my most reassuring smile.

"This is supposed to be *fun*. Your cake should be the least of your worries, and Vic's going to take great care of you." I removed their folder from my green Alexander McQueen handbag. Inside the folder, I had all the details for their big day next month, as well as a bunch of design inspiration photos for their dresses, cake, and decor. They might be working on a tight schedule, but these two had definite ideas about how their wedding should go.

I held open the door to the bakery. It was a sunny little building in Southeast Portland, a longtime fixture in this neighborhood, and was recently under new management as Vic, the baker I usually worked with, had become a partner in the business. But the man himself was nowhere to be seen when we entered the storefront.

Instead, the delivery person who had accompanied Vic on the last several weddings I'd planned was working the counter. A cute blond kid, he'd grown a beard since I'd seen him last. I'd assumed previously that he was in his late teens, but the beard made him look older. And yummier. I'd felt guilty macking on him before, but now I could see he was more like twenty-one, maybe twenty-two or -three if I squinted hard. Still younger than me, but a person could look without shame.

"Hi, Todd," I greeted him. I make a point of learning the names of *everyone* associated with a wedding, even the support staff. It helps that I'm good with names—always have been. That and I enjoy the look of surprised pleasure on someone's face when you remember their name— Todd's eyebrows went up and his mouth quirked. "I'm here with the Ramos-Vienne wedding. Can you let Vic know we're here?"

"Sure thing." He pulled a large glossy binder out from behind the counter. "You guys can look this over while you wait." He had a bit of a Southern drawl and a slow way of talking that made one really pay attention to his words, like each might be extra-important. Not that Todd was much of a talker—our few interactions before, he'd always let Vic handle things.

Thus, I was surprised when a few minutes after we got all settled at one of the tables tucked into the front window area, Todd came back with Vic and took one of the free chairs at the table.

"Hey, Kendall." Vic greeted me with a hearty handshake. I introduced Maria and Leah, who also got handshakes from Vic.

"I asked Todd to join us because I'm training him in more front-counter stuff. I want him to know how we handle a wedding consultation, just in case he has to do one in a pinch." Vic gestured at Todd, who gave a nervous smile that was closer to a grimace. He had a spiral notebook and pen with him, and his expression reminded me of some of my friends facing a test they hadn't studied for.

Vic talked to Maria and Leah about their wedding, a small intimate affair at the Benson, and what they were looking for in a cake.

"Stunning and elegant," I said, taking out the inspiration photos we'd collected. They liked sugar flowers, which was something that Vic specialized in, but they also liked complex yet modern cakes. I couldn't wait to see what Vic dreamed up for them. He started scribbling in his sketchbook, adding and crossing out things as we talked and flipped through the pictures.

"Memorable," Maria added.

"And tasty." Leah laughed.

"Well, we've got tasty covered. Todd, could you fetch the tasting cakes from the case?"

"Sure thing." Todd stood, then hesitated, forehead creasing. He truly was distractingly adorable, even confused. "Hey, Kendall, I've got a carafe of water and cups ready for us. Could you give me a hand?"

He nibbled the corner of his lip and I had a strong feeling he had more than water to hand me. He had that look—the one people get when they're trying to figure me out. Nevertheless, I nodded and followed him to the counter area.

"What's on your mind?" I asked in a low voice once we were out earshot of the others, who were continuing to look at cake pictures. No sense in pretending that he hadn't wanted to talk to me for some reason.

"We work a lot of weddings with y'all." He pulled two plates of samples out of the refrigerated case and set them on the counter. "And I just…" He shrugged.

A prickle raised up my spine. This could get uncomfortable fast, but even as I felt my shields rising, I still gave him the benefit of the doubt and nodded stiffly. "Yes?"

"I want to make sure I treat you with respect," he whispered. "You know, when I think about you and stuff."

"You think about me?" Despite myself, my voice took on a flirty edge, in part to see if I could make him as uncomfortable as I was.

"Umm." He tugged on his left ear, a most delicious pink blush staining his cheeks. Yeah, he thought about me, probably in ways he'd rather not. "I just mean, I've heard Vic recommend y'all to people looking for a planner."

I nodded. I'd let him pretend that was it.

"I want to make sure I'm using your preferred pronouns, you know? I never know what to use when I'm thinking about you."

Well, wasn't that adorable. I'd been expecting something more blunt, along the lines of the oft-asked *Are you a guy or a girl?* But Todd looked so beseechingly earnest standing there, chewing his lip. His eyes were serious, like he actually *cared* about getting this right.

"Pronouns are tricky bastards, but you can use 'he,' " I said. "That's how I identify—a genderqueer gay man." I laid it *all* out there for him, in part because people who took the time to ask questions always wanted to know *everything*, including things that were none of their business, like when I'd first embraced my genderqueerness or whether I identified as both male and female or neither. More than one person had asked for percentages, like I did some complex math each morning when getting dressed. But I also wanted to mess with that little flare of interest I'd seen when Todd said that he thought about me. Did he think about me because he'd read me as female? It wouldn't be the first time. Especially when I left my hair down so that the curls brushed my neck, I got more "yes, ma'am" responses and curious looks. Frankly, I loved rocking my androgynous presentation, even if it did sometimes lead to awkward conversations like this.

Todd's face didn't give away a lot, with his eyes staying serious, but his ears flushed a darker shade of pink. "Good to know," he mumbled, not quite meeting my eyes.

That little bit of avoidance made my spine stiffen and my voice harden. "How about you? You have any labels I should know about?"

"Thought you'd already figured *me* out." He turned his arm over for me, revealing a tattoo on the underside of his forearm. He'd rolled the sleeves of his white bakery jacket up today, but I had a feeling they'd been down the other times I'd seen him as I totally would have remembered that tat—it was a tribal design with a sun at the center, but the sun was rainbow colored.

"Nice." I'd planned Vic's wedding to his husband, Robin, and I knew he liked to hire along the QUILTBAG spectrum, but unlike Todd's assumption, I really hadn't been able to get a read on him. Why would I...

For when I think about you. Oh. Maybe this wasn't just the ordinary fishing expedition that curious people liked to hit me with all the time. Maybe—

"How's the cake coming?" Vic raised his jovial voice.

"Coming!" Todd scooped up the cake plates, leaving me with the water and a lot of questions.

When I got back to the table, Vic had sketched out a gorgeous cake—square base, round middle, and top tiers with a cascade of orchid-like flowers down the side.

"We want buttercream frosting, not fondant," Maria said as I settled back down. "I already know that."

"Their buttercream is *divine*. Try it with the espresso-infused cake." I pointed to a sample on her plate. "And remember, this is *your* day. Go with what you find absolutely delicious for both of you."

"Do you want a slice of something, Kendall?" Vic asked. "Anything you want in the front case, on the house. Todd can get it."

Vic always offered and I usually declined when bringing my clients in, but some little devil made me look directly at Todd. "I think I'll let my brides handle the cake. What do *you* recommend?" I didn't bat my eyes, but my tone was plenty flirtatious.

"I...uh..."

"Todd doesn't eat much sugar," Vic explained, giving me a stern *don't mess with my assistant* look. Whatever. We'd known each other long enough for him to give me a little leeway.

"I like the new paleo muffins." Todd blushed. His Southern accent got more pronounced when he was flustered. "No refined sugar."

"You can bring me one of them, if it's not too much trouble," I said.

"No trouble at all." His long, loping strides took him back over to the display case. He ducked behind it to grab a muffin and put it on a plate. His bakery coat was too baggy for me to check out his rearview, which was a pity. As he slid me the plate, his eyes lingered on my sweater. It was butter yellow, with a loose weave and plunging V in both front and back. It was one of those pieces in my wardrobe that made me feel invincible. And hot. The tips of Todd's ears blushed as he sat back down. Yeah, he'd noticed the hot part.

I tried to return my attention to Leah and Maria and what flavors would best compliment the rest of the reception food, but I was still *aware* of Todd, in a way that I hadn't been in a long time.

* * * *

Over the next couple weeks I thought about Todd and his sweeter-than-buttercream questions more than I would have liked, but work kept me busy—and away from the bakery until a rare lazy Saturday with my bestie.

"I don't want coffee," Freya said once we were already walking away from our building.

"What? Are you feeling okay?" I reached over and touched her forehead. Come to think of it, she *had* been acting a bit off the last few days. "This is what we do. We get coffee."

And by coffee, I meant fancy coffee drinks at our neighborhood place, which let us get in some great people-watching along with single-origin cappuccinos.

"I know, but I'm hungry. I've been doing that low-carb thing again, and all I can think of is *carbs*. Which I can't have."

"You doing the paleo thing like half the city?" I shook my head, making my hair tickle the back of my neck. It was an off day for me, so I'd left my hair natural and hadn't tried to tame the curls with product. Freya did *not* need to lose weight in my opinion, but she was convinced she had too much junk in the trunk.

"That's the one. I miss *bread*."

"Honey, you're *perfect*. Exactly as you are. You don't have to starve yourself."

"Thanks." She gave me a wan smile.

"Well, at the very least, let's find you *something* you *can* eat. The bakery that handles most of my wedding clients has a new paleo muffin. No grains, no refined sugars. It's not bad." Todd's muffins had come to mind immediately. I had a better chance of cheering her up—and giving myself a boost with a possible glimpse of Todd—at the bakery rather than hitting our usual neighborhood coffeehouse.

"Take me there. Now."

"All they have is drip coffee—"

"I don't care. I want muffins."

"Okay, okay." I lived in the newer part of Southeast Portland, but not too terribly far from the older neighborhood that housed Vic's bakery. "We'll have to take my car."

Freya was already turned around and headed for the underground parking at our building. Something about her still seemed a bit not herself, and not simply her sudden craving for carbs. I licked my lips—terrible nervous habit—and then immediately pulled out my clear gloss to fix the damage I'd done before I followed her.

* * * *

Once we found parking on a side street near the bakery, my stomach did this weird rumble. Not hunger. And not unease about whatever was going on with Freya that she hadn't told me about. No, the wobbles were all anticipation—something I hadn't felt since long before Lewis, my ex. I wasn't sure whether I wanted Todd to be working the front or not. I hadn't seen him in the three weeks since our conversation during the Ramos-Vienne planning session. I didn't really have room for a lot of distractions in my life, and I *needed* a good relationship with Vic's bakery—not some weird, awkward shuffle with his assistant. But my uncertainty didn't matter because Todd was indeed working the front.

"Hi, Todd," I said when we approached the counter.

"Kendall! No consultation today, right?" Todd looked…well, he was the sort of guy who didn't really look *eager* about anything in life, but his blue eyes lit up and the corners of his mouth lifted into a not-quite smile. The beard gave him a very roguish air and also made it even harder to read his emotions.

"No, I was telling Freya here about your new paleo muffins, and we'd like two, and two coffees with room for cream."

"For here or to go?"

"Here." I pulled my wallet out to pay.

"That's pretty," Todd said, gesturing to the pink embossed leather. His neck, not his ears, flushed this time. I couldn't tell whether he was uncomfortable complimenting a man who carried a purse and pink Coach wallet or whether he was uncomfortable with himself for liking said wallet.

Regardless, it wasn't my problem. "Thanks," I said and accepted our coffees, passing one to Freya. Todd put our muffins on cute little plates with red flowers on them.

We headed to one of the front tables. "Let me know if y'all need me to adjust the blinds," Todd called after us.

I snorted. Only in the Northwest did we fret over what to do with that strange glowing orb in the sky.

Some of the light in Todd's eyes flickered. "I mean...let me know if there's...well, anything I could do."

"We'll do that, honey." Freya reached across the counter to pat his bicep. She gets away with stuff like that. Me, I don't like my personal space invaded, so I'm careful to not do it to other people, Freya being a notable exception. We'd known each other a million years, and had the sort of comfortable friendship that should *not* have had her shifting around, fiddling with her phone and not meeting my eyes.

I waited until we were seated at a table to say, "Out with it."

"The bakery guy likes you."

"Not that," I said, even though it did make my cheeks heat. "And Todd's simply a nice *kid*."

"He's maybe five years younger. You can *totally* fish in that pool."

"Enough about him, or he'll hear you," I whispered, resisting the urge to look over at the counter and see what Todd was doing. "Now out with whatever's bothering you."

I needed her to tell me so that together we could solve the problem. It was what I was good at—helping my friends work through both major and minor crises. I *knew* I could get her back in a better mood.

"Okay." Freya stirred her coffee over-vigorously. "Here's the deal. I can't do the dance classes with you."

"What do you mean? Classes start in two weeks." Freya and I had planned for *months* to take West Coast Swing dance classes together in prep for a forties-themed charity dinner dance that I had no choice but to attend.

The charity event for the homeless shelter was sponsored in part by my mother's law firm, for which both Freya and my ex-boyfriend worked, Freya as an admin assistant, Lewis as junior associate. I *had* to make an appearance, and I'd been planning to show off some new dancing skills. Well, more accurately, I'd been wanting to not fall on my face or end up standing there alone, both of which seemed likely now. I'd had this vision of showing Lewis exactly what he was missing and not getting back, but that wasn't happening if I had to languish like some Victorian spinster without a dance partner.

"Kayla—you know, my sister in Tacoma—her husband's still deployed, and she just got put on bed rest with her pregnancy. I'm cashing in all my leave at work, and taking three weeks to go be with her until her husband gets back. I'm leaving tomorrow."

"That makes sense." I sighed. No way could I compete with a little sister in need. "Give my best to Kayla. You need anything for the drive?"

"I'm good." Freya gave me a tentative smile. "You're really not mad?"

"Of course not." I waved such a notion aside with a flick of my wrist. "But, what *am* I supposed to do now?"

"You already paid for a couples registration, right? Call around—I'm sure one of our friends will dance with you. Or you never know. Maybe you'll meet someone." Her eyes slid to the counter area where Todd was unloading a tray of cream puffs into the glass case.

"No," I said firmly. "I'll make some calls." But even as I said it, my brain went, *Maybe?* And my heart sped up, just a bit, which was a reminder that any sort of thing for Todd would be an epically bad idea. The memory of Lewis still lingered, more bitter than black coffee, and I needed to be smart if I wanted to avoid that kind of hurt again.

Chapter 2
Todd

I knew soon as I got into work on Saturday I wasn't going to like what Vic had to say. See, he has this look he gets when he's behind schedule or things aren't going his way—reminds me of an angry gator down in Florida, where I grew up. And lately, ever since taking part-ownership, he's had that look more times than not.

"Hey, Todd, I need you to do the Ramos-Vienne delivery on your own," Vic said. "I'm behind on the Mitchell-Abrams wedding cake and the Bellmont christening."

Vic was the kind of control freak who needs to do the weddings all personal. I wasn't sure how I felt about being trusted to do one on my own. But, he's the boss-man, so I just nodded.

"Need me to pack the morning-after breakfast basket for them?" That was something Vic loved doing—a little gift for the couple. Figured I might as well make myself useful while I stewed about everything that could go wrong on the delivery.

"That would help. Then we'll get the cake loaded up." Vic handed me a box, and I started filling it with muffins and pastries. I hadn't always been so good about keeping a job. Vic, he'd done me a real solid, taking me on, but I was always on edge about being let go. Wouldn't be easy for a guy like me to find a new gig.

"Kendall will be there if you have trouble. He'll help you get the cake table situated," Vic said as he returned to the cake he was working on, a pretty teal layer cake with intricate drop lines.

Ah. There it was. The real reason my hackles had been raised all morning. I wasn't one to circle days on the calendar, but in the back of my head, yeah, I'd known I was seeing Kendall again. Kendall, now, he was pretty like the cake—all colorful elegance. And he unsettled me, because I always felt like I was two words away from falling in shit with him. Like last week, when he'd come in with his friend, I'd thought I'd try it on a bit, but my flirting game is crap, and he'd left looking all kinds of pissed. Couldn't tell if it was me or the friend, but I'd thought about that exchange far more than I should've.

And I thought about him again as I drove to the hotel. I'd known I was gay since forever, but Kendall wasn't my usual type. At all. However, something about him had intrigued me since our first encounter. He did it for me in a way no one had in a couple of years even. The way I'd figured it, he'd had to have noticed my scoping him out. Repeatedly. But then, maybe he was used to all kinds of eyeballs on him.

I parked the truck in the hotel's delivery bay and made my way to the banquet room, where chaos greeted me. Unlike most weddings we did, the room wasn't set up yet. Instead, workers scurried around, rearranging chairs and slapping down tablecloths.

"Todd! Thank god you're here." Kendall strode across the room, cutting through the chaos like some video-game chieftain on a rampage. I liked how he always dressed just so for weddings—sophisticated in perfectly tailored suits but with little details like a ruffled top or lace pocket square or dangly earrings that showed utter confidence in his tastes. That kind of confidence was more intoxicating than a fifth of Jack, and made things I'd figured for dead stir inside me.

Today he was wearing a suit that was somewhere between cream, rose, and brown, a silky-looking top with ruffled collar, and a gold band that held his curly hair back. The prettiness of his outfit contrasted with the sureness of his strides and the firm handshake he had for me. The whole package did something for me, made my pulse hum.

"There was a *disastrous* miscommunication with the hotel." Kendall managed to sound both supremely irritated and in control at the same time. This wasn't a person prone to hysterics, and I liked that about him. "They're fixing things, but it's going to be a minute before the cake table's ready. Do you mind waiting?"

I did, a bit, because it would push back my other tasks, but I knew what Vic would do. If Kendall needed us to be the ones responsible for getting the cake arranged, then that's how it would go down. "Not a problem."

"Thank you." The wide smile that Kendall shot me made all sorts of hassles worth it. He had eyes the color of brown sugar, and when he smiled, they sparkled like warm caramel. "How about you and the cake wait there?" He pointed to a little corner out of the way of all the foot traffic.

"Sure thing." I wheeled the cake over there and took out my phone to kill time. I had a new message from Gran.

You home in time for dinner tonight? Chicken pot pie. I'll keep some warm for you if you're doing a meeting after work.

My stomach gave a little grumble, reminding me of all the hours since breakfast. Gran's pot pie sounded amazing, but I supposed I knew what she was really after—wanted to make sure I wasn't skipping my meetings.

Behind on work, I texted back. *Save me a slice or two. And yes, ma'am, I'm doing the regular Saturday meeting at the center. Don't you wait up on me.*

I couldn't really fault her for worrying. I'd had a cold a few weeks back, skipped a couple of meetings and had myself a funk until I got back to my routine. And for all she babied me, I coddled her right back, making sure she got her rest. Woman was busier than a congressman, what with all her causes. Didn't need her burning herself out on my account too.

Across the room, the DJ was setting up, testing the sound system. A jazzy little big-band number came over the sound system. I recognized it instantly as one we'd used back when I was…oh, I must have been ten. Maybe eleven. But all of a sudden I was back there, pre–dance competition jitters coursing through me. And unlike some memories, this particular song held no bitterness for me. Damn, I'd been *good* at ballroom that year.

Step. Turn. I wasn't quite dancing, but I was swaying in place, remembering the routine, powerless to resist the music wrapping around me.

"Zo-mi-god! You can dance, can't you?" Kendall's voice startled me, and I stopped mid-movement, which made me lose my balance—only for a second, but a second was all it took to jostle the cart with the cake.

"Shit," I cursed, moving fast to keep the cake steady. Kendall reached out too, but we were both too late to stop two flowers fluttering loose and the icing on the bottom tier smudging. I stepped back to survey the damage. "Vic's gonna kill me dead. And then fire my carcass."

"No one's getting fired." Kendall's voice was firm. That was one of the things I liked about him—his voice was a sure and steady tenor, the voice of a person who could get things done. "Not you, not me. Did Vic send his repair kit?"

I nodded. I'd never been the one to *do* said repairs, but there was spare icing and some tools on the bottom shelf of my cart. I'd watched Vic do a repair or two, but I was the delivery boy, not a baker. And unlike those other fixes, this mishap was squarely on me. "So fuckin' clumsy," I muttered.

"I don't know, you looked pretty graceful to me," Kendall said with a laugh. "This one's my fault for startling you. The cake table's ready now. What do you say we get the cake on the table, then see what magic we need to work?"

Magic. Yeah, right. I'd stopped believing in magic so long ago my brain forgot what it felt like, and I didn't have nearly Kendall's faith in my ability to fix things. Lord knew, I'd dropped enough balls in my life. But still I followed Kendall to the table, and worked with him to carefully—so carefully now—transfer the cake to the center of the table. Kendall turned the cake this way and that until the smudged part faced the back.

"Now we just need to affix the flowers." Kendall's air of *I've got this* worked to calm the galloping horses in my chest.

I took a deep breath, visualized what Vic would do. I worked best with steps to follow, so I thought it out for several seconds before picking up one of the flowers. Felt like I was performing surgery, and my hands shook, but I got the flowers back in place. Almost perfect. I knew it wasn't *exactly* like Vic had it, but maybe others wouldn't notice. Didn't matter. I still felt like crap, messing up Vic's work.

"And the smudge." If I was the nervous surgeon, Kendall was my bossy scrub nurse, keeping us on track. This part was trickier and needed a deft hand.

"Maybe you should do it," I muttered.

"You've got this. I think Vic's gearing up to train you on decorating next."

"Only reason he's got me working front of the shop is 'cause Danielle's out on baby leave." That and he felt sorry for me, but I left that part out. No doubt Robin had leaned on him hard to get me extra hours. Robin wasn't just Vic's husband—he was my friend too. But that only got me so far—wasn't no one training me for the fancy stuff.

Same as I had for the flowers, I visualized the smudge being repaired, thought about how I needed it to look, then went in with the extra icing.

"Perfect," Kendall pronounced. It wasn't, not really, but it was nice of him to say so.

"If they complain—"

"They won't. And if they do, I'll tell people it was my fault."

"You'd do that for me?" Didn't seem to me that he had any reason to get my back, not when he had a rep on the line too.

"Sure. And really, the fix worked, Todd. You did great."

I nodded, not sure what to do with that praise. "Here." I took out the breakfast stuff from the shelf on the cart. "This is for their breakfast tomorrow. Gift from the bakery."

"I love how you guys always do that." Kendall took the box. "Here, let me walk you out."

"I can find my way back. Sure you've got plenty to do."

A frown flittered across Kendall's face. He seemed to draw himself up taller, shoulders raising. "It's no problem, and I had something I wanted to talk to you about."

Oh heck. Here it came, a lecture about not staring at him. Or maybe I hadn't worded the question about his pronouns the best. I followed him back toward the service hallway, heart thumping double time.

"I really didn't mean to startle you earlier," he said once we were alone in the hallway.

"'S okay."

"*Can* you dance though? You looked like you could."

I paused. Licked my lips. Wasn't sure how to answer. "Lifetime ago, yeah," I said finally.

"Lifetime?" Kendall laughed. "You're what, twenty?"

"Twenty-two." *Barely.*

"Okay, but seriously, how many lifetimes could you have lived?"

He had no clue. None. Not that I was going to enlighten him. "I started with tap and jazz dancing when I was a bitty thing. Then later I did junior ballroom competitions—"

"Oh my god. You *are* perfect." Kendall's face broke into as wide a smile as I'd seen on him before.

"It's no big deal. Haven't really danced in years."

"That's okay. Do you know West Coast Swing?" Kendall wasn't letting this drop.

"Nope. East Coast, but just a little. I competed more in classical ballroom, foxtrot and that sort of thing."

"Here's the deal." Kendall glanced down at the gold watch on his wrist. Undoubtedly, he had more important things to do than talk dance with the delivery boy. "My friend and I were signed up for LGBTQ-friendly West Coast Swing classes that start next week, but she had to cancel. Would you be interested in taking the class with me?"

Well, that was unexpected. *Could* I dance again after all this time? Did I even want to? I'd put myself a million miles and eight years away from that life, that person who had lived for dance. "Why do you want to learn?" I asked, hedging.

"There's a fund-raiser for the shelter on Burnside—the one Vic's bakery supports with so many donations. You probably know the one."

Saved my damn life. But I just nodded, keeping my muscles loose like I wasn't there for meetings twice a week.

"Anyway, it's my mother's law firm's pet charity this year, and they're having a big forties-themed dinner and dance. You wouldn't have to commit to the fund-raiser yet, but it's a great cause."

Any other cause and I probably would have told him to keep on dancing out the door. But the shelter was special.

"And you really need someone to dance with?" I looked him up and down. God, he was gorgeous, and it wouldn't really be too much hardship to imagine him in my arms. But a person like him wasn't for me. "Seems to me you could take your pick."

Kendall laughed. "You're sweet. But this is short notice, and a lot of my friends are already attending the fund-raiser. With their significant others." He sighed heavily, and lord, didn't I know that feeling of it seeming like the whole world was coupled up.

I shuffled my feet, thinking. I didn't really leap into much of anything, especially not these days. I wasn't a fast thinker like Kendall.

"Listen, can I give you my card? I really have to get back to the prep, but I'd love it if you'd think about it." He held out an embossed card with a wedding cake and champagne flutes on it. And his number. Now I had Kendall Rose's number. There was a part of me that gave a little leap at this, but I knew better than to let that sort of hope dance around.

"I'll text you later," I said. "Either way. I might have to check my schedule at work—"

"That's fine." Kendall smiled. He knew how close he had me to a yes. "Text me any questions. And I'll be up late tonight. It always takes me *forever* to wind down from a wedding."

I knew plenty about sleeplessness, but Kendall's words were... *intimate.* Like a little something that I now knew about him that maybe the world didn't.

"I will." Smiles, they don't come as easy to me as they do someone like Kendall, who showers the world with his sunshine, but I tried for one then. "I'll think about it." *Think about you,* is what I really meant.

* * * *

"You're back early," Gran said when I came in. "Let me get your dinner in the microwave for you."

"I can do it." I grabbed the neatly wrapped package from the fridge. "No one going out to coffee these days?"

"Nah." I shrugged. Coffee wasn't really my thing. I'd gone with some of the guys after a meeting a couple of times, but it wasn't my jam. "Mostly, it's people going out to smoke, and since I quit, easier to just come on home. You havin' a pot pie waiting, that pretty much made my choice." I gave her a kiss on the cheek on my way to the microwave.

"I *am* glad that you quit that nasty habit." She shuddered, which was kinda funny since we both knew nicotine was far from the worst bad habit I'd had to kick. "You're so much healthier now. Your color's good, and your weight is up again."

Well, now, healthier was *highly* debatable, and I cringed a little at the weight comment. My inner chubby thirteen-year-old wasn't ever gonna get okay with my weight. And while I wasn't *that* heavy, I was having a hard time getting exercise in, what with my increased hours at the bakery and all, which made me feel out of shape. The microwave dinged, and I took the plate out and sat down at the table. Gran grabbed her tea and joined me.

"I just wish you had some friends your age. Outside of meetings, I mean."

"I *like* meetings."

"I know you do." She patted my hand. "And they're good and important for you. But you're too young to be coming home to an old lady—"

"You're not old, Gran." And I came home to her because of all the years I should have and hadn't. But I wasn't good at articulating stuff like that, so what I said was, "I'll see about getting some friends. Promise."

Uninvited, an image of Kendall crept into my head. 'Course, most of what I wanted to do with him was more than strictly friendly, but dancing would get me out, put Gran's mind at ease.

Later, stretched out on my bed, I texted Kendall about which day and time the classes were on.

Thanks. Hope the rest of the wedding was disaster-free, I replied when he told me the classes were Thursdays at seven.

It was. And they didn't notice the cake, promise. They were in their own little love cocoon.

Love cocoon. Didn't that sound all cozy? And exactly like something I'd never get. An ache bloomed right behind my ribs. *Glad they were happy, I texted. How much are the classes?*

I already paid ;) All I need is you to show up on Thursday ;) Kendall's emoji game was on point, and that wink did strange things to my insides, took that ache and spread it out like warm butter. Maybe I couldn't get that *love cocoon*, not now, not ever, but an in-person version of that wink wasn't really too much to ask the universe.

I'll be there. My heart thumped hard as I hit Send. I wasn't really sure what I was doing, opening myself up to dance again, letting those old wounds dangerously close to the surface. All I knew was that I was willing to risk it for more time with Kendall.

Chapter 3
Kendall

I was alone in my condo when Todd texted that he'd do the class, and I literally squealed so loud I disturbed Rococo, my Chihuahua/Jack Russell terrier mix, from his spot at the end of the couch. He growled softly at me before settling back down. I might have two left feet, but I'd seen Todd earlier—he had an innate rhythm. The kind I lacked, and dearly yearned for. He had the sort of posture that I'd worked for over the years with Pilates and yoga, but all the classes in the world couldn't teach the sort of quiet bearing that Todd had. Once he'd said he'd danced as a kid, I could totally see it. He would have been a little blond cherub with a shy smile and absolute mastery over his steps.

I was still sad about Freya canceling on me, but honestly, this might work out better for all of us—she got time with her sister, and I got Todd, who would make Lewis far more jealous than a few turns around the floor with my bestie. Of course, there was still the possibility of a friendship with Todd making things complicated at the bakery, but the more time I spent around the guy, the less I cared about that. As long as we kept things casual, we'd be fine. Lewis had cured me of any urges for anything more serious. Serious simply wasn't in the cards for me.

I scrolled through my other messages. I was tired and really just wanted to flip on *Shameless* and bask in the exhausted-but-triumphant post-event high, but my clients and friends came first. I took care of some questions about catering, a different couple wanting to switch their colors, and a potential client wanting to know if a circus theme was possible. Of course it was. I'd work the trapeze myself for a high-budget event that pushed the boundaries of typical wedding fare.

Buzz. Oh, not more questions. It seemed like I could never get my inbox completely clear. But I brightened when I saw that this one was from Todd.

I hate to ask this, but could you give me a ride home after the dance class? I live in Northeast. I'm checking the bus situation for that time of night and it's complicated. I can make it work though if you can't.

I smiled. More time with Todd? Absolutely not a hardship. But alone in my car…that sounded like a gateway to places that could challenge my resolution to keep things casual. My pulse hummed. Bring it on.

* * * *

I was almost late to the first dance class because I had a bridal fitting that turned into a tearful confessional, and I needed to do emotional damage control. I left my bride smudged and sniffly, but at least she seemed okay with her dress—and her partner—again. Then on my way to the car, I had a text from the circus-wedding couple. They did want to hire me, so that needed an immediate reply. They were "open to animals as entertainment," so that could get interesting. Most of my clients waved the rainbow flag in one way or another, but as word of mouth spread, I was getting more cis-het couples like the circus-wanting duo. If I pulled off their event, I could count on expanding that market.

If all went well, I could maybe hire an assistant next year. Maybe even steal Freya away from my mom.

When I got to the dance studio, I had to circle the lot, looking for a spot that wouldn't get me towed. Finally, I rushed into the studio at 7:01 by my watch. Clumps of couples stood around the dance floor talking in groups of two and four. Todd stood by himself against the far wall. The smile he gave me when he saw me was almost enough to make me want to keep him waiting more often—the look in his blue eyes was part relief, part pleasure, but his mouth curved more than I had seen before.

"Kendall! You made it." Todd crossed to me. I hadn't seen him out of his bakery uniform of white jacket and faded jeans before, and that was a damn shame because he cleaned up *nice.* He looked ready for a Southern church service—blond hair neatly combed, beard looking freshly trimmed, and dress shoes with black pants and a gray button-down shirt.

"You look great," I said.

"Yeah, well, I knew they'd want shoes with a heel, and it felt weird wearing these with jeans." He gave me another rare smile, this one more sheepish. "You look…awesome too."

I was getting more used to Todd's slower speech and conversational pauses, but I still wished he didn't act as though he was figuring me out like a Rubik's Cube. And I did look nice. I'd read the part on the website about shoes with a heel too, so I'd paired heeled boots alongside skinny jeans with a lot of stretch to them, and an orange sweater.

An older man with a gray ponytail, whom I recognized from the website, clapped his hands. He introduced himself as Chuck and his partner and assistant as Ted. I tried to imagine working on a regular basis with a significant other and had to stifle a laugh—never happening to me. Chuck announced that we'd start with the starter step for the first part of class.

"Now, most people in my classes like learning both the lead and the follower roles, so we'll switch partway through this segment."

I glanced over at Todd. I had a feeling he'd only ever led before, and I had no idea how he'd take to letting someone like me lead. Even with my heeled boots, I was still an inch or so shorter than him. Butch, gender-conforming guys like him often had decided opinions about femme guys and their roles—something that was a large reason why I didn't have more of a dating history.

And true to my expectations, he licked his lips. "You mind if I lead to start? It's what I'm used to."

"Of course." If I was disappointed, I didn't let my voice show it.

Chuck and Ted demonstrated the starter step, which was a six-count pattern. Todd nodded like he was memorizing their motion while they demonstrated.

"Not that different from an East Coast Swing basic," he said in a low voice to me when it was time for us to give it a try. "So it's two triple steps followed by a back rock step. You ready?"

I was still learning what chassés and triple steps and rock steps were, but I nodded. When our hands met for the first time and he put his big hand on my waist, a little involuntary shudder raced through me. His touch was warm and his grip sure. I was clumsier than a drunk goat, but he had a natural fluidity to his motions.

Chuck counted out the steps and Todd repeated the count under his breath.

"You were one of those annoying perfect students in school, weren't you?" I joked as we tried it again.

Todd snorted. "Hardly. I tried hard, sure, but school and me... it's complicated."

I sobered up, reminding myself that learning didn't come naturally to everyone. "I get it. But dance? Were you instantly good at it?"

"I was so bitty when I started, I don't even know. I started competing and getting medals, so mama kept payin' for more lessons."

"That's—*oops*." I tripped again.

"This works better if you actually *let* me lead," Todd said as Chuck called our attention back to the center of the room to learn how to follow the starter step with what he called a throwout.

"Sorry," I hissed as I watched Chuck and Ted. The throwout sounded like some daredevil move out of figure skating, of which I was a major fan, but actually was a subtle sort of turn with Todd releasing the hand from my back and leading me into a quarter turn, ending with us holding hands, facing each other.

"All right, now you give it a try!" Chuck said. "Starter step then throwout."

Todd started us off, and I was so wrong. It was as hard as ice dancing had to be. Harder, in fact. At least I could do a basic glide in skating.

"You need to trust me to lead. I'll get you where you need to be." Todd's voice was more serious than seductive, but my body immediately took his words to the dirty place. Letting others lead wasn't my usual MO, either in bed or out, but Todd's earnest blue eyes made it seem like the most delicious prospect ever.

We tried it again, and I focused on letting him lead, consciously relaxing my tight arms. That attempt went better, even though I still stepped on his foot.

Chuck was coming around, giving individual pointers to the couples. When he got to us, he had a big smile for Todd. "You're an absolute natural."

"Thanks." Todd blushed and looked at his shiny shoes.

"And you…" Chuck turned to me, concern showing on his wrinkled face. "Just keep practicing. Listen to your partner. Watch his cues. Trust."

Todd nodded, giving me a pointed look. Hey, it wasn't my fault that trust didn't come easily to me. The world needed to *earn* my devotion. We ran through the move again before Chuck and Ted pulled our attention back to them.

"Now, we'll do a lead switch. Ted will lead, and I'll follow. And if you choose, you can switch leads with your partners as well."

"We don't have to," I whispered to Todd as Chuck and Ted demonstrated.

"Are you kidding?" Todd raised his eyebrows. "You keep trying to lead anyway. We gotta see if you're more comfortable leading."

I wanted to point out that the issue wasn't what *I* would be more comfortable with, but before I could protest more, Todd moved into the follower's position. He still counted under his breath, but instead of the firm posture he'd had as lead, he went more pliant in my arms. And wasn't that a heady sensation? This bearded baby lumberjack giving up control to me? *I want more of that, yes please.*

I did my best to guide us through the starter step, and surprisingly, it *did* go smoother, mainly because Todd was so good that he covered for a fair bit of my bumbling. When we tried the throwout, he slithered in and out of the turn, giving me a grin as we finished.

"Told you. You just like to lead." He winked at me. "And that's okay."

"You don't mind?"

"Nah. Switching things up keeps everything interesting. I may have not followed very much, but it's fun. Try again?"

I wasn't entirely sure if we were only talking about dancing. His voice was lighter than I'd heard it before, and that wink made my insides wobble. I nodded, and we repeated the move. I had more confidence now, and Todd more flourish as he seemed to embrace this role. Fuck, that was sexy.

We practiced a few more times as Chuck made his way around the room again. This time he had a smile for both of us. "Much better. Maybe keep...zir at the lead when we do the underarm pass next?"

"Kendall prefers he," Todd said before I could. For all Todd seemed uncertain sometimes when dealing with me, he was smooth and confident correcting Chuck.

"Of course." Chuck nodded. I wasn't the only person in the room who skirted the nonbinary line, and Chuck seemed perfectly willing to accommodate my preferences. I liked that. Across the room, a bearded individual in a long skirt danced with a shorter person in a jacket and tie, and Chuck had treated them with deft respect as well. "Now, Kendall, when you lead Todd into the slot, feel free to loosen up on your anchor triple-step. This is supposed to be fun."

I led Todd through the pattern again, and this time it *was* fun, and we both laughed as we finished. Chuck taught us to follow the throwout with an underarm pass.

"Starter step. Throwout. Underarm pass," Todd repeated as we assumed the position with me leading again. "Now I'm taller than you, so be sure and get your arm nice and high. We're not square dancing."

"Maybe you should—"

"I like my feet intact. You're leading. Just don't·strangle me on the pass." Todd laughed again. I loved how the class really seemed to loosen him up, bring him out of the quiet shell he always seemed to be in at the bakery.

We put the three step-patterns together, and while getting my arm up was a challenge, it was one I embraced for the look of joy on Todd's face as he spun.

"I haven't thought of my old dance teacher in years," he said with a wistful laugh. "But I'm totally messaging her to tell her that I missed out. Way more turns in this role."

"You do...*turn* well." I couldn't help it—my voice got flirtier the more fun we had.

Chuck had the class do a lead switch, and I *tried* to be all loose and easy like Todd, tried to embrace the spins, but I still stumbled through the moves.

"Now before our break, let's do a little dancing to the music. Feel the music. Starter step–throwout–underarm pass–throwout–underarm pass, and repeat."

"You lead," Todd said.

It was weird—I was leading, but he had control of the dance, making us both appear more graceful and purposeful with his natural rhythm. When he spun, the movement of his hips and ass was more than a little distracting.

"You're getting good," he praised me on a pass. "You'll have to wear those boots again next week—they make up the height difference nicely."

"Or my heels," I said absently.

"Oh that too. Like pumps with a high heel? Just don't wear anything open-toed yet."

I could have kissed him right then for that reaction. He didn't go all dude bro about the prospect of being led by someone wearing high heels or get embarrassed that I owned said shoes.

"Can I ask something?" he asked after a few more turns. He had that serious look again, but he'd been so cool so far, I was more than willing to risk some discomfort.

"Sure."

"Your lips...they're so shiny...You do a gloss, right? Ever do color?"

His eyes were indeed locked right on my mouth. I got a little thrill knowing that he thought about my mouth.

"I've been known to." At this point, it had been enough years that I wasn't going to apologize for the contents of my makeup case. But unlike when a lot of people asked me about it, I didn't get all defensive with Todd, who seemed more...*thoughtful* in his curiosity than some. "Why? Would you like that next week?"

He was silent a long moment, gnawing on his own lip. I was seriously going to have to get the guy some balm the way he abused the poor things. "Yeah, I think I might." He sounded a bit surprised at himself, giving me a shy smile.

At the break, he fetched me a water, shifting effortlessly from letting me lead to taking charge again, insisting that I take a chair. I was so used to doing those little things for other people that it felt a bit weird, letting him do them for me.

Chuck announced that the second half we'd be learning the sugar-push step, which was supposed to be a basic repeatable pattern.

Todd had that serious, taking-mental-notes look again, so I nudged him. "Sugar push, huh? That sounds more like a designer club-drug than a dance step."

To my surprise, he scowled.

"Sorry. I just meant to be funny."

"You do those things?" he asked as he moved into position to follow me.

"Club drugs?" I laughed. "Nah, I've tried E, but that was a pretty awful couple of hours for me. I'm too much of a control freak to really get into that stuff."

A strange look passed over Todd's face, one I couldn't place. "Good."

We practiced our sugar push, but Todd didn't seem quite as joyful as he had earlier. "Can we add an underarm pass to this pattern?" I asked Chuck when he came around.

"Going for extra credit, eh?" He patted me on the back. "Sure you can."

I'd never been the kind of student to seek out extra credit, much more concerned with doing as many extracurricular activities as possible. My question was less about wanting to impress Chuck, and more about wanting to make Todd smile again, and he had seemed to love doing turns. So when Chuck turned on a longer selection of music for us to practice both the sugar push and the starter step sequence as we wanted, I made sure to lead Todd through a lot of turns, until finally he rewarded me with a grin.

"You tryin' to make me dizzy?"

"Maybe I like watching you spin," I said cheekily.

"Well, keep it up." He winked at me. "You're turning me all kinds of around."

He probably—okay, certainly—meant on the dance floor, but for a second, I couldn't help but wish he meant he was as infatuated with me as I was rapidly becoming with him.

"You want to grab a drink or some food or both before I run you home?" I asked as the class came to a close.

Todd was quiet so long I was afraid I'd overstepped some boundary. "I could eat, but..." He hesitated. "I don't drink. At all."

"Ah." I led him away from the other students leaving the class, and asked in a low voice, "Recovery?"

He gave me a tight nod that said we weren't talking about it more. "But I'd be up for some burgers or something."

I'd been planning on suggesting HUB, the Hopworks Urban Brewery, or another place with local brew, but if he wasn't drinking, neither was I. "Would Grain and Gristle work for you? It's in Northeast. Fabulous burgers and onion rings. They do serve, but I won't drink."

A little smile teased the edges of Todd's mouth but didn't reach his eyes. "You're one of those foodies who knows all the places, aren't you? I'd be just as happy with Burgerville, but sure, bring on the fancy burgers."

Chapter 4
Todd

I followed Kendall to his car, an older black BMW.

"Nice car," I said as I got in on the passenger side.

"Thanks, it's a hand-me-down from my mom." He smiled at me, then put the car in gear. Gotta love a man—*person*—who can handle a stick with ease.

"Nice mom." My insides felt like we were still dancing, all spinning and flopping around. I might be the one with a beard and tats, but Kendall was a total Northwest hipster, taking me to one of those places that probably put the sources of the beef and potatoes on their menus and did all the strange toppings. Back when I'd been with Jake, he'd liked joints like that. Me, I was just as happy with a hot burger and fries from a chain place. Lot of people, they take for granted how nice simple, hot food is. That's why I appreciated Gran's cooking so much—might be plain, but it was plenty tasty. And warmed a body through.

Kendall waited until we were on MLK headed north before he spoke. Liked that about him too—the not needing to fill a silence with mindless chatter. He was good about letting others talk too, like his wedding clients at the bakery.

"So..." His fingers drummed against the steering wheel. "I just want to make sure I don't say or do the wrong thing—"

I had to laugh. I *constantly* felt that way around him. "Join the club."

"Um...okay...how new is sobriety to you? We can go somewhere that doesn't have anything on the menu, if you need."

Him sounding all nervous, like I felt, settled me down some, made it easier for me to answer. "Two years and a month sober. And I'm fine with the restaurant, really. I don't drink, but booze was never my big issue. Drugs were."

"Congrats on making it two years. My sister, Lyndsey, just celebrated six years sober too. She got into some bad stuff in college."

I wasn't really one for trading war stories, but I nodded politely. "That's great for her."

"You'll meet her if you go to the fund-raiser with me. She'll love the way you dance."

Pretty man with his pretty clothes and pretty car and pretty food was *not* introducing me to the family in any universe, at least not like *that*, but my heart still stuttered for a few beats.

"Is the fund-raiser dress up?" I asked, neatly sidestepping the comment about the family, as if we were doing a throwout. "These clothes are about as nice as I own."

"Oh, *please* say you'll let me take you shopping. Please. I know some great vintage shops." Kendall made puppy-dog eyes at me as he circled around Prescott looking for parking. "You'd be fine in whatever you're comfortable in, but, man, you'd look *amazing* in a suit."

That sort of compliment, it can go to a guy's head. Especially when paired with a killer pair of dimples, which Kendall unleashed on me. "We'll see. Have to be one of the cheaper places, though. Some of them 'vintage' thrift stores charge double what you get new."

"I'm the queen of bargain shopping. Trust me." Kendall skillfully parallel parked. Man, there was something so fucking hot about a capable driver.

"Whatcha wearing to the thing?"

"Are you asking because you want to brace yourself for a dress?" Kendall asked as we got out. His words had a bite to them, like someone else had hassled him about what he was wearing.

"Like you said to me, whatever you're comfortable in." I shrugged. "Just was gonna tell you to plan on shoes with a good heel to them. If we're practicing these lessons with you in those"—I pointed to his boots, which had a two- or three-inch heel to them, at least—"we don't want y'all showing up in flat shoes, or all the practice will go to waste."

Also, not to call Kendall short, but him in flat shoes and me in my dress shoes wasn't going to work if he was going to lead. And if we did this fund-raiser deal, it would be nice to switch out. I was a bit surprised how much I'd liked taking the lady's—or rather the follower's—role. I loved how Chuck called it that. Made it so much simpler. Turned out, I *liked* to follow. Liked to spin and move and simply not worry about holding everything steady for a few minutes.

The restaurant was just as I'd figured—low red building with their logo painted on the side. Inside there were exposed wood beams on the ceiling and gleaming hardwoods everywhere else. Like I'd predicted—very hipster sort of retro feel to it. It was late enough that we got a table along the wall easily. Some people next to us were eating what looked like clams with fries on top. To each their own and all that.

I got an iced tea, and Kendall did the same. We both got the burger and onion rings, mine with cheese, his with a fried egg, because hey, Portland. "I had to teach myself to like tea plain out here," I confessed.

"Oh that's right, you're from the South?"

"Alabama. Little town just over the Florida border. And yeah, we drank sweet tea by the gallon." I laughed as I squeezed my lemon into the tea. "My gran, she's the heretic who drinks her tea *hot*. I clown her that they drummed her out of the South, all the way to here."

"She lives in Portland?"

Might as well spread my cards on the table. Wasn't like I was ashamed of my living situation. "I live with her, actually. She moved out here for a job at PCC, but she's retired from teaching now."

"Ah." Kendall stirred his tea with his straw. "I live in Southeast. By myself. Bought a condo last year."

My back muscles tightened. Why was Kendall showing off that he lived alone, probably in some fancy high-rise? Wasn't like this was a date and he'd need to signal to me that he had a place with privacy. Wait. *Was* this a date? We'd done dancing. I'd sure as fuck dressed up for him. Showered too. I didn't rightly know what this was, and that unsettled me, made me play with my napkin.

Fuck it. The people next to us kept glancing at Kendall all funny. Hell, this was Portland. Surely they'd seen dudes carrying purses before—no need for them to look him over like he belonged in the elephant house over at the zoo. And I had no idea what side of the store he bought that orange sweater in, but he looked damn smokin' in it. I gave them Granddad's best *I'm going to the woodshed* threat glare. Like Granddad, I had no intention of following up on the threat, but it served its purpose and got them looking back down at their food.

"It really doesn't bother you, does it?" Kendall asked.

I didn't play dumb. We both knew what I'd been het up about. "Nope. You do you. I like you. Pretty simple if you ask me."

"Thanks." Kendall's eyes were all soft. "You've...uh...had other genderqueer...*friends* before, I take it?"

I had to think on my reply a minute, get it straight in my head how to answer him without offending. "There's a few people who come to meetings at the shelter and all."

"But no...*close* friends? Partners?"

I snorted at this. "Never had someone worth calling partner. And...no, but not because I was...avoiding it." God, I hoped I wasn't making a mess of this. No one, and I meant no one, had ever intrigued me like Kendall. I hadn't really done much thinking about genderqueer individuals before him, but it wasn't the label that had my pulse humming—it was *him* and all the little details that seemed so...*right*. I needed a longer think on why exactly he did it for me, but our food arrived right then.

"This is good," I said after a few bites. The burger had some sort of sauce on it that I wouldn't have added myself, but it gave it a nice taste, and the meat had a good sear on it. "Nice and hot too."

Kendall laughed. "I'd send it back if they sent it out cold." Something in my face must have given me away because he buttoned up that smile. "Sorry, I...uh...forget that not everyone has access to good food."

"Growing up, we had to fend for ourselves a fair bit. Got plenty sick of stuff that didn't need cooking. And then..." I paused, not sure what to share. Wasn't like I was ashamed of my history, but it did tend to make others a mite uncomfortable.

"Yeah?" Kendall's face was relaxed, not all hard and pushy, more like he'd wait for me to explain, long as it took me to find the words.

"I was on the streets some, back when I was using. Food was...learned not to get too picky, that's all. And now, I like my food hot. Fresh, you know?"

"I get it. That's why my mom is such a supporter of the shelter and the services they provide. Hot meals can make a difference."

I nodded, throat tight. "Saved my life. I don't have no real money yet to donate, but if dancin' can help them raise money, well, I'll do what I can."

Kendall reached across the table, squeezed my hand. He wasn't a real touchy-feely person, so him touching me made my throat even thicker. We sat like that a few moments—quiet, holding hands, his eyes all full of emotion, neither of us needing to speak to communicate.

When the check came, I said, "Split?" and hauled out my cash, even though I knew Kendall was gonna try to pay. I might not have much, but I pay my own way.

Kendall studied me as he was considering whether to press the issue, but he took my cash and put it with his card.

"Mint?" he offered, pulling a little tin out of his purse. They were those ones that taste like flowers, but I took one to be polite.

Out at the car, I gave him the directions to my place. He gave me a curious kind of look before he put the car in drive, one that warmed me all the way to my toes. I'd grown the beard in part because I was tired of people treating me like I was fifteen, but Kendall's searching look made me feel *all* adult.

We chatted about food on the way to my house, the way you do after a really filling meal, and we kept talking a few minutes after he pulled up next to the curb. I wasn't in any hurry to say goodnight, and it looked like he wasn't either.

"Hey, you've got a crumb in your beard." Kendall leaned in and before I knew it, his face was right there as he plucked whatever off my beard. He didn't pull back, the way I'd expected him to. Instead his eyes locked on mine, heat arcing between us.

I had a feeling what he was about, but I didn't pull away. It had been so long. Eternities. And in a second, I was going to have to utter the words that would make him not want any more moments like this, but I was going to enjoy this one kiss. His lips slid over mine, cool and firm and fleeting.

"Night," he whispered.

"Night," I whispered, but I was greedy, and leaned in for another kiss, letting him dictate the pace, mimicking his efforts. He traced my lips with his tongue, so I did the same to him, then when he sucked on my lower lip, I gasped, pulling him closer. I kissed like this might be my last kiss. And it might. At the very least, it was our last one, so I put all that longing into the kiss, until we broke apart, both breathing hard.

"I don't have a wedding tomorrow night," Kendall said. "Want to... uh...come over? We could practice—"

"I can't," I said, regret lacing every syllable.

"Oh, all right." Kendall straightened his sweater, not meeting my eyes. "Some other time, then?"

"Kendall..." Oh hell. I'd had to say the words before, but they never got any easier. "I'm HIV positive. I should have told you..." *But I needed to know what you taste like.* I'd needed to know exactly what I couldn't have. Now I was the one who looked away.

"We can still dance," I mumbled when he didn't say anything. *Please don't take that away from me.*

"Of course we can." Kendall patted my knee. "Good to know. And you haven't...*dated* since?"

"Not really. I had this friend from my meetings. Jake was positive too. We hooked up a bit, but it..." I shrugged. Jake had been toxic for me, wanting to take care of me, controlling at the exact moment when I had to stand on my own feet. Before Jake, I'd figured that I'd just stick to other poz guys, but after him, avoiding the whole mess of hookups seemed the smartest plan. Staying sober was far more important than getting my rocks off. "Most guys don't want to get with a poz guy...and the ones who do can be a bit..." I searched for a kind word for weird. "Militant. Easier to just not mess with that stuff."

"I can see that." His usually expressive voice was rather flat.

"Yeah," I said tightly. Man, I did *not* want to be having this conversation, not with Kendall transforming from a potential friend to a social worker interviewing me about my lifestyle and risk factors. "I should be getting in."

"Todd." Kendall stopped me with a hand on my arm. "I really appreciate you telling me. And for what it's worth, I still would have wanted to kiss you goodnight. Just saying."

I nodded, throat feeling like a too-tight wool sweater again. I couldn't speak, but I wanted to let him know how much it meant, him saying that. I leaned in and brushed a quick kiss across his cheek before I headed out of the car. My eyes burned on the walk up the path to the house. Kendall was sweet, but he'd have a think on this, realize that making out with a formerly homeless, poz addict wasn't what he wanted from his pretty little life. Which would be for the best, really. At least I'd gotten that one kiss. That and the dancing would carry me awhile. It had to—as much as I liked him, getting involved with Kendall would be a damn risky move, and I'd sworn off big risks for good.

Chapter 5
Kendall

I won't say that I went home and happily Googled HIV transmission risks based on specific sex acts. No, my mind was much more muddied than skipping ahead merrily to next week's dancing lesson. I'd left things on what I'd thought was a good note with Todd, but I still had some thinking to do. Also, I had to walk the dog, then check my client messages. Vic had a lead for me on friends of his getting married, so I sent a thank-you, not mentioning that I'd been tangling tongues with his assistant not a half hour ago. Or that I'd learned in the space of a few hours that said assistant happened to be a recovering addict who'd spent time on the streets and was HIV positive. Fuck. Did Vic even know about that?

He had to, right? Was the bakery taking a risk with an HIV-positive employee? I touched my lips, remembering the taste of Todd. I'd gone a little cold and wooden after he told me. I knew woefully little about HIV risks beyond understanding that most people didn't die of it anymore, thanks to the new meds which kept viral loads low. I hadn't had that many partners, and had always used condoms. I got tested at my physical each year and that was that. Or that had been that.

Rococo in my lap, I settled in on the couch with my tablet, pulling a fleece throw around us. It seemed like a good night for a blanket fort. A quick search showed me that no, the bakery wasn't taking a risk having him on staff. More searching revealed that kissing him was fine, about as low risk an activity as one could find. And there were plenty of lists of other things we could do. But Google didn't really have answers to the other questions churning in my gut. The first guy I'd been interested in in months, and he came with a whole grocery cart's worth of issues. It wasn't really fair to think like that—Todd had admirably overcome a lot in his life. But I was having a lot of *What does this mean for me?* questions.

Bing. My phone chirped with a new message. It was from Todd.

It's okay if you don't want to dance next week.

I shook my head, getting distance from my pity party. I really could be a selfish prick sometimes. I hadn't even repeated my invitation for tomorrow night after he told me. And I genuinely liked hanging around the guy—dancing with him was fun, watching him eat was practically pornographic with the pleasure he took from simple food, and talking with him was easy and relaxed. Why on earth would I want to run from that?

You do you. I like you. Todd's voice from earlier echoed in my ears as I tried to decide how to word my reply. Todd seemed accepting of me, judgment-free. Maybe he didn't have the most experience with other genderqueer people, but it had been almost endearing, watching him so carefully trying to navigate my fishing expedition about his history. He so obviously didn't want to offend me, but I hadn't exactly repaid the favor when he told me about his status.

Yeah, I had needed a minute to wrap my head around his diagnosis. However, when it came down to it, I was more worried about the risk he posed to my heart than the risk he posed to my body. *Keep it casual and fun,* I reminded myself before typing a reply. We could be friends, perhaps with a side of benefits. That would suit me. After Lewis, I didn't have it in me for anything more serious, but celibacy was damn boring. Maybe Todd was just the middle ground I needed.

Of course I want to dance! Want to practice before next week—we can push the couch out of the way and practice at my place? And no, I wasn't offering my place because it would be easier to kiss Todd here. Not at all.

His reply took a few minutes. *I've got a meeting tomorrow night. Monday after work?*

It's a date :) Funny how just typing that calmed the restlessness I'd come home with. I returned to my internet searching, less scattered and more focused on what would happen if I could get Todd to kiss me again.

* * * *

We worked it out that Todd would take the bus from the bakery to my neighborhood and then I'd run him home after we ate and practiced dancing. I'd cued up several swing playlists and pushed my couch against the wall, exposing the center of the loft-like space for us to practice in. Rococo kept turning in circles, looking for the missing couch. When I buzzed Todd up, Rococo went nuts trying to get out of my arms to greet him when I opened the door.

"I should have figured you for a dog person," Todd said, holding out a hand for Rococo to sniff. "Gran's got two old bulldog rescues. Your dog probably smells them on me."

I wanted to quip that he smelled yummy and that the dog and I had the same taste in men, but Todd seemed wary enough without me making it worse. I set Rococo down and let him and Todd continue to feel each other out.

"Eat first?" Since I'd had a light schedule that day with a lot of phone calls, I'd offered to cook.

Todd nodded and held up a sack. "It smells amazing. I brought a loaf of our sourdough."

"I'll put that in to heat up now while I take the roast out." I loved entertaining and cooking for others, whether it was one person or ten. I'd figured out from our conversation last week that Todd liked classic fare, so I'd cooked a maple and apple cider–glazed pork tenderloin with roasted vegetables while on hold with some vendors.

Mainly, I just wanted an excuse to watch Todd eat. He admired my vintage table and chairs, admired my dishes—I loved how he *noticed* things, whether it was my clothes or my place settings—before turning his attention to the food.

"You made this for me?" His voice was soft as he gestured at the food. I got the impression that he didn't let many people take care of him—and that not many had tried.

"It was no trouble. Something to do with my hands while on hold on the phone, really." I wanted to tell him he was worth a lot more trouble. The way he savored his food with wide eyes and little happy noises had me wanting to cook for him a lot more. That and I wanted to see what else made him make that pleased expression.

After dinner, he insisted on doing the dishes. I wasn't one to leave the sink all week or anything, but I also wasn't one to spring right up after eating, dishcloth in hand. Todd, however, clearly was, even wiping down my counters and stove while we chatted more. I got him to tell me some cute dance-competition stories. I got the impression his mother had been a major stage mother, and he didn't sound close to either of his parents, but his whole demeanor changed when he talked about dance.

"So we had this little neighbor girl who started taking basic ballroom at the place where I took jazz and tap. My mama was best friends with her mama, and they got to talking about how cute we'd be competing together.

Turned out we weren't so bad, so Hailey and I, we did the contests and Disney performances—"

"Wait. You performed at Disney?"

"Just a few times. With groups of other kid dancers. It was no big deal." Todd didn't look up from the sink.

"I think it is."

"When you're dancing in the July Florida heat, it's less than fun, trust me." Todd washed my roasting pan and handed it to me to dry. "And it was a lot of practice. Same as anything else."

"Did you have to miss a lot of school? I follow figure skating and a lot of them end up homeschooled or with a tutor."

"Yeah. It was hard too because dance was easy. Math, that I could do, but readin'—man, that was the toughie. It was easier to just focus on the dance. Mama tried the homeschooling thing for a bit." He made a screwed-up face like that hadn't gone well. "But then my folks split and everything went to hell."

"I'm sorry. My parents divorced when I was so little that I don't remember my dad."

"Relationships are a total crapshoot." Todd shook his head.

"On that we can agree."

"But you help people get married!" Todd sounded like I was confessing to being the Easter bunny.

"Uh-huh. This year, I'll be planning the third wedding for one of my first clients. I've already had a couple of other repeat flyers too. I love special events, love giving people a magical day, but trust me, there's no happily ever after in store for me."

"Amen to not needin' any of those trappings, but you nailed it on giving people a magical moment. That's what you need to bring to the dance. The idea that you're creating a magical moment for the audience. And if you're lucky, some of the fairy dust rubs off on you."

"Shall we, then?" I raised the volume on the speakers from the soft background music I'd had on while we ate. I was glad that we seemed to share a similar cynical view of long-term relationships. It made my kissing plans easier. "I am wearing the shoes for it, after all."

I was wearing my favorite pair of heels—black leather, closed toe with a stacked heel. The rest of me was pretty casual—tight jeans and a gray sweater, but I'd worn the shoes for him.

"That you are." Todd smiled at me before grabbing the remote. "How about not Perry Como?"

He flipped through the playlist before landing on something jazzy that seemed to please him. "Let's start with a little waltz to this one to warm up, then we can go over the stuff from class."

I'd waltzed before, albeit rather badly, but I moved into the follower's position. Todd made a pained expression and reversed our positions. "You lead. I'll talk you through the steps."

"Really?" I was pretty sure no one had ever let me lead a waltz before, including my sister when she'd taught me. And the couple of times I'd danced with someone like Lewis at an event, the other person *always* led. "We're not in class. We don't have to switch—"

"I like you leading," Todd said firmly. "You're good at it. Just pushy enough. I always struggled with being...what do you call it...*decisive*, unless I had a choreographed routine. You've got that though."

"The pushiness?" I raised an eyebrow.

"In the best way." He winked at me and we started the waltz with me leading and him giving tips.

The next song was more up-tempo.

"Okay, now sugar push."

"You should be a dance teacher," I joked.

"How about we get through a song without one of us tripping before you make declarations like that?"

"Spoilsport." I stuck my tongue out at him, and his laugh slid right over me, smooth as the trumpet in the big-band orchestra playing from my speakers. Laughing, we made a full song doing the sugar push.

"Ready for some turns?" His eyes sparkled.

"Yeah," I said as the new song started. "Starter step first, right?"

"Yup. Count it out if you need to." We worked through the starter step and the throwout and underarm pass again.

"Keep your knees softer. Get your hand up higher. Right on my shoulder blade," Todd coached. As I got more confident, the tips got fewer and he started adding little flourishes to his turns, like little kicks and hand movements.

"You totally need to message Hailey and tell her she was hogging all the fun." I laughed as I spun him again, loving how delighted he seemed.

A funny expression crossed Todd's face. "Maybe I'll do that."

It took another few turns before his smile crept out again along with his stream of tips. "Relax your elbows. And smile."

An unhappy thought flitted across my brain and refused to leave. "Do you smile because you're having genuine fun with me, or do you smile because you were taught to do that for the audience?"

Todd's lips pursed. "Both? I mean, there were plenty of times at competition when I smiled even though I wanted to puke. But, with you... it's different. I'm not sure why, but this just feels...freer."

"Yeah." I kind of understood what he meant. Nothing had ever made me feel like this either. Powerful. In control. And...balanced. Which was a corny thing to think since I was always one step away from tripping, but it was true. I was wearing my best heels and taking the lead, and that felt *right* in a way that few things did.

It was similar to how my favorite clothes made me feel—able to take on the world, beautifully. That feeling of invincibility kept me reaching for certain articles in my wardrobe, even when I knew all eyeballs would be on me. Maybe especially then. And Todd made me feel the same way, made me appreciate myself and who I was and the space that he gave me.

The music changed again, this time to a Sinatra song, and Todd's smile got more wistful. "I've only ever done foxtrot to this piece. Man, I loved foxtrot. That was probably my favorite of the ballroom dances."

"Show me," I urged, reversing our hands. "Lead to demonstrate for me, then I want to try."

"Pushy, pushy," he said, laughing. "Okay, I'm going to show you a basic foxtrot."

He led me through the basics. "Slow, slow, quick, quick. Now you try leading."

"This isn't very fancy," I observed as I guided us around the room. "I bet you can do all the trick stuff, right?"

"I can do a little of that." A smile that meant he could do all sorts of things teased at the corner of his mouth.

"Hey!" A thought occurred to me. "If I Google you, will I find all sorts of cute videos of you dancing as a kid?"

"No. I think most of that was pre-YouTube, thank god."

"I bet I could find *something*."

"Do not search me." Todd dropped the dance hold, cupping my face to hold me still. "I'm serious. You want to see fancy dancing, I'll send you some links to some demos."

"I've seen demos. I just want to see *you* strutting your stuff."

"I suppose Gran probably has some video of me somewhere. I can check her DVDs and files. Find something I'm okay sharing—"

"You don't have to." I licked at his thumb, trying ease some of this tension.

"Maybe I want to." He didn't sound too certain, but he kept his eyes locked on my face, gaze dropping to my mouth. The moment shifted, became charged with something far more potent.

I licked his thumb again, this time more deliberately. His breath hitched. Sucking his thumb in, I swirled my tongue around it, sucking hard as I showed that while I might be uncoordinated with my feet, I had no such issues with my mouth.

"Fuck. Kendall," Todd moaned softly and bumped his hips forward.

"Yeah." I gave him a dirty wink before releasing his thumb. I started to sink to my knees, but his hand stayed me.

"No?" I'd never been turned down for a BJ before.

"You really want to?" Disbelief colored Todd's words. "I kinda figured you…that is, thought you wouldn't want anything like—"

I stopped him mid-ramble. "I want to."

Todd licked his lips, nodding even as his eyes were wary. "Are you gonna laugh if I say I want to wait? Like not tonight?"

"I'm not laughing," I assured him, stretching a hand out to stroke his beard. "But…not tonight?" I wasn't sure if this was a brush-off or not.

"My brain needs to play catch-up to my dick. I'm still…figurin' things out. I'm not as fast a thinker as you." His neck flushed.

I really was a selfish prick. This whole time I'd figured that since I'd thought things through, had a Google, bought some new condoms, and moved on from my fears, that sexy-times would be ahead. I hadn't stopped to think that Todd might have his own set of reservations.

"It's okay," I said, and meant it. "No pressure."

"I want to. It's just…" He shrugged. "Gonna sound stupid."

"Not to me." I continued to stroke his bristly jaw, other hand rubbing his tight shoulder.

"Everything's different with you. Dancing, sure, but even eatin' together and stuff like that. I never had that before. Before you, I'd sworn off looking for anything like this."

"This? This is just two new friends dancing. And maybe a *little* more." I gave him a meaningful look. As sweet as he was, I still needed Todd to not make too much of this. My resolve to keep things casual and uncomplicated might be wavering, but the memory of how quickly things had gone from sweet to sour with Lewis still lingered.

"I know. But it's still a far cry from the sort of hookups I've had in the past. I kinda want to go slow. See what I've been missing. Take my time and make it…special."

My chest contracted. I'd never thought of that either—from the little he'd said, his teenage years had been anything but normal. Mine hadn't exactly been Hallmark-perfect either, but at least I'd had dating and friends.

I might not be able to give Todd everything he needed, but I could give him the slower exploration he seemed to crave.

"We can do that." I massaged some of the knots out of his shoulders and neck. "And it gives you more time to think?" I guessed.

"Yeah, that too." He looked so concerned that I leaned in, brushed a kiss across his mouth. "I'd always figured I'd just stick with other poz guys. Easier. I don't wanna hurt you or put you at risk."

"You won't." And because that sounded a bit glib, I added, "And we can talk about risks and stuff when the time *is* right."

"It'll be soon." Todd laughed. His smile was a soft one that felt like a shared secret. "Lord almighty...your mouth. But isn't that kind of the fun?"

"Fun?"

"Yeah, knowin' we'll see each other again on Thursday, but not knowing what we'll get up to..."

"Anticipation, you mean?"

"*Yes*. That's the word I was looking for. I want to anticipate with you."

I was pretty sure no one else ever had taken the time to go slowly with him, and my throat went thick and tight. I had to force out a joke before I got too emotional. "Can you anticipate us making out for a while when I drop you off?"

"I'm counting on it." He kissed me then, soft and sure. Anticipation might be exactly what Todd needed, but it might well kill me.

Chapter 6
Todd

Making out with Kendall in front of my Gran's house had me rethinking my "go slow" request. I'd been surprised by him being all willing to go to his knees for me. Usually, it was the other way around, but without the fancy dinner and dancing first. I wasn't lying—I'd never had anything like Kendall. It couldn't—*wouldn't*—last, but I wanted to enjoy this sweetness. I wanted to see how it worked for other people and wanted to distance myself from a past I wasn't that proud of.

And mainly I wanted to memorize Kendall's taste, the texture of his tongue against mine, the feel of his breath against my cheek. I spent the next few days in a pleasant haze, remembering those kisses.

It helped that Kendall texted me a few times in the run-up to Thursday. Silly stuff like, *I'm dancing with my mop. Practice makes perfect, right?*

My feet thank you ;) I'd replied back with a link to where he could print and cut out footprints for his floor.

Then he'd actually done it and sent me a pic of the dog chewing one of the footprints.

Need a ride to dance? Kendall texted on Thursday. *The bakery isn't too far out of my way.*

I'd been planning on busing it, but I wasn't going to turn down the ride. *Sure. I've got my clothes with me.*

After Marcie and I closed out the front, I went into the bathroom at the back of the bakery with my little grocery sack of clothes and dress shoes. I wasn't going to run out and go purse shopping with Kendall, but I could see the appeal in having a nice bag. It said you respected your belongings. That's one thing I liked so much about him—his actions just seemed so full of care. Like he cared about his table, making it all pretty for our little dinner, and he cared about himself, always being so put together. I wet my hair down, trying to look less like a southern-fried scarecrow for Kendall. Same clothes as last week, but I'd added an old suit vest of Gramps's. Tossed that on because it seemed like the sorta look Kendall might like.

When I got out of the bathroom, Vic was right there in the hallway, hanging up his apron.

"Look at you," he said. "Where are you headed?"

Now that was a tricky question. Would Kendall be cool with me telling? I wasn't rightly sure. But this was Vic, and I didn't want to lie, have him think I was on the hustle or something. "Dancin' lessons."

"Dancing?" Vic looked like I might as well have said leprechaun stomping.

"Yeah. Swing dancing. Kendall does it too," I said defensively. Hadn't meant to toss Kendall in there, but Vic's being all shocked had me testy.

"Oh, that's...great. You getting out and all." Vic rubbed his shaved head. "But, uh...Todd...you should be...*careful*...with Kendall."

"I told him," I said to the wall over Vic's shoulder. "*Everything.* Okay? And we're just dancing. Nothing serious."

"No, no, that's not what I meant." Vic held up his hands. "I meant watch out for *you*. Kendall's coming off a bad breakup, and I don't know if he's the steadiest of people."

"I'll be fine." I crossed my arms over my chest. Kendall had made it clear he wasn't looking for serious, but neither was I. Matter of fact, I was still sorting out exactly what I was doing here—taking the kinds of risks I'd sworn not to. I didn't need Vic's warning to guard my heart, because I planned to lock that sucker up right tight.

"I'm sure you will." Vic didn't sound convinced, and that irked me. Just tell it to me straight, you know? And I kinda looked up to Vic. Not in a crush sorta way or hero worship, more like he had his shit so together that I couldn't help but respect that. And it hurt a bit, him not being more supportive.

"I gotta get going."

"Todd?" Vic stopped me when I would have brushed by him. "Good luck. Really. You deserve something you enjoy. I hope dancing can be that for you."

I nodded curtly, but I still had a bit of a head of steam as I slid into Kendall's car.

"You look *amazing*." Kendall grinned at me. "Really. We *have* to go shopping for the benefit. You wear vintage so well."

"Thanks." I was still pouty, but I remembered my manners. "You look real nice too."

He'd worn reddish-pink lip stain of some sort, and it made him look hot as fuck, those luscious lips all full of sin. He was wearing a slinky tunic thing over skinny pants, and the whole package, especially coupled with his competent driving, revved me up out of my bad mood in no time at all.

At class, Chuck had us start with the sugar push and a review of the starter step. "You've been practicing," he said as he came by, offering pointers.

"We have." Kendall gave me a meaningful look, one that seemed to promise more kisses. A hot little shiver raced up my spine. *Yes, please.*

"All right, now we're going to learn how to whip, and several variations. And I don't mean the *Fifty Shades* kind." Chuck laughed at his own joke. But it got me wondering, was I holding Kendall back, wanting to go slow? Was he into more of that fancy stuff? Whips and harnesses? Me, I'd never been one to need accessories for sex, but maybe Kendall...

"*Psst.* Time for us to practice." Kendall nudged me. "Where'd you go?"

I assumed the follower's position before I answered. "Just thinking. . . about...stuff." I knew I was blushing.

"Oh, do tell." Kendall dropped his voice. He led me into the eight-count pattern, but for once I was the one to bungle it all to hell.

"Fine. You into...what Chuck said?" I whispered as we tried it again.

"Whips?" Kendall's eyebrows shot up like twin rockets. "Uh. No. Very much no. You?"

"Nah. I like things...simple."

"Simple's good." The heat in Kendall's eyes went a long way to covering my embarrassment. "*Very* good, actually."

"Kendall, elbows up! Try dragging Todd less," Chuck said as he came by. "And, Todd, as you go into your coaster triple step, bring your right foot forward more."

I coughed because I hadn't been doing anything close to a coaster step, too distracted by Kendall and our conversation. We tried the move again as Chuck watched, and this time, I got it. Man, I wasn't ever gonna get tired of Kendall turning me around.

"Lead switch," Chuck announced a few minutes later. "And if you choose, you can switch with the couple closest to you. Make new friends!"

Only one I really wanted to be friends with was Kendall, but I dutifully looked to the couple to our left—two men in near identical khakis and dress shirts. They pretended not to see us, but the taller guy's eyes slid toward Kendall with a sour expression. That was unexpected, but fine. More Kendall for me.

"You can keep leading, *babe*. You're damn good at it," I said loud enough for the judgmental assholes to hear.

"You're an even better champion than Rococo." Kendall laughed. "Down, boy. I'm an acquired taste. Lots of people think people like me give gays a bad name."

"What?" I blinked. "By being too pretty and confident? That's BS. Fuck the haters."

"You're a treasure." Kendall's eyes went all soft as he led me into the turn.

"Am not." I waited until we were close together to whisper, "Lots of guys say the same nasty things about poz guys like me. Like we're confirming stereotypes."

"Fuck the haters," Kendall said firmly.

Chuck showed us how to add some turns to the basic whip.

I couldn't help laughing when we practiced the move because it just felt so good and right. Fuck Vic and his warnings. Fuck the judgy couple. Fuck whatever norms said that I should lead. Fuck the haters, man. This was simply too good to be missed.

"You know, you're making me want to try following again." Kendall smiled indulgently at me. "You make it seem like so much fun."

"It is."

"Okay, okay, let me try," Kendall said when Chuck announced another lead swap. "Spin away."

The whip was similar enough to some other moves I knew that I picked up the pattern quick enough to lead, turning Kendall easier. "That's it. Trust the motion. Trust your feet," I coached. *Trust me.* I still loved following, but that moment when Kendall trusted me enough to move fluidly in and out of the turn, that was pretty damn sweet. Made my chest swell with unfamiliar feelings.

We did a water and coffee break, and I got my guy a water. And yeah, I knew it was very temporary, but it still felt damn good, having a person to fetch for, to take care of.

After the break, we practiced more variations on the whip. I loved watching Kendall come alive as the leader. His movements were becoming surer, his posture even more confident.

"You two are such a pleasure to watch," Chuck praised. "You work your slot so gracefully."

Kendall waited until Chuck moved away, then snorted. "Yeah, well, I want to do very dirty things to your slot."

"Hush." I felt my ears burning, even as I thrilled to the words.

"So you want to grab food after? I was thinking maybe we could get takeout Indian, go back to my place?"

My nose wrinkled up. "No."

"Oh well—" Kendall's face fell.

"I meant no on curry. I don't like it." I felt like such a hick confessing that. "But you can get it for you. I'll worry about myself later."

"Don't be silly. Do you like pizza? We could get half with whatever you like and half with spinach and artichoke and no cheese for me. I love that combo. And we can pick it up on the way back so that we know it's hot."

"Thanks." My chest muscles tightened up, not up to the pulsing of a too-heavy heart. "Pizza's great."

We grabbed the food on the way back to Kendall's and my pulse thrummed as I held the hot box on my lap, just knowing that we were probably going to kiss before much longer.

Kendall and I took the elevator to his ninth-floor condo. He let me in, then scooped up the dog, who started barking. "I better take him for a fast turn around the block. Help yourself to anything to drink in the fridge, and plates are in the upper-right cupboard."

I was still taking in the view of the city at night through his huge windows, but I nodded and headed to the kitchen. The kitchen occupied all of the rear wall of the condo, and like the rest of the place, it was a mixture of space-age contemporary with glass and gleaming stainless steel, and classic with cherrywood cabinetry. The breakfast bar was open to the rest of the loft-like space, but Kendall seemed to favor eating at the little dining nook he'd created with a vintage table and chairs and a circular rug.

Instead of just tucking into the pizza like I was half tempted to, I set it on the center of his table, then got out two plates and forks for the salad that we'd gotten to go alongside. I had a feeling Kendall was trying to sneak more vegetables into me, which made me smile, him looking out for me like that. I made us both glasses of ice water. It wasn't as pretty as how Kendall would do it, but it looked all nice and homey laid out like that, and Kendall's smile when he came in confirmed that it had been the right call.

"Thanks." He kissed my cheek before sitting down. His pizza looked all naked with just the vegetables on it, but I liked how we'd compromised so easy.

While I chewed, I stewed over how to ask him about the ex Vic had mentioned. I wanted to know more, but I wasn't the best at lead-in questions.

"Everything okay? Pizza hot enough?" Kendall asked.

"It's great." I took a sip of water. "So...you ever dance with anyone else?"

Kendall groaned. "Who told you about Lewis? Vic?"

I nodded. "Sorry. I'll stop being nosy."

"No, it's okay." Kendall waved my apology away with a flick of his wrist. His short nails had been painted black last week, but now they matched his lips. "You'll probably meet him at the benefit. He works for my mother. We're supposedly still friends. It's all very civil."

"Civil sucks." I picked a piece of tomato out of my salad, set it aside. "See, you break up, you're supposed to get your anger on. Hate on them for a while. Healthier than this we-can-be-friends BS."

"You still friends with the guy you mentioned the other night?"

"Jake? He was a friend who became a hookup who went back to being a sort-of friend. It's complicated, but we weren't ever boyfriends or anything like that."

"Sort-of friends pretty much defines Lewis and me. We went to college together at Reed, ran around in the same crowd. He went to law school down at Willamette, but we stayed friendly. Then he started working for my mother and we got...tangled up. And now it's *all* a bit of a mess."

"Was he...did he...how'd he feel about..." I struggled to find the right words to ask what I wanted to know.

Kendall mercifully took pity on me. "It's okay. You can say genderqueer, you know? And you're curious about if that was an issue between the two of us?"

I nodded.

"It both was and wasn't. I always knew that I didn't exactly fit into a predetermined little box, but when I joined the campus LGBTQ group, I met others who identified as genderqueer, and it was like...a light went on. It gave a name to everything I'd been feeling for years, and hanging around those people, I got more comfortable expressing myself, especially my fem side. I think Lewis thought it was a phase at first, didn't really understand that this *is* me."

"Of course it is." I really couldn't see Kendall any other way. His genderqueerness was as much a part of him as his smile or his generous personality.

"You're sweet." He gave me one of those million-watt smiles. "But after a while, especially once we started publicly dating, Lewis kept asking me to tone it down."

I shook my head. "Idiot. He should have been proud to be seen with a person like you. Didn't deserve you."

"Sadly, most people seem to think it's the other way around." Kendall sighed. "Including my mother. She tries, she really does, to accept my genderqueer identity, but I'm not sure she entirely understands it, and she certainly was...disappointed when Lewis and I broke up."

"He wasn't good enough for you." I ripped off a piece of pizza crust with more force than necessary. "Is Lewis gonna have a...date at the benefit, you think?"

"Oh, most certainly." Kendall sighed. "I saw him recently with some tanned and toned personal trainer type. But if you're asking if there will be other queer couples dancing at the benefit, yeah, there should be plenty. We won't stand out."

"You always stand out," I teased. "In a good way. You hoping to make him jealous with your dancing skills?"

"And my hot date." Kendall winked at me. "He was a bit of a prick to me last time we spoke. I know it's petty, and I'm going to have to keep dealing with him because of my mom, but yeah, I'd love to make him jealous."

I wasn't anything to be proud of like that. I guess I looked passable enough, but I wasn't special. Not like Kendall and his fancy friends. I could, however, dance. "Maybe we should practice more."

"You don't have to be nervous. But yeah, we should." He went for the remote to his stereo and I started clearing the table. The couch was still pushed back from other night, which gave us a nice-size rectangle of shiny hardwood to work with.

"You don't have to do dishes!" Kendall tried to take them from me, but I wouldn't let him.

"No sense in leaving them." I made quick work of getting the plates in the washer and crushing the pizza box to fit in his trash.

"Mint?" Kendall offered me one from his tin.

"Is this your way of sayin' we're kissing later?" I took one, resolving to get my own box of non-flowery mints if this was a thing for him.

"Maybe." He winked at me and started the music. He'd lowered the lights, which created a soft glow around the long, open room.

For a few songs, we worked the sugar push and the whip, and the variations on the whip with the turns, but when the playlist slid into a sultry, bluesy number, I gathered Kendall up closer.

"Let's not practice for a song. Just slow dance with me."

"I can do that." He wrapped his arms around my neck. I suppose I was leading, but it felt more like we were equally sharing—no, *surrendering*, standing there swaying. He was wearing chunky boots with a lower heel than his pumps, which put his lips right against my neck. Not really a kiss, but distracting as fuck. His hair brushed my face, and I loved how he was always doing such different things with it. He'd straightened it some today and it hung loosely about his face in gentle sheets. I couldn't resist touching the back of his head, where his hair brushed his collar. *Soft.*

I wasn't really intending it, but the movement of my hand brought his lips millimeters from mine. And I couldn't *not* kiss him. It was one of those perfect moments, the kind that usually happens to other people. Still swaying to Ella Fitzgerald and Louis Armstrong, we kissed, lips sampling each other as our bodies sang like the trumpet in the song. One song bled into another and we still kissed.

It felt like I'd been waiting my whole life for that one kiss, that one moment with that one person who wrapped me with his magic. Kendall tasted like mint and lip gloss and joy—pure joy. I'd tasted passion before, and sex plenty, and a few times I'd caught an edge of seduction, but this was the first time I tasted happiness and joy. I wanted the moment to drag on forever.

But eventually, my body became a bit pushier. Seemed like my cock wasn't amused that my lips were getting all the action, and my hips started rocking against Kendall's, looking for purchase.

He groaned and tumbled us backwards onto his sofa, landing on top of me. "This okay?" he asked, eyes searching my face in the low light.

"Yeah." I buried both hands in the soft mass of his hair, pulling him down for another kiss. Kendall on top of me was hardly *okay*. More like necessary. I *needed* his warm weight pressing down on me, needed his kisses. Oxygen. Water. Kendall. And I might be willing to trade water for more Kendall.

On the stereo, the softer part of the playlist continued, and as Louis Armstrong crooned, I floated along, letting Kendall lead, surely as if we were dancing. He undid the first few buttons on my shirt so he could kiss my collarbones before returning to my neck and ears. Even my eyelids got blessed with little kisses.

We were rocking together, both hard as broom handles, but it wasn't the kind of purposeful club grinding where everyone knows where things are going. From the feel of him, Kendall was seriously packing, and while my body had several ideas of what to do with that knowledge, my brain was content to let Kendall lead us into more dizzying kisses.

Finally, he broke away, lips swollen and face flushed. "Should I run you home?"

My cock throbbed and ached, but I nodded.

"Fuck." Kendall sat up, head falling back against the sofa. "You're going to kill me."

"Sorry. Want me to—"

"No." Kendall gave me a hand so I could sit up too. "This is torture, but what a way to go."

"Yup." I grinned at him.

"You better wipe the lip gloss off your face before I take you home." Kendall laughed. "And *please* tell me I don't have to wait until Thursday to see you again."

"You don't." I leaned in for a quick kiss.

"What are you doing Sunday afternoon? We could go shopping?"

Now, I wasn't one to think of shopping as some relaxing thing, but he'd mentioned it enough times I knew it was important to him. "Yeah, you can get me all dolled up for the benefit."

"You're going to be perfect." He grinned at me, but I was anything but sure about that.

Chapter 7
Kendall

Hanging out with Todd was seriously going to kill me. I was pretty sure that no one had ever died of a hard-on, which just meant I'd be the first. I was used to being one-of-a-kind. Might as well be a medical mystery too. I'd been dangerously close to coming in my pants the other night when we'd made out for what felt like hours on my couch, and then we'd kissed a long time in the car too. We'd texted about nothing later that night—like kids who hated to fall asleep alone.

Sunday I had a wedding consultation over brunch, so I was a bit dressy when I went to pick Todd up, but I also wasn't expecting his grandmother to open the door.

A short woman with a long gray braid and a shirt advertising a presidential candidate I'd never heard of, she blinked several times, whether because of the sunshine or my white sweater and pearl bracelet, I wasn't sure.

"Kendall?" she asked, eyes still narrower than I liked.

"Yes." I gave her a smile anyway. "Is Todd around?"

"Here." Holding his shoes, Todd strode into the front hall in jeans and a T-shirt with a flannel over it. Guy made Portland basic look hot. Hell, even his bare feet turned me on.

"Hey, come in for a sec. Gran found something you're going to get a kick out of."

Gran didn't look like she got a kick out of *me*, but I dutifully followed both of them into a pleasantly cluttered living room.

"Do you want a coffee, Kendall?" Todd's grandmother asked. "I just made a fresh pot."

"I just had a vat at brunch. More and I'll float away. Thanks."

"Any friend of Todd's is most welcome here. And he's been so happy since starting the dance classes with you."

"The classes are pretty fun." I sent Todd a look that said that what happened *after* class was more interesting to me.

"And it got me to thinking of some of Todd's dance pictures when he was bitty." She opened the binder up to reveal a smiling cherub in a shiny costume and tap shoes. She handed me the binder. Todd hovered on the arm of the couch like he couldn't decide whether to squeeze in next to me or run away from the kid pictures.

"So cute!" I leafed through the pictures, watching him grow through several bad haircuts. In the first ballroom pictures, the girl, Hailey, was taller than Todd, so I teased him about that. Then he hit the awkward early teen years, full of puppy fat and acne but the same earnest smile, until the last picture when he was maybe fourteen or fifteen and so sad—deep circles under his eyes and pale skin—that I wanted to reach through the book and give him a hug.

"Anyway, it's just pictures." Todd shut the book and handed it back to his grandmother.

"Thanks for sharing it with me," I said to him, really wishing I could hug him right then, erase the hurt in his eyes. He was always so ready to do battle on my behalf, but I would have gladly taken up a sword against his past.

"We should probably get going, right?" Todd shoved his shoes on.

"Yeah, it was nice meeting you," I said to the grandmother.

"Will you be back for dinner? Kendall, you're welcome too. I've got a League of Women Voters meeting this afternoon, but I shouldn't be out too late."

"We uh..." Todd scratched the back of his neck. "We'll probably eat at Kendall's."

"Ah. Don't wait up?" She laughed in a way that eased my tension toward her but made Todd blush bright red.

"Nope." I joined the laughter and hauled Todd out of there before his face literally caught fire.

* * * *

My plan was for us to hit several of my favorite vintage stores—Red Light, Avalon, and Hollywood Vintage, plus others if we had time. We started at Red Light because it was closest to Todd's house, where, no surprise, Todd found a rack with a lot of Pendleton plaid shirts. He held up two, one a red-and-black and one a blue-and-white with a thinner stripe of purple.

"That one." I pointed to the blue. "Unless the purple puts you off."

"It's a color, not a political preference. Or a vegetable." Todd laughed and tucked the blue shirt under his arm. "Now, I've been thinkin' that I need a bag of some kind. Like a backpack but cooler. What do you suggest?"

I studied him as carefully as I would one of my clients. I loved helping people find their personal style. "I've got it," I said and led him to the bags, where I sifted and sorted until I found a battered leather messenger bag. "Something like this."

Todd nodded. "Like an explorer. I dig it. It'll carry my shoes for dance class nicely."

"Now let's build on the look you wore to class Thursday—more throwback casual maybe?"

"Been so long since I spent like this. Maybe ever." Todd looked a bit overwhelmed as I showed him different options.

"Should we stop?" I hadn't really thought about budget much, and I should have.

"Nah. I got cash." Todd shrugged. "I save most of my money from the bakery other than what goes for my doctors and meds and then to Gran for the food. Gran calls me a hoarder. But when you ain't had it..."

"I get it. Don't let me pressure you into spending too much."

"You won't. I just meant..." He dropped his voice as he fingered a tie. "It's kinda like with kissing. You show me what I've been missing. Make me wanna live that little bit more."

My sinuses burned, and it wasn't because of the musty clothes. "You're getting more of that later," I warned.

"Bring it on."

"Oh my gosh, I *love* your bracelet. Did you buy that here?" A young woman with pastel hair reminiscent of cotton candy grabbed my arm.

"Nope. Nordies." I gave her a smile, even if I'd rather focus on Todd.

"Can I snap a picture of you for my People of Portlandia Insta-gram account? I just *love* your whole outfit."

"Sure." I grabbed a very red-looking Todd and wrapped my arms around him before she snapped the picture. I'd go hunt down her In-stagram later. It would be nice to have a souvenir of the day.

"That happen to you a lot? Total strangers wanting pictures?" Todd asked in a low voice once she'd moved on.

"Some. It's Portland." I shrugged. "Most people are cool. Some tourists seem to think I'm part of the local experience, but I'll take curiosity and compliments over rudeness like that couple in our dance class." I'd been at this enough years to have run the gamut of reactions from people, and it didn't faze me anymore. Living here, more often than not, was a positive experience, and that was all I really cared about.

Where Red Light had had more everyday stuff for Todd, Hollywood Vintage and Avalon's vintage suits were perfect for the benefit. I found a few pieces for myself too at our various stops, but my main focus was Todd. We found a gray wool suit jacket with the right vibe at one place, then paired it with suspenders and darker gray pants from another, and a shirt the color of old paper from a third place. I was mindful of his limited budget and really worked to find him bargains that would look amazing but not break the bank.

"You're good," Todd said when we were walking from the garage to the elevator to my place. "The way you pull things together. Can't wait to see how it's all going to look."

"Oh, you are totally giving me a fashion show back at my place while I cook." I'd already volunteered to make us pasta.

"I'm not all that." Todd blushed and looked at his sneakers.

"Hot bearded tattooed hipster who looks fuckable in vintage? Sweetheart, I'm not sure where you've been, but there are whole In-stagram and Tumblr accounts devoted to guys like you."

"Fuckable?" He gave me a little smile. "That mean I'm gettin' kissed later?" He pulled something from his pocket. "Brought my own mints and everything."

"You are *so* getting kissed." I chased him into the elevator. I would have happily chased him all the way to the bedroom, but Rococo greeted us with a lot of barking and an I-need-outside dance. Todd laughed though and set down our bags while I grabbed the leash.

"I'll come too," he said.

I tried to hurry the dog up as we went on the fastest turn around the block ever.

"In a hurry?" Todd asked as I jingled the leash, giving me a hot look that said he wouldn't have minded my chasing-in-the-bedroom impulse.

"For you? I'm the Queen of Patience." I shot him what I hoped was a beatific smile.

"And it's appreciated." Todd looked around the street, then leaned in. "Have you thought any...that is...if we *do*, there are...risks."

I saved him from his rambling with a quick kiss. Funny how uncomfortable I could be with others in my space and how comfortable I was with Todd.

"Yes, I've thought about that. *A lot.* But you're on the new meds with a low viral count, right?"

He nodded.

"Then I figure condoms for anything involving penetration, but I'm not going to worry too much about lower-risk stuff. Promise I'm not going to freak if I get your spunk on me or something." I kind of guessed that that had been part of what was holding him back the other night.

Todd blushed so hard his beard almost changed colors, and nodded. I grabbed his hand and squeezed, and we stayed like that with a quiet sort of heat between us as we walked back to the condo. Todd was right—there really was something delicious about anticipation.

Thus, I didn't jump him the second the door shut and I let Rococo off his leash, instead saying, "Fashion show? Let's see how everything looks and whether anything's going to need tailoring."

"Tailoring?" Todd blinked.

"It's not a dirty word. It's how you make clothes look their best."

"That how come you always look cute as hell? Tailoring?"

Now it was my turn to blush. "If the pants need hemming or something, I'll do it for you. I do most of my own alterations."

"No pins," Todd said.

Ah. He was worried about risks again. Sweet. I nodded. "No, I've got chalk. Now get to changing while I grab the chalk and my measuring tape."

"Right *here*?" he squeaked as he gestured to the bank of windows.

"We're on the ninth floor. No one can see, but if you're really uncomfortable, we can go to the bedroom." I picked up one of the sacks and headed that way. "I think you just want a tour of my room."

"Maybe." Todd snuck up on me to hug me from behind.

I grabbed my sewing supplies from the hall closet and went to perch on the end of my bed.

"Uh." Todd paused partway through unbuttoning his flannel. "You going to watch?"

"Oops." I gathered up my stuff. "I can wait in the living room."

"No, it's okay…just never given someone a show before." The back of his neck was a dusky pink and his eyes studied the shag rug under my bed.

"Here. I'll try on my new pants too." I grabbed a pair of cigarette pants from my bag. "That way you're not the only one stripping."

"And now I ain't gonna be able to concentrate." Todd's eyes went to my groin. "But yeah, that works. Just wasn't so sure about having an audience."

"It's okay." I brushed a kiss across his cheek. Then, leaving my sweater on, I made quick work of my pants.

"You wear boxers?" Todd sounded surprised. He'd gotten as far as getting his shirts off. And man, he was tasty, pale skin dotted with golden freckles and a decent amount of blond fuzz over his pecs. Rosy nipples several shades darker than his lips peeked out from the fuzz, making me want to touch and taste.

"Usually." I shrugged and picked up the pair of pants. "They're the most comfortable. Why? Were you expecting panties?"

"Wasn't rightly sure. Seem kinda bulky for your tight pants." Todd's hands stilled on his belt buckle. "Whatever's comfortable, you know?"

"If it turns you on, you're allowed to make special requests." I'd had a lover with that fetish, prior to Lewis, and hadn't minded one bit shopping for a few pretty things to drive him wild.

"Not sure." A pale flush crept up Todd's neck and his eyes went wide as he looked me over with barely disguised heat. Yeah, he was into the idea. "I might have to do more shopping." I gave him a wink as I pulled the pants on. "Fuck. Too tight. I knew I should have tried these on at the place."

"Can you take them back?"

"Yeah." I nodded even though I was as likely to end up donating them as I was to return them. I slid them back down and shifted my attention back onto Todd, who had finally removed his pants, revealing utilitarian black boxer briefs. Impressive bulge, but I didn't let my eyes linger there because I didn't want to make him uncomfortable.

He pulled on the dress pants, the shirt, and the jacket. It didn't matter that we had nowhere to be—there was something magical about watching another person dress up. That was part of what I loved about my job, although watching my clients transform never turned me on like watching Todd get all dapper did. Even with a few alterations needed, he totally looked like hipster porn.

"Pants are a bit loose." He tugged at the waistband.

"They're supposed to be with suspenders, but let me see." I grabbed my chalk and measuring tape and went into tailor mode, checking the length of his pant hems and the fit of the waistband and jacket.

"Kendall?"

"Yeah?" I tugged on his sleeve.

"This is torture." His eyes had drifted shut, and a quick glance downward revealed that his pants were decidedly more snug than they'd been three minutes ago. Huh. I guessed my hands *had* been all over him. Smiling, I took the last measurement I needed for the jacket sleeves, then very deliberately ran my fingers against the skin of his wrist.

"Problem?" I said all casual.

"You're evil," he ground out.

"Yup." I pushed the jacket off his shoulders. "We don't want this to crumple."

"'Course not." His voice was breathy. "Better take the shirt off too before I sweat in it."

"Let me." I could have made short work of the buttons, but instead I took them one at a time, caressing and teasing each new inch of exposed skin until the shirt hung open and Todd was breathing hard.

I skimmed the shirt and suspenders off his shoulders and took my time to neatly fold the shirt and the jacket on the side chair in my room, as much to make him wait as anything else. When I returned to his side, my fingers swept all around his waistband, giving him ample time to say no before I went to his fly. I loved how he was totally surrendering to my ministrations, but I also didn't want to push him too far too fast.

I pushed the pants down slowly, reaching around to caress the curve of his ass. He stepped free of the pants, and we both stood there in our boxers, bodies almost but not quite touching. Grabbing the hem of my sweater, he whispered, "You too?"

I nodded and pulled the sweater off and set my bracelet aside on the dresser. Grabbing his hand, I led him to the bed. "I just want to feel your skin. We don't have to do anything you're not up for, but I'd love to lie here and kiss you for a while."

He nodded, teeth digging into his lower lip, then stretched out next to me on top of my comforter. It felt...sacred almost, that moment when our bare skin touched for the first time, the swift intake of his breath as his fuzzy chest met my smoother one. Finally, my lips met his, and it felt like a homecoming, like I belonged right here in this moment with this man.

We were both hard, but I stayed true to my word and didn't let my hands venture below his waistline, instead sweeping my touch up and down the muscles of his back while we kissed and kissed. He kissed me hungrier than before, making these needy little growls that made my cock throb. Gradually, we went from lying on our sides facing each other to me half on him, still kissing and touching, his hands roaming over my back and sides.

He discovered how sensitive I was along my ribs, and I discovered that the little patch of bare skin by his ear made him shiver. When my lips returned to his, he was more aggressive, sucking hard on my tongue. His hands found my ass, maneuvering me until I was between his legs, our dicks grinding through our boxers.

"Fuck, you feel good," I moaned.

"Yeah." Todd's voice was strained, his neck muscles tight as he pulled me even harder against him. "Need...fuck...I need skin. Want to feel you."

"Oh yeah." Reaching down, I shoved my boxers off, and rolled so he could do the same. I kind of expected him to push me the rest of the way down and climb on top, so I was a bit startled when he tugged me back over him.

"Ahhh," he groaned when I settled myself back between his legs, our dicks lining up.

"Fuck." I rocked my hips instinctively, and he brought his knees up around my hips.

"Kiss me," he demanded.

I claimed his mouth a bit roughly, desire making me clumsy. But it seemed like my lack of finesse only inflamed him, made him buck beneath me. His dick rutted against my stomach.

"Kendall," he panted. "God, Kendall, I'm close."

"Yeah, that's it, sweetheart. Go for it." My lips found the spot behind his ear that made him moan.

"Never came like this before, but *god,* kissing you is so good."

"Come on." I rocked my hips harder against him, getting a hand on his hip to pull him closer against me. "That's right. You come for me."

"Kendall. Kendall. *Kendall,*" he chanted as his whole body shook. "Kiss me. God, please kiss me."

My lips found his again, tongue fucking his mouth, which seemed to drive more moans from him.

"Ung." Panting, he wrenched his mouth away right as a splash of warmth hit my stomach. I had been so focused on Todd that I hadn't realized how close I was myself until I watched him come. Power, the likes of which I'd only felt a few times, surged through me. I was doing this—me taking charge caused this pleasure in him, and he was all mine, at least for this moment. I wanted to memorize how he said my name, how his eyes rolled back when he came, how his hands dug into my back and ass.

My balls lifted, and I fucked hard into the groove between his thigh and hip for a few thrusts, then I too was catapulted into a panting, moaning orgasm.

"Fuck." I rolled to my back. "You okay? Didn't mean for things to get there so fast."

"Oh, I was right there with you." He laughed self-consciously. "I don't want to be a buzz kill, but we should probably shower, right?"

"Told you I wasn't going to freak if your spunk touched me." I leaned over and kissed his mouth softly. "Give me a second, and then yeah, we can shower before I cook for you."

"You already got laid and you're still cooking for me?" Todd joked, but his eyes were wary.

Oh, baby, you're worth so much more than people told you you were. My heart broke a bit for him, and I stroked his jaw, my throat too tight to do more than nod. I didn't want to feel this tender for him, not this fast, not when he was still supposed to be temporary, but hell if I could stop the throb of my heart.

Chapter 8
Todd

Kendall had a real nice shower—one of those deals with a separate tub with little lights above it and then a large stall with a big glass door. Plenty of room for two. If I wasn't still so boneless from coming, we could have had some real fun in there. As it was, we stood there and kissed after we washed, until the water ran cold and my cock started getting interested in things again.

It could wait though, as I was still sorting out how it felt, having come with Kendall, having opened myself up like that. I never did that before—the rubbing and the kissing—and I surprised myself how much I wanted that exact thing again. Kendall, he gave me a taste for all sorts of things I never knew I liked.

Like pesto. After we showered, Kendall pulled on a pair of these soft pants and nothing else, so I followed his lead and just put on my jeans. It was right cozy, sitting at his breakfast bar while he chopped and worked on the dinner.

"Give me something to do," I said, hating him doing all the work.

"Can you dice an onion?" He passed me a cutting board, knife, and large red onion.

"Yup. What's that?" I gestured at the bright green puree whizzing around in his high-tech food processor.

"You've never had pesto? It's delicious with roasted tomatoes and onions in this sauce over fusilli."

I figured fusilli was his fancy noodles. Roasted tomatoes, those were fancy too. "Nope. But I'll try it."

"You'll like it, promise. And it's not too spicy."

"Thanks. Sorry for being such a food wimp. It's just that growing up we always had real simple foods. Never got a taste for the fancy stuff."

"Your mom didn't cook?"

"Nah." I shook my head. I tried to slice the onion into neat little cubes, the way Kendall would. "She works as a waitress. Always said the last thing she wanted to do was be in the kitchen at home."

"How did you afford dancing?" Kendall clapped his hand over his mouth as soon as the question finished. "Sorry. Ignore that. I need a filter."

"Nah. It's okay." Others had wondered that too, and even Gran and Gramps had gone on about how the money should have gone to other things. "My dad, see, he's a car salesman. Decent money, so Mama's money, that paid for the dancing classes and the competitions and stuff, until they split and then there wasn't money for lessons."

"They split when you were a teenager?" Kendall's eyes narrowed. I had a feeling he was thinking about how I'd transformed in the last few pictures in the photo album at Gran's. Damn but I hated those pictures. I looked...hollow, and knowing Kendall had seen me that way made my stomach all queasy despite the wonderful food smells.

"Yeah. Things started going bad when I was twelve or so, and by the time I was fifteen they were split and the money was gone."

"Is that...ah...when you..." Kendall made a vague gesture as he added the onion I'd chopped to his sizzling skillet.

"Got into drugs? It's okay, you can ask." I shrugged as I grabbed a paper towel from the roll on his counter, cleaned the counter where a bit of onion juice had escaped off the cutting board. "Yeah. See, I started getting heavier. Hailey and the other kids at dance made fun of me."

"That's awful." Kendall sounded ready to smack Hailey with the wooden spoon he was stirring with.

"Eh. We were kids, you know? Anyway, Hailey told me her mama had a secret for stayin' skinny. Gave me these pills. Made me feel like I was flyin'. That was the start. Eventually, she couldn't keep pinching her mama's stash, so I turned to an older kid to get me some of that. He said he had something even better."

My stomach churned as I remembered those years, the slow, inevitable slide toward harder and harder drugs as I went from being up all the time to needing something to sleep to not knowing who I was without the drugs.

Kendall shook his head. "I want to scream at those kids. I really do. How'd you end up out here, away from your parents?"

"Pretty common story, really. Mama and Dad were so concerned with the divorce, neither wanted to deal with me and my issues. They sent me out here, hoping if I got away from the bad crowd that I'd get clean. I didn't though. Lord, did I put Gran, and Gramps too when he was still alive, through the wringer."

"But you *did* get help. And you guys seem close now." Kendall was cute, all willing to rush to my defense.

"Yeah, we are. Friend of mine died, and I decided that I didn't want that to be me, Gran up there cryin' over me. She got me into rehab once I started going to meetings, let me move back in once I was clean. She's…" My throat filled with golf balls as I thought about how much she meant to me.

Kendall reached across the island, squeezed my arm. "I'm so glad you got help."

"Me too." And I was. Glad I was there with him, eating his fancy food, and I was even glad that I'd told him more about me. Felt good, being honest with him. It also felt like something that couldn't possibly last. The talk was a good reminder of that—I couldn't ever have a stake in something that could push me back to that desperate place if it ended, and eventually, Kendall would see enough of these ugly parts of me and would turn tail and run. I had to be ready.

* * * *

Thursday was our third class, and I was looking forward to it all day. I'd seen Kendall for a short time on Tuesday—long enough to eat a late dinner, practice, and then rub off together on his big, soft bed same as we had a second time on Sunday night before he ran me home. I had a feeling that Kendall wouldn't mind doing something different, but as for me, I loved the novelty of rubbing off, how close I could feel to him, and how simple and good it was.

But before I could get to the good parts of my day, I had to get through work.

"We've got a big wedding coming up Saturday," Vic reminded me toward the end of the day. "I'll be working on that cake all tomorrow, but I'll need you to do the delivery because Robin and I are guests."

"I remember. It's your friend Robby from that coffee cart downtown, right?" I knew him from my deliveries.

"Right. Kendall's the planner for him and his fiancé, David, but you don't want any…" Vic made a vague gesture with his big hand.

"Vic. You trying to say not to fuck around on the job? You do know I wouldn't do that, right?" I got testier with him than I ever had before.

"I know." Vic sounded a bit put out. "Just trying to help you. Stay professional and all. And speaking of, if you dress up in those dancing clothes of yours for the delivery, you could stay for the reception food—Robby told me to extend the invite to you. He says you're his favorite delivery person."

"I'll look sharp. Not sure if I'll stay though—don't want to intrude." Or throw Kendall off his game, but I wasn't giving Vic any more fodder for his *stay professional* cannon.

"Do you want to help with the cake? They're doing two cakes, so it's all hands on deck tomorrow. I can show you how to crumb coat," Vic offered.

"Maybe," I hedged. Last thing I needed was to screw up his big order. Vic had offered before to show me some decorating stuff, but I'd always found something to do up front or an order to deliver. I hadn't quite sorted out in my head if I was good enough to help him. See, this voice in my head, the same one that told me that Kendall and I couldn't last, it said that I wasn't worth a damn and that as soon as Vic figured that out, I'd be out on my ass again. Better to keep my head down, not aim for stuff above me, like my daddy always said.

"You think about it," Vic said. "And uh…enjoy your class tonight." He looked like he had something to add about Kendall and me, but Marcie came in from the front, needing me, and he waved me off.

After work I arrived at the dancing lesson minutes before it started. I'd made sure to wear some of my new clothes. For once Kendall had beaten me there, and he was talking to the couple with the person with a beard and a love of dresses. I gave them all a nice smile. Even if I wanted Kendall all to myself, it was nice to watch him charm others too.

"Micky and Danny here are thinking of a fall wedding," Kendall said when I came up behind him. "I was just telling them about the bakery."

"Vic does a real nice cake," I said. "Y'all should come in and taste some samples."

"You know, you should think about doing some of the decorating," Kendall said. "You've got a steady hand and a nice eye for detail."

Not you too. I was kind of done with people making me out to be more than I was, but I blushed and looked down at my shoes. "Think you got me confused with you. You're the one who makes everything all pretty."

"You're such a cute couple," the bearded person said, voice higher than I would have expected. "How long have you been together?"

"Oh, we just started taking this class together." Kendall made an airy gesture that set me on edge. It was the truth, but still made my back muscles tighten. Not like I could—or *should*—expect more, but still part of me wanted to be claimed by him.

I didn't have much chance to dwell on that because Chuck and Ted called our attention to the front of the room.

"We're working on more whip variations this week with the reverse whip, basket whip, and a few others, but first let's review."

Kendall was wearing his pumps again, but he'd paired them with slim pants and a big fuzzy sweater that made me want to cuddle him close. Even though my body was galloping ahead to after class, I tried to keep my head on, letting Kendall lead me through the starter step and throwout. We worked the sugar push and whip before Chuck demonstrated the basket whip, which had a crossed-arm component that Kendall struggled with.

"Walk, walk, triple step, walk, walk, triple step," Chuck counted out.

"Argh," I gagged as Kendall caught me right in the wind pipe with our joined hands.

"May I?" Chuck came over to us. "Let me lead Todd and show you."

It was a bit weird, dancing with someone who wasn't Kendall and letting him lead. Seemed like my body only really enjoyed this *following* business with Kendall. Still though, I tried to be a good sport for Chuck, letting him pass me into the basket position with arms crossed, and back out again.

When Kendall got me back again, it felt like he held me a bit firmer. I liked that, that little hint of jealousy and competitiveness. This time, when he passed me into the arms-crossed position, he did so with confidence.

"Coming back with me after class?" he asked, eyes full of dirty promises.

"You feeding me?" Funny how much I was coming to like that, the way it wasn't just sex for Kendall, the way we could eat and talk together. I never once felt cheap with Kendall, and that hadn't always been the case with previous hookups.

"Of course. I left some stuffed shells in the fridge to heat up when we come in."

I pretended to think about it. "Italian? Yeah, I'm coming."

"I'm making you eat salad too," Kendall warned.

"Still coming." I laughed and gave him a wink on the next dance pass.

* * * *

Back at his place after we walked the dog, I discovered that Kendall had set the table all pretty for us with fresh flowers and blue plates. It made my chest ache, the way he went to such trouble for me.

He slid a foil-wrapped casserole dish in the oven. "Now should we practice for another forty-five minutes or so or…"

"Or." I pulled him to me.

Kendall wrapped his arms around my neck. "I was hoping you'd pick that." He started to tug me toward the couch, but I shook my head. Still hadn't made my peace with those windows of his. "Bedroom?"

"I love your bedroom," I said, and it was true. I loved the light lavender wall color, the darker purple accent wall behind the bed, the white wood bed and dresser, and of course, the big fluffy bed that reminded me of some fancy hotel with its thick white comforter and lots of pillows. Mainly, though, I loved the way Kendall sent the covers and pillows raining to the floor before he pushed me down on the bed, intent clear in his eyes.

Just like on the dance floor, he became more confident and bossy with each encounter, and I relished his take-charge attitude.

He left me there, sprawled on his bed, while he stood in front of me and stripped. Unlike me, Kendall had no issues giving a show, as evidenced by the naughty little smile teasing his mouth. He raised and lowered the hem of his sweater a few times, giving me flashes of skin.

"Time's a-wasting," I grumbled.

Kendall just laughed and stripped off the sweater, millimeter by millimeter until finally he gave a little shimmy and it fluttered to the floor. Eyes locked on mine, he slid down his zipper, and I saw the reason for this little show.

"Holy fuck," I said as he revealed black lace outlining his hard cock. I guess you'd call them short boxers, but they were lacier and shorter than any boxers I'd ever seen, and the way they hugged his cock was obscene.

"Thought you might like these." Kendall laughed. "I wanted something that was still comfortable but a little...prettier."

"Love you all pretty," I growled, and rolled toward him so that I could grope his ass, pull him toward my eager mouth.

I mouthed him through the lacy cotton, making him gasp. We hadn't ever done this, but right that moment, I wanted to do it for him, not because I was good at it, not because he was feeding me and taking care of me, but because I wanted to know the taste and weight of him on my tongue and I wanted to give pleasure to my guy. And those undies...good lord, they drove me more than a little crazy as I nuzzled his balls and cock through the fabric.

"Gonna suck me?" Kendall's voice was full of toppy authority, not really questioning my willingness.

"Hell, yeah, I am." I pulled down the waistband of his underwear so that the head of his dick sprung free. I started to lean in for a lick, then remembered. "You want a condom for this? I don't have any sores or cuts in my mouth, but whatever makes you the most comfortable."

"I'm good..." He gasped as my tongue made contact with his shaft.

I laughed before I licked all around the head of his cock, licking along the waistband of his underwear too, sorta pushing it down with my mouth, until most of his cock was exposed for me to tease. His cock was a gorgeous shade of dusky rose, darker near the root and balls, pinker near the uncut tip.

"Enough teasing." Kendall bumped my face with his cock, message clear.

"Want something?" I asked innocently.

"You know I do. Suck it." Kendall's voice was a firm command that I felt all the way to my own balls.

Complying, I closed my mouth around his cock and slid forward until I'd swallowed him to the base.

"*Fuck.* You're full of tricks, aren't you?"

I wasn't necessarily proud of my cock-sucking ability, but I was glad for it right then because it made him moan and gasp as I worked him over. I milked him with my tongue while I started a slow, deep slide. I'd been paying attention to Kendall, and it wasn't speed that usually got him off. Rather he seemed to like a slower rhythm with a lot of stimulation, so I tried to give him that, fingering his balls through his underwear, working the underside of his cock with my tongue, and rubbing his ass with my other hand.

Something peaceful and seductive came over me, made me feel like I'd sipped some potent drink that made every move pleasurable, made me *feel* each breath of his, each moan, and amplified his taste until I was moaning along with him, desperate for more of it.

"Yeah, like that, don't you?" Kendall rocked his hips like he was searching for something and not quite getting there. I knew what he wanted and released his dick before flipping to my back with my head over the edge of the mattress.

I wrenched open my fly, got my dick some breathing room before I motioned him forward.

"Fuck, yeah. Jerk yourself off while I fuck your mouth." Kendall's voice was rough and needy.

I didn't need to be asked twice. I started a hard pull while he slid back into my mouth and got my free hand on his hip so I could feel his rhythm. Fucking slow, hard, and deep, Kendall's breathing sped up and we both moaned. I sucked hard on the upstroke, trying to keep him in my mouth longer, playing games with my head to hold my breath longer. It was its own kind of high, giving myself over to the fuck, seeing how deep and hard I could let him go.

"Right there. Oh fuck. Yes. Going to come."

I moaned in response, hand speeding up. His legs started to shake and he made little groans and whimpers right before he shot down my throat. I sucked hard, letting the taste of him carry me over the edge until I was coming too, moaning around his cock as I spurted all over my belly.

"Oh my god." Kendall tumbled onto the bed next to me. "Oh. My. God. I think you ruptured my brain."

"I'm glad." My voice sounded like it had bounced around in a cement mixer.

"Oh, hell. Between this and almost strangling you while dancing, I really do owe you some ice cream or something, don't I?" He laughed.

"I'll take it."

He rolled over, dropping a lazy kiss against my pant leg. "Next time's on me."

Even though I'd just come hard as a semi rushing a yellow light, my body still shivered. More anticipating. "Counting on it."

Chapter 9
Kendall

Todd took a fast shower while I got the food out of the oven and onto the plates.

"You want a pair of sweatpants?" I called as the shower shut off. I had a feeling he'd gotten spunk on his dress pants and I knew he was fastidious about stuff like that.

"Nah. I had my work jeans." He came out toweling off his hair, jeans riding low on his bare hips. No shirt. He winced and gestured at the clock on the microwave. "Jeez, it got late, didn't it?"

I'd been hatching a plan while he showered. "I don't have an early appointment tomorrow. I could take you to work if you wanted to sleep over."

"Friday's a long day for us. Have to be there early." Todd took a seat at the table, inhaling deeply as he smiled at the food. God, I loved the way he appreciated things I did for him.

"I don't mind. Gives me an excuse to grab a fancy coffee before I get to work instead of sleeping in." In truth, I was more of a night owl, but I really wanted to sleep next to Todd for reasons I didn't want to take out and examine too closely.

"All right." He nodded solemnly and dug out his phone from his pocket. "Let me text Gran, make sure she didn't need anything doing tonight."

He blushed while typing, which was freaking adorable. "Feel like a kid sneaking out," he muttered.

"We better make it worth your while." I winked at him. And hell, I really did owe him after that epic blowjob. I'd never had *anyone* who could deep-throat that easily—or enthusiastically. His phone beeped and he turned redder. "She says to have fun."

"She's remarkably accepting of you being gay. Was she always that way?"

Todd made a face, pausing with his fork in the air. "Just because people are from the South doesn't mean they're all conservatives. She's a lifelong liberal poli-sci professor. Now, my daddy, he didn't take to me being gay so well, and blamed mama and the dancing, but Gran's always been great about it." His Southern accent always got stronger when he got worked up about something.

"Sorry. I didn't mean to imply. And trust me, I know all about people and assumptions."

Todd reached across the table, patted my wrist. "I know you do. And that's what I lo—*like* about you. You know people are gonna judge, and you just be yourself anyway. Strong. I dig that."

His near slip of the tongue warmed me all the way through. As much as I kept telling myself that this was casual, I was already more than a little infatuated with him, like walking along the beach at the Oregon coast—buildings getting smaller and smaller and risks getting bigger. And I liked that he saw me as strong. I didn't always see myself that way, and it meant something that he saw the me I tried so hard to be. "Thanks."

"I'm serious. You know what you want to do with your life. Like you've got...*purpose*." There was a wistful tone in his voice that nicked me close to my heart.

"I didn't always want to do this," I admitted. "And my mom is still irked that I didn't get a safe degree, like law or an MBA, a 'real' job. But I got into event planning with groups in college, then friends started getting married." I shrugged. "Turned out I was good at it, and I'm the sort of person...I need to work for myself."

What I really meant was that I wasn't willing to deal with having bosses with opinions about my gender nonconformity. In my line of work, people saw me as "eccentric," but also didn't see me as a threat, someone to spirit their partner of choice away, which was a double-edged sword. I was a character to them, not always a person. I liked how Todd always seemed to see the person, had right from the start.

"Wish I knew what I wanted or needed. Gran wants me to go back to school, get my GED, think about college, but hell, that's not me." Todd chased his food around with his fork.

"What would you do if you could do anything in the world?"

"I guess I don't know." He sounded so sad about that that I squeezed his hand. "I like making people smile. Doing something nice for them. But that's not really a *career*."

"It's a start. Why not let Vic teach you some of the decorating stuff? That makes people smile. And good customer service is a valid career choice. You don't need fancy suits to be worthwhile."

"He keeps getting at me about learning, but Kendall, what if I suck at it?" Todd's voice was little more than air.

"He's not going to fire you," I said firmly. "And what if it turns out that cake decorating is what you're good at? That that's your purpose?"

"'Fraid of that too," he said to his plate.

"Hey"—I gestured with my fork—"none of that. You're great at following directions. You'll do terrific."

His eyes were big blue pools of emotion. "That means something. You believin' in me."

"I do." I squeezed his hand again, and our eyes met and held. It felt like walking on that unknown beach—like we were leaving a trail behind us of little moments like this one, just hoping we weren't about to get swept out to sea. But if we were, I was sure as hell going to admire the scenery as long as I could.

"Want to watch a movie in my bed to fall asleep?" I asked as we took the plates to the sink.

"Want to watch *you*." Todd replied the way I'd hoped he would, and we made fast work of the kitchen, because he insisted, before we raced to the bed, leaving a trail of kisses and clothes in our wake.

Like we'd been doing it a dozen years, we snuggled together naked under the covers, kissing and touching with unhurried ease. He smelled like my shampoo and soap, something I found strangely sexy, and he tasted like the peppermint mints he'd taken to carrying.

I rolled him so that I could kiss the back of his neck and the tops of his freckled shoulders. My hand snaked around to stroke his cock.

"What do you want?" I whispered. "Anything."

He gave a soft chuckle. "This is pretty nice right here. Love being surrounded by you."

"Okay if I make my hand slick?" I reached in the bedside table for my lube.

"Yeah...we can...if you want..." He bumped his hips backwards, but his nervous rambles told me that he wasn't really ready for that.

"We'll get there." I kissed his shoulders again. "Right now, I just want to go on your back while I jerk you off. That sound good?"

"Oh yeah."

Using the lube, I slicked both of us up, then nestled in close behind him, dick riding the top of his crack

"Fuck, that feels good," he moaned. "Kiss my neck more."

"Yeah, that's it. Tell me what you need." I was never getting tired of how much he loved being kissed and touched and held. Like with dancing, it felt like something slid into place, a balance I hadn't known I needed. I needed someone like him to hold and take care of like this.

I loved the feel of him in my hand, hot and heavy, and loved the needy sounds he made as I thrust against his back. I listened to his little pleas and groans, learning how he liked my grip—tight around the shaft, looser over his cockhead, and with plenty of speed.

"Close. God, Kendall. I'm close. Please."

"Yeah, that's it. Come for me." I sped up my hips against his back, holding him tight, lips against the base of his neck.

"Hold me. God, hold me." He shuddered, voice breaking as he came. I stroked him through it, and a few thrusts more and I joined him, gasping his name, orgasm washing over me in gentler waves than earlier. I kissed his back and shoulders over and over as I drifted back down from the haze.

We were in desperate need of a towel, but I was loath to let him go.

"Man, that was...*intense*." Todd snuggled against me, not his usual leap away to shower. "Felt so close to you."

"Me too." I moved so I could give his mouth an awkward kiss. "Me too."

And hell if I knew what do with that feeling of closeness, this *need* that had opened up inside me for this man, for this connection we had.

* * * *

I dropped Todd off early, not intending to see him again until he dropped off the cake for the Saturday wedding of my clients, David and Robby, but we ended up with an emergency that sent David and me to the bakery in the early afternoon.

Todd was loading croissants into the front case when we came in.

"Kendall!" His eyes went wide and his mouth quirked, as if he weren't quite sure what to do next, and I shared his indecision. I wasn't really sure how to greet him at his place of work. With a close friend like Freya, I'd expect a hug. With a boyfriend, I'd assume there would be some sort of affection, but the sudden awkward energy between us underscored the strange limbo we were in. After last night, I was no longer so sure that I wanted—or could do—casual, but opening myself up to admitting that had had me fretting about traffic that morning when I dropped him off, not talking about my feelings. All of a sudden, I *needed* Todd, and that terrified me, and I was certain that terror showed in my eyes.

"Is Vic in?" I saved us both more uncomfortable staring. "I left him messages, but we were in the area and thought we'd stop by. We're in a bit of a quandary."

"Vic ran out for a salad for his lunch. But the cake is looking amazing. Coming along right fine."

"That's a relief." David shifted around next to me, all restless energy. "But that's not what has us concerned. I just learned that my sister and her kids have given up all gluten, and I'm worried they won't have anything for dessert when we cut the cake. I was hoping Vic might have an idea. I don't want the kids to feel left out."

"Hmm." Todd nodded, considering. "We've done a gluten-free cake before, but that's special order. Not sure if he can do one on short notice, because we've got a couple of weddings this weekend, and I'm not sure what's on hand."

"Oh well, maybe we can get something at New Seasons—"

"Wait." Todd's eyes narrowed. "They still eat some sugar? Like frosting? 'Cause I've got an idea."

"They're kids. I'm pretty sure they'll eat frosting," David said.

Todd grabbed a plate and a paleo muffin from the case. "What if we turned these into decorated mini-cakes to match the big cake?" Slicing the top off the muffin, he turned it upside down on the plate. "See? I can see if Vic has got time to decorate it up in your colors."

"That's brilliant," I said to Todd.

"And I think you should help. You can crumb-coat the mini-cakes for me." Vic emerged from the back, big smile on his face as he addressed Todd. "I've got some more paleo mix, and we can do it a bit sweeter than the muffins, without the berries and nuts."

"I knew you'd come through," I said.

"We aim to please." Vic laughed. "Want a peek at the main cake? I'm really pleased with how it's coming."

"Sure," David said, and we followed Vic and Todd back. I noticed Todd was limping slightly.

I tugged on his sleeve, stopping him. "What happened to you?"

He shrugged and made a face. "Took a tumble off the loading dock. Don't worry, I'll be fine for dancin' next week."

That wasn't why I asked, and I opened my mouth to explain that, but Vic was motioning us forward and David was happily exclaiming over the cake, and the moment passed. Todd moved away from me, going to the far side of the cake. Hell. If he was having a crappy day, I wanted to hear about it, give him a hug, but if he wanted distance, I didn't have any right to push. And if he wanted us on the down low, could I really blame him, when I hadn't given him any reason to think we were more than friendly fuck buddies?

I needed to focus on David and Robby's wedding, but even as I went through all the other last-minute tasks, my thoughts still lingered with Todd and the way he'd moved away from me. Maybe it was for the best that I hadn't spoken up. My history had taught me that needing someone the way I needed Todd only led to disaster. Maybe it was time to pull back before one of us got hurt.

Chapter 10
Todd

Soon as I'd slid off the loading dock, turning my ankle, my first thought had been how disappointed Kendall would be if I couldn't dance. Would he even want to hang out if I couldn't dance at the benefit? What other value did I have for a guy like Kendall?

Such thoughts got me in a grumpy mood that carried me through work all Friday. Vic had one of the other assistants do the batter for the paleo cupcakes for Kendall's client, but true to his word, Vic made me help.

"You're precise. You'd be good at running the mixer in a pinch," he said as he set me to watching the batter. "And crumb-coating is something we always need a hand with."

I wanted to be helpful, I really did, but I also couldn't help feeling like Vic was setting me up for a test I couldn't possibly pass. Disappointing him would be almost as bad as disappointing Kendall. I stewed even as Vic worked his magic on the mini–paleo cakes, and my quietness continued through my Friday night meeting.

"You okay?" Robin, Vic's husband, asked as we put the chairs away after the meeting. Even though he was my sponsor, I couldn't tell him about my fear of failing at the bakery. He'd stood up for me to get the delivery job. Didn't need to shake his faith in me too.

"Yeah. I'm fine. Messed up my ankle earlier, and it's got me crabby."

"I know a great sports medicine clinic. Want me to get you their info so you can get it looked at?"

"Nah. Just turned it, is all."

"Are you going to stay for the food at the reception tomorrow? Vic told you that Robby said you were welcome to hang around after you deliver the cake, right?"

"Right." I didn't say that I probably wouldn't.

"I'm sure Kendall would be happy to see you." Robin was clearly on a fishing expedition but I wasn't taking the bait.

"We'll see," I said. Kendall needed to focus on his work. He didn't need the distraction of me, not when I wasn't sure I could give him the one thing he needed me for.

* * * *

When I went to deliver the cake on Saturday, I was still in a bad mood. Bum ankle was stiffer and more painful than I'd hoped, and Kendall hadn't texted me goodnight like he usually did. I knew he was busy, but I still felt off even as I loaded up the cake.

The band was warming up when I got to the rooftop lounge and conference center in Northwest Portland that David and Robby had picked for their reception, but I wasn't about to make the same mistake as last time and give in to the rhythm, even if my ankle had been doing better. The view of the Northwest skyline through the large bank of windows created a nice balance for the cream-and-light-green decorations. Along one wall was an elaborate coffee and drink station—a nod toward Robby's job running a coffee cart in downtown Portland.

The cake table was flanked with fresh plants and an artfully rumpled cloth. Wheeling the cake over, I looked around for Kendall, but I didn't see him. One of the catering staff came over to give me a hand sliding the cake over.

I was about to give up and leave the box of breakfast goodies with one of the catering people when Kendall showed up, grooms in tow.

"Look at our cake!" Robby, the shorter of the two men, the one who hadn't been at the bakery, rushed over to the cake table. "And look, David, the baby cakes for your sister's family are adorable."

"They turned out great." David offered me his hand, so I shook it. "Good work."

"It was all Vic, but they sure look pretty." I grabbed the box from the bottom of the cart. "And this is from Vic too, for your breakfast tomorrow."

"Thanks so much," Robby enthused. "Now are you going to slip off that coat? Have a coffee and some food? The other guests should be arriving any moment."

"I can't believe that the ceremony went off without a hitch." Relief tinged David's voice. And the way he looked at his new husband...man, everyone should get that look at least once in their lifetime.

"Of course it did," Kendall said. "And you should stay, Todd. There's plenty of food in the buffet, and you can mingle with Vic and Robin."

Something about how he said my name set me on edge. It was as if he'd set up a fence blocking off our friendship from the outside world, and I didn't like that any.

"Nah." I shrugged. "Gotta get the truck back and all. You guys have a great evening though. Congrats."

Seeing how they beamed at each other was its own kind of torture. I wasn't ever getting that kind of connection in my life, and for the first time I really *felt* that loss, wanted to share that bond with someone. Wanted it with Kendall if I was being honest, and that made my gut clench around the emptiness inside me.

* * * *

I saw Kendall a couple of times over the next few days, but that distance between us seemed to be getting worse, not better. He finished messing with my new dress clothes for the benefit, which had me all antsy about the event next week. Old worries kept dogging me: Maybe Kendall had gotten freaked out about HIV, or maybe he was having second thoughts about being with someone with my sort of baggage. A braver person than me would have *talked* to him, but I couldn't find the words, even for a text. Didn't want to look that needy.

Thursday was the next dancing lesson, and thank goodness my ankle felt strong enough to go. I arrived before Kendall, wearing a pair of pants that he'd hemmed for me. Gave me a strange sort of thrill, him taking care of me, and I just wished I could enjoy it more.

I chatted a bit with Micky and Danny, who had decided to hire Kendall for their wedding. I surprised myself talking cakes with them, how passionate I got about fondant versus buttercream. I described, in all sorts of detail, the white-on-white wedding cake from David and Robby's wedding. I guess Vic and the bakery were changing me more than I thought.

Chuck came in without Ted and headed straight to where we were talking.

"Todd, can I ask you a favor?" he said.

"Sure," I said warily.

"Ted has a cold and stayed home tonight. Could I use you to demonstrate? We're doing the Texas Tommy. Your whip looked so good last week that I think you'll pick it up fast."

"Yeah, I can do that," I said, but inside I groaned. Funny how things had changed for me. When I was younger, I loved showing off for the teacher, being her special assistant, knowing I was good at stuff. But, dancing was different with Kendall. With him, it was pure fun, following him, dancing together.

I wasn't sure I was ready for dancing to be work again.

"Kendall can dance with Danny while you demo. I don't mind watching." Micky, the shorter of the two, adjusted his gold vest before grabbing one of the chairs off to the side.

Kendall came in just then, and looked a bit put out by this plan, which made me strangely happy. Good. I preferred dancing with him too.

Chuck led me through the Texas Tommy several times to show the hand change and spin. He was more forceful than Kendall, and I kept over-rotating, which made it hard to demonstrate the rock step that came next. I was concentrating so hard on my moves that I almost missed Kendall laughing at something Danny said. Danny was wearing a long black dress, and the two of them made a pretty picture, dancing together. Kendall looked like he'd come from one of his client meetings—cream-colored suit, no tie but subtle lace on the shirt. Real nice.

Danny easily followed Kendall, and I should have been all proud of him for picking it up so easy, but instead I was pissier than a gator in winter, watching someone else earn his smiles and laughs. Which was crazy, I knew.

"Okay, why don't you give this a shot with Micky?" Chuck suggested as he released me so that he could go around the room and give pointers.

What I really wanted was Kendall back, but I nodded and walked over to Micky. "You mind if I lead?" I asked as I held out a hand to help Micky up.

"Oh, I usually do," Micky said and easily assumed the leader's position. Hell, I might be willing to follow Kendall anywhere, but I didn't like being passed around like this. Micky had an aggressive style, one I hoped Danny appreciated because I sure as hell didn't.

I caught Kendall's eye on a turn. *Save me.*

"Having fun?" he asked.

No. "Oh sure. You?"

"Danny and I have matching shoes." Kendall laughed like this was the best news all week. Of course, he had no clue the knots I'd been in all week. *Talk to him*, I lectured myself. *Tell him how twisted up you are.*

Finally, Chuck called for a lead swap and we changed back. "I'm leading," I said, all testy-like.

"Okay," Kendall said, brow wrinkling.

I was too firm, too commanding as I led Kendall around, pulling and pushing him more than I needed to.

"Ow," Kendall said and pulled his wrist free. My gut churned. I hadn't meant to hurt my partner.

"Sorry," I said and grabbed his hand to rub it, but Kendall didn't give it over, instead shooting me a wounded look that speared me right in the soft bits.

Chuck needed me to demonstrate the closed and open variations of the Texas Tommy, showing how to come back out of it with a reverse whip, bringing in what we'd learned last week. The whole time I just ached to make things right with Kendall, and I practically raced over to him after Chuck released me.

"You can lead," I said, voice full of as much apology as I could stuff into three words.

"Okay." Kendall released Danny, then took the lead with me, gracefully leading me into and back out of the turn. "What's gotten into you? You haven't been yourself all week."

"Not sure," I said truthfully. "Just feel off."

"I know what you need."

You. I just need you. I nodded.

"Pho. A nice big bowl of soup will help you reset. It always does me, and there's a place in Northeast, not far from your grandmother's."

Ah. I guessed we weren't having any sleepovers tonight. And I wasn't any too sure that noodle soup would fix me up. I'd had it before, and I liked the meat and broth okay, but I wasn't as gaga for it as it seemed half the city was. Still though, I needed to make things up with Kendall. "That sounds fine."

I tried to follow him extra close the rest of class, declining the lead swaps, and hovering over him with a water bottle at the break. But he was more into talking wedding plans with Danny and Micky, which was understandable as that was business.

Still, by the time we were in the car heading to dinner, I was more rattled than I'd been in months. Damn, I needed tomorrow's meeting. That would be more of a reset than the soup. I hated being this kind of unsettled with Kendall.

Speak up. Tell him how you feel. I knew that was what I needed to do, but I couldn't seem to make my tongue work. What I did know was that we couldn't continue like this—me this rattled was a slippery slope for my sobriety, and no meeting could fix the way Kendall had me turned around. This was exactly why I hadn't wanted the risk of a relationship.

The restaurant that Kendall had picked, Pho Oregon, was popular with a section of the hipster crowd despite the unassuming outside. I'd been there before with Jake. I ordered what I'd had before—the beef soup and some spring rolls, which were like baby egg rolls with a too-sweet sauce.

"Want to come over and practice tomorrow?" Kendall asked while we waited for the food.

My chest loosened a bit. At least he still wanted to dance. That was something.

"Yeah." I tried not to look pathetically grateful and was saved by the arrival of the food.

"Bring some clothes and I can run you to work before I have coffee with Freya on Saturday."

"That I can do." I couldn't hold the grin in.

"There's that smile. See, I told you soup would help." Kendall grinned at me.

I wasn't telling him that it was the prospect of sleeping all night next to him that had me happier, not the food. One more sign that we had to talk. I was falling for him, exactly the sort of risk I'd sworn to avoid, and I couldn't stand the way he made my emotions swing like the pendulum of Gran's old clock.

Pho is a challenge to eat, so we were quiet for a bit, which suited me and my uneven mood just fine. We were finishing up and about to pay when in walked Jake and some other guys I knew from meetings.

"Todd!" Jake was tall, taller than me by several inches, and he practically hauled me up out of my seat with a big meaty handshake. He was wearing a T-shirt advertising the local AIDS fundraising run that he helped coordinate each year. He didn't spare Kendall more than half a glance. Typical Jake. "How's it going, man?"

"Jake. Long time no see." Didn't point out that I'd taken to purposely going to meetings at times when I knew he usually didn't attend.

"Too long, man. Listen, I'm having a get-together at my place tomorrow. You should come by—gonna grill."

"I've got plans. With Kendall." I gestured toward him since Jake seemed so intent on not noticing him.

"Kendall, huh?" Jake offered Kendall what looked like a bone-crushing handshake. "You two…"

"We're just friends," Kendall said quickly, and *rip*, there went my heart, right into two pieces.

"Don't keep your friends waiting on our account," I said to Jake, voice stiffer than Gran's ironing board. "We need to get going."

I stayed quiet while we each paid our share, then slunk out to Kendall's car. I was half tempted to walk, but I just didn't have the diva-fit in me. Besides, I wasn't airing my dirty laundry where Jake could see out the windows.

"So that was your ex?" Kendall said as he put the car in gear.

I made a noncommittal sound in response.

"What *is* your problem? You've been in a mood all week. Is everything okay?"

"Why do you care?" The bitten-off question snapped out before I could recall it.

"Because we're fr—"

"*Friends.* Yeah, I got that memo, thanks."

"You don't want to be friends?"

I shrugged and made a frustrated noise. God, I didn't want to be having this conversation. No, no, I did *not* want to be Kendall's *friend*, and why the hell couldn't he see that? *Friends* was too damn dangerous for me, and if he didn't feel the same way I did, then I had to get out now.

Chapter 11
Kendall

Something was dreadfully wrong with Todd and I wasn't sure what. And he wasn't exactly talking either.

"Are you mad that I told your ex that we're friends?" I was at a red light and glanced over at Todd in time to see him nod almost imperceptibly.

In truth, I'd seen Todd's ex and known immediately that *all* Todd and I could ever be was friends. Nothing more. Jake was Todd's real type, tall and broad shouldered with ham-sized hands, and a macho voice and presentation. He was a clear alpha dog. And he was HIV positive—something Todd had said more than once was important to him. He hadn't planned on ever dating negative guys, and that was just more reason why Todd and I couldn't work out.

Now, maybe Jake wasn't the *exact* guy Todd needed, as he also seemed like a major dick, but eventually he'd go back to that type of guy. Lewis had run so fast back to the gym-and-muscle-shirt crowd that I was surprised he hadn't sprained something. This was why I'd pulled back all week—I knew deep down that I couldn't be what Todd needed in a relationship.

So instead of reassuring Todd or laying claim to a status that could only be very temporary, I doubled down on the self-preservation. "I kind of figured you wouldn't want me to advertise that we're sleeping together."

"'Course not. Wouldn't have expected more from a guy like you," Todd said softly when I pulled up near his grandmother's house.

"Exactly," I said, my throat feeling raw and itchy. *Guy like you.* "We make good friends with benefits, right? No sense in making this out to be more than it is."

"I can't do this." Todd's voice sounded strained, like he was trying to hold back a river, same as me. I reached for his hand but he shook me off. "I'm not fancy like you, and I don't fit in your fancy world, and I can't let this gut me. I *won't*." Todd's fists were clenched tight. "So no, I can't be your friend, sorry."

With that, he was out of the car, sprinting up the walk.

I could have gone after him, but I knew deep in my heart I was doing the right thing to let him go. So instead I sat there for a long time, sinuses burning, hands shaking, head swimming. I heard the slam of a door from within the house. His pained words had made it clear that he thought somehow that *he* wasn't good enough for *me* when in fact the opposite was true. I ached to reassure him. My hand inched toward my phone before I pulled it back. He didn't want to be hurt, and that was all I could really offer either of us. It was better that we end things now.

* * * *

In a bit of awful timing, I had a wedding consultation with the circus-wedding couple the next morning. Bailey, the bride, and I were scheduled to tour a few venues, then brainstorm over lunch. No time to mope, I had to be Kendall, the happily-ever-after guru. God, I hated life sometimes. I couldn't really make myself care about much more than coffee though, pulling my hair up into a half-assed bun, and wearing a pair of gray dress pants and a white shirt only because showing up in sweats was *not* an option.

Bailey showed up at the Portland Art Museum with two of her friends in tow.

I pulled their folder out of my bag. "I scheduled us here first, because I really think this is going to be the best choice for the type of pageantry you want," I said to Bailey. "Now, who have you brought with you to help you pick?"

"These are my girlfriends, Gina and Louise." Bailey made the intros. "But I'm sad. I told them *all* about you and what a *character* you are, and you go showing up all...*plain*." She fake pouted in that way that twenty-two-year-old sorority girls have perfected.

I blinked. This was hardly the first time I'd been called a character, but I hadn't slept much at all the night before, tossing and turning and missing Todd, and I was simply...*weary*. Guilt for that hurt look on Todd's face dogged my every step. So very weary. "You wanted a dress?" I raised an eyebrow. An unplucked eyebrow. I hadn't exactly been in a landscaping mood—hadn't shaved either, and I almost never skipped that.

The girls all tittered. Yeah, they'd wanted a dress. "We just want a super fun wedding experience," Bailey explained.

"You'll have a great day." I had to work hard to sound even halfway sincere.

"I was totally picturing you in a sparkly costume for the circus. You know, something short, gay, and fabulous." Bailey ended with a hand flourish that made her friends all laugh and my stomach cramp. I was not equipped to handle this today.

"I'm a wedding planner. Not an entertainer." I kept my voice level but firm.

"Awww." Bailey's friend made a face.

"Is it extra to get you in drag?" Bailey tapped around on her phone. "I'd kinda assumed that was part of the package—"

"I'm not a drag queen. It's not costume with me. I wear what I want to wear and what makes me feel good about myself that particular day." My chest ached, remembering how easily Todd had understood that distinction. "And my…boyfriend broke up with me last night and clothes were the last thing on my mind this morning. I can't guarantee what I'll wear to your wedding, and if you need that, maybe I'm not the planner for you."

Felt weird calling Todd my boyfriend when I'd been so against defining us that way, but there was no denying I had a post-breakup hangover happening.

"Oh my gosh. I'm *so* sorry." One of the friends patted my arm. "He broke up with you? Why?"

"We weren't going to work out." I shrugged, trying to make myself believe it.

"Well, I'm not sure we will either." Bailey had the glassy-eyed bridezilla look I knew only too well. She had a vision for her wedding, and it involved a fun, happy gay caricature, and she wasn't going to be denied that.

"I don't know any wedding planners who do drag themselves, but I can get you the number of some drag acts, if that's the direction you want to go." I finally let every ounce of weariness into my voice.

"Yes! A drag revue as part of the circus. If you can arrange that, you can stay."

I needed this job and its big fee and its potential referrals badly. But I just couldn't take another few months of being a prop. Not today. "No," I said. "I'll get you a list of other possibilities for your planner. But first, would you like me to stay long enough to introduce you to the museum people?"

I was dying a little inside, forcing that amount of professionalism out, and my whole body shook with relief when Bailey tossed her head. "Don't bother."

I walked away from the museum, not sure where I was headed, just that I needed to get away from everything. Todd had never once looked at me like Bailey and her friends did—like I was an oddity, something that belonged in an exhibit, not a person with real thoughts and feelings. I meandered through the park blocks, passing families and other pedestrians out enjoying the mild spring weather.

Had I made a huge mistake? My phone beeped in my pocket. *Todd. Please let this be a sign from the universe.*

But it wasn't. It was Micky from dance class, who was also my newest client. *Can you PLEASE tell Danny that zie can wear a wedding dress if that's what zie wants?*

I typed back quickly. *Of course zie can. I know just the vendors to take you both to. No worries. We'll get you both looking fabulous.*

Inside, however, I crumbled a bit more. Danny and Micky were such a great couple, and they loved each other exactly as they were. This was the sort of wedding I loved doing, but today, for the first time, I had deep pangs of *Why not me?*

Across the path from me, a toddler was standing on another bench while his mother took a photo. After she snapped the picture, she held out her arms and the toddler jumped into them, absolutely fearless.

Leap. That was what I had to do, or else I'd be here ten years from now, still secretly pining over romances like Micky and Danny's. Still letting my hurt over Lewis keep me from *real* happiness. I wanted a sign from the universe, but the universe wasn't going to just hand me my happy ending, if such a thing existed. Lewis and my few other lovers hadn't been worth leaping over—they wanted too much of me or not enough, but what if Todd was different?

You know he is. That's what scares you. If he was worth the fall, maybe it was time to sprout wings.

Chapter 12
Todd

Kendall was waiting for me when I got done with work. Don't know why, but I'd been kind of expecting that. Not that it meant I wanted to see him or that my heart did a little dance. Nope. None of that. Just that I'd been figuring he couldn't just leave things be.

He was standing by his car when I came out the back of the bakery. I shook my head at him and kept on walking, heading to the bus stop.

"Wait." He chased after me. He looked like hell, frankly. Hair all twisted up on his head and plain face and clothes. Pained me to see him looking like I felt. "Could we talk?"

"Free country." I shrugged but kept walking. "I've got a bus to catch."

"Could I give you a ride home? I really want to talk to you. Apologize—"

"Nope." I stopped and swiveled to face him. "You don't got to do that."

"Yes, I do."

"See, I did a lot of thinking last night. And the way I figure it, I might not be the best catch, but I'm worth something. I have to be. I can't go back to feelin' like trash and not worthy all the time. Too much risk to my recovery. I deserve someone who's not ashamed to be with me."

Almost made me want to vomit, spewing all that out, but I'd lain there half the night, torn between anger and craving a fix, and longing and more anger. Finally anger won because I was *not* going to let this be the thing that undid the last two years of sobriety for me. Maybe Kendall didn't want to claim me, but someone would. I was worth that. The last few weeks had shown me that I had more to give than I'd thought.

"I'm *not*." Kendall grabbed my arms. "I'm not. I thought…I thought it was the other way around. You needing something…*more* in a relationship. Something I couldn't give you."

I blinked. Hadn't occurred to me that maybe he was just as twisted up as me. "Why would I think that?"

"I'm not like Jake. At all."

"And that's a good thing. He might be good-looking, but he's a judgmental, controlling bully at times. I didn't want any part of that when we were hookin' up, and I don't want it now."

"It's the good-looking part that threw me. I'm not…I'm not your usual type, am I?" Kendall's voice was soft and small, and I'd want to hold him if I wasn't still so ticked at him.

"Nah. But you're like pesto."

"Pesto?" Now Kendall was the one to blink.

"Yup. Never even thought I'd like the stuff before you. Walked right by it in the grocery store a hundred times. But then you fixed it for me, and lately, I crave the stuff. I want to try it all sorts of ways."

"See, that's what I'm worried about." Kendall's grip on my arm was still tense. My explanation didn't seem to have worked. "I don't want to be a novelty for you. Flavor of the week."

"You're not. It's more like…you're what I didn't know I was missing. What I need. Like dancing back in my life and pesto and salad and *you*. But"—and this next part near killed me to say, but I forced the words out—"I don't want to play games. Either you trust me that this is real, or you can't and we move on. I can't be believin' enough for both of us."

I just wasn't that strong to carry this thing if he wasn't going to be able to trust me.

"I don't want to play games," Kendall said, but his eyes were still all shifty. "It's just…you're so perfect—"

I snorted because we both knew I wasn't all that.

"Perfect for me," he insisted. "You let me lead. You eat my cooking. You make me feel…needed. I think I got scared that anything this good can't last."

"It won't if you go shoving us in boxes, tryin' to not get hurt." I still had my dander up over how he'd friend-zoned me in front of Jake.

"Fair enough." Kendall's grip relaxed into something closer to a caress. "I'm sorry that I hurt you. I can't promise that I won't be a dick again in some other way or screw this up, but I won't deny us. I want this. Want you."

I nodded, very aware that we were on the street and I wanted to be done talking. "Yes."

"Yes?"

"Yes, you can give me a ride." I turned and headed back toward his car.

"Wait. What?" Kendall struggled to catch up. "Is that a yes, we can try again?"

"That's a yes, you can give me a ride to your place. One step at a time. I'm still workin' out how I feel."

All I knew was that I was now even more confused than I'd been all day, something I hadn't thought possible, and I needed to touch Kendall in the worst way.

* * * *

I knew that going back to Kendall's meant we were going to fuck. There was too much tension between us not to, and what I couldn't say with words, I needed to say with lips and hands and bodies. I kissed him the second his door closed, pushing him back against the door. Usually, I left the leading up to him, but I wasn't feeling particularly like following right then.

Grrrr. Kendall's dog had his own ideas, worming his way between us, growling.

"Fast walk?" Kendall pulled away from my mouth.

"Lightning," I ordered, grabbing the leash from the hook next to the door and tossing it to Kendall.

The last few times we'd walked the dog, I'd felt like such a couple, talking and holding hands, and sharing secret smiles, but this time things were still weird between us and the distance between us wasn't something that linked hands could cure. Kendall hurried the dog along, and we were quiet on the elevator back up to his condo.

"Now where were we?" Kendall linked his arms around my neck, pulled me close. It was pretty clear that he wasn't as conflicted as me, and that made me angrier. How come he got to hurt me last night and come back around all apologizing today? No, fuck that noise. I kissed him aggressively, lips firm and hands grasping.

"You make me crazy," I whispered against his mouth as I pulled him toward the bedroom. "Don't know which way is up."

"Does it help if I say that I feel the same way?" Once we were in the bedroom, Kendall worked the buttons on my flannel shirt.

"Nope," I said, honest.

"I'm sorry." He kissed my neck below my beard, kissed my collarbones, lips going lower, over my chest. "So sorry."

Kendall touched my neck and shoulders as he pushed my shirt the rest of the way off, dropping little kisses here and there before he sank to his knees. "This okay?"

I nodded. "Want a condom?" I felt for my wallet, but Kendall pushed my hand aside.

"Nope. We're good." He smiled at me, making my insides all flippy. I knew the risks were almost nil, but it still meant something, him being willing to do this.

Unzipping my fly, Kendall took my dick out. My dick didn't care how conflicted my emotions were—it was hard and ready. Yeah, it might not be very well done of me, but I needed this, needed him on his knees for me, needed him looking up at me with those big dark eyes, needed his hot and eager mouth.

Kendall didn't tease, simply swallowed me down, hands gripping my hips to pull me closer. My pants and boxers fell down to my knees, but I could give a fuck about them.

"Mmmm." He made happy little noises around my dick, moaning when his nose tickled my pubes. Fuck, I loved that, him being all eager for my cock.

"Yeah," I moaned. "Take it."

He sucked hard in response, setting a demanding rhythm that had me too close too fast. His tongue did something on the underside of my cock, got me panting.

"Close. Too close," I muttered, wanting this to last, but my body charging ahead.

"Come for me." Kendall urged me with a hand on my ass.

Maybe he needed this every bit as much as I did. I liked that thought, and it got me closer to the edge. His fingers traced my crack, and I bucked into the touch.

He laughed around my dick, probably at how damn needy I was for that. Sure enough, as soon as his fingers circled my rim as he sucked hard, I was coming. My knees almost buckled and my vision swam—felt like a motorboat crashed into me, leaving me churning in its wake.

I stumbled to the bed when he released me, and kicked my pants the rest of the way off. Kendall took deep, shuddery breaths as he stood and shed his clothes with shaking hands. Fuck, but that was a turn-on, him so undone.

"Fuck me," I said, nodding at his bobbing dick.

"Really?" Kendall raised an eyebrow even as he was rooting in that drawer of his for a condom and lube, which he tossed on the bed.

I know some guys aren't into getting fucked once they've already come, but I kind of dig it—feels nice, having already gotten mine, and the oversensitive feeling inside lights me up, often gets me up for a second round, and even if it doesn't, I like basking in the feelings, watching the other person go, knowing he cared enough to see to me first. Maybe that makes me selfish, I'm not sure—I just know that I've been left wanting enough times to prefer it this way.

"Gimme." I held out my hand for the lube. This part I liked doing myself, and I got everything all slick, working my fingers in, while he rolled on the condom.

His hand was still shaking and his voice wasn't much steadier. "I… uh…haven't topped much. People don't usually want that from me—"

"Thought we'd established that I'm not most people."

"You're not. And I love that." Kendall gave me a tentative smile that went a good ways to defusing my temper. "I just meant…tell me what you like. Help me make this good for you."

"I like it like this." I scooted backward, leaning against the pillows, letting my legs fall open and drawing them back. "Face to face. Kiss me?"

"Gladly." Kendall stretched out on me, but didn't try to push in yet, instead capturing my mouth in a blistering kiss that made my dick start to get hard again. Reaching up, I tugged his hair free, buried my hands in the thick, curly mass, pulling him even closer.

He fucked me with his tongue, something he knew by now drove me crazy, and he worked it until I was wiggling beneath him.

"Fuck," I panted. "Now, please now."

"Yeah." Kendall raised up enough to get a hand on his cock, gently pressing forward.

"Come on, come on." I tilted my hips, pushing back onto him.

"Oh fuck. You feel amazing," Kendall gasped. His balls brushed my ass, and I groaned at how good he felt all the way in. He might not top much, but he had a good natural instinct for hitting my spot as he slowly rocked his hips.

"Kiss me," I demanded, stretching to meet his mouth.

I'd done enough fucking in my life, but very seldom like this with the kissing and the touching and the whispered praise as he told me how good I felt. Each kiss made me feel like I was flying, high on some beautiful drug. Wrapping my legs high around his back, I held him tight as I dared.

Kendall broke the kiss long enough to brush the hair off my face. "You're amazing," he whispered, wonder shining in his eyes. Right there in that moment, I believed him. The fuck shifted, became something else as I let myself believe him, believe in us. Believe in this.

I'd waited forever to feel like this while fucking, safe and cared for. Sure, I was turned on as fuck and fully hard again, cock pressed between our bellies, but my dick was secondary to how *needed* I felt. The warmth and tenderness in Kendall's eyes undid me more than the roughest fuck, got me closer to coming than a fist on my dick. I could happily drown in the sensations, and I held his gaze, let myself wallow in it.

Kendall's breath hitched, and he moaned. "Tell me you're close. Please."

"Gonna come for me?"

"God, yes. Want to. So close." His hips sped up, hitting my gland with each thrust, making lightning explode behind my eyes. I wormed a hand between us, gave my dick a little extra pressure. Didn't take much more than that to have me on the edge.

He growled, and I didn't know what it was about that sound, or maybe it was his fierce expression or the hard grip on my thigh, but Kendall turned up the aggressiveness, and my whole body keyed up, everything tensing, and on the next hard slam, I was coming, this time a slower build that seemed to peak over and over.

"Kendall. Jesus. Kendall." My body shook with aftershocks. Took me a second to realize that he'd come too. He collapsed onto my chest, breathing hard. He kissed me over and over—my forehead, my cheekbones, my ear. Little nuzzles. I'd never had that after sex, and I wanted to stay right here forever.

We hadn't said a lot of words that needed saying, but I was more at peace than I'd been in weeks, and I snuggled into his embrace, let go of the last of my anger. And it wasn't because of the fuck, good as it had been. It was the look in his eyes, even now, half-asleep. He saw me, really saw me, and wasn't running.

"Stay with me," he whispered. "Stay tonight."

"Yeah," I said, my mouth finding his because even now I couldn't get enough of his taste. "I'll stay."

Chapter 13
Kendall

"You ready?" Todd called through the door of my bathroom, waiting for me to get ready for the benefit. He'd been ready since five minutes after our shared shower.

"In a minute," I called.

Things with Todd had been…tenuous all week. Not bad, not strained, but also not as free and easy as they had been prior to our argument. Or, more precisely, prior to me being a fool. He seemed a bit quick to agree, a bit too cheerful at my suggestions, whether it was for sex or food or dancing practice.

Dancing was the high point. Whenever we practiced for the benefit, everything else seemed to drift away, all the questions about a future for us, all my missteps and mistakes, all his wariness. It all fell away until it was simply us, my swing music mix, and the increasing ease we had moving together. We took turns leading, same as in class, but like in bed, more often than not I took the reins, and that was just fine with both of us.

I was working on trusting that this was what Todd genuinely wanted and needed—a chance to let go. Like with dancing, topping seemed to bring a weird yet wonderful sense of balance inside me. No one else had seen past my love of pretty things and my genderqueer identity to let me experiment much, but Todd made it seem as natural as me leading him through the Texas Tommy. I liked topping; he liked bottoming. It really was that simple. Or at least it could be when I got out of my own way.

I took a final, critical look at myself in the mirror. My mother was likely to roll her eyes at my ensemble before sighing in resignation, but I was more concerned with whether Todd would like it.

I'd curled my hair under in classic forties style and added just a hint of makeup, especially the lip color that seemed to do it for Todd, but I'd paired my hair and makeup with a suit of sorts—pants, because those were easier to dance in, heels because I needed the height, and a jacket with a bit more of a feminine cut. A bow instead of a tie was the finishing touch.

"Wow," Todd said when I opened the bathroom door.

"You like?" I preened and gave him a spin.

"Love it. It's very you." He smiled indulgently. With anyone else, I'd take the "it's very you" comment as minimization or a dig, but with Todd, it felt more like a compliment. He understood my genderqueerness in a way that few did.

"Are you nervous?" I asked. He was shifting about, tugging at his sleeves.

"Not about the dancing." He gave me a grin that was no doubt designed to make me stop pressing him.

"But?" I wasn't going to be distracted.

"But the rest of it...you look so done up, and me, I'm just my scruffy self—"

"Hot as fuck," I interrupted. "And I'm removing that suit with my teeth once we're back here, promise."

He turned pinker than my lip gloss. "Maybe. But I'm still all wound up about meeting your family and all. What if I disappoint you?"

"Is that what you've been uptight about all week?" I wrapped my arms around him, held him close so he was forced to look at my eyes, see how little I was worried about this.

"Well, yeah." He was stiff in my arms, eyes flitting away. "You could do better than me. What if they all see that?"

"Then they're idiots." My voice was firm. "And I'll tell them that because you're exactly—*exactly*—what I want."

"Really?" He grabbed on to my arm, but it felt like my heart he was squeezing. "Everyone else there is gonna have fancy degrees—"

"Look, I'm not going to deny that my mother's money has helped me." I gestured to encompass the condo. "But it's not *me*. And I'm proud of you. You work hard at an honest job, and you're working to figure out what's next for you. Nothing to be ashamed of there."

"I let Vic show me some stuff the other day," he admitted. "Liked it more than I thought."

"There you go." I smiled up at him.

"If...if the bakery is all I want, you still going to stick around?"

"I'll still love you regardless of how you make your money. If you found your passion in tie-dye for Saturday Market, or picking up trash on I-5, I wouldn't care. And I think being with a baker is kind of cool, actually."

He sucked in a breath, and I realized that I hadn't said the L-word aloud yet. It had been in my heart with every kiss and every dance and every shared meal, but I hadn't managed to say it until it tumbled out. "You love me?" he asked so tentatively it was clear that he was expecting me to recant.

"Yes." I kissed him soundly, lipstick be damned. "I do. It kind of crept up on me until it's all I think about when I see you."

"Think I'm falling for you too," Todd said softly. "Never felt this way before. Not ever. It's…"

"Terrifying," I finished for him.

"Yeah. That. And pretty cool at the same time. Like I don't ever want to stop feelin' this way, even if it hurts in the end."

"It won't." I grabbed his face. "I promise. I don't want this to end. Not now, not ever. No matter what happens tonight—even if we don't dance a step or my family is awful, I'm still in this thing, okay?"

He nodded and finally—*finally*—the tension in his muscles seemed to ebb. He kissed me more tenderly than I'd thought possible. Reverently even. If this was what love felt like, I could get used to it in a hurry.

Chapter 14
Todd

The benefit was held at the Hilton, a place I'd delivered to with Vic for a wedding once, but I'd never seen the grand ballroom all gussied up like this. A swing orchestra was set up on a platform at the head of the room, with a wooden dance floor in front. Upbeat swing music wafted through the whole big space. Reminded me a bit of places I'd been for dance competitions as a kid. Tables lined the back of the room with what Kendall called a silent auction. Seemed like there were prizes up for grabs if someone wrote their price down on a little gold clipboard. Nothing was remotely in my price range, but Kendall bid on a getaway at the coast.

"Think Vic would let you have a day off if I win it?" he asked.

"Yeah. I could probably work that out." I followed him away from the auction tables, a bit flustered, me having a boyfriend who wanted to take me on a trip.

The gold and black draped tables in the center all had little cards saying who had sponsored that table. It probably cost more than I made in a week to buy a whole table. I really didn't want to know. Despite what I'd told Kendall, I was still plenty nervous. I didn't really fit in here.

Kendall was rather obvious in trying to make me feel like I did, though. He kept pointing out other bearded dudes and people with tats. There seemed to be a good percentage of QUILTBAG folks representing though, including several gender-nonconforming people. Kendall knew a lot of the people we passed, and faces quickly became a blur for me—this couple were former clients, that person went to college with him, and so on. We recognized a few faces from dance class too, including the stuffy couple who wouldn't trade partners with us. Them we didn't go over and say hi to.

When he did introduce me to people, he kept an arm around me and called me his boyfriend. I hated that it had taken an argument to get us here, but I thrilled a bit, being so publicly claimed by a guy like Kendall. That coupled with the words he'd said back at the apartment made me feel really solid about us.

Vic had told me earlier in the week that he and Robin would be there, so I scanned the room looking for them. Saw them over talking to some other folks from the shelter. Vic was the only person in the room who looked more uncomfortable in a suit than me, but Robin looked like something out of a magazine in a sharp tux. I gave them a wave.

"Kendall! Here's our table!" A woman who had to be his mother called to us from several tables over. She had the same hair as him—but hers was in a fancy updo—and Kendall's dark eyes. Her red dress looked like something an old-fashioned movie star would wear. Her eyes widened as she took in Kendall's outfit, and mom or no, I was prepared to tell her where she could shove it if she dared say a word against how smoking he looked.

But she just sighed, a heavy exhale that said she was tolerating Kendall but not exactly thrilled about it. That wasn't okay with me, but before I could decide whether to speak up, Kendall was hugging her and the woman next to her in a blue halter dress.

"You look marvelous," the blue-dressed woman said. She had enough of a family resemblance around the eyes that I figured her for the sister, Lindsay. And her I liked right away, and not just because she complimented Kendall. She had a big, easy smile and a teasing lilt to her voice that made it hard to hold a grudge long. "So this is the new boyfriend, eh?"

"Yeah," Kendall said and made the introductions.

"So do I get to steal you to dance?" Lindsay asked.

"Kendall's the better leader," I said, giving him a little smile just for the two of us, because man, did I ever love it when he led.

"Loyal *and* hot? Kendall, I think you have a keeper." She laughed. "Why can't the cute ones ever play for my team?"

"Later I'll introduce you to some single men from that accounting firm I mentioned," the mother said, laughing too. To me she said, "I'm sorry for these two. It's nice to meet you."

We made the small talk I'd been dreading about where I worked and how I liked it, but it went better than I'd thought, with both of them having heard of the bakery and neither of them looking like they thought I wasn't worthy of Kendall. Then a dapper fellow strutted over. Had to be Lewis, the ex. I could guess just from how he carried himself and how he looked at Kendall, part possessiveness, part disgust.

I stepped a little closer, put an arm around Kendall. This guy, he definitely had the you're-not-worthy look before Kendall even spoke to introduce us.

"Kendall, nice to see you here," he said in haughty, East Coast tones. "And this must be your...delivery boy. Heard a rumor you were with someone." His look dismissed me in a single glance, but I surprised myself and stood firm.

"I'm the boyfriend, yes," I told him with a look of my own that said I had what he didn't. Maybe I didn't have his pricey degree or sophisticated life, but I had something better—Kendall. Who had told me he loved me and seemed to mean it. I could bank on that. Lewis-the-loser didn't have anything near as fine.

"Mine is around here somewhere." He gave a casual flick of the wrist. "Probably waiting for me to dance already."

Kendall grinned at me. I grinned at Kendall. "Shall we?" he said.

"Absolutely."

"Sorry, Lewis. We love this song." Kendall's grin got wider as he turned to his mother. "Mom, we'll be back in a few minutes. Don't wait on us for food."

Bye, Lewis. I didn't give him a backward glance as we strode to the dance floor. The trumpet player was really good, and all around us were people of various ability levels trying out their moves. We were ready.

"Sugar push?" Kendall asked as he assumed the lead.

"Let's do this." We started slow, but as the trumpet player got to wailing, we unleashed some of the fancier moves we'd practiced. And right there, as Kendall spun me, I knew that I'd never been happier. I'd say that Kendall gave me dance back, but really Kendall gave me *myself* back—the self who had been waiting right here for this moment with this person.

* * * *

Six months later

"They're ready," Vic pronounced, scrutinizing my cupcakes from every angle. I'd been practicing decorating our famous cupcakes for weeks, but this was the first order I'd taken charge of start-to-finish.

"They better be." I still hadn't mastered spun-sugar butterflies and flowers like Vic's, but my piping skills improved by the day. Turned out he was right, and I did have a steady hand for this sort of work.

"What time is the party?" Vic asked.

"Seven," I said as we carefully packaged the finished cupcakes. "Kendall's mom eats late."

It went without saying that I was still a bit nervous, heading to her Pearl District condo that was larger than most people's houses. Doubly so since it was Kendall's birthday. His friend Freya would be there, along with other assorted friends and family. Food was being catered because his mother joked that her big kitchen skill was knowing how to order in, but we'd have my cupcakes for dessert.

"You know, Robin's been after me to sell my car, get a truck to make all the Home Depot trips easier. Think you might be interested with fall coming? I could make you a good deal."

I laughed. "You're just jealous that you don't look as good on a bike as me." I'd figured out a good bike route from Kendall's condo to the bakery. Getting me to part with the scratch for a commuter bike had been hard enough. Vic was going to have an uphill battle to convince me to take his junker off his hands.

"He's picking you up today though, right?" Vic studied the cupcake box like I was seriously considering strapping it to my rear rack.

"Yeah." I checked my phone and carefully lifted the pink bakery boxes. "Should be out there now, actually."

Sure enough, Kendall lounged near his car as I came out, moving to open the trunk for me.

"I feel like we need a seat belt for these," he joked as we loaded up the cupcake boxes.

"Not a bad idea," I said, wedging things around the boxes so they wouldn't slide so much.

Kendall wrapped his arms around me as I straightened. He looked fabulous in a metallic tunic and slim pants and chunky boots. Me, I was going to need every second of the fast shower I was planning back at our place. *Our.* Still got a little thrill thinking that. Last few months when I'd handed Kendall a check for my share of expenses had me so proud. Maybe it wasn't earth-shattering, but I'd found my purpose in contributing to a shared life with Kendall. It was more than enough, so much that sometimes I thought my heart couldn't hold it all.

"I'm sure they're great." He looked down at the boxes before shutting the trunk.

"They are." I was working on having more confidence in my work. "Three flavors too, because one's never enough for you."

"Oh yum." He stole a kiss. "There's something for you on your seat."

"What's that?" I faked anger. "It's *your* birthday. You can't go getting me stuff."

"It's my present to me." His grin was unapologetic. I went to the passenger seat and discovered a paper with a bow on it.

"Receipt for more dance classes?" I read aloud as I sat down. "Advanced swing?"

"We're getting rusty, just us in our living room. Thought it would be fun." He slid into the driver's side.

"It will be." Now I was a bit put out that I hadn't thought of that as a present for him. My pout must have shown because he pulled me in for another, longer kiss.

"The only present I really need is right here," he said when he came up for air.

"You're getting sappy in your old age." I looked away, as if that could help disguise my blush. I did, however, have one additional surprise for him waiting back home in an envelope of my own. He hadn't won the coast getaway at the silent auction, but I'd pulled a bunch of extra hours to get us a night away in Seaside. I'd wrapped it up all cutesy with a pair of swim goggles for the pool.

"I'm serious." Kendall squeezed my hand. "You. More dancing. Cupcakes. I'm ridiculously happy."

"I love you." The words practically flew out of my mouth. I didn't say it as much as he did, but sometimes the words just bubbled over like my chest got tired of holding them in.

"That. That is the best present ever."

"You're supposed to say it back." I nudged him.

"Love you too." He laughed and I hauled him in for one more kiss. I didn't care if Vic or anyone else saw us making out in the parking lot. This was our moment, and I was going to savor it, add it to my little pile of memories we'd made these past few months, each moment another step in the beautiful dance we're making up as we go along.

About the Author

Annabeth Albert grew up sneaking romance novels under the bed covers. Now, she devours all subgenres of romance out in the open—no flashlights required! When she's not adding to her keeper shelf, she's a multi-published Pacific Northwest romance writer. Emotionally complex, sexy, and funny stories are her favorites both to read and to write. Annabeth loves finding happy endings for a variety of pairings and is a passionate gay rights supporter. In between searching out dark heroes to redeem, she works a rewarding day job and wrangles two toddlers.

Annabeth can be found online at annabethalbert.com, @annabethalbert on Twitter, and Facebook.com/annabethalbert.

And don't miss these other titles by Annabeth Albert!

Some like it steamy...

PORTLAND HEAT

SERVED HOT

ANNABETH ALBERT

In Portland, Oregon, the only thing hotter than the coffee shops, restaurants, and bakeries are the hard-working men who serve it up—hot, fresh, and ready to go—with no reservations...

Robby is a self-employed barista with a busy coffee cart, a warm smile, and a major crush on one of his customers. David is a handsome finance director who works nearby, eats lunch by himself, and expects nothing but "the usual"—small vanilla latte—from the cute guy in the cart. But when David shows up for his first Portland Pride festival, Robby works up the nerve to take their slow-brewing relationship to the next level. David, however, is newly out and single, still grieving the loss of his longtime lover, and unsure if he's ready to date again. Yet with every fresh latte, sweet exchange—and near hook-up—David and Robby go from simmering to steaming to piping hot. The question is: Will someone get burned?

From its famous coffee to the mouthwatering fare at its cafés, restaurants, and bakeries, Portland, Oregon, has a lot to whet the appetite, including the hard-working men who serve it all up—hot, fresh, and ready to go—with no reservations...

Vic Degrassi is a baker on the rise, and it's all thanks to his rare ability to make—and keep—his New Year's resolutions. Whether it's losing weight, giving up smoking, or graduating from culinary school, Vic goes after what he wants—and gets it. This year? He wants Robin Dawson, the sweet-hearted hottie who volunteers with him at the local homeless shelter. When he learns that Robin is suddenly single after being unceremoniously dumped, Vic is more than happy to offer a shoulder to cry on—or at least a fresh-baked pastry to bite into. But it's been a long time since Vic's gone on a date, and he's nervous about risking his friendship with Robin. So when their flirtation turns into a steamy night together, Vic and Robin have to figure out if they're friends with benefits or lovers in the making, and if Robin is ready for something more than just a rebound. There's only one way to find out: turn up the heat...

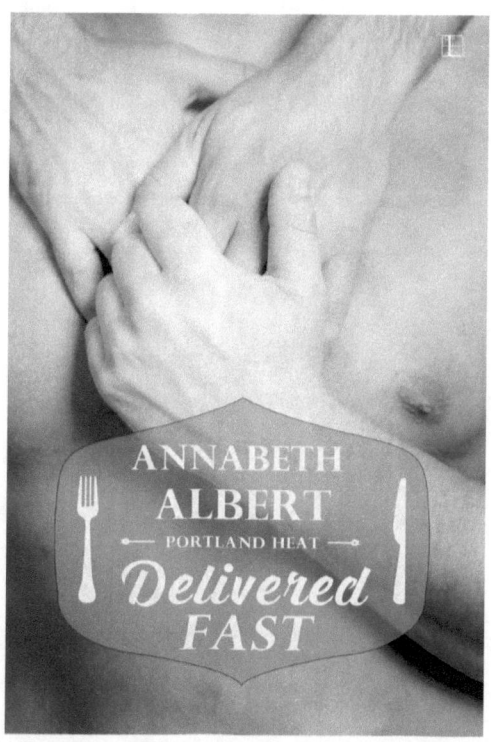

ANNABETH
ALBERT
— PORTLAND HEAT —
Delivered
FAST

Portland, Oregon, aka Hotlandia, where the coffee shops, restaurants, and bakeries are ready to serve everything piping hot, fresh, and ready to go—like the hard-working, hard-bodied men behind the counters—with no reservations…

Sure, Chris O'Neal has problems. His restaurant is still co-owned by his ex. His flannel-and-tattoos style is making him accidentally trendy. He can't remember the last time he went out and had fun. But he's not lonely, he's driven. And the hot bakery delivery boy is not his problem, no matter how sweet his buns.

Chris is old enough to know Lance Degrassi's sculpted good looks and clever double entendres spell nothing but trouble. Lance is still in college— he should be hitting the clubs and the books, chasing guys his own age, not pursuing some gruff motorcycle-riding workaholic. Especially when he'll be leaving for grad school in a few months. But Lance keeps hanging around, lending a hand, charming Chris to distraction. Maybe some steaming hot no-strings indulgence won't hurt.

Then again, maybe it will…

He's all about this bass...

TREBLE MAKER

PERFECT HARMONY

ANNABETH ALBERT

On *Perfect Harmony*, the ambitious competitors heat things up on stage and off...

Cody Rivers is determined to be a rock star, but couch-surfing between bar shows gets old fast. Joining an a cappella group for a new singing competition show could be his last chance at real fame—unless the college boy from the heart of the country messes it up for him. Lucas Norwood is everything gothy, glittery Cody is not—conservative, clean-cut, and virginal. But when a twist in the show forces them together, even the sweetest songs get steamy as the attraction between them lights up the stage. Lucas wants to take it slow, but Cody's singing a different tune—and this time it may be a love song...

There's no way he'll shake **this** *off…*

Trevor Daniels is feeling aimless. A recent college grad, he's not sure what to do with his useless degree, and his family all but abandoned him after he revealed the truth about himself. But a friend's suggestion that he take his chances on a reality show aimed at finding the next big boy band strikes a chord with him—until the show's producers convince him to act like he's in a relationship with a guy who's not at all his type. It isn't exactly love at first sight for Jalen Smith either—but lust just might push them in an unexpected direction. If only their secrets weren't even more twisted than their sheets, threatening to cost them the win— and each other…

Giving true love a spin...

Michelin Moses is a country music star on the rise. With a hit single under his Texas-sized belt buckle and a sold-out concert tour underway, his childhood dreams of making it big are finally coming true. But there's one thing missing—a promise to his dying mother that he'd find it—him—when the time was right. With a little luck, he won't have to wait too long...

Lucky Ramirez is a hunky boy toy who dances at The Broom Closet, one of West Hollywood's hottest gay bars. He loves what he does, and he's good at it—almost as good as he is at playing dumb when he spots Michelin Moses at the bar. What happens next is off the charts—and keeps Michelin coming back for more. He's just not sure it's the right move for his career. But if Lucky gets his way, Michelin will get Lucky—and no matter how the media spins it, neither of them will be faking it...